HOOD

JENNY ELDER MOKE

HYPERION
Los Angeles   New York

First Hardcover Edition, June 2020
First Paperback Edition, May 2021
10 9 8 7 6 5 4 3 2 1
FAC-025428-21078
Printed in the United States of America

This book is set in Fairfield LT Std/Adobe
Designed by Phil Buchanan

Library of Congress Control Number: 2019009842
ISBN 978-1-368-05231-3

Visit www.hyperionteens.com

TO ANNA AND CHRISTINA, FOR EVERYTHING

CHAPTER
ONE

Isabelle took great pride in herself that she did not cry once during the whole wretched, messy ordeal. Not when the soldiers barked their orders at her to stand down; not when they grabbed her up like a common criminal and threw shackles on her wrists; not when they shoved her in this moldy makeshift prison cell that once served as a potato cellar; not even when the strips of light leaching in from outside grew longer, and thinner, and then disappeared altogether. She held her head high, gritted her teeth, and glared malevolence at the warped wooden boards of the door and the rough voices of the men beyond.

And when even they faded away, and she began to fear they'd forgotten about her or planned to leave her behind, and fear twisted itself into panic, she would not give in. She thought of her mother in full prioress regality, stern and powerful and threaded through with iron, and wished for her strength. But as the night wore on, the cold stealing its thin fingers up her ankles and calves, she just wished for her mother.

She'd almost forgotten the door was there by the time the heavy bolt screeched open, a stab of torchlight blinding her after hours of complete dark. She curled into herself instinctively, the shackles dragging and clanking against each other as she raised her hands to block the light. She steeled herself for another round of brutal questioning from the soldiers, summoning what little well of strength she had left. But after hours of fear, hunger, and churning panic, it only took one word to undo her.

"Isabelle!"

She lifted her head, her face twisting.

"Mother?" she whispered, and promptly burst into tears.

Marien swept across the small space, enveloping her in warmth and softness and the smooth, sharp scent of lemon verbena. "Shhh, 'tis all right, child." She kissed the top of her head, murmuring into her hair. "Oh, my Isabelle. Oh, you willful child. Are you hurt?"

"I am so sorry," Isabelle said through a hiccuping sob as her mother lifted her hands to unlock the shackles around her wrists and examine the angry red welts underneath. "I am so very sorry. I can explain, I swear it. I know you forbade me from leaving the priory while everything is so tumultuous, but the people in Kirkleestown were starving, Mother. I knew we had the grain, but Sister Catherine would not let me share it. She said the sisters needed it to keep up their strength, but there was plenty to go round! She was just being greedy—I know it is an unkind thing to say, but it is true. She would rather watch these families starve than open her heart. So I thought if I could go hunting, even just for a brace of rabbits, I might be able to help feed them for the night."

"Hush now, child," her mother said, not unkindly. "I know your heart, my love. I know what you meant to do. But I am afraid it is worse than that now. Something terrible has happened."

Isabelle shuddered, not from the cold in the air but from the chill in her mother's voice. "What do you mean? What has happened?"

Another light appeared at the cellar door, drawing her mother's attention away. Isabelle knew the man holding the torch, a kindly farmer who had often come to the priory for her mother's healing teas in the past year since they had opened their doors to the people of Kirklees. The flames threw deep shadows along the creases in his brow as his gaze flicked into the darkness behind him, his fingers worrying at the fabric of his woolen leggings.

"Please, mistress, we don't have much time," he said, his voice wobbly. "They'll be back soon, I expect. If they know I've helped you—"

"Yes, of course, thank you, Frederick. The Lord shall bless you for your service." Marien turned to Isabelle, eyes dark like an oncoming storm. "We must go. Quickly and quietly."

"But, Mother—"

Her mother shook her head. "There is no time for explanations."

They hurried out of the cellar into the field beyond, which Isabelle now realized was part of the land Frederick tended. The farmer stayed behind, his torchlight growing dim as they ran through the freshly plowed and seeded barley fields. Her mother moved like a wraith, swift and silent, her footfalls light and instinctive. Isabelle tried to match her movements, but her own steps were clumsy and loud in comparison, the fear and fatigue dragging her down.

Night transformed the woods into a stranger, webbed in shadows and clawing branches, tearing at the thick wool of her habit and snatching tendrils of her golden curls with sinister whispers. An owl swooped low with a keening hoot as they moved through the trees, Isabelle's heart pumping hard at every unexpected sound. More than once she caught a toe on a root or ran a shoulder into a low-hanging branch. But her mother, if it was possible, seemed even more at home among the trees, flitting between pockets of darkness like a shadow, making it difficult for Isabelle to even keep track of her. Where had her mother learned to move like that?

They emerged from the woods beside a wide road, the deep ruts of passing wagons glittering in the half moonlight. Isabelle took a deep breath, trying to free the knot of tension coiled in her chest from their breakneck pace through the trees. But the coil only tightened at the empty stretch of road in either direction.

"Mother," she whispered, her voice feeling large in the quiet night. "Where are we? Where is Kirklees?"

"We cannot return to the priory," her mother said, searching through the limbs of a nearby tree and pulling down a tidy bundle made of Isabelle's cloak, which had been secreted away in its branches. A cascade of orange-and-yellow leaves scattered to the ground, their edges curling and brown.

"Why can we not return?" Isabelle asked. "Where would we go instead?"

Her mother did not answer as she loosened the cloak and withdrew Isabelle's quiver and bow, the polished wood gleaming gray in the moonlight. She removed a burlap sack with a small tin from the folds of the cloak, the earthy fragrance of the salve within the tin stirring Isabelle's senses. Marien rubbed the remedy into Isabelle's raw wrists with quick, gentle strokes.

"Comfrey?" Isabelle said hopefully, trying to distract herself from the twisting in her gut with an attempt at their old game.

Her mother gave a patient smile. "Yarrow root, dearest. Comfrey has a much more floral scent."

Isabelle shook her head. "Of course. I should have remembered that."

"God calls us all in our own ways, dearest," Marien said as she worked, reciting the maxim that had framed Isabelle's childhood. "This will help the pain. The wounds are thankfully superficial.

You should have enough salve to last you until you reach your destination."

The simmering dread that had been souring Isabelle's stomach all day turned to a full boil. "What destination?"

"I cannot keep you safe in Kirklees any longer," her mother said, quickly wrapping Isabelle's wrists in white linen. "There is no one here we can trust, not now. The truth will come out soon, and I cannot protect you from it."

She tucked the rest of the salve and more linens in the burlap sack before sweeping the cloak around Isabelle's shoulders. She cinched it tight against the chill night air, Isabelle following her motions perfunctorily, slinging her bow and quiver over her shoulder in a daze. Her mother hesitated, taking Isabelle's face in her hands.

"You are in grave danger," her mother said, white puffs of breath obscuring her face. "You must leave Kirklees tonight."

Isabelle's voice pitched up in protest. "All this because I . . . embarrassed some lowly soldier? I know what I did was wrong, but he was no better. Those people were no threat to them. It was rusty threshers and makeshift cudgels against broadswords and crossbows. They never would have stood a chance. I know the people attacked those soldiers, and the soldiers must defend themselves, but the villagers were only hungry! I cannot imagine if King John knew the true state of his people starving here that he would approve of such brutality. Surely, if we speak to someone in charge, perhaps if I promise to apologize—"

"It is far beyond that," her mother said with a firm shake of her head. "I wish I had more time to explain, but they will be after you as soon as they realize you are gone. You must leave now, immediately. Cover your tracks, leave no trace. Just as I taught you."

"For hunting, not for . . . being hunted," Isabelle said, numbness settling over her despite the rapid pace of her heart. "Mother, these are soldiers! Not rabbits or poachers. I could not possibly outwit them, even with your help."

A quiet breath slipped out of Marien. "I cannot go with you. You must go alone."

Isabelle's jaw sagged. "What? I cannot go on my own. I have never even been outside Kirkleestown!"

"If there were another way, any other possible way, I would do it," her mother said, stroking her cheek. Isabelle wished she could curl up and take refuge from this nightmare in her mother's even tone and sure hands.

"But why can you not go with me?" Isabelle begged.

Marien would not meet her gaze. "Because I have other business here. I cannot leave, and you cannot stay. You will have to be strong, my child, even when the worst comes for you. You will have to be braver than you feel."

"What do I have to do?" Isabelle whispered, her voice trembling on the edge of exhaustion.

Her mother gestured down the main road out of Kirklees. "Go south until you reach the town of Huntingdon, three days' journey from here. Stay to the woods and keep out of sight. Do not seek help from the towns or travelers you pass along the way. Find the Blue Boar Inn at the split in the road, and ask for Thomas. Tell him that I sent you. He is an old family friend and you can trust him. He will know where to take you." She hesitated again, a tremor going through her hands. "Tell him the Wolf has returned."

Something in her mother's tone and the crease of fear deepening between her eyebrows chilled Isabelle more than anything else that had happened that day. She clung to her mother's hands, all pretense of bravery abandoning her.

"Mother, please—"

But a solitary shout went up from the direction of Frederick's farm, slicing between them and severing their conversation. They cut their gazes to the impenetrable darkness of the woods, but nothing emerged from the shadows. Yet. Isabelle held her breath, willing herself into quiet stillness as they waited. Another shout rose, and then another, drawing closer.

"You have to run, Isabelle," her mother whispered, her voice vibrating.

Isabelle tried to move her feet, but they wouldn't obey. Her chest fluttered with little breaths, her head spinning. The next shout came close enough that she could make out the words clearly.

"Find the girl!"

"Run, Isabelle," her mother whispered harshly, pushing her toward the road. "Run!"

And so she ran.

CHAPTER
TWO

This couldn't be the place her mother meant. Three days of running for her life, half starving and living off foraged berries because she couldn't risk a fire to cook any meat, sleeping in snatches and waking up soaked in terror sweats, her legs already moving to run, to bring her to . . . a tavern?

The Blue Boar Inn—if it even *was* an inn, she thought it must be of the most unsavory kind—shone like a sweaty, foamy, frothy beacon of male indulgence. If she had imagined the opposite of the priory in Kirklees, this was the kind of place she would have envisioned. Woodsmen the size of plow oxen crowded around tables made from felled tree stumps, their beards hanging down over their tunics like fur, and their legs thicker than tree trunks in their rough woolen hose. The low-slung building behind them vibrated with calls for ale and off-key singing of songs that would make even the most worldly of the sisters turn red with shock. The only door into the inn, as far as she could tell, was on a direct path through the men, swinging open and shut like a curtain caught in a wind, stuffing so much humanity inside she thought the building would burst.

All this Isabelle watched from a stand of trees down the road, hunkered among the sparse brush, shivering and starving and on the verge of tears. Her skirts were splattered with mud and torn along the hems, her hair snarled and peppered with leaves and branches that made her scalp itch something terrible. The fine linen her mother had wrapped around her wrists had long ago disintegrated into black tatters. No doubt these men would cry ghost if they saw her emerge from the woods in such a state, a haunted soul denied the afterlife.

Now all those times she'd sworn to leave the rocky walls of Kirklees to seek the outside world struck her as exactly what they were—the foolish, naive fantasies of a child. Oh, how Sister Catherine would crow if she could see her, the old shrew. No doubt she was even now lording Isabelle's arrest over Marien, as if it proved that her impulsive choices had finally got the better of her. A pang of guilt stabbed her gut at the idea that Sister Catherine might, for once in her miserable miserly life, be right.

She couldn't do it. Even though the luscious aroma of stew slipping in between the smell of pine and dirt made her stomach beg for just a small spoonful, and her feet ached for a chair and her back for a soft bed, she couldn't scrape together the courage to march through all those men just to find this Thomas.

"Maybe it will be easier in the morning," she whispered to herself, running her fingers over the fletching of an arrow for the hundredth time that night. "Surely they must have . . . trees to chop, or boars to wrestle, or . . . whatever it is these men do."

But she knew better. She knew she would have no more courage come sunrise and she didn't have the time to wait. She'd heard the hooves up and down the road as she hid in the trees, light on the balls of her feet and sticking to the heavier parts of the underbrush as her mother taught her. She might even be too late now, and the soldiers might have already made their way here and were even now lying in wait for her inside. Though she did not think these foresters would take kindly to a contingent of soldiers in their midst, so perhaps she still had time. Not much, though.

A crowd of young men half the height and size of the other forest-ers approached the front door as she watched, many of them with cheeks and jaws still soft and chubby. Not that they acted like it. It seemed the smaller they were, the bigger their voices and bravado, so that even the youngest among them swaggered around like the only cock in the henhouse. The others mostly ignored him, but it gave Isabelle an idea.

She tore into the burlap fabric of the knapsack her mother had given her, a few crumbs from her last precious meal two days ago spilling on the ground as she twisted the fabric into the rough shape of a hat. She piled her hair into a thick knot on top of her head and scrunched the hat down over it. The burlap itched and slid around with the weight of her hair whenever she moved, but it covered what it needed to cover.

Changing her clothes was a challenge on another level. She still had her cloak, which covered much of the habit she wore under-neath, but the bottom edge of the skirt swished out with every step she took. It pained her to lose the warming layers, but the skirt had to go. She took an arrow from her quiver and used the sharp edge of the head to cut into the fabric with a ripping determination, tearing the hem up to the knee and slitting through the middle to form wide, loose legs. It wouldn't fool anyone in the light of day, but hopefully it wouldn't attract the attention of a few drunkards by firelight. She tucked her mother's salve into a fold of her habit and slung her bow and quiver over her shoulder as if preparing for battle.

The young boys were still gathered around the entrance, shout-ing down their insecurities with a swaggering bravado that was easy for her to adopt. The older and wiser of the foresters had long since turned their backs on the boys, but that only seemed to rile up the young men even more. They elbowed into one another, pummeling shoulders and knocking heads and swigging back mugs of ale like they'd never catch up. They reminded Isabelle of the herd of goats Sister Margaret tended in the back fields of the priory, locking horns over the slightest transgressions. She headed straight for them and the entrance beyond.

"Oi, you couldn't land a slap on the broad side of a pig," one of the boys called, as thick as he was tall. He smacked the smallest of them on the back, the boy Isabelle first noticed when they arrived.

The small boy turned a deep red. "Maybe I ought to practice on the arse end of a horse first, Samuel. Lend me your face, will you?"

The other boys broke up into shouts of laughter, pounding Samuel on the back so hard he spilled some of his ale. He puffed up like a guinea hen, shouldering his way toward the smaller boy just as Isabelle tried to swagger through their ranks. The two of them bounced off each other, knocking Isabelle into the smaller boy.

"I'll clock the both of you," Samuel growled, bearing down on them and curling his thick fingers into fists.

The small boy, sensing the trouble coming his way, shoved Isabelle toward Samuel and disappeared into the flickering shadows.

"Who the hell are you, mate, and what the hell do you think you're doing?" Samuel demanded, getting right in her face. "They'll be cleaning up your parts for days round here when I'm done with you."

Had she been full of belly or sound of mind, she might have apologized and slipped out the same way the smallest boy had gone. Had she not been running in fear for her life the past three days, she might have been cowed by the boy's browbeating bravado. She was no stranger to the bullying ways of others; Sister

Catherine had waged a campaign against her of backbreaking manual labor ever since Marien was elected prioress over her, and she loved nothing more than to punish Isabelle for the slightest infractions with a brutal caning in front of the other sisters. Isabelle knew how to grit her teeth and bear it, and had spent the last five years doing so.

But she was not full of belly or sound of mind after the events of the last three days. And so, when a drop of spittle from the thick boy's lips landed on her cheek, wet and warm and disgusting, it was like a key in the lock of a secret door. She could almost hear it click in her mind, feel the door swing open as a wave of red poured out of its dark recesses. The boy never even saw the punch coming as it connected with the soft flesh under his jaw, his teeth clacking together as he sprawled back into the arms of his friends.

"I'm your worst nightmare, mate," she gruffed, her voice low and raw with anger as she mimicked the accents of the boys around her. "Come for me again and I'll show you where I'm from. You want a sparring dummy, go find your friend. You want someone who will put up a real fight, stand up."

She regretted the words as soon as she said them, for the boy was probably twice her weight and could easily flatten her out. The other boys egged him on, dragging him up and shouting for him to do all manner of unpleasant things to her face. For a moment she considered running for her life and forgetting about the Blue Boar Inn completely. But her mother's words echoed back to her, steeling her spine and giving power to her resolve.

Be braver than you feel.

She would not let this red-faced, thick-necked, beardless boy get the best of her. Even if it meant she got pummeled to a pulp. Which she most certainly would. But she would do it with pride. She clenched her fists hard, bringing them up in front of her as the other boy did the same. The first punch had been lucky; she'd never punched anything in her life, and already her knuckles ached from the impact. They certainly hurt worse than the other boy looked, eyes gleaming like a wild hog's. His friends closed in around them, yelling and shoving each other and tossing coins on the ground as bets against her.

Yes, this had definitely been a terrible idea.

"For the love of Saint Peter, shut up, you lot!" someone shouted, cutting across their little fighting ring with a roar. A thick man with hair the color of a first snowfall shoved through their ranks, hauling Samuel up by the collar of his shirt. "I told you last time, Samuel, I caught you stirring up trouble round here you'd be banned for life."

"It weren't me, I swear it!" Samuel squeaked, his face turning even redder as he clawed at the edge of his tunic where it cut into his neck. "It's that fellow there. He started it! Tell him, boys."

Some of the boys nodded their support, but most of them disappeared into the night the same way the small boy had, leaving Isabelle standing on her own, her hat dangerously askew.

"Yeah, it's always someone else starts it, but it's always you I find in the middle of it." The man gave Samuel a good shake. "That's enough, then. You're banned from the Boar."

"You can't do that!" Samuel whined, all bravado gone. "I'll tell my da, I will!"

"You go on and tell him, then. See if you don't end up with a backside blacker than a chimney stone." The man raised his voice to the few boys still standing about. "That goes for the lot of you, you hear? I find out even one of you's been sneaking drinks for Samuel here, the whole lot of you is banned. You understand?"

"Yes, Thomas," several of the boys muttered, avoiding eye contact with the older boy.

"Now get, the lot of you," Thomas said, shoving Samuel away. "Go on and tell your da; if he's got a problem, he can come see me anytime."

As the older boy slunk away, on the verge of tears and muttering about justice, Isabelle was so relieved to not have her face smashed in that at first she didn't register the white-haired man's name. And when she did, he was already pushing through the door leading inside.

"Please, sir, are you the barkeep here?" she asked, darting around several patrons to catch up to the big man. She didn't bother keeping up the low voice or the swaggering stance. "Thomas of the Blue Boar Inn?"

The man looked down at her with a frown. "Depends on who's doing the asking. What's it to you?"

She scrabbled for a hold on his sleeve. "Please, I need your help."

Thomas rolled his eyes, shoving through a thick patch of men singing a bawdy song loudly and off-key. The noise inside was near deafening, the heat and press of the men nauseating. "Not another of you. Listen, lass, you're not fooling anyone round here, least of all me. If it's work you're looking for, we're full up. If it's the Merry Men you're thinking of joining, I don't know them and I don't care what your sad story is. You're best off crawling back to whatever farm you left and giving your mum a hug and telling her you're sorry for ever tearing off in the first place. All right?"

"You do not understand," Isabelle said, trailing after him determinedly. "I am not from any farm. I come from the priory of Kirklees."

Thomas stopped so suddenly she ran right into him, a single golden curl tumbling out of her makeshift hat into her peripheral view. She tucked it up hastily as he stared down at her, hawk eyes raking over her face. She felt exposed in the bright firelight, but she didn't turn away. Not even when his gaze shifted and he let out a curse under his breath.

"I knew your hands looked too soft to be a farmer's," he said.

"My name is Isabelle. The prioress of Kirklees sent me." Her voice wavered at the thought of her mother, her heart hammering away at the inside of her chest, but she cleared her throat to continue. "She said to deliver you a message of great urgency."

Thomas grabbed her by the arm, pulling her in close and darting a glance around the crowded tavern. He spoke low and fast to her. "Not another word, lass. There're always ears listening. Come with me."

He barreled through the crowd with her in tow. From outside she had longed for the warmth and comfort of the fire, but inside the heat and stink of sweating bodies was far too overwhelming. Combined with her exhaustion and the hunger still gnawing an escape route through her stomach, it was enough to make her light-headed. When Thomas finally reached the bar and ushered her behind it to a small trapdoor below, she jumped into the cool recess gratefully. He followed more slowly, clambering down the short ladder to fit himself between barrels of ale and stacks of mugs.

"What is it, then, lass?" Thomas said after he'd secured the trapdoor above, crossing his arms over his round chest. If he sat still enough, she might mistake him for one of the ale barrels. "What message did Marien send?"

It was odd enough being crammed into this clandestine space, dizzy from hunger and carrying a secret message of grave importance. But to hear her mother's name spoken so casually, so intimately by a complete stranger, it was almost more than Isabelle could believe. Perhaps she'd fallen into a fever dream and was even now writhing about on her pallet back in the priory while her mother squeezed cool water over her brow.

"You said it was urgent," Thomas said in a flat, slightly impatient tone, snapping her back to reality. However strange this reality was.

"I . . . Yes, yes, it is. My mothe—the prioress said to tell you . . ." She took a deep breath, the rush of air making her sway on her feet. "I apologize. It has been a trying few days."

"No more trying than these few minutes," Thomas muttered, but he disappeared between the barrels and reappeared wielding a long, flat loaf of bread. "Here, lass, before you expire in my storeroom."

"Thank you," Isabelle breathed, biting into the loaf and nearly losing a tooth in the process. It was tough, and cold, and utterly devoid of taste, but she would have eaten a dozen of them if he had handed them over. Her jaw ached by the time she finished the first few bites, but at least her head no longer spun.

"Now, this urgent business that couldn't wait?" Thomas prodded.

She chewed through the tough bread hastily, wishing for a cool spot of ale to wash it down, but too scared to ask. "She sent me to tell you that the Wolf has returned."

For a moment Thomas did not move, not even to blink or breathe. The moment stretched out awkwardly as Isabelle chewed the last few bites of bread and darted her gaze from the barrels to Thomas and back, thinking that actually he was even wider than the casks beside him. And still he said nothing, his eyes fixed on a spot just behind her, his gaze distant. The only thing that changed was his pallor, the color draining from his features until he was almost as white as his beard.

"Is that . . . Does that mean something to you?" she finally asked when she couldn't bear the silence anymore.

"I have to warn Robin," he whispered to himself, as if he'd forgotten she was there.

"Robin? Who is Robin?"

His eyes drew back up to her as he frowned. "What more did Marien tell you? Where is the Wolf now? Is she safe?"

Isabelle shook her head. "I do not know anything else. Who is the Wolf? Who is Robin?"

But he was caught in his own thoughts, muttering to himself. "The child. What did she say of the child?"

Isabelle wasn't sure he was talking to her until his gaze landed on her. "What child?"

"Marien's child. Where is the child now?"

She shook her head again. "I do not . . . Do you mean me?"

Thomas's eyes widened. "*You* are Marien's child? But you're . . . Has so much time really passed? How old are you, lass?"

"Sixteen years this past spring," Isabelle said, more confused than ever. "I do not understand. What do I have to do with this?"

"She didn't tell you? Your mother didn't tell you who you are?"

"What do you mean, who I am?"

He stepped closer, his eyes glittering in the half-dark. "You are the daughter of Robin Hood. And if the Wolf has returned, he'll be coming for you."

CHAPTER
THREE

Isabelle could not decide which life-changing bit of information to process first, so she simply stared at the big barkeep, mouth slightly ajar, fingers turned to ice. Her heart seemed to be the only part of her responding, thumping away wildly in her chest and churning her stomach into a frenzy. Thomas took her by the shoulders and gave her a gentle shake.

"Did you hear me, lass?" he asked. "Are you all right?"

Isabelle might have asked how anyone could be all right in this particular moment, except they were both interrupted by a crash overhead. The lively buzz of the taproom dropped into a tense quiet as heavy footfalls creaked across the floorboards, each one like a whip crack in Isabelle's ears. She closed her eyes and imagined they were nothing more than rabbits foraging in the brush, separating each distinct pair of steps until she could mark every one with an arrow if she needed.

"Seven," she breathed to herself, forgetting about the barkeep until he replied.

"And more waiting outside, no doubt," he whispered. He shook his head. "It'll be a mess of blood and teeth to clean up all morning for me."

The temporary lull in conversation erupted again in angry tones and hard thumps against the floorboards, every sound making Isabelle jump. She slid her bow off her shoulder as her other hand sought the fletching of an arrow from her quiver, her eyes fixed on the trapdoor overhead. She should have kept running. She should never have stopped, no matter what her mother told her. Now she was trapped in a cellar with a legion of soldiers overhead and only a few drunk foresters between them and her. She was doomed.

"Wait here, lass," Thomas said as snatches of insults and barked orders from the soldiers sifted down with the dust. He pushed at the trapdoor, and she instinctively slunk behind the nearest ale barrel. The big man moved quickly, crawling through the door and lowering it without a sound to leave Isabelle in the dark once more. From the angry buzzing overhead, it was only a matter of moments before someone threw the first punch. Maybe she could slip out in the chaos, run until she found the ocean. Or the highlands. But anywhere she thought to run, her mother's shadowed eyes and Thomas's tense words would follow her.

If the Wolf has returned, he'll be coming for you.

What if the company of soldiers in Kirkleestown had been no coincidence? What if they had been sent by someone to find her? Who was this Wolf? What kind of power must he wield to have an entire company of soldiers at his command? What did he want with her? And what in the name of the Almighty did Thomas mean, she was the daughter of Robin Hood? *The* Robin Hood? The criminal mastermind and perpetual thorn in King John's side? The man Sister Catherine swore to the rafters only existed in stories, to give the common wretches hope for a better life? The highwayman that she had overheard Sister Eleanor and Sister Margaret whisper about in dreamy snatches during mealtime before Sister Catherine glared them into a respectful silence?

How could she be the daughter of a man that no one was even sure existed?

Someone shouted overhead, nearly making her jump out of her skin as a heavy object slammed against the floor, and soon the whole taproom exploded in noisy ferocity that rained down dust and other, chunkier objects she'd rather not examine too closely. Thomas came thumping down the stairs into the cellar, grinning like a madman.

"That oughta keep them tied up for a bit," he said as the floor shook with violence. "Come on, lass, follow me."

He wound through the stacks of barrels, dragging her along as the way grew narrower and the light dimmer. More than once she caught her hip on a crate corner or stubbed a toe against a barrel, anchored to the world only by Thomas's fingers wrapped firmly around her wrist. She'd never considered herself afraid of small spaces—there were so many wonderful, forgotten corners of the priory she could fit into and escape the soul-crushing work of scrubbing stone floors—but down here under the Blue Boar Inn, wedged tight between kegs with the ceiling threatening to cave in above, she might have to reconsider.

"Where are we going?" she huffed. "Should we not be attempting escape?"

"That's exactly what we're doing, lass," Thomas said, his voice loud in the confined space. He dropped her hand. "Watch your head through here, it gets right narrow."

Isabelle thought it already *was* narrow, but soon enough her forehead knocked against solid earth, forcing her into a half crouch as they continued on. The fight in the taproom receded into the distance, the light completely gone no matter how hard she strained her eyes to find it. She couldn't imagine how Thomas could fit in such a space, but every time she reached a tentative hand forward she met with the ties of his apron. Her heartbeat settled as they slipped farther from the soldiers.

"Is this . . . Are we going to meet . . . him?" she whispered.

Thomas grunted. "Of a sort."

Which started her heart pounding away again. Robin Hood. Her father. *Her father.* She didn't even know she had a father to wonder about. Plenty of other young women came to the priory with no father to give them a name, and she had not considered herself any different. At least not until just after her mother became prioress and Sister Catherine had sought to expend her fury on Isabelle by assigning her the worst parts of kitchen duty. She had picked up a pot of boiling water too soon after it was taken off the fire, the metal searing the flesh across both arms, and dropped it with a screech. The water spilled everywhere, soaking into the soft boots of the nearest sisters and burning their toes inside the leather.

Sister Catherine had screamed until her face turned red, calling Isabelle all manner of heinous things, but it was the last that sent her running to her mother for answers. *Treasonous bastard spawn.* She hadn't known a single one of those words, and when she asked her mother what they meant, the prioress had only asked who had spoken them, then disappeared to the kitchens. Sister Catherine was put on kettle duty after that, and Isabelle learned only later the true meaning of what she had been called. She could not imagine her mother committing any kind of treason, so Sister Catherine must have been talking about her father. But every time Isabelle attempted to ask her mother about him, Marien suddenly found pressing business in her duties as prioress that took her away, and Isabelle gave up on ever having a private moment to ask her again.

Which she never would have done if she'd known the answer.

"Here we are," Thomas said just as Isabelle ran right into his backside. "Steady now, lass."

"Apologies," she breathed. "I did not know we were stopping."

"Soldiers shouldn't be this far out from the Boar, but keep your wits about you," he said. "I'll go up first. Wait for my signal and follow after."

She didn't want to let him leave, considering she had no way to know how to follow him, but his ale-foam scent drifted upward, a sliver of moonlight dropping into the tunnel from above and illuminating the hard edges of a ladder. A few moments later he gave a soft whistle down into the tunnel, which she hoped meant *Come along, lass* and not *Run for your life, lass*.

The night's chill settled on her immediately as she emerged from a hollowed tree trunk into the woods. Thomas lowered a curtain of moss over the hollow, draping it so that no one would even know the opening was there unless they were already looking for it. She couldn't see the Blue Boar Inn from here, much less hear it, and she took a deep, cleansing breath for the first time since spotting the inn what felt like years ago. Thomas gave a trilling whistle that she would have mistaken for a birdcall if she weren't right next to him.

They stood perfectly still for several moments, waiting for what, Isabelle couldn't fathom. She glanced between the barkeep and the thicket of trees around them, waiting for something to change, but the night grew colder and her stomach grew louder and still nothing happened. Even Thomas looked annoyed.

"Bloody idiots probably carousing half in their cups by now," he muttered, releasing another sharp whistle, this one louder and more impatient. "What's the bloody point of a signal if no one's listening for it?"

"Who are we whistling to?" Isabelle asked, because it seemed safe enough to talk now.

"Nobody, apparently," Thomas groused, staring hard at the trees. He glanced down at her, his features softening at the complete befuddlement on her face. "Sorry, lass. This is all probably a bit of a shock for you, eh?"

"Yes," Isabelle said faintly. "Yes, it is."

"Robin would do much better to explain the whole business to you," Thomas said, his gaze sweeping the trees. "If he would show up."

"He is . . . Robin Hood is coming here?" Isabelle puffed out a few short breaths, staring hard into the trees like she could pierce the veil of night with her anxiety. "But I . . . Does he even know I exist? Does he know who I am? Is he expecting me?"

Which was a foolish question, for of course he would not be expecting her. Perhaps he didn't even want to see her. She didn't know the first thing about how she ended up at a priory with her mother and he ended up the king of the outlaws. Maybe she was about to be a very unwelcome intrusion. Her stomach gurgled loudly in sympathy.

"I can't—" Thomas began as a distant whistle cut through the trees, nothing more than the call of a nightingale. But Thomas grumbled at the sound. "Finally, the fools."

"Is that him? Them? The . . ." What had Thomas called them? "The Merry Men?"

"Better be," Thomas said, crossing his arms.

"I thought you said you did not know them," Isabelle whispered, but he held up a hand to silence any further inquiries.

Another call rose up, distinctly unnatural, and raised the hairs along the back of Isabelle's neck. She reached for an arrow over her shoulder on instinct, her fingers sliding into the well-worn grooves of her bow as the nock in the arrow snapped into place. Several birdcalls flitted across the distance like a flock taking wing, but Isabelle couldn't tell which might be real and which might not. Which, she supposed, was the point.

"Bloody hell," Thomas muttered, uncrossing his arms. "The soldiers must be in the forest. Stay here, lass, and hide in the tree. You'll be safe until I can fetch you."

"Should I not stay with you?" she asked, half afraid to be alone and half determined not to give in to her cowardice.

Thomas shook his head. "You're safer here. Besides which, Robin would string me up like a hare if anything happened to you on my watch. I'll come for you when it's safe, just listen for my whistle. You understand?"

Isabelle nodded, though she didn't understand, not really. She hadn't understood a single thing since her mother found her in the potato-cellar prison several days ago. But she climbed through the tunnel opening and down the ladder as Thomas settled the moss back into place, leaving her in more than one kind of darkness. She paced the small space, absently stroking the grooves in her bow, the wood worn smooth over the years from the oils in her hands.

Her ears strained toward the mossy opening overhead as her mind darted from one question to the next, trying to fit the pieces of her incomplete puzzle together into something that would make sense. If she were back in Kirklees Priory right now, it would be close to the matins hour, the sleepy first prayers of the day, leaning heavily against her mother as one of the sisters droned their prayers at the head of the chapel. She wished for the thousandth time that her mother were with her to sort everything out. God's teeth, she'd even take the comforting familiarity of Sister Catherine's nasally whine if it brought some semblance of balance to the world.

Something terrible has happened.

She'd never heard such a quaver in her mother's voice. Not when she fell from a window in the dormitory when she was six and knocked herself unconscious. Not even when she got lost in the woods for an entire day the first time she snuck out of Kirklees, just after her mother was elected prioress and Sister Catherine had threatened to put Isabelle in the stocks for mixing up wild carrot and hemlock and nearly killing Sister Margaret. They hadn't found her until after sunset, long past tears, shivering and huddled beneath an alder tree. Even then her mother had gathered her up, knocked the dust from her small habit, and murmured soothing promises that all was well as she carried Isabelle back to the refectory for a late supper.

Her mother was fashioned of the same material as her bow—flexible and smooth on the surface, but unbreakable at her core. She couldn't imagine anything that would actually scare the prioress, and the idea that something—or someone—could put such fear into her mother left her feeling that maybe the world was more chaotic and dangerous than she ever suspected.

"Oh hell, Isabelle girl," she hissed, the curse coating her tongue. "Pull yourself together. You're no good to anyone if you fall apart at the first sign of trouble. I don't believe Robin Hood is known as the king of the outlaws because he bends so easily to fear."

And even though she had yet to meet him, somehow the thought of the rogue outlaw close by, perhaps charging gallantly through the trees to tie up those soldiers in a snare of trickery, gave her the courage to square her shoulders and stand up. She was not just Isabelle of Kirklees; she was the daughter of Marien, prioress of Kirklees, and Robin Hood, the not-so-mythical outlaw king of Sherwood Forest. Or so the barkeep said. Still, it was a comforting idea if she was meant to face down seasoned soldiers with nothing more than her bow. She donned her parentage like a cloak of chain mail and climbed the ladder up to the base of the tree to listen for Thomas's signal.

It wasn't long before he returned, his heavy footsteps crunching over twigs and rustling tree branches. He'd said to wait, but Isabelle was too eager to prove her bravery. She slipped out of the tree, careful to drape the moss back in place as he'd done before. It was a very Robin Hood thing to do, she thought, to pay attention to the details. Her father would be proud, she hoped.

She turned to face the barkeep as he emerged from the trees, the faint creak of a poorly oiled metal joint the first and only warning of her hasty mistake. For it wasn't Thomas who appeared, but a young soldier, his sword drawn and pointed at her.

CHAPTER

FOUR

Isabelle froze, instantly regretting every single decision that brought her there. She should have waited for the signal; she should have listened more closely to the gait and pacing of the footsteps; she should have insisted on staying with her mother; she should never have taken that shot at the soldier in Kirklees, no matter how heinous his treatment of the villagers. Although she really couldn't bring herself to regret that last one, even if she'd ruined her own life in the process.

"You there, what are you doing here?" the soldier demanded, the tenor of his voice betraying his youth.

Isabelle nearly sobbed in relief. He didn't know who she was. She'd almost forgotten the hat that hid her hair and the modifications she'd made to her habit before entering the Blue Boar Inn. Her knees still shook like they were submerged in freezing water, and he still had her at swordpoint, but at least he hadn't called for anyone else to drag her away in chains. There was still a chance. A slim one, but a chance nonetheless.

"Oi, what's it to you what I'm about, then?" Isabelle asked gruffly, mimicking the aggressive nonchalance of Samuel from the tavern.

The soldier narrowed his eyes. "You are speaking to a soldier of the king's army, boy, and you will do so respectfully."

Isabelle snorted. "Not bloody likely, mate."

The soldier sucked in a sharp breath. Too far.

"I was only taking a walk, see," she continued hastily, letting a little of the rebellion out of her tone. "To take care of . . . of, uh, personal matters, see? I was just finishing up my business when you came about, like to startle me right down me britches."

The soldier turned his head to the side with a disgusted sneer. "That is far more information than I required, boy."

Isabelle cleared her throat, her cheeks warming. If only the sisters could hear her right now. She had earned at least a day of penance for her actions this night alone. "Yeah, well, you asked, mate."

"Yes, to my misfortune," the soldier muttered. He cut a glance back at Isabelle, his gaze probing in the darkness. "Where did you come from just now?"

"I told you—"

"No, before that," the soldier said. "Where were you that you needed to . . . take a walk?"

"Oh, uh . . ." Isabelle's mind blanked on any reasonable response. She couldn't say the Blue Boar Inn, because he might think she was trying to escape the fighting there. But she knew nothing of the land around here, and if she answered with something wrong or nonsensical, he might see through her cobbled disguise and arrest her anyway. "I was, uh . . . with my mate. Samuel."

"And where is this Samuel now?"

Isabelle scratched at her neck, a thin trickle of panic sweat winding down her back. "Well, uh, probably doing the same, sir. He's a . . . tiny fellow, you see, can't hold more than a thimble at a time. Mean as a hungry badger when he's in his cups, though. He'd even pick a fight with the likes of you."

"Is that right," the soldier said flatly. He glanced back toward the trees where he had first appeared, as if he would rather be back at the Blue Boar Inn cracking pates instead of discussing bodily functions with her. "I suggest you find your way back to your friend and keep him out of trouble, then, boy. There's enough of that going around this night."

"Yeah, sure, 'course," Isabelle said. The soldier had already turned away from her, as good as a dismissal, and Isabelle was so relieved and pleased, she committed her second mistake of the night. "None of the Boar for us tonight, sir!"

The soldier paused, and in the half turn it took him to face her again, all her hopes sank into a well of panic.

"What was that about the Boar?" the soldier asked, each word carefully crafted and laid out.

"What?" Isabelle asked, her voice edging higher.

"Would that be the Blue Boar Inn to which you are referring?" the soldier asked, his tone so very casual, his gaze so very not.

"I don't . . . I didn't . . ." Her heartbeat spiraled out of control. "No, I don't know a thing about a Blue Boar, or any other color boar. I said . . . what I said, what I meant, was no—no more for us. That's not—I don't know any Blue Boar, sir. Is that . . . What is that?"

It got worse as she went along, but the words kept bubbling up out of her as the soldier lifted his sword and advanced across the small space. His gaze cut through her disguise, his shoulders tensing and his eyes crinkling with determination. The world spun around and she feared she might faint, but still the words kept flowing, an endless stream of nonsense.

"I don't . . . look, I don't want any trouble here, sir," she said, stumbling back a step and bumping her hip on the tree. Only after she said it did she realize she'd forgotten to disguise her voice. She cleared her throat, muttering a few more gruff words, but it was too late.

"Put down your bow and stay where you are," the soldier said, the point of his sword only inches from her face.

"Yeah, sure, of course, mate," Isabelle said, bending down and placing her bow on the ground. "Don't want no trouble, none at all."

She waited until the soldier had lowered his sword to spring forward, barreling into him and knocking him flat on the ground. He coughed in surprise, stunned into momentary inaction, and Isabelle took the brief advantage to scramble up and snatch her bow, sprinting into the thick of the woods. She crashed over bushes and ricocheted off trees, raising an unholy racket that would do more to bring the soldiers down on her than the shout of warning from the one she'd left behind, but it couldn't be helped. She was spooked like a deer with an arrow through its haunch, leaving a bloody trail of noise even an amateur could follow.

Her chest heaved, her lungs screamed, but she could not stop. She was lost before she even knew it, running blindly at the contingent of soldiers for all she knew, but still she could not stop. Her heart or her lungs or both would have to explode before she could be brought down. She'd hunted a fox like this for hours once, the injured thing so desperate to escape she found it lying on its side, legs still twitching, eyes roving about madly. She'd sat with it and smoothed the fur behind its ears until it quieted down, then stilled forever.

If I escape this alive, I vow to never hunt another fox again, she thought, though she already knew the answer. The foxes were safe from her either way.

In the end, it was not a soldier or an expired heart that brought her down, but a lowly tree root, snagging her toe and sprawling her face-first in the dirt. She lay there in the sudden quiet, her ragged breaths muffled in crunchy, half-moldered leaves, her body refusing any command she issued. She could not have lifted a finger if an angel came down from on high and offered her eternal salvation. A wretched, broken sob slipped out of her, the last of her energy wasted on self-pity. She had just enough time to miss her mother, and the safety of Kirklees, and even the wretched Sister Catherine and her hatchet-like nose, before she heard the crunch of approaching footsteps.

Somehow, some way, she dipped into a well of strength she did not think existed to drag herself to her feet and draw up her bow. She might not be able to escape the soldiers, but she would be damned if they found her lying facedown in shame. She set an arrow and lifted the bow, focusing her attention along the narrow line of the shaft, stilling her breath and her heart and the maelstrom churning within her, to confront her fate.

"I know you are out here, girl," said the voice, off to the right, the brazen confidence in it sending a tremor through her hands. "Your . . . *friends* at the Blue Boar Inn have already been dealt with. Do not make me do the same to you."

Oh, poor Thomas. What had she brought down on him? On all those men in the tavern? How many lives tonight had been ruined—or worse, ended—because of her? Because of something she still did not understand. What hope did she have of saving herself if even those fearsome foresters could not stop the Wolf?

Moonlight glinted off the shoulder plate of the approaching soldier, only a few steps away, when a shadow dropped in front of her on silent feet, taking her by the waist and tossing her up into the branches as if she were nothing more than a sack of feathers. Another set of shadowy hands caught her, hauling her up and clamping a hand over her mouth to stifle her scream of surprise. She thrashed her legs, clawing at the figure to release its grip.

"Stop that or you'll knock us both out," a voice hissed in her ear, young and male and irritated.

Isabelle thrashed harder, biting into the hand still pressed against her mouth. The boy growled, doubling his grip on her waist in one sharp jerk.

"Would you stop that?" he said. "We're here to bloody *help* you."

Had she the freedom to speak, Isabelle might have protested, but below them the soldier stepped into view, eyes raking the trees for any sign of her. She stilled, her captor doing the same, neither of them daring a breath with the soldier mere feet below. Suddenly she was grateful for the hand over her mouth, for she wasn't sure she could stop the squeak of terror rising up from her belly otherwise.

"Where the hell has she gone now?" the soldier muttered, turning in a half circle. "One damn girl and we're combing half the country looking for her. A bloody mess, it is. The Wolf's lost his mind."

She sucked in a breath at the mention of the Wolf, her captor pressing his hand more firmly against her mouth to stop any further sounds escaping. Isabelle prayed to every saint she knew and a few she made up on the spot that the soldier would not look up, or even stop to rest. Already her thighs trembled from holding her position for so long, and she didn't think she could stand it much longer. The boy holding her must have sensed it, because he drew her back against his chest for support.

"Steady on, sister," he said, no more than a breath brushing against her ear that sent a single shiver over her. "I've got you."

Isabelle pressed her eyes closed, all of her attention fixed on one breath in, one breath out, steadying her nerves as her mother had always taught her when hunting. One thumb rubbed over the smooth polish of her bow handle, pressed against her side where the boy held her, the arrow caught under her arm and digging into her side. It would absolutely ruin the fletching, she was sure, but that was the least of her worries at the moment.

"Come on, Little," the boy muttered. "Do your job."

Something crunched through the forest off to their left, loud and clumsy like a wounded animal, or like a terrified young woman fleeing for her life if you didn't know any better. The soldier whirled toward the sound, sword raised on alert.

"Who goes there?" the soldier called out, but the crashing continued away from them, deeper into the trees. The soldier grunted, sheathing his sword and running off in the same direction. Still Isabelle did not dare to move, nor did the boy loosen his hold on her, until both the crashing and the soldier's pursuit faded into the night.

"I'm going to release you now," the boy said slowly, carefully, as if speaking to a small child or a wild animal. "You're not going to scream, you're not going to make any sudden movements, and if you bite me again, I'll bite you back. Understand?"

Isabelle nodded slowly, cutting her eyes to one side and then the other to try and get a better look at him. All she could make out was a pair of long legs clad in deep green, the hose thick and woolen and likely much more comfortable than her skirts tangled about her legs. Slowly the boy lifted his hand off her mouth, the other clamped firmly on her arm, but shifting so she could sit on her own. Moonlight dappled his face, hiding and revealing brown hair that rolled like waves on the sea, and dark eyes, his jaw sharp and his teeth a flash of white in the darkness.

"Well, you certainly increased our evening's entertainment," the boy said with a smirk.

"Who are you?" Isabelle asked, her voice shaky, her heartbeat pulsing through each word. She'd never been so close to a man who wasn't begging for food or trying to arrest her, and as her panic receded, something else rose to replace it, an odd hyper-awareness of every point of contact between them and the distant last time she'd been able to wash. There was something different about this boy, something stronger and leaner and more danger-ous than the foulmouthed boys from the tavern or the boys back in Kirkleestown, who always stank of muck and sweat. Something that set her pulse on an uneven rhythm again.

"I'm Adam," he said, oblivious to her racing thoughts. His eyes flickered over her, appraising her disheveled appearance. "And I'd guess from the look of you, you're the sister Thomas has been tear-ing up our forest looking for."

"Thomas." Her stomach flipped and she clutched his arm reflex-ively, shoving back her extended analysis of his jawline and the waves of his hair. "Is he all right, then?"

"Oh, I'd say so, probably half into our roasted duck by now. None too pleased with you, either, I'd guess. Didn't he tell you to stay put in the tunnel?"

Isabelle darted her gaze away, relief tumbling into a growing sense of guilt. "There were extenuating circumstances."

Adam chuckled. "Oh, I'd like to see you tell him that."

"How do we get down from here?" Isabelle asked, wishing to change the conversation and put some physical distance between her and the boy.

"We don't," Adam said, pointing higher into the tree. "We go up."

"Why would we . . ." she began, but trailed off as she followed his direction. For above them, several more feet into the foliage, she could just make out the shape of a rope bridge tied to the sturdy tree trunk, spidering out in every direction to the neigh-boring trees. She would never have noticed the ropes from the ground, twisted as they were in the leaves and branches, but from here they were unmistakable, and they were everywhere.

"What in the name of the Almighty . . ." she breathed, her eyes going round in fascination.

Adam grinned at her from the shadows. "Welcome to Sherwood Forest, sister."

CHAPTER
FIVE

Getting up to the rope bridge was a task more easily imagined than executed. Adam scaled the branches as if he were strolling up a hill while Isabelle struggled to follow with a maximum reach several inches shorter than his. She was used to climbing the neatly manicured trees of the orchard and had done so to slip out of the priory on several occasions, but these trees were different. Older than the kings themselves, these trees had stood guard over all that came to pass in Sherwood Forest since the first bud had sprung, and their massive branches did not suffer fools or beginners. She was still two branches below the bridge when Adam crouched down, perfectly balanced on the rope's edge, and lifted a brow at her.

"Need a hand, sister?" he asked.

"I . . . believe . . . I can . . . manage," she grunted as a strip of bark came away in her hand, nearly tumbling her to the ground far below.

"Yeah, I can see that," Adam said, but he didn't offer her help again.

It took several more tries, and a littering of bark on the surrounding limbs, but she finally managed to reach the thick line of rope and haul herself up. There wasn't much to support her, a single rope the thickness of her foot and two smaller ropes at waist height for balance, but it was better than scrabbling up the tree trunk. The rope swayed under her feet, the hard soles of her boots giving her no purchase.

"Takes some getting used to," Adam said, reaching out a hand to steady her until the rope stopped swaying. She could feel each one of his fingers pressed into her side, their heat suffusing the fabric of her habit. "Might help if you took those boots off."

"I . . . am . . . fine," Isabelle said, her heart hammering away with each wide sway of the rope. She'd rather fall a few dozen feet than bare her legs to him right then. "Where are we going?"

"Well, if you can get your balance, we're headed to the camp," Adam said, eyeing her boots doubtfully. "I suppose I could carry you."

"Absolutely not," Isabelle said, heat blossoming over her cheeks as she gripped both hand ropes until her knuckles were white. She pulled her shoulders back, willing the rope to stay steady under her feet. "I am fine. Shall we?"

His only answer was a raised eyebrow and a half smile, but he turned and led the way forward. He moved over the rope like it was wide as the king's road, his step sure and quick. She did her best not to rock the bridge, mimicking his movements by sliding her feet forward rather than picking them up. Still, she had to stop several times to regain her balance before she could continue on.

"What of the soldier?" she huffed, her concentration glued to the ropes as they reached the next tree where the rope bridge connected to another.

"Who, that tin head?" Adam glanced back at the forest floor. "He'll be fine. Little's probably led him halfway to Scotland by now."

"And the others?" she asked, hugging the trunk of the tree to slide to the next rope bridge. "The Blue Boar Inn?"

Adam gave a little huff of laughter. "I wouldn't worry about that lot. It's the king's lapdogs you should be worried for. They know better than to come round here. These lads must be green and hungry to bother the Boar."

But Isabelle knew why they had come. She swallowed back a lump of guilt, following in silence for several moments, the rest of her concentration going to keeping her footing on the rope. There were plenty other questions she could ask, but just watching the confident, economical movements of the boy reminded her how much of a fool she'd already made of herself. She didn't need to add to her humiliation with a thousand silly, ignorant questions. Even if she desperately wanted to ask them.

They had crossed several more trees, enough that Isabelle could navigate around their trunks without pressing her face against the rough bark, when Adam stilled, holding up two fingers for quiet. Isabelle wiggled behind him, taking shelter in the solid expanse of his shoulders while doing her best not to sway the rope as she searched the surrounding shadows for whatever had alerted him. Finally she heard it, a faint rustle drawing closer. Her heart pounded, her hands tightening on the rope, until Adam gave an exasperated sigh.

"You're doing it again," he called out.

"Doing what?" came a voice from below.

"Letting your arms swing."

"I am not!"

"You are! Old Man Jeffers could hear you coming."

A boy unwound from the darkness below, so tall and lanky Isabelle thought he must have been crafted from the same material as the trees. His hair gleamed a deep red in the faint moonlight, and he crossed his arms as he glared up at Adam. "That old turkey wouldn't hear the Four Horsemen coming, and I wasn't swinging my arms."

He hauled himself into the branches, vaulting up through the canopy until he landed on the rope bridge with a speed that left Isabelle breathless. He leaned past Adam to give her a grin. "Hello again, sister."

She regarded him with wide-eyed surprise. "Have we met?"

"Not properly, no, but once you've tossed a lass into a tree you're practically related, don't you think?"

Isabelle turned a furious shade of pink, glad for the darkness. "I see. That was you."

His grin widened. "That was me. Allan's the name, though everyone calls me Little."

She took in the sheer height of him. "I cannot possibly imagine why."

Adam chuckled, glancing at her over his shoulder. "His da is Allan A'Dale. Believe it or not, he's the littler of the two."

"For now," Little grumbled in a voice that indicated it was a sore subject for him.

"The soldier, Little?" Adam prompted.

"What? Oh, right. Him. Be picking his way out of Sherwood for the next year on."

Adam gave a nod, glancing over his shoulder at Isabelle. "See, sister? Nothing to worry about."

There was plenty to worry about, but she wasn't going to tell him that.

"Come on, then," Little said, bouncing up and down and setting the rope bridge moving in a way that made Isabelle queasy. "I'm near to starving and all the best bits will be gone from the feast by now."

Isabelle's stomach awoke from its slumber at the mention of a feast, grumbling loud enough that Little raised both eyebrows at her.

"That you, sister?" he asked.

She considered letting go of the rails and plunging to the ground rather than answer his question, but Adam saved her with a shove on Little's shoulder.

"Get on, then, if you're so hungry," he said. "It's you blocking the way."

They followed the bridges through the canopy, the single rope widening into a ladderlike structure of multiple ropes bound together, which made it far easier for her to walk along. Ahead the bridges connected to small wooden platforms encircling the trees, the planks fanned out like the rays of the sun to allow for easier passage between the bridges. She even thought she spied some larger structures, almost like houses, built around the trees in the distance, though she couldn't imagine how that would be possible.

But all of that faded to insignificance after the first whiff of roasted suckling pig came wafting through the trees. It took all her propriety not to shove the two boys aside and race across the bridges toward the source of that smell, so fatty and meaty and delicious. Some sigh of desire must have escaped her, though, for Adam glanced at her over his shoulder with a curious look.

"Are you all right, sister?"

All she could manage was a nod, her salivary glands flooding her mouth in anticipation. She barely registered the walkways expanding around her, knitted through the trees like a spider web, extending out to cheery little houses that were, in fact, built high up in the canopy around the tree trunks. She didn't even startle as other people appeared outside those houses and along those walkways, men and women and children going about their business, stoking cooking fires and hanging laundry and hauling braces of hares back from a long evening of hunting. All of them wearing the same deep green as Adam and Little.

But even in her hunger-induced stupor, Isabelle drew up short as the trees thinned out into a clearing filled with a feast the king himself would envy. She had never seen so much food, not even at harvesttime. There were a dozen stone tables patched in moss on the forest floor below, covered in platters of food so heavy Isabelle doubted she could lift one. It was enough to feed Kirkleestown three times over for the remainder of the year. Each table teemed with foresters, shouting and laughing and lifting flagons of ale like there wasn't an entire contingent of soldiers scouring the woods just then.

"Where are we?" she breathed in awe.

"The outlaw camp," Adam said, as if it were the most natural thing in the world. "Come on, let's get you something to eat before Little opens his mouth and inhales it all."

He led her to a break in the platform where a ladder extended down the trunk to the ground. If anyone was curious about her, they hid it well, their glances sliding past her to more interesting sights. Sure enough, Little had already elbowed his way into a table still piled high with food. He waved a turkey leg in her direction and she nearly bit his hand off.

"Come on, sister," he said, mouth full. "Don't be shy, I know you're hungry."

She didn't even have the capacity to be embarrassed by the observation because she was too busy tearing up the nearest loaf of bread and shoving chunks into her mouth. Unlike the indigestible disappointment of the bread Thomas gave her, this bite dissolved into a heavenly, buttery mess in her mouth, and she closed her eyes and moaned with pleasure before devouring the rest. Little watched the proceedings with wide eyes.

"Never seen a girl eat like that," he said. "Don't know whether to be impressed or afraid."

"I'd better tell Thomas we found the sister," Adam said. He pointed a finger at Little. "No fighting."

Little spread his arms wide, the portrait of innocence. "What do I have to fight about?"

"You always manage to find something. Keep an eye on the sister here, would you?"

Isabelle was too consumed by the delicious feast to note his departure. She dove into each dish with abandon, hardly tasting some of them in her eagerness to fill her empty belly. The genial conversation of the outlaws washed over and through her, and as her hunger dropped to a low growl, she was able to take stock. She wouldn't have guessed these people to be outlaws were she not sitting in their hidden camp, eating what was probably stolen food. Despite all the tales she had heard of Robin Hood and his Merry Men, she didn't expect to find an entire community of men, women, and children thriving within the wilds of the forest. In an odd way it reminded her of Kirklees Priory, a community isolated from the greater world, though with far more men and meats.

"So, sister, what is it you've done to bring the king's wrath down on you?" Little asked, gnawing thoughtfully on the remaining bits of meat still clinging to his turkey leg.

Isabelle's stomach lurched. "What makes you think I've done anything?"

Little shrugged. "No one comes to the camp on a lark."

Isabelle took another bite of the roasted pig, chewing slowly to consider the various answers to that question. Had he asked a few hours ago, she would have thought the answer far more simple;

but the revelations from Thomas threw everything she thought she knew into confusion. She swallowed the meat, deciding on the easiest of the answers she could give.

"I shot a soldier off his horse," she said.

Little perked up. "Go on, then, you did not! That's bloody brilliant!"

Isabelle winced. "It did not feel brilliant at the time. I only meant to spook the horse, but the fool pulled his reins at the last minute and the horse reared, and the arrow caught him right in the shoulder, just between the armor."

Little gave a boisterous laugh that drew the attention of half the clearing, and Isabelle sank down behind the carcass of the suckling pig. "Oh, I bet he screamed like a bloody girl. They always do."

"Always?" Isabelle lifted her brows. "Do you make a habit of shooting soldiers?"

"We're the Merry Men, sister. It's part of the job."

"Don't let him fool you," said a wry voice edged in an Irish accent. A young boy no taller than Isabelle plopped down in a vacant spot across from them, his smile open and welcoming. "He's never shot a man in his life. All those long limbs, wasted on bad aim."

"I shoot all right," Little said, looking upward in contemplation. "If it's the broad side of a barn you're aiming for."

The boy laughed. "Your strength lies in the staff, Little." He looked to Isabelle with a serious expression. "The Almighty help the man who gets close enough to test it."

"I am not sure the Almighty concerns himself with the petty nature of men fighting," Isabelle replied. "He is, after all, a just God. I would think he supposes if one were to take up such a challenge, one would deserve such a thrashing."

The boy laughed. "You sound like Father Donnell, my old tutor, whenever I found myself on the thrashed end of a scuffle. Welcome to Sherwood. I'm Patrick."

Isabelle nodded in greeting, taken aback by the easy camaraderie in his tone. Were all the outlaws so friendly? "Isabelle."

Little leaned forward gleefully. "The sister here was just telling me how she shot a soldier off his horse."

Patrick looked to her in surprise. "You're a sister?"

She matched his look. "That was the most astonishing part of what he said to you?"

"There you are," came Thomas's voice from the crowd. He threaded through the outlaws, Adam close behind, bearing down on her like an angry bull and thrusting one accusing finger at her. "You were supposed to stay put."

"I did," Isabelle protested, her voice pitching up in an effort to cover her guilt. "But you were gone so long I was afraid something might have happened to you. And then I heard something, and I thought it might be you—"

"Even though you didn't hear the signal," Thomas interjected. "Which I told you to listen for."

"Well, yes, but I thought you might have forgotten. Or maybe you could not give the signal because you were in danger."

Thomas crossed his arms over his chest, glaring down at her. "And so you thought the best idea was to leave the safety of the tunnel and put yourself at risk as well?"

"No!" Isabelle fumbled with the heel of a loaf of bread. "I mean, that was not my intention at the time."

Thomas blustered through a curse as Little let out a booming laugh. "A sister after my own heart."

"I am not actually a sister," Isabelle said reflexively, staring at the table.

"That's enough, Little," said another forester, stepping forward beside Thomas. He towered over the barkeep by at least a head, and considering the sharp slope of his nose and the red tint to his hair, she guessed he must be Allan A'Dale. "Don't you boys have some cleaning to do?"

"Cleaning?" Little snorted. "Since when have we cleaned—"

"Since now," Allan said, in a tone that brooked no refusal. He turned his stern expression on Patrick. "I trust you will keep my son out of trouble?"

"Sure," Patrick said, looking not at all sure, and hopped up from his seat. "Uh, why don't we see about clearing the tables down there, Little?"

"Clearing tables?" Little stood up, shaking his head. "We're bloody outlaws, not maids. Next you know he'll be asking us to wash our own laundry. Then what would my mum do?"

His protests trailed off as Patrick led him away, and Isabelle somehow felt more exposed without the two of them there. Allan turned his attention to her, his expression grave if not unkind. "I understand you have need of the Merry Men, lass."

Isabelle straightened, her mouth going dry as her stomach threatened to eject the bounty of food she had just shoved in it. There was so much she wanted to say, to ask, that she could only manage a simple "Yes." She glanced at Thomas, unsure of what she could reveal. "I have a message for Robin. Robin Hood."

"Small trouble there," Allan said, looking apologetically to Thomas and back to her. "He's not here."

CHAPTER

SIX

*H*e *truly is real,* Isabelle thought, at the same time that Thomas gave a curse.

"Where's he bloody gone this time?" the barkeep demanded.

"North," Allan said apologetically. "To York, to talk with Tuck. He thinks King John will go back on the charter he signed at Runnymede, which means the country is headed for war. And if there's a war between the king and the rebel barons, we all suffer. Robin's hoping Tuck might be able to talk some sense into the rebel barons."

"Of course he is," Thomas grunted. "When's he due back?"

Allan shrugged a shoulder. "I'm not sure. He said, and I quote, 'Diplomacy is a snail's race.' I took that to mean it might be a while before he returned."

"Bloody hell," Thomas said, glancing at Isabelle. "This can't wait. Can you get a messenger up there to him?"

"'Course I can," Allan said.

"I could go tonight," Adam offered. "Wouldn't take me more than a week."

Isabelle stood up. "And I shall go with you."

"No," the three men said simultaneously.

Allan tapped his chin thoughtfully. "I'd tell you to take Little with you, but that might be more trouble than it's worth."

"Excuse me!" Isabelle said, indignant at being so summarily dismissed.

"You'll stay here, lass," said Thomas, patting her on the shoulder. "Safer that way."

"We could cut through the forest to Lincoln, take the king's road from there," Adam said. "It's a risk, but it's the fastest route."

"Excuse me," Isabelle said more forcefully. "But I will not be staying anywhere. With all due respect, you cannot keep me here."

Allan managed to look chagrined as he answered. "All due respect, lass, but we surely can."

Adam crossed his arms and looked at her. "You'd only slow us down, sister. The king's men are thick between here and York, and we can't spend all our time rescuing you."

"You would not have to rescue me," Isabelle said, heat rising along her neck. "I am perfectly capable of taking care of myself."

The three men looked at each other.

"When was it exactly you were taking care of yourself?" Adam asked. "When we saved you from that soldier back there because you didn't stay put like Thomas said?"

"I was—that was . . . different," Isabelle sputtered, glowing like an ember.

"This isn't a game, lass," Thomas said, his voice both firm and gentle. He took her by the shoulders, turning her to face him. "You were as brave a lass as any, bringing word this far. You do your family proud. But these are Robin's men, and you must let them do their work. They'll get your message to him, I can promise you that."

"I do not doubt they can find him. But you cannot truly expect me to sit around, twiddling my thumbs, while . . . while . . ." She glanced around the clearing, dropping her voice so only Thomas could hear. "While the Wolf hunts me down. You said that Robin is my . . . please, Thomas. You have to understand why I must go."

"You'll be safe from the Wolf here, lass," said Thomas in an equally low voice. "The Merry Men will protect you, and they'll bring Robin back. You'll have your time, lass, and your answers. This is the best way. Marien sent you to me for safekeeping. I won't betray that trust."

Isabelle felt her chances slipping away, powerless to change their minds. And after all, were they wrong? Would she really not be a burden? What value could she bring to these trained forest-ers, more at home in the world than she and far more skilled in stealth and combat? Should she really risk her life—all of their lives—just because she wanted to meet the man Thomas said was her father?

"I'll pack some supplies for you," Allan said to Adam. "And you'd best take Little along. Just make sure he's not so deep in his cups he can't walk this time."

Adam gave him a flat look. "He's *your* son, Allan."

"Which is why I know you'd best hurry if you've any chance of stopping him early," Allan replied.

"I'll take Patrick as scout, which means Helena will insist on coming as well," Adam said. "We could use her bow arm if things get sticky."

Isabelle leaned in, scenting her opportunity. "I can shoot."

Adam glanced at the bow still slung over her shoulder. "I'm sure you can, sister."

"I could be a bow arm for you. I can hunt, and track."

Adam took a deep breath, speaking slowly. "We don't need a hunter. We need an archer."

"I can shoot," Isabelle insisted. She looked between the three men. "Give me any target, any test. If I can outshoot anyone you pit against me, will you consider letting me go?"

"No," Thomas said flatly.

"Hang on, Thomas," said Allan, his gaze turning thoughtful. "The sister has a right to try and earn her place among the Merry Men if that's what she wants."

"Earn a place?" Thomas grunted, rubbing his forehead in frustration. "Allan, you can't actually be giving the lass credence, can you? She's a child, and a nun. She's already got a calling. She doesn't know aught about the world out there, and she's been put in my charge. I'll not throw that duty to the wind on account of her shooting a few hay bales."

"We are sisters, actually, not nuns," Isabelle said. "And I have not taken vows. My mother has not allowed it."

"But you think she'd allow this?" Thomas asked.

"I . . ." Isabelle glanced at the foresters. "Perhaps. If it were necessary. Which I would say it is, as she has sent me all this way."

Allan gave Thomas a patient look. "We don't turn away anyone who wants to join the cause, isn't that what Robin himself has said? There've been plenty who have come to us younger and knowing less. What makes this girl any different?"

Thomas stared at him for a long moment, his nostrils flaring in irritation as he considered his answer. Isabelle did not dare to speak, not even to breathe, as she waited for what the barkeep might reveal in his reply. He had clearly not told the outlaws about why she was there, or who she was, which meant Robin had kept her existence a secret from them. Something stabbed her chest at the thought of her father sharing his life with all these men and never once mentioning her. Did he really care so little for her? Or did he not even know of her? Her mother had certainly kept her share of secrets. Could Isabelle's very existence have been one? Her gaze flickered to Adam, his dark eyes moving over her thoughtfully in a way that made the heat rise to her face once more. Why was he staring at her?

"This is madness," Thomas finally grunted. "Sheer idiocy."

"But you'll let me do it?" Isabelle asked, clasping her hands together.

He stared at her balefully. "Don't seem I have much choice, does it?"

Isabelle gave a little clap, bouncing up on the balls of her feet. "Oh, thank you, Thomas. Thank you."

She threw her hands around his neck on impulse, giving him a hard squeeze. He grunted at the affection, patting her back heavily.

"I shall be fine, I promise," Isabelle said, pulling back.

"You haven't actually passed the test yet," Adam said dryly.

"Oh, yes, right," Isabelle said, smoothing her hands down the front of her habit, her palms suddenly sweaty. The confidence she'd felt just a moment ago bubbled into a nervous energy that made her jitter. "Where shall we compete?"

Adam lifted a brow at Allan. "This was your idea."

"The range," Allan said firmly. "Get Little and Patrick to help you set up the arrows and clear the targets."

As the outlaws disappeared to prepare for the competition, Thomas turned to her. "I suppose it's time you and I had a chat."

Isabelle swallowed around the lump in her throat. "Please do not try to talk me out of it. You of all people should understand why I must go."

"Oh, aye, that I do," Thomas conceded. "You're wily as your da and stubborn as your ma. But you might as well know what you're coming up against, best as I can tell you. Robin could explain a sight better, but of course he's gallivanting about the country playing the hero."

"Does he . . . does he know about me?" Isabelle asked.

"Course he does," Thomas said with surprise. "You're the reason all this happened."

Isabelle's stomach fluttered. "What?"

Thomas glanced around at the outlaws gathered in the clearing. "Come on, then. This isn't a conversation for general ears."

He led her away from the clearing toward a small stand of trees with several trunks cut to low stumps, perfect for sitting. The camp, so lively and full of noise, was like an upside-down world from the priory, where she was used to the muted snoring of the sisters and the quiet rustling of night beyond the dormitory. Little bonfires twinkled throughout the trees, keeping the late-autumn chill at bay, and the houses overhead flickered with lamplight and movement. It lent a magical glow to the trees, dispelling the intimidating shadows she'd faced earlier.

"It's only fair you know what you're walking into," Thomas said. "I don't know the whole of it, mind you. The nobility tie themselves up in all kinds of rules that don't concern me. But your da has told me enough about the man hunting you."

"You mean the Wolf," Isabelle said, heart pounding at the mention of the mystery man.

"Aye, the Wolf." Thomas made a face as if pronouncing the name left a foul taste in his mouth.

"Who is he?" Isabelle asked, not sure she really wanted the answer.

"You'd know him by the name of Sir Roger of Doncaster."

"Sir Roger . . ." She studied the pattern of the fallen leaves on the ground, chasing a faint memory. "I feel as if I have heard the name before."

"I should think so, considering he's the king's right-hand man."

And then it came to her, draining the blood from her face and gripping her chest so that she could not breathe. A name only spoken in hushed tones by the townspeople of Kirklees, quickly smothered under bowed heads and hasty hands. A name even the soldiers who locked her up spoke with reverence, no trace of their previous arrogance on display.

"Sir Roger," she said, her voice no more than a whisper, her head spinning.

"Most powerful man in the country, second only to the king," Thomas said gravely. "The *most* powerful if you ask the right people. Nothing happens Sir Roger don't know about. Even John's afraid of him, and that fool don't have the sense to be afraid of much. Sir Roger has earned himself a reputation for carrying out the king's dirty business these past twenty years."

"But what could he possibly want with me?" Isabelle asked, her gaze skittering over the surrounding trees as if they might come alive with soldiers at any moment.

"It's not to do with you, lass," Thomas said sadly. "Your da, Robin, he made a powerful enemy in the king back when John was just a prince lusting after his brother's throne."

"How could Robin have made an enemy of John?" Isabelle asked. "What happened?"

Thomas scratched at his beard. "That's where my know-how gets a bit fuzzy, lass. Far as I could understand it, Robin was some hoity toity fella in the nobility back in his youth. John thought your da was a threat to his campaign against Richard the Lionheart, so he sent the Wolf to take care of it."

"Take care of it?" The earth moved unsteadily beneath Isabelle's boots. "Do you mean—"

Thomas sliced a hand across his throat, clicking his tongue in a crude approximation of an ax strike. "He was supposed to kill your da and your ma, and you still in your ma's belly. Thought he got the job done, too, didn't he? Only they escaped."

"I do not understand," Isabelle said, shaking her head. "Why did my mother not tell me any of this before? How could my father just leave us in that place, and come here to play at . . . what? Being an outlaw? Why not come back for us? For me?"

Thomas shrugged. "You'd have to ask him that yourself. But what I do know is there's old blood between Sir Roger and your da. Bad blood. It's him Robin's been outrunning these past sixteen years, hoping this day would never come. But if it has—if the Wolf has found out Robin's still alive—nothing will stop him now. He'll have every tin head from here to York hunting you."

Isabelle's head swayed, and she braced both hands against the tree trunk to keep from falling. How had her life turned so inside out in a matter of days? All because she shot that stupid arrow.

"I should have stayed in the priory as Mother told me," she whispered. "She was trying to protect me, and I was too selfish to see it. I just wanted to help, and now I've made everything worse. I'm such a fool."

"You're not a fool, girl," Thomas said quietly. "You've the impatience of youth on you. You can make a better choice now and stay. You're safer here in Sherwood surrounded by the Merry Men than you will be out there."

But she'd already seen what the Wolf's forces did to people who got in the way of what they wanted. She'd stood between the soldiers and the townspeople, the only thing that stopped them from trampling innocent people beneath their horses' hooves. She couldn't put these people at risk, even if they were the famed Merry Men. She shook her head resolutely.

"I will go," she said. "I will find Robin."

"If you win," Adam said from behind them.

Isabelle turned around to face the young outlaw leaning against a tree, a ghost of a smile across his face. He was so at home in the wilderness, his eyes gleaming like a nocturnal hunter. Her heart started its hammering again, racing for a different reason at the sight of him. He seemed to sense the catch in her breath because his smile widened slightly, bringing more warmth to the cool night air.

"We're ready for you, sister," he said.

She nodded, a soothing numbness falling over her as her body went through the motions of following Adam around the camp, past the remains of the feast to a long stretch of open field with three targets set up at varying distances, their centers lost in the murky darkness of predawn. The carousing outlaws had abandoned their feast for a greater entertainment, clustered around the edges of the shooting range. They cheered when they saw her, the naive challenger. Allan A'Dale stood before them, raising his long arms to the sky.

"Merry Men of Sherwood," he called, "there is one among us who wishes to join the notorious ranks of the fellows of Robin Hood!"

Several more cheers peppered through the crowd at that.

"Does it have to be such a spectacle?" Isabelle muttered.

Adam looked down at her, amused. "You haven't met Robin. This is subtle."

The comment stung for reasons she couldn't properly rationalize, and so she hunched her shoulders as Allan continued.

"As you know, no man or woman, however desperate their plight, can wear the Lincoln greens without earning them. This lass, Isabelle of Kirklees, has challenged for a place among the Merry Men! Only by defeating our champion at a shooting competition will she earn her place and deserve the title of true outlaw."

As the outlaws cheered, some shouting bets among them, Allan

A'Dale held an arm out, calling her forward. After a brief moment, Adam set his hand on the small of her back, giving her a little push.

"Go on, then, sister," he whispered against her ear. "Show us what you've got."

"Now, Isabelle, as the challenger, you have first choice of bow," Allan said, sweeping his hand to the side to indicate a rack full of bows. He gave her a wink. "Choose wisely, lass."

Isabelle examined each bow, all of them finely crafted and well used, many of them taller than she was. She wondered how many, if any, Robin had previously wielded. She stepped back, clearing her throat.

"I shall use my own bow."

Allan raised both brows dramatically, the bets among the men shifting and swaying at her proclamation. "The lady shall use her own bow! And now, Merry Men, for our challenger!"

The crowd roared as Allan swept his hand to one side, right past Isabelle. She turned, giving Adam a questioning look, but he shook his head.

"Oh, not me, sister," Adam said, stepping aside. Behind him the crowd parted as Patrick dragged a young woman forward, small and compact, her expression as sharp as the short sword she wore at her belt.

"Who in their bloody ale-soaked mind challenged me to a shooting contest?" the girl groused, whipping a long, dark braid over her shoulder.

Isabelle's jaw went slack at the sight of the girl, dressed in the same garb as the men and loaded with twice as many weapons. She wore them with a comfort that suggested she knew how to use them, and the look the girl pinned on Isabelle made her suddenly doubt every shot she had ever made. For a brief, ludicrous moment, she imagined Sister Catherine trying to assign penitentiary chores to this girl, and the thought made her want to laugh aloud.

"Helena," said Adam to the girl, not bothering to suppress his smile. "Meet Isabelle. Isabelle, this is Helena. Our best shooter. Well, second best, but Robin's not here, is he? The sister would challenge you for a place in the Merry Men, Helena."

Isabelle cleared her throat, the manners her mother instilled in her taking over as she stepped forward and gave a small nod. "Pleased to meet you, Helena."

Helena looked her up and down. "Not bloody likely. Whose joke is this? If Little's still sore about the last thrashing I gave him, this isn't much of a punishment."

"No." Isabelle faltered, glancing at the others. "I do not . . . This is not a joke. I wish to challenge you for a place among the Men."

Helena crossed her arms, her lips pressed thin. "Well, then, I hope you've got somewhere else to sleep tonight, sister. Let's shoot."

CHAPTER
SEVEN

"**O**ne arrow per archer at each target," Allan said, waving to the three targets set up down the range. "Helena will shoot brown, Isabelle will shoot white. Whoever's aim is truest wins the challenge. Are the archers ready?"

Isabelle chanced a glance at Helena before nodding. The girl did not return the glance, her eyes trained on the bales down the range, the first set at ten paces, the second at twenty, and the farthest one at thirty paces. Patrick trotted to stand outside the range near the first target, giving a wave when he was in position to call the winner.

Allan raised his arms. "As our champion, Helena will shoot first."

Helena stepped up to the line in front of the first target, nocking the arrow with brown fletching and lifting the bow without preamble. Isabelle had to admire her stance, wide and strong, not even a tremble of emotion before she loosed the arrow. Her shot flew straight to the center of the target even though she'd hardly sighted down the range. The men gave up a cheer when Patrick confirmed the hit, but Helena merely grunted. She looked at Isabelle expectantly.

"Your turn, sister," she said, tossing the last word out like an insult.

Isabelle stepped up to the line and planted her feet resolutely. She had half a mind to take the same careless approach to her first shot, but she suspected Helena had done it to lure her into making a mistake. She would take her time and plan the shot. Her heart pounded against her chest even though she'd made such simple shots thousands of times. They'd never meant anything like this before, though. Now, as she checked the strength of the bow and ran her fingers along the fletching of her arrow, the full import of her actions hit her. She was not only shooting to prove herself worthy, she was shooting for the right to fight for her family. One false move, one moment of hesitation, would end her chances.

"For Mother," she whispered, sighting down the range and letting the arrow fly.

The arrow hissed through the air, striking the target with a resounding thunk. A murmur rippled through the gathered onlookers as the white fletching nestled next to brown, so close it seemed they had sprung from the same shaft. Helena rolled her shoulders and straightened her spine, eyeing Isabelle guardedly.

Patrick squatted before the target, his head jerking back in surprise as he turned to the crowd. "White takes the target."

Isabelle pressed her lips together to suppress the smile that rose up, her toes curling in her boots with the victory. Conversation rumbled through the outlaws, several of them shoving forward to get a better look at her. Isabelle met Adam's gaze, her chin lifted high. One side of his mouth curled up and he gave her a wink that made her flush.

"I suppose that little bow has a bit of power to it after all," he murmured.

Allan motioned to the next target. "Isabelle takes the next shot."

She stepped up to the line in front of the second target, taking the same care and precision before letting loose her arrow. It thudded into the center straight on, raising a murmur of appreciation from several of the outlaws. The attitude toward her shifted as Allan clapped her on the back. The sisters had never treated her skill with the bow as anything other than an irritating necessity, a means of procuring meat and keeping her out of their way. But here, among the outlaws, it was a skill worthy of praise.

Helena stepped up to the line and took her stance, this time lining up her shot carefully and sighting down the range toward the target. There was no flippancy in her movements, no casual dismissal of the challenge. She was alert and focused, her hand drawing back to her ear as she stretched the bow into a deep curve. When she let go, the arrow whistled with deadly precision toward the target, hitting the center beside Isabelle's arrow. Patrick trotted to the target to examine the results.

"She's just nudged out white," he called out. "Right down the center. Point goes to brown!"

Helena smirked, drawing another arrow and casually checking the fletching. Isabelle let out the breath she was holding with a deflated sigh, the confidence once again leaching out of her. In any other situation, she would have admired the outlaw girl's prowess with the bow, might have even asked her for insight into her technique. But now she only wished the girl were not so much better than her at her only useful skill.

"The score stands one to one," Allan declared. "This is our final shot, for the win. Helena shoots first."

Helena stepped up to the line, sighting down to the final target thirty paces away. Even in the pinkening light of dawn the target was no more than a suggestion of an outline, a patch of red and white in the deep shadows. Isabelle stared hard at Helena's rigid shoulders, willing her to miss. The outlaw girl took care, bending the bow in a narrow arc as far back as her arm would allow. The arrow flew straight and true, sinking several inches into the red center of the target. The outlaws gave a rousing cheer of support for their champion. It seemed a foregone conclusion to them that the battle was won.

Helena leveled her gaze at Isabelle. "Beat that, sister."

Isabelle stepped up to the line, holding her bow down while she considered her options. From where she stood, the arrow looked dead-on, and she could do no more than hope to hit the same shot. Even if she split the arrow, it wasn't enough. She needed not just to win, but to win them over. She needed something more dramatic, something to play to their theatrical tastes. A shot to best all other shots.

She studied the target for several moments, anchoring its location in her mind. The wind blew gently, tickling a stray curl against her face. In that moment her senses stilled, weeding out the distractions of the outlaws' reveling and her thudding heart until there was nothing but the target and her bow.

"A blindfold," she called out, loud enough to silence those closest to her. She turned her gaze to Adam. "If you would be so kind as to provide one."

Adam looked incredulous, but Isabelle did not waver. A murmur passed among the Merry Men, sounding their doubt and surprise and begrudging respect that she would attempt such a feat, even if they did not believe it possible she could complete it. She kept her gaze locked on Adam, a challenge passing between them. Finally he shrugged one shoulder, waving to the Merry Men.

"A blindfold for the challenger!" he called out.

Someone brought forth a long strip of cloth. "I hope you know what you're doing," he murmured, securing the blindfold over her eyes. He was close enough that she could smell the crushed pine needles and fresh earth on his clothes, his fingers brushing the back of her neck as he tied the knot.

"As do I," she replied with a small shiver, but the cloth was secured and she could not turn back.

The foresters dropped into a silence so full it weighed on Isabelle's bones, and it took all her effort just to lift the bow. She reached for the quiver on her back but fumbled the arrows, the wood clacking together as she struggled to grab one. Helena snorted next to her, several isolated snickers peppering the crowd behind her, but Isabelle did not heed them.

In her mind's eye, she reconstructed the shooting range, the milky target with a drop of red swimming into view. The wind rustled again, adding definition to the trees in her mental picture and pinpointing the target before her. She set her feet in the spongy earth, her rib cage settling low and grounding her. She nocked the arrow and drew the string back, the creak loud and close. She drew in one deep breath before releasing the tension in her fingers, the arrow whistling away to seal her fate.

She couldn't bear to remove the blindfold, but she didn't have to. A collective gasp sounded behind her, followed by a roar. She lifted one corner of the blindfold, squinting down the range even as Little swooped in and lifted her up on his shoulders. All she could see was white fletching against the red.

"You split her arrow!" Little shouted, dragging her into the thick of the welcoming outlaws. "You split her bloody arrow blindfolded! Welcome to the Merry Men of Sherwood!"

Isabelle squatted, pulling at the thick woolen hose that clung to her calves and thighs, the material scratchy and rough against her skin. The tunic wasn't much better, though she was used to such coarse material under her arms and across her shoulders. Her limbs were light, no longer weighed down by the heavy skirts, but somehow she was still warm in the cool dawn. The boots were wondrous, soft and molded to the pads of her feet. She bounced on the balls of her feet, luxuriating in the freedom of movement.

"I must say, Isabelle, the Lincoln greens do favor you," Patrick said, hauling a knapsack full of supplies to the edge of the camp.

Isabelle preened at the compliment, squaring her shoulders and adjusting her meager bag of supplies across her chest, a few slices of bread and the healing salve from her mother tucked away in a new burlap sack. Her bow hung over her shoulder, nestled beside a quiver fully stocked with arrows courtesy of the Merry Men. Adam appeared with a bundle of weapons, tossing a pair of daggers to Patrick while looking her up and down with a faint smile.

"Certainly a sight better than what you were wearing before," he said.

Isabelle flushed, but refused to let him take away from her victory. "A prize well-earned is worth its weight in gold, even if it is fashioned from scratchy wool."

Adam tilted his head in concession. "Just do yourself a favor and try not to look so smug about winning when Helena gets here. She's a bit sore."

"She'll get over it," Patrick said, patting Isabelle on the arm. "No one's ever beaten her. You were quite the shock to her confidence."

"It was bloody brilliant," Little said, appearing through the trees with a wide grin. "You smashed it."

"It was a lucky shot," Helena snapped behind him, her expression harsh in the early morning light. She glanced at Isabelle. "And she only won because my arrow was already dead-on in the center."

"Come, now, Helena," Patrick said in a conciliatory tone. "It was a brilliant shot. Doesn't mean yours wasn't, too."

Helena grunted a nonresponse, dropping her pack on the ground to check through its contents once more before they left. Isabelle's hopes that they might make friends were quickly dwindling in the shade of the other girl's dismissal. It would not be the first time she had been shunned by another of her gender, but somehow this stung worse than any new arrival at the priory avoiding her company once Sister Catherine got hold of them. The easy welcome of the Merry Men had made her feel on the edge of being a part of something for the first time, but Helena's reserve reminded her of what she truly was—an outsider. Could she find no place where she fit in the world?

Allan A'Dale appeared with Thomas, both men grim and resolute in the early morning light. Thomas gave Isabelle a long look, huffing a breath at the sight of her in the Lincoln greens, but he did not try to talk her out of going. She figured it was the closest she would get to his approval.

"Cut through Sherwood up to Lincoln and follow the king's road north to York," Allan told Adam, before landing a meaningful look on his son. "No taverns, no towns, keep to the trees and move quickly. Last we heard from Tuck, the soldiers are thick through those parts. Check in with David at the Wounded Lion in Lincoln. He'll get you food and supplies to get you up to York. But *no drinking*."

"Well, if you're gonna make it a bloody chore," Little muttered, but he didn't meet his father's eye.

"Little," Allan warned.

"Yeah, all right, Da, no drinking," he said, rolling his eyes skyward. Patrick and Adam shook their heads.

"We're overlooking the obvious here," Helena said. "Just leave him behind."

"Oi, don't you start on me," Little said. "If anyone's getting left behind, it's the one just lost a shooting match to a bloody sister."

Helena turned an impressive shade of crimson, her fists balling up as she started for Little. Only Patrick's intervening stopped them from falling into a brawl. Allan shook his head.

"What a fool's errand this is," he said. "I ought to keep the lot of you here."

Adam clapped a hand on his shoulder. "We'll be fine, Allan." He glanced back at his crew. "Probably."

"Go on, then," Allan said, resigned. "You're losing the day."

Thomas took Isabelle by the shoulders as the others hefted their packs and prepared for the journey through the woods. "Know this, lass—the man you're up against, he is capable of any evil, and he has eyes and ears everywhere. For your safety, for Robin's safety, no one can know who you are, or who Robin really is. Not even these lads here. The more they know, the more he can use them against you."

Isabelle nodded, heart thudding. "I understand. Thank you, Thomas. For everything you have done."

He nodded. "Good luck and God speed you, lass."

Adam quirked a brow at her as she stepped back. "You ready, sister?"

She gave a nod, lifting her chin. "Let us go."

CHAPTER
EIGHT

They followed the eastern road to Lincoln under the cover of the trees, tracking along its dusty curves at a safe distance. The sky lightened to drifts of white clouds against a cerulean backdrop as they traveled, the sun bringing the warm tones of autumn to the trees. Isabelle's step lightened with the sky, the full splendor of day warming her bones and lifting her spirit.

"Where did you learn such a crack shot, sister?" asked Little after they had cleared the outlaw camp.

"Yes, tell us where you learned such a dramatic and useless shot," muttered Helena.

"Don't be sore because she beat you square," said Little.

"I didn't need a blindfold to hit my target," Helena said hotly.

"I imagine if you'd had one you would have won," Adam said mildly. He turned to Isabelle, his gaze warm and curious. "Where does a sister learn to shoot like that?"

"My mother taught me," Isabelle said, running her fingers fondly over the bowstring as she had many times while wandering through the woods outside of Kirklees. "There is an old peddler that comes through the priory every few months, always giving me little gifts of figurines or sweets. He gave me this bow when I was five and said a girl with knees as scraped as mine should know how to use one."

"My da said as much to my little sister Camilla when she was that age," Little said, tilting his head. "Though I suppose he regretted it when her first shot went wild and caught him in the leg. A dulled tip, but I bet it bloody hurt. Ma was fit to blacken his backside when he came limping home."

Isabelle smiled. "I do not think my mother was any more pleased than yours that he gifted me a weapon as a child, but she taught me how to hunt, and how to track animals through the woods. I would sneak out to practice and get lost, and she would inevitably have to send the sisters to search the woods and bring me home. They used to get so cross with me, until they realized I could supply the entire priory with meat from my hunting. Then I think they were relieved to send me out. At least until recently, when the hunger among the people in town began to grow to violence. Then Mother forbade me leaving the grounds alone."

"How is it you ended up in a priory anyhow?" Little asked.

"I was born there," Isabelle said. "My mother came to the sisters before I was born, and Prioress Rosamund had compassion on her and took her in."

Of course, now she knew the simple explanation her mother gave her as a child was no longer so simple. What had Prioress Rosamund known of her mother's past? What had she known of Robin? Had Marien really just appeared at the gates of the priory, heavy with child and seeking refuge, for Rosamund to take her in with unquestioning generosity? Or had the prioress known more than she ever let on to Isabelle? A deep seed of doubt and anger took root in her chest, blossoming into the realization that everyone she had trusted had lied to her.

"And what about the bastard that left you a bastard?" Little asked, tugging at that root of doubt and anger in his offhand manner.

"Little," Patrick said, shocked. "You can't ask her questions like that."

"What?" Little asked, spreading his hands wide. "I'm just making conversation."

"You're not making conversation," Patrick said. "You're prying. And insulting Isabelle in the process."

"'Tis all right," Isabelle said, not wanting to draw any more attention to the question than necessary. "The truth is I never knew my father. My mother never said."

Until now.

Little smiled. "Well, you don't need him. To hit that target's hard enough, but blindfolded? Bloody brilliant. You're the best shot I've ever seen."

Helena kicked one booted foot at his shin. "Don't let Robin hear you say that," she warned.

Little hopped on one leg a few paces, moving out of kicking range. "I'm including Robin in that, and I don't doubt he would agree with me."

"There's none like Robin," Patrick said. He bowed his head to Isabelle. "Not to take away from your well-earned victory. But he could shoot a fly off a horse at a hundred paces."

"What is he like?" Isabelle asked, unable to help herself. "Your Robin Hood. What kind of person is he?"

"Robin's the best," Patrick said, his voice steady and earnest. "He's jolly when you're in a foul mood, he's smart as a whip crack, and he can charm the coin out of any pocket here to Dover. He's always pulling tricks on everyone in the camp, and on the tax collectors and such. He once posed as a washerwoman for two weeks before Will Scarlett found him out."

"He shot an apple out of my hand because I slipped it from his plate," Little said. "And a loaf of bread. And a cheese I was really looking forward to."

"Perhaps you should have learned after the first go," Adam said dryly.

Little shrugged. "I was hungry."

"Is he . . . kind?" Isabelle asked.

"He gave our entire store of grain to Hempstead one winter because a blight wiped out their crop," Adam said. "Of course we had to eat old oats the rest of the winter to make up for it. If you've ever chewed on old boot leather, you'll know the taste and texture."

"He rescued my sister Camilla from drowning in the river when she was just two," Little said. "My youngest brother convinced her she could cross the surface of the water if she ran fast enough. Luckily, Robin was out on one of his walks, heard her screaming as the river swept her away, and scooped her up before she hit the falls. Da blackened my brother's hide for that little trick."

"And him crying the whole time it was you convinced him to do it," Adam said. "I believe you got your fair hiding for it as well."

Little grinned sheepishly, rubbing the back of his neck. "Forgot that part of the story."

"He carried my father back from York so we could bury him proper in Sherwood," Helena said, surprising Isabelle by speaking up. "Wouldn't let anyone else do it. Pulled the wagon the entire way and dug the grave himself. Told my mother that my father was his greatest friend, and his death was a terrible loss to the camp."

Helena's voice was calm, straightforward, but Isabelle could read the tension in her shoulders and the hard set of her lips. She had seen what it was to soldier on despite devastation, and what it did to your soul anyway.

"I am so sorry for your loss," Isabelle said softly.

Helena rolled one shoulder as if to shrug it off, but some of the tension left her lips. Isabelle glanced at the other members of their crew. "Are you all children of the outlaws?"

"Second generation," Little said proudly. "My da came to the Merry Men after Robin helped him rescue my ma from being forced to marry an old codger. Don't know if she found living in the woods better than living with a man twice her age, though."

"I would imagine any number of women who might prefer it," Isabelle said.

Little shrugged. "She seems happy enough."

"Twelve children is more than happy enough," Adam said.

"Thirteen, near enough," Little said. "Ma's due to drop any day now. Probably have a new brother or sister by the time we return."

"And you, Patrick? Are you also a proud son of an outlaw?" Isabelle asked the young Irish boy.

"Of a sort," he said, tilting his head to one side. "Though not the sort Robin would ever welcome with open arms. My da was a traitor to his people, tried to sell them out to the Normans and had to flee to England when they caught wind of his betrayal. His ship crashed in Liuerpul, and I was the only one to survive. There was a priest there, Father Donnell, he took me in and raised me as his own."

"How did you happen to join the Merry Men?" Isabelle asked.

"Father Donnell died," Patrick said with a small shrug that spoke volumes. "Nearly four years ago now. I had nothing and no one, and the people in Liuerpul were none too kind to the son of a drowned Irish traitor. I was starving my way through the country-side when Robin and Little John found me. I was like a stray animal, I suppose. They fed me once and I followed them home."

Isabelle looked to Adam. "I hesitate to even ask your circumstances."

He gave her a faint smile. "No one finds their way to the Merry Men easy, sister. You learned that yourself."

All their stories were crafted from tragedy, and even though he moved with the same easy stride, there was something about the distant, shadowed look on his face that made her think his was no different. But she wanted to know his story most of all, her chest already aching in sympathy for whatever pain had driven him here. She decided to start on easier footing.

"Do you have family in the camp like Little and Helena?" she asked.

"No, my family's back in Locksley," Adam said.

Isabelle did not know where Locksley was, but she imagined the distance from Sherwood to Kirklees and how many times her father could have traveled it and did not. "Do you visit them often?"

Adam's smile twisted down into a hard line. "No. I don't."

Isabelle glanced at the others, afraid she had made some misstep, but Patrick showed her pity. "Adam's father does not approve of the company he keeps."

"He doesn't approve of anything," Adam said, his voice hollow and bitter. "Were it up to men like him, John Lackland would have us all strung up by the neck and my da would pull the lever on himself. He's more terrified of changing than he is of fighting to be free."

Isabelle dropped her eyes to the ground in the silence that followed, a feeling of guilt twisting in her gut. All she had wanted since running from Kirklees was an end to the nightmare and a way back home. But these outlaws were fighting for something greater, something they were willing to sacrifice their whole lives on. What would Adam think of her if he knew the truth? Would he judge her with the same scorn he held for his own father?

"And just how is it you found your way to Sherwood, sister?" Helena asked, her suspicious tone breaking into Isabelle's thoughts. Though Isabelle supposed she did most things suspiciously.

"She shot a soldier," Little said gleefully.

Adam raised both eyebrows at her, lifting the shadows off his face. "Is that right?"

"It sounds far more sensational than it was," Isabelle said, feeling silly. "They were attacking the villagers of Kirklees, and I happened to be there. I had no choice but to intervene."

"You had a choice, sister," Adam said gravely. "Don't forget that. There are plenty who choose to do nothing while King John takes whatever he likes."

For a moment Isabelle saw the true rebel in him. She had wrestled with her choices over the past days, fearing every twig snap and distant clatter of hooves; perhaps she had not done the right thing. Perhaps she should have stayed out of it, or tried to reason with the soldiers another way. But looking at Adam's fierce expression, the resolve built into the core of him, she felt for the first time that she had done the right thing. It was like something fit together, finally, within her. She had done the right thing.

"Well, you're a welcome member to the Merry Men," Patrick said. "Even if you hadn't made that shot."

"But she did," Little reminded him.

Helena rolled her eyes. "Would you let it go?"

Little grinned at her. "Never."

"How far is it to Lincoln exactly?" Isabelle asked, wishing to move the conversation away from her reasons for coming to Sherwood.

"A day's walk," Adam said, giving Little a pointed look. "Less if we don't have to stop every few hours to eat."

"I'm a growing man," Little said, patting his midsection. "I need food to sustain me."

"The amount of food you take in could sustain an army," said Helena.

"It's another two days to York from Lincoln on foot," Adam continued. "Less if we're lucky and David can find us mounts. We've got a smaller camp outside York, we should find Robin there."

"Should?" Isabelle asked, picking up on the slight emphasis.

"Robin has a way of . . . disappearing when you want him," Patrick said ruefully. "He always reappears when you need him, though. It's like he's got a sixth sense about it."

"And what's this terribly urgent message we're supposed to be carrying to him?" Helena asked, looking to Isabelle. "Since we're risking our lives and all."

Isabelle let her gaze skitter to the dappled leaves underfoot, her new boots making barely a sound as she walked. Thomas's warning about Sir Roger vibrated through her bones, bringing a deeper chill than the morning warranted. Helena was right; they were risking their lives for her. But she would not risk theirs by putting them any further into the Wolf's path than she already had.

"It is about the soldiers attacking the town of Kirklees," she said, clearing her throat around the half-truth. "Their incursion is only the latest hardship the people have faced. My mother had to open the doors of the priory to serve the town because they were half-starved and begging. Many of the sisters were unhappy about the change, but she saw no better way to serve God than to help his people."

"It sounds like your mother would make a fine addition to the Merry Men," said Patrick with a slight smile. "We've tried to do much the same thing around here, taking from those who have too much and sharing it with those who would starve without it."

A small frown line crinkled the bridge of Isabelle's nose as she spoke. "But that is stealing."

"And what do you call it when these people break their backs to earn their coin and men like King John come take it out of their pockets in the name of taxes, all so they can pay to fight their losing wars or fill their tables to excess?" Adam asked. "You only think it's stealing because they've told you so. They put themselves in charge and set all the rules, and now we're the ones breaking the law just to keep our families from starving."

Isabelle had no argument against that, despite the twist of moral guilt in her gut. Stealing was wrong, but so was letting people starve when you could help them. Her mother had opened the priory to the community because they had food enough to share; but what about those who did not? What were they meant to do?

Little spat to the side, his mouth twisted in a scowl. "The high sheriff here is the worst of them, bloody Phillip Marc, treating all of Nottinghamshire as his personal pillaging grounds. Taking whatever he wants from whoever he wants. The barons think they'll stop him with this charter they made the king sign, as if he'll honor some piece of parchment."

"What charter is this?" Isabelle asked.

"They're calling it the Magna Carta," Adam said. "The Great Charter. From what I've heard, it's basically a list of demands from the rebel barons for John to stop bleeding their coffers dry and losing their lands in France."

"I don't know why he keeps picking battles with the French," Little said, shaking his head. "The man couldn't fight his way out of an empty sack of grain, much less command a whole army. The barons ought to just declare war on him—losing is the only thing he's good at."

"And if the barons go to war, what about everyone who gets caught in between?" Patrick asked quietly. "What about the poor farmers and villagers who have already lost their homes, their families, their very lives, because of the king? Do they not matter?"

"'Course they matter," Little said. "But their lives aren't getting any better under John Lackland, are they?"

"Fighting is not always the answer just because it's what you like best, Little," Helena said. "I'm not any more in favor of John remaining king, but if the barons think they can stop John's worst impulses with this charter, then I say we give them a chance. Anything is better than war."

"Not anything," Adam said firmly. "Not the way things are going round here. Not if it means starving and dying so men like John and Phillip Marc can build another castle."

"So are you in favor of war, then?" Isabelle asked. "You see no chance for peace?"

Adam took a deep breath, staring straight through the trees around them as if he could see his way to a clear answer. The others walked ahead, but Adam slowed his pace to match hers. "We have to do all we can to protect the people who can't protect themselves. That's why Robin founded the Merry Men. I don't want a war, but I think that's what it will take to stop King John. He's a beast, and he'll crush everyone who opposes him under his boot."

Isabelle shivered, the panic gripping her until she was afraid she would cry out from the tide of rising fear. Adam glanced at her as if he could sense the waves rolling off her.

"You all right, sister?"

"Yes, of course," she said, shaking her head as if she could rid it of these clawing thoughts. "It is only that I did not . . . I could not have imagined what it was like for the rest of the country. For you. I had no idea things could be so bad. That they might get worse."

For the country and for her, though she could not say so to Adam. But she did not have to, because something in the dark depths of his gaze seemed to look right into the heart of her and find all she lacked. She might have confessed everything right then, under the scrutiny of that searching look, were it not for Patrick and Little calling for them to catch up. But the feeling stayed with her as they continued through the forest toward Lincoln. The feeling of the hangman's noose tightening around her neck, dragging her toward an inevitable fate.

CHAPTER
NINE

Late-afternoon sunlight stretched out in long rays of orange when the trees began to thin, the road showing in patches to the east as they approached Lincoln. Isabelle had never been outside of Kirklees, much less to a major city like Lincoln, and the growing volume of traffic along the road was easily more people than she had met in her entire life. She only hoped it was a large enough city for them to slip in unnoticed by any prying eyes.

"What sort of township is Lincoln?" Isabelle asked, her nerves doing little somersaults through her stomach.

"It's a cesspool of mercenaries and beggars," Adam said.

"Oh." Not quite the response she expected.

Adam glanced at her. "Not all townships are, mind you. York's quite nice. But the castellan of Lincoln is good friends with King John and overly fond of hangings. You would think having a lady in charge would soften things up, but Nicholaa de la Haye is a dragon of an old lady. Got a first-rate dungeon, though."

"The floors could be cleaner," said Little. "And the food tastes like sawdust."

"Probably is sawdust," Adam replied. "*When* they bother to feed you."

"You have been in the dungeons at Lincoln?" Isabelle asked in surprise.

"Oh, aye," Little said, scratching at the back of his head. "A few times. Fighting and the like, mostly. The castellan's a real stickler for no fighting, thinks it brings a . . . What's she call it?"

Adam gave a small smile. "An unsavory element. Never mind that the fighting is started by all these mercenaries King John keeps hiring to fight his wars. The fool can't build his own army, so he finds the filthiest pigs the trade has to offer. They'd cut up their own grandmothers for a few coin, and Lincoln is crawling with their like."

What she had considered the worst moment in her life, being trapped in that potato cellar, these outlaws spoke of as nothing more than an inconvenient night out. Perhaps she had made a mistake, insisting on joining their ranks. She was not made for tavern brawls and dungeons. Isabelle swallowed against the bile rising in her throat. "And we think it wise to travel to a city crawling with these men?"

"It's not so bad as they're saying," Patrick said with a stern look at Adam and Little. "If you know to stay out of the taverns and the black markets."

"What's the point in that?" Little asked.

"You're scaring the sister," Patrick said under his breath.

"She ought to be scared," said Helena, nodding toward the road. "We all ought to be. Something's going on at the gates."

Isabelle had been so engrossed in their talk of dungeons that she had not even noted their approach to the city itself. The city wall rose high and imposing against the slender trees around Isabelle and her party, awash in the deep orange of the setting sun, the far edges tinged in red. The mass of people crowding the roadway at the main gates could have easily encompassed the entire population of Kirkleestown. Carriages trundled past farmers' carts loaded with vegetables, peddlers pushed their wares forward with a clanking of pans, children ran wild and screaming around the legs of the crowds, and everywhere there were people on foot pressing forward toward the gates.

"I've never seen so many people in my life," Isabelle said, instinctively pressing closer to Adam as the hordes of people milled about and shouted complaints. Beggars gathered on the grassy edges with their hands out, their skin so filthy it was difficult to tell where their rags stopped and their flesh began. "Lincoln must be enormous."

"It's not that enormous," Adam muttered. "Patrick?"

The Irish boy nodded, disappearing into the press of the crowd. Isabelle went up on her toes but could not see past the crush of people to the gates themselves. Little followed her motion, shielding his eyes with his hand to get a better look.

"Can you see anything?" Isabelle asked.

"I can see plenty of things, sister. Just not what's taking so long. Seems like they're stopped up at the gate. Maybe a cart overturned or some such thing."

Patrick returned a few moments later, his face grave. "It's not good news."

Adam frowned. "What is it?"

"Soldiers. They're questioning everyone coming through."

Isabelle's heart began to pound as Adam spat an impressive curse. "Bloody Nicholaa de la Haye. How many are there?"

"Too many to slip past," Patrick said. "And from the talk I heard, more on every gate into the city. Might just be Nicholaa putting on a show of power, or it might be something else."

It could not be the Wolf, Isabelle assured herself even as her stomach turned and her heart pounded, prickles of panic biting at the flesh on her arms. It was not possible he knew which direction they traveled, or where they meant to go. Still, she shrank back farther into the protective shadow that Adam and Little cast, wishing she could make herself invisible.

"We could go around Lincoln," Helena said. "Avoid the gates altogether."

Adam shook his head. "If we don't get word to David that we're here, Allan will worry."

"Worry?" Little snorted. "Probably send half the bloody Merry Men after us."

"No, we need a way in," Adam said, scratching at his chin as he scanned the gathered crowds. His gaze narrowed on something, his spine straightening. "Little, how much coin have you got on you?"

"A few ha'pennies," Little said guardedly. "Why?"

Adam lifted a brow, turning to his friend. "A few ha'pennies?"

"Well, all right, I might have a silver piece. But it's from Robin, and it's special to me."

"Then how about you keep the one that's special to you and give me the other one I know you have."

"I don't . . ." Little gave a huff, digging into a hidden pocket in his tunic and producing a dented coin. "Fine, here you are. But that's one you owe me."

Adam turned back to the crowd. "Considering you stole this one from me, I think that makes us even."

Little threw up his hands. "I knew I couldn't trust Patrick not to tell you. I should have told him I put it back."

"You did tell me you put it back," Patrick pointed out.

"Well, you should have trusted that I did."

Patrick shook his head. "Clearly not."

"What's this plan of yours involve, Adam?" Helena asked.

"Because I'm not putting on those beggar rags. I'll have lice crawling all over me before we clear the gate."

Adam grinned. "I promise it won't be that uncomfortable. Probably."

Isabelle wriggled in her hiding place, a thin slat of light from the fading sun cutting across her eyes through a break in the sides of the apple cart. There were apples everywhere—nobbled against her spine, covering her face, crowding her boots, and one overly familiar fruit pressed right against her mouth. The wheels groaned under the excess weight of their cargo, exuding the smell of harvest season at the priory with every rut they hit. From somewhere on the other side of the cart Helena gave a yelp.

"Little, you idiot, your boot is right in my face," she hissed.

"It's got nowhere else to go," Little whispered. "I'm folded in quarters as it is."

"Well, fold yourself in eighths and get your boot out of my face," Helena said.

"Both of you shut up," Adam said, giving the cart a jostle. "I'll be hard-pressed to explain talking apples to the soldiers at the gate."

"Hurry it up, then," Helena said. "Before I bite his toes off."

Patrick sighed somewhere close to Isabelle's ear, and she would have smiled if it weren't for the apple trying to fight its way past her teeth. The apple seller had been delighted to exchange his paltry goods for an entire silver piece, and Adam had scrunched the four of them into the cart despite loud and prolonged complaints from both Little and Helena. Isabelle's stomach grumbled at so many ripe apples within reach, her mind setting a feast of apple tarts and preserves and a host of other dishes they would prepare during harvest season at the priory, but now was not the time to give in to temptation. Though their meager afternoon meal of cold cheese and hardened bread seemed ages ago.

The smell of unwashed bodies filtered in through the apples, the mill of people pressing in tighter around their cart as Adam dragged it one slow step forward. The crowd at the gate only grew despite the chill evening air. Several merchants grumbled about losing market time, and even the driver of a carriage shouted about delayed trips and important occupants.

"Move it along!" shouted a man close by whom Isabelle guessed to be one of the soldiers guarding the gate. Her toes curled tightly in her boots, one hand wrapping around the firm flesh of an apple as she tried to steady her rapid heartbeat. The guard's tone was bored and impatient. "Keep it moving! Gates close at sundown!"

A protest arose from the crowd, but the soldier shouted them down. The cart creaked and groaned to a stop, Adam setting it down with a huff. Isabelle held her breath, willing every muscle in her body to stay still as she sensed the guard's scrutiny of the cart.

"Name and purpose for visiting Lincoln this day," came the soldier's voice at a regular volume. Adam stepped up beside the cart, the patchwork cloak that he bought from the apple seller showing through the slat in Isabelle's view.

"Stephen of Moorehead," said Adam in a jolly, rounded accent. Isabelle hardly recognized his voice, and had to remind herself not to move to catch a better view of him and confirm it was actually Adam speaking. "I've come to town this day to sell these here apples I've got in my cart. Full load it is, too, sir, we've been blessed with a harvest this year. Trying to sell them 'fore they go bad. You ever smelled rotted apples, sir?"

The soldier's distaste seeped through the layers of apples. "Certainly not."

"Well, then blessed you've been, too, sir. Stinks worse than my brother rolling round in the pig slop. I can't eat them no more on account of smelling them so much, but these lot are fresh and ripe as the day. Would you like one, sir?"

"No," the guard said emphatically. "Move along. You're holding up the line."

"And a good day to you, sir," Adam called out, hefting the cart up and dragging it through the city walls.

"Hang on there, you," shouted another soldier, and Isabelle's heart beat an erratic rhythm she was sure would tumble the apples right off her when Adam brought the cart to a jerking stop. Any number of terrible scenarios played out in her mind in the tense seconds that passed—someone had spotted a boot among the apples, they would all be arrested and thrown in Lincoln's dungeon, the Wolf would find her, she was doomed. They were all doomed. The smell of the apples stung her eyes and she squeezed them shut, not daring to breathe. Somewhere under the mass of fruit her bow and quiver waited, too far out of reach to bring any comfort in the moment.

"Yes, sir, good sir?" Adam asked in his rounded accent as the soldier approached, chain mail clinking.

"Where's your tariff, then?" asked the soldier, his tone gruff and impatient.

"Tariff, good sir?"

"Your tariff, you dumb farmer. Everybody pays a tariff to come through these walls."

"I've been here many a time, good sir, and I don't recall no tariff for certain," Adam said. "Meaning no offense, 'course. Only, I paid my last good coin in West Chestershire for a room for the night. And that was to bunk along with the cows, good sir, who'd have liked to eat my cart here, stem to seeds."

"I wasn't asking for your life story, peasant," sneered the soldier. "If you can't pay the tariff, you don't pass. You lot always come in looking for alms or thieving from the markets, clogging up the city with your begging so decent folk can't even feel safe walking the roads. You're a burden on the rest of us."

A tremor rippled through the cover of apples, and Isabelle sensed the others growing uneasy in their hiding places, which did nothing to bring down the tension singing through her.

"Well, sir, if it's a tariff you be needing, I could pay you in these here beauties," Adam said. "Fresh from the orchard and finest of the bushels. Take as many as you need to pay your tariff, sir. I'm a simple man with simple needs. Only, my brother's come down with a terrible illness and we need the coin to pay the healer for a spot of salve. Horrible cut he got falling out of a tree picking these very apples. Gone green and yellow and stinks like an animal carcass, always seeping out of his hose. Might lose the leg altogether if the thing keeps festering."

"Enough," the soldier barked, cutting across his words. "Bloody peasants. Always got a story. Pay the tariff on the way out, then. Hell, I'd pay the tariff for you to not hear one more word about your brother's wound."

"Well, and that's right kind of you, sir," Adam said, relief pulsing through his words. "I'll be happy to pay on my way out, I will, and my brother will be happy for his salve. Thank you for your kindness, sir."

"It's not you I'm paying the kindness to," the soldier muttered as Adam picked up the cart again, pushing it through the city gates and into Lincoln proper.

CHAPTER
TEN

Isabelle waited until the sounds and smells of the city magnified tenfold around them to release the breath that burned through her chest. Bustles of bright red and yellow skirts and deep purple cloaks swirled past her little peephole, and even the close proximity to the apples could not overpower the smells of wet wool, roasting meat, unwashed people, and trash that filled Lincoln. After the relative tranquility of the forest, Lincoln was like a battlefield.

A lingering nausea tilted Isabelle's insides as the cart trundled on, the assault of so many common smells buffeting her in the prison of apples. Adam found an empty pocket between stalls to park the cart, the noise simmering to a buzz as the market swirled around them. He knocked on the wooden siding and the fruit shifted around Isabelle as the others dug their way out of the cart. Isabelle found herself under a mountain of apples as Little leapt out, and for a panicked moment she feared they might leave her behind.

The apples tumbled away from her as Adam's face appeared in the sudden light above, a slight smirk curling the edges of his mouth. "All right, then, sister?"

She nodded, taking his proffered hand as he dug her out and

helped her over the side of the cart. His hand lingered at her waist and she half turned away, her face warming. "I believe I shall never be able to stomach the thought of another apple again."

"I reek of them now," Helena said, holding her arms out and smelling the fabric.

"There are worse things you could reek of," Patrick pointed out.

"Let's find David," Adam said. "The sun is nearly set and the guards seem rather serious about locking up after dark. If we want to make it out of here, we'll need to leave sooner rather than later."

"Hang on," Little said, stopping them as they made for the main thoroughfare. He pointed at the cart. "What about this lot?"

"Leave them," Adam said. "Some enterprising merchant will take care of them."

"Hey, I paid good coin for these!"

Adam shrugged a shoulder. "Then sell them yourself."

Little glared and stuffed his pockets with as many apples as he could carry, the bulk standing out on his lean frame. Helena eyed his shape critically.

"You look a fool, Little," she said simply.

"You'll feel a fool when hunger comes for you later and I'm feasting on these beauties," he said, tromping toward the road resolutely.

They delved into the roiling mass of the city, the lingering scent of apples wafting from their tunics and blending with the stronger smells. Isabelle pressed in close to the others, resisting the urge to take hold of Adam's tunic like a small child. In Kirklees the lanes were wide enough to allow a line of people to pass each other without rubbing shoulders, but here in Lincoln she could barely squeeze through without bumping someone.

"Is it always this busy?" she asked Patrick beside her, pitching her voice to be heard over the general noise of the city.

"This is mostly quiet," Patrick replied, ducking the swinging hands of a fishmonger selling his wares. "You should see this place after the shearing. Lincoln is a hub for wool merchants, you couldn't spit without hitting a skein of Lincoln wool here."

Everywhere there was activity, from the flying fish of the fishmongers to the swinging cleavers of the butchers to the shining beads of the jewelry carts. Isabelle could hardly keep her feet underneath her at the constant flow of foot traffic carrying her along. Adam and Little carved a path for them, pressing into the heart of the city.

"The soldier," Isabelle said hesitantly, her eyes tracing the confident movement of Adam's shoulders through the throngs. "The way he spoke to Adam, the things he . . . Are they . . . Do they always treat the people so?"

Patrick lifted a brow. "You mean poorly?"

"Why would King John allow it?"

"Allow it? He encourages it." Patrick shook his head. "The only way for the nobility to hold the power is if they've got someone to hold it over. And John's the biggest bully of them all. Anything he does is to line his own pockets and indulge his own whims."

"But he is supposed to be our . . . our leader! Our protector." Isabelle knotted her fingers together, wrestling against the tide of feelings rising within her. "I am sure if he could see what is going on in Kirkleestown, how the people are starving and scared. . . . How could he not change his mind? He should be king for all, not for his own interests."

Patrick gave her a wry smile. "Try telling him that. The rebel barons did, for all the good it's done them. Men like John Lackland don't have a better side to appeal to."

"Then how can anything change?" Isabelle asked, her voice faint.

Patrick's expression settled into grim lines of worry. "The way it always does. War."

Isabelle had thought the incident in Kirkleestown an isolated one, a clash of emotions between the scared townspeople and the soldiers. She never imagined the fear was so widespread and the violence so endemic to the system of nobility. Her mother oversaw the priory with compassion and fairness, and Isabelle had assumed the rest of the country was no different. She realized with a sickening start that King John sounded far more like Sister Catherine than he did like her mother. Capricious, vindictive, and mean. How much worse would her life have been if Sister Catherine had been in charge of the priory? How much worse were the lives of ordinary folk at the hands of King John?

The flavor of the crowd shifted as they reached the taprooms located deep in the city's twisted center. Clustered around the eastern edge of the market were buildings with discreet signs advertising rooms upstairs, entire alleyways that smelled of stale ale, and what was surely a black market of goods stolen from the real market.

Leery-eyed men stomped between the taprooms, their scars marking them as mercenary fighters, the only crown they pledged their loyalty to stamped on a coin. There were others, disconsolate drunks and women in scandalous attire, but they mostly kept to themselves in the dark corners between buildings. Isabelle edged closer to Adam, eyeing a drunk slumped over in a corner singing a sea shanty that made her ears burn.

"This is where your friend resides?" she asked. A stout man with rounded shoulders and a bandage over one eye swooned close to her, and Adam put a hand protectively at her back. A spark of awareness tingled along her skin at the contact, her spine straightening. Adam seemed to sense it, for he drew his hand back quickly and cleared his throat.

"David is a good man," he assured her. "And a loyal friend of the camp."

He led them to a bar with a sign bearing the image of a lion in the throes of death, roaring as a myriad of arrows protruded from its mane. Isabelle had acquaintance with only one other tavern in her life, and the inside of this one was in direct contrast to that vivid memory. It was easily twice as large and only half as full, and a distinct lack of windows plunged them into darkness when first entering. It still smelled of sweat and sour beer and metal, but there were no cheery undertones of crackling wood to warm the place up.

Whereas the Blue Boar had seemed alive with masculine energy, the mood of the Wounded Lion slunk in the shadows like a vulture waiting for its prey to die. The men looked desperate and edgy in their drunken states, leaving large gaps between their seats at the bar. It was quiet enough to hear the clack of the mugs as the barkeep stowed them away beside the barrel of ale. Several men hunched around a table in the corner, their eyes cutting over Isabelle and the others with a practiced precision that made Isabelle wish she still had her cloak to cover her face. Their weapons were chipped but sharp, their faces and hauberks showing an intimate knowledge of battle.

"This place does not seem very . . . friendly," she whispered to Adam.

"The sister's right," Little said, his eyes sliding around. "I don't see a friendly face in sight. It's not usual in the Lion."

"We're not here for the company," Adam replied. "We're here for the barkeep."

The barkeep, a stoop-shouldered man with thinning hair and enormous forearms, broke out in a wide grin at the sight of them. He gave a laugh, loud and ringing in the relative quiet, and several drunks lifted their heads in wary confusion.

"Adam of Locksley, as I live and breathe," he said, dropping a heavy hand on the younger man's shoulder. "And Little Allan A'Dale as well. How fares your da?"

"Still a pain in my arse," Little said. "How fares it with you, David?"

The barkeep spread his arms wide, encompassing the full length of the bar. "I could complain, but what a bore that'd be. What brings you good-for-nothings to Lincoln?"

"Just passing through," Adam said, giving David a meaningful look. "Could use a spot of stew for dinner and supplies for the road."

Little leaned in beside him. "And a mug or two of ale."

"No ale," Helena and Patrick said at the same time.

"One little pint won't hurt nothing," Little said in a wheedling tone.

"It's never one little pint with you, though, is it?" Helena asked.

Isabelle glanced back at the table of mercenaries as Little tried again to negotiate for his ale. She knew she shouldn't look, shouldn't give them a reason to look back, but she couldn't help herself. There was something about them, something so menacing, like a cloud of intent hanging over their table. She suppressed a gasp when she met the eyes of one of the men, already staring at her. He smiled, though it was more like a feral animal baring its teeth than any kind of greeting. She whipped her head around, pushing closer to the bar.

"Adam," she whispered as Little argued with Helena and Patrick about the ill effects of half a pint. "I think we should leave."

He frowned down at her. "Why?"

She cut her eyes toward the table, not daring to turn her head again. "Those men over there are staring at us."

Adam's dark gaze flicked up and back, so quick she would have missed it were she not looking directly at him. "Never mind them," he murmured. "They've probably never seen a girl who looks like you. I'd stare, too, if I were them. They won't bother you unless they think you're worth a coin or two."

"That is not . . ." Her cheeks warmed under his casual assessment. "I do not think that is why they are staring."

How could she explain without admitting that she had not told them the full truth? Perhaps Adam was right, and she was only being paranoid. Except, when she stole another look, the mercenary was still watching her. And he'd actually stood up, his hand drifting toward the sword strapped to his waist. Isabelle swallowed hard, clutching at his forearm.

"Adam, we need to go," she whispered urgently. "Now."

Adam darted a glance down at her, frowning at Little's vocal objections, but then his gaze hardened as it traveled over her shoulder to the cluster of mercenaries beyond. He raised a hand to the others and their conversation stopped midsyllable, all their attention drawn toward him.

"Isabelle, when I say run, you run," Adam said, his gaze never leaving the mercenaries.

She nodded, her mouth dry, her stomach rioting. She dimly registered that it was the first time he'd used her given name, fear sharpening her senses enough that she knew the mercenaries had left their table and stood a few steps behind her, weapons drawn. Adam rose from his stool and the others followed suit, Helena drawing her short sword with a sharp hiss and Patrick producing two wicked knives from the folds of his tunic. Little pulled his heavy staff from over his shoulder, the end whistling as he twirled it around.

"Put your toys away, lads," said the mercenary who had been eyeing Isabelle. "This isn't your fight to win. We only want the girl." He cocked his head at Isabelle. "You're a long way from the priory, ain't you, sweetling?"

A jolt went through her at the man's familiar tone. How could he know who she was? But she knew the answer to that question, and it sent a spiral of panic straight down into her core. Adam took a smooth step in front of her, blocking her from the man's view.

"She's with us," Adam said, his voice cold. "You can move along, or we can move you along."

"What, you and your little cubs back there?" the man taunted. "That's a cute sword, lass, maybe I'll let you scratch my back with it."

"Maybe I'll scratch more than that," said Helena through a clenched jaw.

The man grinned at Helena, his gaze shifting back to Adam. "You're on the losing end of this, mate. The city's crawling with us, and there's only a pocketful of you. Give me the girl and I won't break both your arms and make her watch."

Isabelle couldn't stop the shudder that went through her at the promise of violence in the man's eyes as they latched on to hers.

"Come on, then, sweetling, come to old Blade."

"Isabelle, run!" Adam said, just before swinging his sword at the man's neck.

The mercenary caught Adam's blow with his own sword, thrusting it off and twisting around to deliver a fierce strike. But then Little's staff was there, crunching into the man's nose, while Helena whirled into the action whipping her blade like lightning. Patrick was just as fast, silent and lethal as his knives caught two of the mercenaries across the ribs. It was close, and loud, and violent, and Isabelle could not even think fast enough to breathe.

"Isabelle," shouted Adam, his face swimming into focus before her. He gave her a hard shake. "Run!"

"This way, lass!" David called, taking her by the arm and dragging her toward the back of the tavern. A narrow stairwell led up to a dark hallway lined with doors, each one painted with a different number. The old wood squeaked as David thundered up the stairs, Isabelle tripping along after him, glancing at her friends fighting for their lives and hers.

"She's going out the back!" yelled Blade.

"Bloody mercenaries," David muttered, pushing open the door to one of the rooms. It looked like many years had passed since it had last been used, a cottony web of dust covering the moldered pallet on the floor. David pushed the door closed, dropping a heavy iron latch into place before dragging a chair into the corner of the room. Isabelle watched in a daze as he stepped up, pushing at a square of thatched ceiling. The thatching gave way to a patch of sky bloodred with the light of the setting sun.

"All the roofs are connected around here," said David, holding out a hand to her. "There's a potter's shop at the end of the row, low enough to get you to the ground. Go for the cathedral, tallest building in the town. You can't miss it. Ask for sanctuary."

"I cannot leave them," Isabelle said, turning toward the thuds of metal and grunts of pain below. "This is my fault. I need to help them."

"The best help you can give them is to be as far from here as possible," David said. "Your friends will find you at the cathedral. You've got to go, lass. Now."

Isabelle lurched forward, taking his hand and letting him haul her up through the narrow patch onto the roof of the tavern. Outside was absurdly quiet after the explosion of fighting she just left, a faint background symphony of drunken conversation leaking from the surrounding taverns. Every part of her fought to go back downstairs and help the others, but David was right. She would only be putting them in greater danger by staying, never mind that they were in this danger because of her. She needed to get away, needed to draw the mercenaries off them.

She ran across the roof in a crouch, taking a deep breath before daring the narrow plank of wood connecting the Lion's roof to the building beside it. It wobbled beneath her boots and she threw her arms out in panicked circles, trying to regain her balance, until the beam stopped tipping. She slid her feet forward, not daring to lift them from the wood until she reached the neighboring roof. No one came crashing out of the Lion's door below, but she didn't know if that was a good omen or a bad one.

The rest of the beams proved more stable, and she crossed each roof as fast as she could until she reached the last one, the potter's shop. It was a shorter building than the Lion, but staring at the distance from the edge to the ground made Isabelle woozy. She had a very different idea of heights than David did. She closed her eyes, leaning back from the edge to take a shuddering breath.

Be braver than you feel.

The memory of her mother laid a cool hand against her cheek, bringing Isabelle's surroundings into sharp relief. She would get down from the roof, because she had to get down from the roof. She had stood up to the soldiers in Kirklees, faced the foresters in the Blue Boar, and won her place with the Merry Men. She could handle a jump. She opened her eyes, standing tall at the edge of the roof, ready to make the leap.

"Oh, no, you don't," someone said behind her, hauling her back into an iron grip.

CHAPTER
ELEVEN

"Not so quick now, sweetling," Blade breathed into her ear, his arm like a steel band around her ribs. "Got someone wants a word with you."

Isabelle couldn't scream if she wanted to, so tight was his grip. She couldn't get enough of a breath in to keep the edges of her vision from going black. Panic seized her lungs and set her arms and legs thrashing, her whole body desperate to break the ale-soaked, rotted-breath grip he had on her. She kicked back, her heel connecting with his shin and scraping down the length of it. Blade cursed against her ear, squeezing until she thought she would pass out.

"I only like it more when you fight back," he breathed. "So go on, give me a show."

"Let me go," she said in a high, thin voice. "Please."

"I'll let you go when I've got my coin. Now we're going to jump off this roof, you and I, and if you try to run, I'll take my time with you. Understand?"

Isabelle nodded, going still despite the trembling in her arms and legs. Blade stepped up to the edge, his arm still tight around her waist, and eyed the street below. With a grunt he shoved her forward, the roof dropping out from under her feet as she plunged toward the ground. She landed hard on her side, the shock reverberating up her spine and down through her legs, the air knocked out of her lungs from the impact. By the time she could suck in a breath, Blade was there, crouching over her and hauling her up.

"Not very graceful a lass, are you, now?"

She wished she were like Helena, sharp and quick and brave, so she could spit in his eye or slice his throat. But one good shot didn't make Isabelle like the outlaw girl, not really, and so she went along as he hauled her up. She only fought him once, when he took her bow and quiver, tossing them in a nearby pile of trash. But his grip on her arm made her bones hurt, and the threats he promised were so heinous and specific that she went limp as he dragged her through the street into the main market. Most of the tradesmen were packing up for the day, eager to be out of the streets before nightfall, and if any of them noticed her distress, they did nothing to intervene. She lost track of the twists and turns they took through the city, the shadows growing longer as the evening sun faded into an early twilight. By the time they reached a respectable-looking building with cheery fires burning next to the guard stations, she was completely lost.

"Got someone here the man would care to see," Blade said to the guards, shoving Isabelle forward.

The guard looked her up and down. "Don't look like much from here."

"Well, it's not you that needs to do the looking, is it? Tell him I've got the girl."

The guard's expression didn't change, but he turned to the doors and disappeared inside. Isabelle wished for her bow, for her mother, for Adam, for the mythical promise of her father. But no such salvation came and the guard reappeared, waving them through the doors. She jumped when they clanged closed behind her, fighting the urge to throw herself against the heavy wooden beams and beg for her release.

The interior of the building was cool and dim. In a strange way it reminded Isabelle of the priory, with stone walls arching overhead and meeting in a wooden support beam that kept the rocks from tumbling down on them. Darkened entryways studded the halls, alluring in their aura of freedom, but she knew there would be no escaping these hardened soldiers. She tilted her chin up, doing her best to mimic the cool authority her mother exuded as prioress.

They turned down a narrow hallway that ended in another heavy door guarded by more mercenaries. Blade nodded to the men standing guard and rapped on the door, waiting with his head tilted for a response. A faint voice sounded from within and Blade pushed the door open, dragging Isabelle forward.

"Found the girl, sir," he said.

The room was surprisingly small, most of it occupied by a massive wooden desk covered in neat stacks of parchment. It reminded her of the writing desks where the literate sisters would copy manuscripts. Behind it sat a thin man with gaunt cheeks and hair heavily streaked with gray. His fingers were almost skeletal as they moved between the stacks, scratching out letters in a quick, sure hand. His surcoat was crafted of fine silk dyed a deep blue. He did not lift his head as they entered, but held up one hand to wave them forward. Blade shoved her toward the desk, standing behind her to prevent any attempts to flee. Not that she could, with another dozen mercenaries standing guard throughout the building beyond.

"You may go," the man said, his voice low and droning, but with an odd hollow quality to it, like it was the echo of a person long ago forgotten. He folded the letter in thirds and dribbled hot wax on it, pressing his seal into the wax to mark the letter. Isabelle caught a glimpse of a wolf's head, teeth bared in anticipation.

"You don't want me to stay, sir?" Blade glanced at Isabelle. "In case the girl tries anything?"

The man looked up, pinning Blade down with eyes like black winter ice. "You think I cannot handle a single female child?"

Blade cleared his throat, his cocksure tone wobbling. "No, sir, I didn't mean it like that at all."

The man watched the mercenary, his expression unchanging, his chest so still Isabelle wondered if he was even breathing. "Then why are you still here?"

He did not raise his tone or change his inflection, but the hardened mercenary did not dare to question him again. He gave a muttering bow and backed out of the room, closing the door behind him. Isabelle tried to keep her legs from trembling, but her body was in revolt, her eyes darting around the room, looking for any kind of help—a window, a weapon, even a candlestick. Something to make her feel she wasn't completely at the mercy of this man.

"Please do not waste my time or insult my intelligence by thinking you can escape," he said, leaning back in his chair and lacing his fingers together. "You know who I am?"

She didn't want to say it, didn't want to manifest her fear with those words. But she needed to know, to be sure. "You are the Wolf. Sir Roger of Doncaster."

He gave a brief nod, and in that confirmation her heart sank. She was doomed. The Wolf had her, and whatever he wanted, there was nothing she could do to stop him. Her friends were on the other end of town still fighting, possibly hurt or worse; her mother was miles away in Kirklees, counting on her to get word to

Robin, not knowing the battle was already lost; and her father . . . she would never even meet the man. Somehow that felt like the greatest defeat.

"You have proven a difficult girl to find, Isabelle."

His men had thrown her in prison, chased her like a stray dog for days, upended her life, and stripped away everything she had ever known. He might have her, but she would not be cowed by this man. She tilted her chin, looking down the length of her nose at him.

"If it is an apology you expect, you will be kept wanting."

His lips pressed together in a flat line. "I see you inherited your father's penchant for insolence." His dark eyes swept over her dispassionately. "And your mother's beauty. Wasted in a priory, of all places. As if God could save her from me."

Her stomach twisted and she lurched forward a half step. "Leave my mother alone."

"Ah, no witty retort? No arrogant proclamations? Perhaps there is not so much Robert of Huntingdon in you after all. Such a shame, I did not expect you to break so easily. Do you even know who your father is, child?"

"Of course I do," she snapped, but it was too quick, too hot. Too defensive.

The Wolf clicked his tongue. "How very like Huntingdon to abandon his wife and unborn child in a dusty priory on the edge of nowhere and never return for them."

She tried not to let the insult find its target, but it slipped under her defenses and needled at her resolve, because of course he was right. How could her father just abandon them, leaving her isolated from the world and defenseless against the likes of Sister Catherine? And why did the Wolf keep calling him Robert of Huntingdon?

"He did not abandon us," Isabelle said, clenching her fists in determination. "He put us there to keep us safe from the likes of you."

The Wolf gave her a faint smile. "Is that what your mother told you? Or those heathen friends of yours? How very little you understand, child."

"I understand enough to know I would trust those heathen friends over anything you say," Isabelle retorted. "If you mean to arrest me for the incident in Kirklees, very well. Put me in your dungeon and be done with it."

"Oh, I intend to do far worse than put you in a dungeon if you do not cooperate," said Sir Roger, turning the air cold with his resolve. "I do not have the time or inclination to play these childish games. I want Robert of Huntingdon, and you will tell me where to find him. If you do not, I will hang your mother."

Isabelle's mouth fell slack, the distinct sensation of tumbling down a deep well unbalancing her where she stood. She could not possibly have heard him right. He would never . . . No one would *ever* harm her mother. This was . . . It was madness.

"Close your mouth, girl, you look like a simpleton," Sir Roger said, disdain dancing over his tone.

"Please, you cannot do this," Isabelle whispered, her bravado crumbling like dead winter leaves. "Do not hurt my mother. I do not know where my father is."

"Do not bother with lies, girl," Sir Roger said. "I already know Robert is not hiding among the townspeople of Kirklees. My soldiers made sure of that before your intervention. And if your mother saw fit to send you out alone, there is only one person she would trust with your safety. It is charming, if ultimately futile, that you wish to throw your life on the sacrificial altar for a man who has given you not a thought since ridding himself of you."

"Please, I promise, I do not know where he is," she said. "Truly."

"Then you will find where he is, and you will bring him to me."

"Why are you doing this?" Isabelle whispered, her voice thick with tears. Tears that spilled out and down her cheeks in shame. She did not want this man to see her weakness, but she could not stop it.

Sir Roger leaned forward on the desk, swallowing her up in his cold gaze. "Because your family should have died sixteen years ago. Consider it a gift that I am allowing you and your mother to live now. But Robert of Huntingdon is a threat to our king and country, and I will not let him live."

"My father has been gone for sixteen years," Isabelle pleaded. "He is no threat to you anymore. None of us are."

"As long as Robert breathes, he is a threat," said Sir Roger. He looked her up and down in disgust. "If your poor choice of attire is any indication, he has sought his refuge among the arrogant outlaws of Sherwood Forest, no doubt stirring them up into rebellion against the king. Always a thorn in my side. Shall I have the forest burned down? Shall I put your friends in the stocks until they starve? What tragedies will you have on your hands before Robert is in mine?"

Isabelle shook her head, slouching forward against the desk to stop from falling to the floor. All of the running, joining the Merry Men, it was all for naught. She could not be braver than she felt, for she felt everything and nothing at all. This man had her trapped like a fly in ointment, struggling against a foregone conclusion. She barely heard him continue over the rushing in her ears.

"Your mother is being held prisoner in Kirklees. Bring Robert to me within seven days or I will hang her for your crimes against the crown. And then I will find you, and your father, and make sure you both stay dead this time." He waved a hand at her, returning his attention to the letters before him. "Now you may leave. I have other business."

Isabelle stumbled out in a fog as the mercenaries led her back through the building. She wasn't even sure how or when she reached the front doors, but at some point she was in the cold, the cloak of night falling over the city and shrouding it in sinister shadows. She shivered against a gust of wind, but the cold did not come from outside. It came from within, deep down in her bones.

Betray her father to save her mother. She could not let her mother hang, not for her crimes, not for a stranger Isabelle had never known. She would do anything to save her.

CHAPTER
TWELVE

The dark made a menace of the city as she tried to find her way to the cathedral, stumbling for hours through alleys and abandoned streets until she was sure she was trapped in some lower hell as punishment for her sins. By the time she did find her way to the cathedral, she was so exhausted she slipped on the steps, slamming her elbow against the hard ground and collapsing across the stairs in sheer exhaustion, empty from the inside out. She didn't even know who or what she would find there, if her friends had escaped the mercenaries at all. But she had nowhere else to go.

"Well, it's about bloody time."

Isabelle jerked upright as Adam approached the stairs, a deep cut over his right eyebrow and a bruise blossoming across his cheekbone, but otherwise alive and well. The sight of a friendly face, even with a scowl on it, was enough to break through the fog, and she hauled herself up, launching into him and wrapping her arms tight around his neck. He staggered back a step, catching her around the waist.

"I am so glad you are safe," she said, pressing her face against his shoulder to stop the tears from rising. She didn't deserve the embrace, not for what she was contemplating, but she could not seem to pull herself away.

"Maybe I should find myself in mortal danger more often," Adam murmured, but he didn't set her back. Instead he stroked her hair gently. "What the hell happened to you?"

"I got lost," she said, her words smothered in his tunic. "Very, very lost."

"I'd say, we've been tearing up the city looking for you."

Isabelle drew back. "The others are . . . They are not harmed?"

Adam gave a small shrug. "Little's got a black eye and maybe a cracked rib, and Patrick and Helena got banged up a bit, but nothing we couldn't handle. Mercenaries are mean, but they're not fast." He took her chin in his hand and tilted her head up toward him. "Are you all right? You look as though someone's tromped over your grave."

Not my *grave,* she thought, but it was too much too soon. She pushed the thought away, suddenly desperate to be anywhere but within the same city walls as Sir Roger.

"Are we ready to leave?" she asked, stepping back.

Adam crossed his arms, eyeing her critically. "Where's your bow?"

"I must have . . . I must have lost it when I was running away."

"From the mercenaries." Adam's expression narrowed. "Who were looking for you."

Isabelle swallowed hard. "I don't know what you mean."

"That really how you want to play this, sister?"

"I am not playing at anything," she said, though she could not quite meet his gaze. "Perhaps the soldier I hit was important. These are trying times, as you said. If word got out that a simple priory girl could unseat a soldier from his horse, it could cause havoc in the countryside. They need to maintain their order through the law, do they not?"

Adam wasn't buying a single thread of her tapestry of lies, but he did not press her for the truth, which somehow only made her feel worse. Thomas might have told her to keep the truth from them for their own protection, but the longer she kept quiet, the more it felt like a cowardly lie. She had no doubt that any of the others would swoop in, mount a gallant battle of wits and swords, and get the upper hand on the Wolf. She wasn't fit to wear the Lincoln greens, which chafed at her skin as if they knew she was unworthy.

"We'd better go," Adam said finally. "The others are waiting."

"Will David be all right?" she asked, hurrying after him as he descended the steps and headed toward the north. "Will they not come after him, now that they know he helped us?"

"David can look to himself," said Adam. "Won't be the first time he's on the wrong end of Nicolaa de la Haye. He'll get word to Sherwood that we made it out safe. He even managed to find us a few horses to get out ourselves."

"I have never ridden a horse before," Isabelle said, chewing at the side of her lip. "We could not afford them at the priory. Will that be a problem?"

"Only for your backside," Adam muttered.

"Where the hell have you been?" Helena demanded when they reached the northern gate. "We've been sitting out here like chickens ready for the slaughter for over an hour. If you were looking to get us all arrested, you've done a bang-up job of it."

"We had some delays," Adam said, not looking at Isabelle. "Where are the horses?"

"Here," Little called, navigating around the surrounding building on a large brown stallion. "David could only scrounge up four mounts, and it nearly cost me my front teeth trying to get them out of the stables. I think you'll like yours. She's tied up round back."

"Why is she tied up round back?" Adam asked.

"She was scaring the other horses," Patrick said, appearing around the corner on a dappled gray mare. He led another horse by the reins, handing them over to Helena. The outlaw girl vaulted up into the saddle as if riding were second nature to her—yet another skill for Isabelle to envy.

"Glad to see you made it out safely," Patrick said to Isabelle with a nod.

"Yes, you certainly disappeared quickly enough once the fighting started," Helena said in a flat tone. Isabelle's cheeks exploded in a blush that suffused her entire body.

"Helena," Patrick admonished. "Adam told her to run. She's not trained like the rest of us."

"That's all right, Patrick," Isabelle said, keeping her eyes down. "Helena is right. I should have stayed and fought with you."

"You would have only been in the way," Helena said, relenting. "You might be a decent shot, but I don't guess you're much use in hand-to-hand fighting."

Isabelle wished she had been, then perhaps she could have escaped Blade's grasp.

"Sister, you'll ride with me," Adam said as a high-pitched whinny sounded in the open streets, followed by a solid thump as if someone had knocked a wall down.

"Perhaps I should ride with one of the others," Isabelle said, eyeing the shaking wall of the building that hid the horse.

Adam gave Little a dark look. "Switch with me."

"Not on your life, mate," said Little, his grin widening. "After all, you're the one always bragging about your way with the mares. Maybe you could put your touch to this one, give her the old Adam of Locksley treatment."

"Oh bloody hell," Adam muttered, disappearing around the corner. The building shook with a heavy impact, followed by a grunted curse and a high-pitched whinny. Isabelle winced at the series of blows the building sustained thereafter, each one harder and stronger than the last. But after several moments Adam came around the corner, leading the roving-eyed mare on a tight rein with his teeth gritted.

"I'm giving this beast to the first starving family I see," he muttered, tugging her reins. She snuffled a nasty response as he swung into the saddle. But she didn't rear up, nor did she try to bite him as he reached for Isabelle's hand. "Up you go, sister."

Isabelle wavered beside the massive beast, caught in the circle of its black eye. "Perhaps—"

"*Now*, sister," Adam said, grabbing her arm and pulling her up. She slid in behind him, her thighs nestled so close to his that she was sure Sister Catherine was muttering a curse against her indecency right then. The horse took off at a slow walk, jostling Isabelle sideways as she slipped against the smooth leather.

"Arms around my waist," Adam said over his shoulder. "Otherwise she'll throw you the first chance she gets."

Isabelle hesitated, leaning back against the lip of the saddle for stability and an inch of breathing room. She'd never been this close to anyone but her mother in her life, and certainly not a young outlaw she barely knew. *The flesh is far weaker than the will*, Sister Catherine would say. What would she think of Isabelle now? What fresh insults would she hurl? Some of them Isabelle might even deserve, because the truth was she wanted to slide her hands around Adam. She wanted to know where he felt soft, and where he felt strong, and if he always smelled of the forest even in the thick of the city. Sister Catherine was wrong; the will was as weak as the flesh, both parts of her leaning toward him against more rational thought.

"Promise I won't bite," Adam said in a low voice, drawing her closer. She thought she detected a small vibration through his words, an imbalance to his usually steady tone, but he turned away before she could search his face.

She shivered as she put her arms around him, trying to maintain some small distance, but it was impossible on the swaying back of the horse. She laced her fingers together, hoping that keeping them tangled in each other would stop the itching desire to lay them flat against his chest. He *did* smell of pine, and woodsmoke, and something else warm and comforting that made her want to bury her nose against his neck. But more than anything, the straight line of his shoulders and the slight curve of his spine made her feel safe. She knew he could not stop the might of the Wolf, but here in this moment, on this particular horse, she believed that they could outrun a galloping horde. That they could keep riding long past York, off to the distant wilds of the highlands. And she believed Adam might just be daring enough to do it.

But the fantasy chilled along with the frosty morning, brought back to harsh reality by the needles of discomfort already working their way under her thighs. If she were to run away, where would that leave her mother? The Wolf had given her a choice that was no choice at all—betray her father or let her mother die. What else could she do? Gladly would she throw herself in the hangman's noose to spare her mother, but it was not *her* neck the Wolf wanted. What kind of person would she be if she betrayed a man so many others were willing to die for? True, he had abandoned her and her mother to the priory and left her with a lonely and fatherless childhood. And he was already a wanted outlaw; how long until the king's men caught up with him anyway?

The Wolf's cold voice and dispassionate eyes haunted her long after they had passed through the city gates to the freedom of the open road. Even the surrounding trees seemed shadowed with eyes watching her as they headed north, Helena and Patrick's idle conversation easy and light in the wee morning hours. She had no doubt the Wolf could reach her anywhere in the country, no matter how far she ran or how deep she hid. And she knew with a crushing certainty that he would kill her mother without a moment of regret. She doubted he was a man given to regret. He had not become the king's most powerful advisor by doubting his choices. He had given her a choice, however impossible, and she had made up her mind.

She would give the Wolf what he wanted. She would give him Robin Hood.

CHAPTER
THIRTEEN

S leep was the furthest thing from Isabelle's mind when they left Lincoln, the Wolf's gaunt cheeks and thin lips mocking her each time she closed her eyes. But the steady sway of the horse's hooves and the solid reassurance of Adam's back lulled her into a light, blessedly dreamless sleep. It was the most rest she had gotten in the days since leaving Kirklees, and when the horses slowed and Adam's voice rumbled under her cheek, urging her awake, she responded by burrowing deeper into his back.

"Much as I'd be pleased to serve as your pallet the rest of the trip, sister, I've got a powerful need to relieve myself," Adam said, his voice full of amusement.

Isabelle drew back sharply as if someone had dumped a bucket of freezing river water over her. "Oh dear," she said. "I am terribly sorry. I don't know what I was thinking."

"Or dreaming," Little said with a wink.

"Shut up, Little," Helena said, sliding off her horse. "Your mind is always mucking about in the latrines. Give the sister some peace."

Little raised his eyebrows, as surprised by Helena's defense of Isabelle as Isabelle was herself. But he said no more, dismounting and following Helena and Patrick past the stand of trees where they had stopped. Adam swung a leg over and hopped down, holding up a hand to Isabelle.

"You'll want to be careful here, sister, seeing as how—"

But Isabelle did not want his help or his touch right then, and she set her foot in the stirrup and swung her other leg over just as he had done, intent on getting down by herself. Her leg muscles seized up, though, protesting the long hours in the hard saddle, and she tumbled forward with a small yelp. Adam caught her against his chest, lowering her the rest of the way until she could stand.

"As I was saying," he continued dryly, "you'll want to take it easy coming off the horse since it's your first time. Saddle riding can be hard on the backside."

Hard on the backside was a gentle way of putting it. Her entire body ached, from the crick in her neck where she had slumped against him down to her sore rump and through the pads of her swollen feet. She tipped her head up, doing her best to regain a modicum of dignity.

"I am fine," she said, though she would have preferred to curl up in a ball on a soft patch of hay and sleep the rest of the afternoon. "'Tis no worse than a day spent scrubbing the refectory floor, and I have done more than my fair share of that."

Adam lifted a brow. "If you have personal needs, see to them now. We won't stop for long."

Isabelle picked a trail through the denser parts of the surrounding trees until she found a quiet spot to relieve herself, her grumbling stomach reminding her it had been nearly a day since she last ate. She thought it would have adjusted to its new life of hunger by now, but it rumbled more insistently and she foraged through the undergrowth for anything she recognized as edible. If she'd had her bow, she could have picked up a hare or two, but as it was she had to console herself with edible roots and leaves. At least she hoped they were edible.

"Are you looking to cure a sore tooth?" Adam asked, eyeing the bundle in her tunic when she returned. "Because otherwise that yarrow root won't do you much good."

"Oh blast," Isabelle said, letting the little bundle tumble out. "I thought it was a wild carrot. I always mix those two up. The healing arts were never my strong suit."

"A sister who can't heal?" Adam shook his head. "No wonder you joined the outlaws."

Isabelle smiled faintly. "Besides my mother, Sister Catherine is our true expert, but she refused to teach me after I accidentally slightly poisoned Sister Margaret when I mixed up wild carrot and hemlock. She said I was a menace to the healing arts. Although I cannot say I blame her in this instance. I do not have the memory or the patience to be a healer. They agreed kitchen duty was a better application of my strengths."

"You don't look the kind who much enjoys hauling massive pots of gruel around, either," Adam said, pulling a few apples from his horse's travel bags. He tossed one to her, and she bit into it gratefully.

"It was a sight better than tending the gardens or mending habits," Isabelle said around a mouthful of apple. She took a seat on a fallen log. "Plus, I was closer to the food. Not that Sister Catherine would allow me to sneak anything when she was on duty. She would crack a wooden spoon over my hands if they strayed too close to the hearth."

"Sounds like most of the sisters I've been acquainted with," Adam said, sitting beside her. He took a bite of his apple, wincing halfway through and stopping to rub his jaw.

"What is it?" Isabelle asked, straightening up.

Adam shook his head. "Nothing worth bothering over. One of those bastards caught me with a blow to the jaw when I wasn't looking. Still smarts."

"Let me see," Isabelle said, standing before him.

"It's not much to look at, really," Adam said with a wave.

"I shall judge that for myself," Isabelle said, taking his chin firmly in her fingers and tilting his head to the side. A reddish-purple bruise covered his cheekbone, the edges spreading up toward his temple and down to his ear. She imagined it must have hurt terribly, even though Adam treated it as a minor inconvenience, and once more the guilt of knowing she was the cause of such a wound tore at her.

She brushed her fingertips over the bruise, gently palpating and checking for any breaks in the bone beneath or cuts on the skin. A small muscle stood out along his jaw as he clenched his teeth together, and she moved her fingers away from the bruise to his hairline. His skin was smooth along his temple, growing rougher with the few days of stubble from his ear down along his jaw. Her fingertips crackled with little frissons of energy as she moved them down his jawline, the stubble playing at her sensitive skin in ways that made her heart slow and then race. Adam had gone very still beneath her hands, his chest barely rising. When he caught her gaze it was like plunging into the deepest lake, jolting her awake.

"I have something for that," she said, stumbling back, her fingertips prickling. She turned away, rubbing her hands against the rough wool of her tunic to stop the sensation.

"As long as it's not wild carrot," he said, his tone wry.

"My mother made it. You are safe from any accidental poisonings." She riffled through the saddlebags until she found her travel sack, pulling the small container of salve out of the bag and letting the pungent herbal bouquet wash the smell of him from her nose.

She took a deep, steadying breath before trusting herself to face him.

"So what encounters have you had with sisters of the order?" she asked as she dug her fingers into the salve, looking for anything to distract from the roughness of his skin. "You said Sister Catherine sounded like every sister you had met."

"My sister, Abigail, she's in a priory," Adam said, keeping his eyes fixed on the ground. "Well, an abbey. Is that the same thing?"

"Not exactly, but I do not think you are interested in a lecture on the particulars of ecclesiastical hierarchy."

Adam gave a half smile. "Not in the slightest."

"What brought your sister to the abbey?" Isabelle asked, her fingers lingering over his jaw of their own volition.

Adam hesitated. Isabelle had seen her fair share of sisters come to Kirklees, their reasons as varied as their backgrounds. Sister Catherine had always advocated for courting royalty and only accepting girls of noble backgrounds and the large dowries that often went along with them. But when Isabelle's mother became prioress, she opened Kirklees to girls of all status, wanting to provide shelter and a better life for those whose opportunities were limited or whose circumstances were unbearable beyond the priory walls. Isabelle feared, from the look on Adam's face, that his sister was of the latter.

"I am sorry," Isabelle said after a long moment. She stepped back, her fingers soft and oily from the salve. "I should not have pried. It was not my place."

"She thinks I should move past it," Adam said, working his jaw carefully side to side. He lifted his brows in surprise. "That actually is better. My thanks to you and your mother."

Isabelle shook her head. "My mother is the true healer."

"I think you did all right."

Isabelle turned away from him, the heat of his gaze spreading over her back. "I am happy to help. Especially for the brother of one of our own."

"Now you sound like Abigail."

"Then she sounds like a lovely girl. I am sure I would like her."

Adam grinned. "Oh, she'd love you. She's only a year younger than me, and if she could have had her way of things, she would have been born a boy, same as me. She got into more scraps than I did, and me always having to haul her back out before she did any real damage. We ran everywhere, did everything together. Fishing, sword fighting with dead branches we'd haul out of the woods, tearing apart my da's workshop until he kicked us out. I think it was a rude awakening for her when we got old enough that it was obvious she wasn't a boy and her body didn't listen to any of her demands otherwise."

"What kind of workshop does your father have?" Isabelle asked, warmed by the image of a young Adam chasing a little girl with wild braids. She had no siblings herself—at least none that she knew of—and hearing him speak so lovingly of his sister brought a sharp pang of loneliness for her childhood self.

"My da is a tanner," said Adam, testing the edges of his bruise. "Cures leather and the like."

"That is it!" Isabelle said on a spark of inspiration. "That is what you smell like."

Adam gave her a horrified look. "You think I smell like a tanner's shop?"

She frowned. "Is that a bad thing?"

"Only if you've ever *smelled* a tanner's shop. They smell of urine and rot on a good day, and worse when it's hot. It's a nasty process, making leather. Poisons the water and stinks to the heavens." He pulled the neck of his tunic away from his body, exposing his collarbone and the top of his chest. Isabelle quickly cut her eyes away, her face warming. "Is that really what I smell like?"

"No, no, of course not," she said hastily. "I only meant you smelled of leather. In a good way. Like a fresh pair of gloves. Or a well-oiled saddle. It is a nice smell."

She turned toward their horse to hide the blush creeping up her neck and across her cheeks, packing away the salve. What was she saying, telling him of his own smells? What was wrong with her mind? If Adam noticed her discomfort, he didn't remark on it.

"So long as I don't smell of the shop," he said. "I swear it took years to get the stink off me after I left Locksley, like it grew into my skin and came out of the roots of my hair. Even Abigail said she still woke up from dreams sometimes smelling the pits of blood and dung where my da washed the skins when they first came in from the butcher."

"Is she the reason you came to be at the outlaw camp?" Isabelle asked quietly over her shoulder.

"Oh, aye," Adam said, a dark current rippling through his words. "I never forgave the men who hurt her, but I did find them. Tin heads, of course, propped up on their own importance and swimming in ale. There were three of them and one of me. They didn't think I stood a chance."

Her breath caught at the unspoken violence in his voice, his pain still so fresh, his rage crackling. She sat beside him, wanting to take his hand, to wrap her small fingers around his as much for her own comfort as his. She'd heard enough versions of his sister's story from those who sought shelter at Kirklees, and it never failed to break her heart that women could suffer such violence at the hands of men.

"I'd snapped two of their arms and smashed one of their noses by the time their friends heard the fighting and pulled me off them,"

Adam said, his gaze hard on the ground. "Not even a cut on me. At least not until they got me to the stocks. Then they had their way, the cowards."

A faint white scar followed his hairline down past his temple to just above his ear, right where she had applied the salve. She wondered if the soldiers had given it to him.

"What about your family?" she asked, her voice soft.

Adam gave a laugh that chilled her. "My da came to visit me, once. Just after they'd left me practically for dead. Told me he was ashamed. That I'd let my impulses rule my head and put all our family in danger over one daughter. He said if anyone ever came to let me out that I could find my way to another home and not give a look back. Not that there was anything for me to look back on. My father had the shop, my mother had my little brothers and sisters to look after, and Abigail was gone. There was nothing for me in Locksley anymore."

Isabelle's heart tightened into a knot, the tension aching through her entire chest. Adam shook himself as if coming out of a reverie, taking a deep breath.

"Anyway, that's where Robin and Little John found me. They were passing through towns like mine, wrestling any idiot foolish enough to try his hand against Little John. Got me out of the stocks and I joined up on the spot. Never looked back, just like my da said."

Isabelle studied her hands, lacing and unlacing her fingers, but it was not quite the same as holding his. "My mother would say forgiveness is essential to leading a peaceful life."

"Maybe," Adam said, stretching back. "But it's not peace I'm looking for. Robin always says we help those the king would rather use up and forget, people like Abigail. The king doesn't look at people as precious, he looks at them as a commodity. Somebody to work his lands and fill his coffers and clean his boots." He leaned forward, his eyes narrowing. "But his time is coming to an end."

"How can you be so sure?" Isabelle whispered. "He is a king, with an entire army at his disposal."

"An army bought and not yet paid for," Adam said. "You can buy a sword, but you can't buy loyalty. John will find that out soon enough. His days on the throne are numbered."

Looking at Adam just then, his jaw set and his eyes blazing, Isabelle could almost believe it. She could almost believe that Sir Roger was only human, fallible and beatable. She wanted to believe it, so desperately, that these rebel outlaws could actually change the country if things had really gotten so bad as they were in Kirkleestown. But it was easy to fight for ideals, and much harder to face the reality of their consequences. Consequences that her mother would pay if she did not do what the Wolf demanded.

"We should keep moving, should we not?" she said. "If we want to reach York in time."

Adam nodded, standing up from the log and tossing his apple core into the woods. And even though it had been Isabelle's suggestion, she regretted it as soon as he left to find the others. She could have sat with him for hours, talking of his family and Robin and the Merry Men. If it had been another time, another set of circumstances.

She sighed, standing and following after him toward the sound of wood striking against wood, followed by a vibrant string of Gaelic curses. She found Adam at the bank of a wide creek where Little and Patrick faced off, Little wielding his staff and Patrick holding a crude approximation of one that looked fashioned from a fallen tree branch.

"I keep telling you not to look where you mean to strike, Patty," Little said, swinging the bottom of the staff forward to meet

Patrick's low blow. "I know what you're doing before you do it every time."

"I didn't think I was looking," Patrick grunted. He brought the bottom of his staff forward again in a strike to Little's knees, but before the wood could make contact, Little parried the blow. "And what have I said about calling me Patty?"

Little tilted his head thoughtfully. "To keep doing it?"

"To *stop* doing it," Patrick said, groaning as another of his blows slipped off Little's staff. "I swear you must be cheating somehow."

Isabelle kept clear of their fighting area, not wanting to find herself on the receiving end of a wayward blow as Little deftly blocked Patrick's strikes with friendly taunts. They were both covered in a fine sheen of sweat from their practice. Little caught sight of Isabelle and Adam, waving with one hand as he put the tip of his staff to Patrick's chest and shoved the Irish boy into the water.

"Oi, Adam," Little called. "Come and fight me. I need a real challenge."

"Don't make me lob a stone at that thick head of yours," Patrick spluttered, coming up out of the water.

"Come on, then, Adam, give us a go," Little said, drawing his sword from the scabbard on his belt. "Unless you're worried I'll trounce you in front of the sister."

Adam sighed, giving her a small shrug as he pulled his own sword. He swung it around, opening up his shoulder, as he approached the tall boy. "The only thing I'm worried about is the crying I'll hear from you for the rest of the day. Guard up."

They faced each other with sword hands low, the tips dancing through the air as they moved on light feet around the small clearing. Patrick dripped his way over to where Isabelle stood, watching. He nodded to Adam, whose relaxed stance and slight smile didn't make him look like a man ready to fight.

"This is the only form of retribution I'll get for Little's pounding," he said to Isabelle.

Isabelle started to ask what he meant by that, but Adam opened their sparring with a swing toward Little's left shoulder, the blade arcing so fast it glinted like lightning. Little barely escaped the blow, dodging to the right and countering with his own strike to Adam's ribs. Adam blocked Little's attack with even more boredom than the tall boy had shown Patrick, easily turning his blade to the side and sliding down to nick him in the hand. Little gave a shout, pulling back his sword arm.

"That hurt," Little grumbled.

"I told you to use the guard to your advantage," Adam said, sounding thoroughly unapologetic.

They sparred for several minutes, Little working up a true sweat in his efforts to find a hole in Adam's defense. Adam, for his part, turned more aggressive as they fought, tapping Little several times on the shoulder or in the ribs to let him know when he was caught. Isabelle watched the gleaming swoop of his blade, the sword a natural extension of his arm. He moved with fluid grace, his lean muscles flexing and relaxing as he executed each movement with careful explosions of energy. He never once lost his footing, or missed the mark of his attack, or took his eyes from Little's gaze. It was a breathless dance of violence that held Isabelle transfixed.

Little dropped his sword arm, the tip dragging through the dirt as he raised his other arm over his head and backed away. "I give, I give," he panted, dropping both hands to his knees with a heaving breath. "It's a good thing you're on our side, mate."

Adam smiled, his own chest rising and falling rapidly now that the fight had drawn to a close. "I'm always on your side, Little. Until I'm not. Then you'll never see me coming."

"Bah," Little said, waving him away. "The Merry Men never turn on their own. Thicker than blood, eh?"

The Merry Men never turn on their own. Isabelle's stomach turned at the reminder of what she had to do. What she had chosen to do.

"You all right, sister?" Patrick asked, frowning. "You look a bit pale."

"Only exhaustion," she said, mustering a faint smile.

Patrick nodded sagely. "I could use a warm fire and a spot of stew myself. I'll be glad once we reach the camp in York."

Isabelle could not share his enthusiasm. The closer they got, the tighter the noose around her neck. And eventually, she knew, her neck would snap.

CHAPTER
FOURTEEN

Isabelle could find no peace in sleep after that, but the droning pace and uneventful passage of their trip did lull her into a numbing complacency as the scenery shifted from heavy forests to rolling hills. She grew so content that when Adam's horse stopped abruptly she nearly tumbled out of the saddle and had to scrabble at Adam's waist to keep her seat. She peered over his shoulder at what had spooked the horses.

"What happened?" she asked, but Adam held up a hand.

"She smells something," he said in a low voice, and the others had reined in their mounts as well, all of their ears pricked up for what the horses had already detected.

"Patrick," Adam said, but the Irish boy was one step ahead. He tossed Helena his reins, slipping down on silent feet and running toward the closest hill for cover. They waited, quiet and tense, Adam's horse giving a low whinny. Patrick came running back.

"Highwaymen," he said. "Over the next rise."

Isabelle jerked back at the mention of thieves along the king's road, but the others looked as if it were no more than an irritating inconvenience.

"Bloody hell," Adam said, letting out a breath. "Ours?"

Patrick shook his head.

"How close are we to York, do you figure?"

"Pretty close," Patrick said, waving at the hill behind him. "I can see the castle from the hilltop."

Adam tapped a finger on the pommel of the saddle. "Do you think you could get word to Little John? They're taking a risk, ambushing this close to our territory."

"We can take them," Little said, already reaching for his staff. "It's been ages since I've had a good row."

"You had one not a day ago," Helena said. "And you fought on the way here!"

"Yeah, but that doesn't count, does it?" Little replied. "Neither of those was a proper thrashing. Come on, Adam, let's crack some heads."

"Not with the sister here," Adam said, shaking his head. "We can't risk her getting hurt."

"All I require is a bow," Isabelle said with far more confidence than she felt.

He cut his gaze over his shoulder. "And where is yours now?"

She flushed, looking down at the ground. "I misplaced it in Lincoln."

"Exactly."

"They don't look like much," Patrick conceded. "Farmer's axes and a few cudgels among them. No more than six."

"Are you all just spoiling for a fight?" Adam asked incredulously.

"Well, if it's one we could win," Patrick said, trailing off with a shrug.

"Idiots," Helena said, closing her eyes and lifting her head skyward.

"All right, look," Adam said. "Little and I will go up the road.

Helena and Patrick, you flank to the left and right. Isabelle, you take Helena's bow and find a vantage point."

"You want me to give her my bow when she just admitted to losing her own?" Helena demanded.

Adam pinned her with a look. "Would you rather give her your sword and let her take up the action instead?"

Helena narrowed her eyes at him but did not argue again, holding out her bow for the other girl. When Isabelle made to take it, though, Helena drew it back an inch. "You take care of her, do you understand?"

"Of course," Isabelle promised, cradling the bow as she took it.

"Stay out of the fighting," Adam warned her. "Anyone comes for you, shoot them. If you can't do that, you run, fast as you can. Everybody understand?"

They all nodded, Helena and Patrick dismounting and leading their horses off to opposite sides of the road. Isabelle slid off Adam's horse, her legs so sore she could cry, shouldering the bow and quiver and cutting across the hill in the same direction Patrick had disappeared. Adam and Little continued forward as she crept up the hillside, kneeling at a vantage point as the two horses crested the hill and dipped down into the valley below.

"Halt!" someone shouted from ahead. Six men swarmed the road, surrounding Adam and Little in an instant. Patrick had been right, their weapons were crudely fashioned, but they wielded them with a grinning eagerness that made her breath come in short, panicked bursts. One of the men, with more gaps than teeth and a woolly black beard, swung his ax and let out a whooping shout that sent Adam's horse into a frenzy.

"Well, hello, mates, what a fine evening we're having," the man with the black beard said, his words mushy through his missing teeth. "You? Not so much."

"Clever," Adam said flatly. "What is it we can do for you fellows this evening?"

"You can start by giving us those fine horses of yours," said a man with yellow hair and a trimmed beard. "And then we'll be taking those swords, and whatever coin you've got. And don't think to be hiding nothing from us, because we're bloody men of the highway. We get what we want."

Adam leaned forward over the pommel of his saddle, eyeing the ragtag group of men assembled. "I'll tell you what. You move out of our way and let us pass without any trouble, and I won't knock the last of your teeth out of your head."

A few of the men laughed at that, which only incensed the blond man further.

"Don't you be threatening me! There's six of us and two of you lads. That don't make for much of an advantage."

"Perhaps," Adam said with a tilt of his head. "If there were only two of us."

Patrick and Helena appeared over the hills to the left and right, weapons drawn, flanking the men and boxing them in on the road. A few of them looked decidedly less eager, their cudgels dropping toward the dusty road. The blond man puffed his chest with a snort.

"A girl and a boy with nothing but fuzz on his cheeks? That don't worry us much."

"Then you're not bloody paying attention," Helena said. "Call me girl again and find out how worried you should be."

The man lifted his ax menacingly. "You give us those horses or I'll cut you down. I'm not afraid of a few children playing at swords."

"Finally, some fighting," Little said buoyantly, brandishing his staff. "Come on, then, show us what you've got. Come cut me down."

The man hesitated, his fatal mistake. "Let's get what's ours, men!"

Isabelle ignored the pounding in her chest and drew down an arrow just as he lifted the ax, letting it fly right for the handle. It knocked the ax out of his grip, the weapon landing in the dusty road with a thud. The man gave a sharp yelp as he snatched his hand back, scanning the hills for the source of the shot. Isabelle crouched low, holding in a deep breath.

"Looks like your advantage keeps narrowing," Adam said in an even tone. "Perhaps you'd like to take what little remains of it and get out of our way?"

"Get them!" the man barked, snatching up his ax just as a deep horn blast shattered the air around them. For a moment nothing happened, the highwaymen frozen in midattack, the horses' heads down and ready to charge, and Isabelle wondered if she had imagined the sound. But then a shadow crested a hill several hundred feet away, dipping into the valley and rising on the next hill, the bulk of the shadow expanding upward and outward until she was sure it must be two men side by side or standing on each other's shoulders.

"God's teeth, it's Little John," said a skinny boy with dung-colored hair and freckled cheeks. Isabelle had rather the same reaction to the colossal man striding toward them in the Lincoln greens.

"Hold steady," said their leader, though his face paled considerably, and the arrogant confidence drained out of his features as the behemoth approached. "He is only one man."

"Only one man who could crush our skulls together like cheap pottery," whispered another of the men, his ax trembling in his hand. "Loudon, we've got to go!"

"Hold fast!" Loudon replied.

Isabelle watched in wonder as the man crested the last hill. In all her life she had never seen a man so large, his arms heavily muscled and thick as trees. He had a dark brown beard, giving his face the appearance of a beast that had caught the scent of his prey. He closed the long distance between the hill and the road in three strides and came to a stop before them. His bright brown eyes swept over the scene, picking apart the situation without speaking a word. He gave a short nod to Adam and let his heavy gaze settle on Loudon. The blond man seemed to shrink under the weight of that gaze.

"Loudon," he said with a nod, his baritone voice coming from the depths of his belly.

"John," said Loudon, dragging his shoulders up with an effort. His men made no such attempt at gathering their pride about them, and many had already backed up to the edge of the roadway.

The big man took another sweeping look around the scene, and the men backed up a half step more. He leaned on his staff the size of a small sapling, chewing on some invisible cud. "What are you doing?"

"Conducting my business, same as you," said Loudon. "The king's road is free territory and you know it."

John nodded, his jaw still working up and down slowly. Loudon's men had now stumbled back onto the rocky knoll of the nearest hill, looking ready to bolt at the first sign of trouble. "You've got a problem, lad. These are friends of mine."

Loudon bristled as a deep shadow fell over the roadway. Fat clouds rolled in, and a far rumble made several of his men jump. Isabelle had lowered her bow at the approach of the big man, but her fingers were still pressed tight against the grip, digging in farther as thunder crackled in the clouds above.

"Friends of yours or not, they're on the main road. Which makes them fair game."

Little chuckled, shaking his head. "You said the wrong thing, mate."

John straightened again to his full height, his chest expanding on an intake of breath that sucked the wind from the clouds. He gave his staff one whistling whirl before taking it up with both hands, his bright eyes fixed on Loudon. The other highwaymen lost all courage then, breaking formation and scattering along the hilltops until they were nothing more than distant specks. Loudon was clearly agitated by their noisy departure.

"All right, then, Loudon," said the big man, a hint of pleasure seeping into his tone. "Take what you want. If you can."

Little leapt from his horse and brandished his staff beside the big man. "Let me have a go at him before you crack his pate open, fair enough?"

The blood drained from Loudon's face, his ax head dropping to the ground and digging a little trench in the dirt as he stumbled back a step. It was difficult for him to try to maintain his dignity in retreat, but he gave it one last valiant effort.

"This slight will not be forgotten," he said, raising his ax to shake it at the big man. "You will pay someday for the disrespect you have shown me."

John limited himself to a grunt and another swing of the staff, the whistle cutting through the air. Loudon colored, making his sandy brows stand out on his forehead as he stalked away after his men. John spat on the ground after them.

"Useless chuff," he said. "And more of them every day."

"Perhaps a war will clear a few of them out," Adam said, swinging one leg over to dismount. He held out a hand. "Little John, well met as always."

John clasped his forearm and gave it a hearty shake. "Well met, Adam. It's been a while since I've seen your face round these parts."

"We've been busy with our own scourge," said Adam. "You remember Little?"

"Allan A'Dale's lad," he said with a nod, shaking Little's hand. "You taller than him yet?"

Little stood up a bit straighter. "Nearly."

Adam turned back to where Isabelle still crouched, waving an arm at her. "It's all right now, sister. John's one of the Merry Men."

Isabelle rose and picked a path back down to the road, the bulk of the man they called Little John growing with each step she took. She couldn't imagine what it took to feed such a man each day. When he shook her hand, he nearly tore her arm from its socket.

"Isabelle of Kirklees," she said. "Well, formerly of Kirklees. Of nowhere at the moment, I suppose."

Little John rubbed at his beard. "Kirklees, you say? Seems as if I've heard tell of it at some point. Your mother wouldn't happen to be a prioress there, would she?"

Isabelle colored as Patrick and Helena drew closer, the former frowning at the big man. "How do you know about Isabelle's mother?"

"A prioress with a child is a rarity," Isabelle said hastily. "No doubt he has heard of her by reputation."

Little John regarded her with a look that brought her close to confessing everything. She bit down on the inside of her lip to keep her mouth closed, silently pleading with the big man. But he only gave a grunt, flipping his staff over his shoulder to stow it away in its sling.

"Aye, that must be it," he said, turning his attention to Adam. "What brings you round to our parts? Everything all right in Sherwood?"

Adam nodded. "For now. The sister has urgent news for Robin. We came to find him."

"If all goes according to plan," said Little John, "you can see him tonight and tell him whatever news you've got to share."

Adam crossed his arms. "The words 'according to plan' don't bode well here."

John scratched at his beard, his hand disappearing into its depths. "Robin's a bit tied up at the moment. In York Castle. In the dungeons."

Adam sighed. "And there it is."

CHAPTER
FIFTEEN

"Oh, for bother's sake," said Helena, throwing up her hands in disgust. "Men."

"Brilliant," Little said with a grin. "What was it this time?"

"This time?" Isabelle said. "Is this a regular occurrence?"

"Not regular, I wouldn't say so, no," John said in the same steady tone as if he were discussing the wheat crop. "Every few months, maybe."

"Every few months?" Isabelle cried. "How is getting thrown in dungeons something one makes a habit of?"

"For us, it's an occupational hazard," Adam said. "What happened?"

John shrugged. "Well, things have been a bit tense round here, as you might expect, especially after Tuck was ousted."

"Who is this Tuck you all keep mentioning?" Isabelle asked.

"An old friend of Robin's," said Patrick. "One of the Merry Men back in the day. Tuck is the archbishop of York now. Or was, apparently?"

"The king never did take well to him," conceded Little John. "Never wanted him for the position in the first place, and now, with all the goings-on with the barons, I guess he thought Tuck needed to go."

Isabelle pinched the bridge of her nose. "Are you saying the archbishop of York, the second most powerful man in the English Church, was once in the Merry Men?"

"Was the archbishop," said Little John. "As I said. Still a Merry Man."

Isabelle shook her head. "Next you shall tell me Robin once dined with the pope."

"Don't look so impressed," Adam said. "Tuck was just a lowly friar when Robin met him. What's Tuck's ouster got to do with Robin taking a turn through the dungeons?"

Little John tapped his massive staff against the ground. "The way Tuck had tell of it, some of the castle guards got rough with him when they were delivering the letter from the king, and Robin took exception to their handling. There was a scrap, and Robin got pinched."

"What are we going to do?" Isabelle asked. "We cannot let them hang him."

"Oh, no, we'll get him out," said John. He turned his face up to the heavy clouds overhead. "Though this weather won't make it easy on us."

"I'll get him out," Little said confidently. "You've got some armor lying about somewhere, right? I'd make a right perfect tin head."

"You've certainly got the lack of brains for it," Helena said.

"We'll help whatever way we can," Adam said. "Patrick's the best scout in the camp, and Helena's our best bow arm."

"Second best now," Little said, grinning.

"Test it and find out, Little," Helena said, glaring at him.

"We've got a plan," John said. He eyed Isabelle critically. "Though you could actually be of some use, lass. If you're willing."

"Me?" Isabelle asked in surprise. "Yes, of course. Whatever you need."

He tilted his head to the side. "Maybe you should hear what it is before you say so."

They followed Little John back to the York outpost of the Merry Men as a peal of thunder rippled through the sky overhead, the clouds low enough that the tops of the trees were lost in their iron weight. The men gathered here were a tenth the number of the camp in Sherwood, with no women in sight, and their beds were no more than mossy ground coverings in place of the elaborate tree houses of the other camp. But as Isabelle drew deeper into the camp, John and his men pulled at a network of hidden ropes, raising thick nets laced with leaves from the ground for camouflage, revealing deep cooking pits and stockpiles of weapons. And the men were just as merry as those from the Sherwood camp, the energy buzzing among them friendly and comfortable.

Little John clearly ruled the camp, sending men off on various errands to prepare their evening meal and shore up their shelters against the impending rain. Isabelle trailed him as he ordered the men about, not wanting to be forgotten in the furor of activity. She had no intention of sitting out her own father's rescue, not when he was so close at hand. The big man finally turned to her, crossing his massive arms over his chest as he surveyed her from his great height. She fought the urge to shrink into herself under the weight of his gaze.

"You're Robin's daughter," he said, no hint of a question in his tone.

How odd, after all these days of secrecy, to have it stated so plainly by a stranger. Isabelle swallowed reflexively, nodding. "Yes. I am."

He tilted his head toward Adam and the others where they stood with the Merry Men, gathering supplies and discussing plans for the rescue. "And they don't know about it?"

"It is better for them that they do not, at least for now," said Isabelle, trying to convince herself as much as the outlaw.

"You're in danger, then," John said. "Your message for Robin got something to do with it?"

Isabelle considered feeding him the same lie she had given the others, that she was only there to warn Robin about the growing unrest in Kirklees. But there was a certain weight to his gaze, a clarity that told her he would sort out her untruths faster than she could tell them. So she told him the simplest version of the truth she could.

"Yes. It is imperative I find him—my father."

The big man nodded once, as if her plight was all the proof he needed. "You're sure you want to help?"

She nodded firmly. "Yes."

He reached into a nearby trunk and pulled a bright bundle of blue-and-white cloth from within, tossing it to her. "Put this on, then."

She held the fabric up. "What is it?"

"A disguise. We need someone to distract the dungeon guards."

"Oh," she said with disappointment. Then, as she plucked the loose strings holding the bodice together, recognition dawned and spread like a wildfire over her face. "Oh."

Little John lifted one brow. "You could stay at the camp if you prefer."

If only her mother could see her now. If *Sister Catherine* could see her now. Reduced to playing the strumpet to free her outlaw father from the dungeons of York. No doubt the old crone would crow her delight to see Isabelle fill such a role. *No good in you but the riddance,* she always said.

Little John left her to the privacy of a copse of trees dense enough to shield her from the camp, returning to the others to finalize their plans. She held the dress out, a loose collection of silky fabrics and a low neckline she suspected had been designed for generous tips. It would hardly protect her from the wet chill filling the air, and she already missed the warm comfort of the Lincoln greens.

"How in the name of the Almighty do they expect me to be a . . . a barmaid?" she muttered, draping the dress over a nearby tree branch to stare at it critically. "How seductive am I meant to be if I am shivering? What do men find attractive about a barmaid anyhow?"

"They're cheap and easy," came Helena's voice through the trees. The girl appeared a moment later, surveying the dress as if it were an enemy soldier.

"Little John sent me to help you into this contraption. As if I know about skirts and bodices any better than you." She inspected the dress critically. "Not much to it, is there?"

"I was rather thinking the same thing," Isabelle said, chewing her bottom lip. "It's quite possible this plan will fail spectacularly."

"I'm in agreement with you there. You're too skinny and proper for most men I know."

Isabelle closed her eyes on a sigh. "That is not improving my confidence in the matter."

Helena grunted. "Look, whether or not I think you're any good at this isn't the point. The point is, we need someone to distract the dungeon guards while we slip in and get Robin. You'll certainly do a sight better than me with those big blue eyes of yours. Men love a good damsel in distress—something about her helplessness makes them feel even manlier. Which is pathetic, frankly, because it takes a real man to handle a woman who can speak her own mind."

Isabelle smiled. "My mother once said a man should measure

his worth not by the women he has tamed, but by the ones he has let run free."

"Your mother, I like. Now put this thing on before those idiots try to leave without us."

Between the two of them, they managed to get the dress over her head and secure the waist with a thin rope belt. The neckline plunged low enough that Isabelle turned pink at the prospect of parading about in it, and for a brief moment she wondered what Adam would think. They gathered her hair in long ringlets over one shoulder, the curls intertwining and locking into a loose knot. Helena stepped back to survey their handiwork.

"You look enough the part, though a bit of color round your cheeks and lips wouldn't hurt. No help for it, though. Do something . . ." She waved her hand vaguely. "Seductive."

Isabelle blushed. "What would that be? I come from a priory, not a brothel."

Helena threw up her hands. "How should I know? I'd just as soon shoot them an arrow as a kiss. Tilt your head down and look up through your lashes. No, not like that. You look as if you've been brained with a cudgel. Move your chin to your shoulder and try it. Tilt your head more. No, that's too much, now you look like you've snapped your neck. There, that's better. I suppose."

Isabelle sighed. "This will never work. I have no idea how to willfully attract a man."

"You're willful enough about everything else," said Adam from behind her. He leaned against a tree, arms crossed. His gaze raked down the front of her dress in a way that set the chill night on fire. "You certainly look the part."

"I do not feel the part," she said. "I feel . . . exposed. And ridiculous."

"You wanted to help, sister," he said, spreading his hands. "And this is helping. If you would rather abide in the camp and keep the fires warm . . ."

"You will not be rid of me so easily," Isabelle said, straightening her spine. The dress slipped precariously close to one shoulder, and she snatched at the fabric, bringing it back to a more modest angle.

"You certainly blush more than most barmaids of my acquaintance," Adam said, the thrum of a laugh rippling through his words.

"I have better things to do than listen to you two go on," said Helena, rolling her eyes. "If you need me, I'll be unavailable somewhere else."

"Helena, wait," Isabelle called after her, twisting her hands together. "Thank you. For your help."

Helena looked her up and down. "I'm not actually sure I did help. Good luck, sister."

She disappeared through the trees, and for once Isabelle wished the outlaw girl back. Something about the way Adam watched her made her feel like a deer caught in an open meadow. He pushed himself up and started a slow, wide circle around her.

"It's not completely unconvincing," he said. "I suppose we could work with this."

"Are you so practiced in the art of female seduction?" she asked.

He gave a half smile. "You would be surprised. Soften your shoulders and roll them forward."

"I do not know that I would be surprised," she said, looking away from him as she tried to do as she was told. "You are an outlaw, after all."

"As are you now, sister," Adam said. "That's better. Now tilt your head as Helena said. Don't look at them straight on; it's too challenging. Guards are a simple breed. They prefer their women loose, dumb, and submissive."

"I suppose all men do," Isabelle said, trying to look up at him through her lashes without straining her eyes.

"Not all men," Adam said, his voice a murmur as he drew closer to her. "Sway your hips when you walk, and don't be in a hurry to get anywhere. And purse your lips a bit."

"I feel an absolute fool," she said.

"So long as you don't look it."

She stopped, facing him and putting her hands to her hips. "Will this really work?"

Adam surveyed her appraisingly, his dark eyes warming to a deep mahogany. Isabelle's heart thudded at the look, her breath hitching in her chest. "At this rate, I'm inclined to believe it myself."

He stood only a few inches from her now, close enough that she could see the dark shadows along his jaw forming into a beard from their days of travel. Heat radiated off his skin, drawing her a half step closer. The darkness overhead dropped low and weighty around them, blanketing them in a sacred space. Her breath came quick and shallow.

"Careful, sister," Adam murmured, tucking a stray lock behind her ear. "There is such a thing as too convincing."

Isabelle shuddered in a deep breath. "So long as it works, right?"

CHAPTER
SIXTEEN

If it was possible, York stank even worse than Lincoln. The offending odors of human and animal waste mixing in the open air and putrefying in ditches and pits carried over the gentle hills as they approached the city, a sprawl of buildings cropping up like a mouth full of crooked teeth. The industry within the city flourished despite the filth, the wool and wine trade thriving since the king granted York a petition to self-govern the previous year. They set their own laws and taxes, elected their own officials, and prospered even as the rest of the country flailed under the king's tyrannical rule.

King John's mercenary army had not yet reached York, and so the people still moved freely about the city trading wares and raising mugs in the taverns Isabelle and Little John passed without a care for who was watching. And many watched, too many for Isabelle's comfort. She clutched her arms around her chest as Little John guided her through the mass of the city toward the looming York Castle, the keep on a massive hill that towered above the city. She felt no less exposed than that castle keep, her dress thin and the eyes of the men they passed lascivious and searching. Somewhere in the deep shadows of the night, the others followed after them, silent sentinels.

The plan was so simple Isabelle feared it was doomed from the outset, though she would not say so to the others. She carried a full wineskin over her shoulder, drawing from her limited herbal knowledge to brew a potent concoction her mother had called dwale that would put a grown man into a deep sleep. She had mixed up hemlock, wild neep, lettuce, opium, henbane, and vinegar to lace the wine. She only hoped she had remembered the proportions correctly and would not accidentally kill someone.

"We'll be coming up on the castle soon," Little John said in a low voice.

Isabelle nodded, too nervous to speak. Between the carousing crowds of two rival taverns, she caught glimpses of the castle, the keep looming like a monolith on its high hill. A wide, deep moat surrounded the castle, formed by the confluence of two rivers, the only break in the glittering expanse a narrow wooden bridge stretching across the water to the castle bailey, the enclosed courtyard surrounding the keep. Figures moved along the top of the wall in rhythmic fashion, their armor winking in the firelight. Her heart hammered at the sheer size of it. How could they possibly hope to get through the main gate, much less get Robin out of there?

"Steady on, Isabelle," murmured a voice in her ear, a solid presence suddenly at her side as Adam took her elbow. "You'll do just fine. No need to panic."

She wasn't aware she had been panicking, but of course her breathing was loud and fast, her heart threatening to burst from her chest. The steadiness of his hand at her elbow released the tension from her muscles, and for a moment she wished she could curl into him and beg him to take her away from there. But she had come too far; she needed Robin too badly. She could not give in to her fear, not when it meant her mother's life. So she pulled her elbow free with a slight tug, giving him a nod of confidence.

But he was already gone, melted back into the surrounding dark.

Isabelle and Little John reached the edge of the moat, the buildings around them thinning out as the massive island of York Castle filled the skyline. The castle had been built in the middle of two rivers, a natural protection against ancient invaders. But tonight there was no army, just a handful of Merry Men and a girl dressed as a lowly barmaid. John paused under the eaves of a shop, his eyes fixed on the castle.

"We'll part here, lass," he said. "And meet back up outside the dungeons. Do you remember your role?"

Isabelle's stomach knotted, squeezing the air out of her lungs. "Yes. I will tell the gate guards the mayor sent for me, and once inside, the dungeons are located to the northeast corner. I am to . . . incapacitate the soldiers on duty there."

"We'll swim the moat and find our way inside the bailey," Little John said. "When you've taken care of the dungeon guards, give the signal and we'll go in for Robin."

Isabelle bobbed her head nervously. "Yes, I understand."

Little John gave her a steady gaze. "You sure you want to do this, lass?"

Her father would not back down, she was sure of it. And somewhere on the other side of that castle wall, he was waiting. "I can do this. I want to do this."

Little John nodded. "See you on the other side."

And then the big man was gone and Isabelle was alone. Goose bumps rose on her arms as the wind cut through, the air so heavy with moisture it felt like breathing underwater. Somehow the rain had held off, though she worried their luck would not keep for long considering the ominous roll of thunder overhead.

I can do this. I must do this. For Mother, for myself. To finally meet my father. Robin Hood.

What would he think of her? What would she think of him? If this ludicrous plan succeeded, if they freed him from the dungeons, she would at last come face-to-face with the missing half of her history. Her nerves jangled as much from excitement as from fear, the weight of the Wolf's terrible decision a distant threat for the moment.

What if he does not like me? What if he finds me a disappointment? What if Sister Catherine was right all these years, and I was born in Kirklees because there was no one left to love me outside of the priory walls? How could I live up to a legend like the infamous outlaw Robin Hood?

Time stretched out before her, stealing her nerve as the cold stole her resolve. What had possibly convinced her she could do this? March into a heavily guarded castle, trick the dungeon guards, and waltz out with their most prized prisoner? She was a fool. They all were. This plan was bound to fail. And if it failed, she failed her mother.

She could not let that happen. She might not have the cunning of her father, or the steel will of her mother, but she would use what little skill she had to make this plan work. Because she could not accept the alternative. She would not let her mother down. She would be brave, braver than she felt, and she would rescue her father.

The first step on the castle bridge was the hardest to take, a threshold she could not cross back over until the purpose of this night was done. At least the smell across the moat was better than the city itself, the natural flow of the river carrying away the most offensive of the waste dumped into it. Still, she did not envy the others swimming through its muck.

"Halt!" someone called out from atop the gate as she approached. "You there, stop!"

"Hail and a blessed Lammas Day to you!" she called out, slurring her words as Little had told her people do when deep into their cups. She jutted a hip out, giving the soldiers a playful glance even though they were nothing more than shadows along the high wall. "And how do you gentlemen fare this fine evening?"

"Get back where you belong, wench," called one of the soldiers down to her. "It's not even Lammas Day."

"Is it not?" she called, pressing her fingers against her pouting lips. "Have I missed the feast, then?"

"Bloody barmaids," the soldier groused. "Go on back to your tavern, lass, or you can dry out in the dungeons."

Well, that was certainly one way to get to her father, but she would prefer not to take such a drastic route. So instead she let a foolish little giggle bubble up to the surface, waving to the soldiers.

"I'm here to see the sheriff," she said, weaving slightly to one side. "Or was it the mayor? What did he call himself again? Hardcart? Harness?"

"Harcourt?" the soldier called out in a flat, uninterested voice.

Isabelle perked up. "Yes! That was his name. Harcourt. William de Harcourt, he said it was. So handsome, too, such a gentleman. He told me to come to the castle and he would give me a personal tour."

"Bloody Harcourt," muttered another of the soldiers. "Only just took the office and already inviting these wenches up."

"Just let her through," said a third soldier. "What's one drunken lass to us? Let her be his problem, not ours."

"All right," said the first soldier, raising his voice to her. "Get on, wench."

"Blessed Lammas Day to you!" Isabelle cried out, her voice soaring with relief as she hurried across the last few boards of the bridge onto the solid ground of the castle courtyard. She slowed her steps after the shadow of the gate passed overhead, reminding herself to play the drunken barmaid, but a quick glance over her shoulder proved the soldiers had already dismissed her from their concern. They didn't even turn from their posts to watch her go.

The interior courtyard was surprisingly large, filled with buildings much as the city had been. There were stables with teams of grooms brushing down horses and hauling hay; forges with massive kilns and men in heavy leather aprons working the bellows; a bakehouse, a brewery, and a kitchen pumping out an intoxicating stew of smells. Isabelle hurried past it all, past the harried servants and roaming soldiers, keeping her head down to draw as little attention to herself as possible. It would have been easy enough to get lost in the massive castle grounds were it not for the keep on the raised hill acting as her North Star, anchoring her and guiding her in the hectic activity of the courtyard.

Two men stood guard outside the entrance to the castle dungeons, thickset fellows so rounded in the middle that in their armor they reminded her of two fat teakettles. Out of their helmets poured the black steam of twin curly beards, their faces red and weather-beaten in the torchlight. Behind them stood a simple iron gate set into the deep stone of the castle wall, the entrance to the dungeons buried beneath the walls. Isabelle drew the wineskin from her shoulder and pulled the cork from the top.

I should have taken a drink of this for courage before we drugged it, she thought, but there was no time for regret now and she swung into the outer reaches of the torchlight with the wineskin brandished high.

"The knight so brave and gallant didst love his maiden true," she sang, spinning about on a clumsy foot. "And for the love of such a lass he swore 'twould anything he'd do. La da, da da, da da, da da, I can't recall the words! La da, da da, da da, da da, the gallant knight withdrew."

She pulled up short at the sight of the guards, sloshing a bit of the wine down the front of her dress in a deep red stain. She gave a gasp that sounded halfway to a hiccup and pressed her hand to the sopping mess on her chest. The nearest guard's eye followed the wet trail hungrily down.

"What have we here, Edgar?" asked the guard of his friend.

"Seems a lost little birdie, Ned, a lost little birdie indeed," said Edgar.

"Good heavens, sir, do not sneak up on a poor girl in such a way!" she cried, tossing the wineskin around and sloshing more liquid on the cobblestones. She wavered unsteadily on her feet, rounding her shoulders and dropping her head to glance up at the guard through her lashes. "I frighten most easily."

Ned grinned, his teeth stained brown. "Well, then, there's plenty to me would raise the hairs on that pretty little neck of yours, birdie."

Isabelle had no idea what he meant, but Edgar gave a rotund kind of laugh and so she laughed along with him, giving a twirl that sloshed her nervous stomach. She hummed through another few bars of her song, dancing with the wineskin, and stumbled a few steps for good measure. She pictured Little's face that first night in the forest and adopted what she hoped was the same moony, blissful expression.

"And a happy Lammas Day to you, handsome sirs!" she said, lifting her wineskin.

Edgar chuckled. "Lammas Day's long past, pretty poppet."

Isabelle gave him a smoldering glance over one shoulder. "All the more reason to celebrate, then, wot? Have a drink with me, and toast to the great Saint Peter!"

Ned sidled close, reaching for the wineskin with glowing eyes. "And are you the virgin, then, to be sacrificed for our pleasure?"

Isabelle curled one side of her mouth into a tiny smile, pressing her lips hard together to hide their trembling. This had been much easier with Adam. "Such bold words, good sir, and not even a toast drunk on Saint Peter's behalf. You must drink to good health and a prosperous year, or see your crops blighted and your coffers shrivel."

"Well, we wouldn't want anything to shrivel," said Ned as Edgar gave a wicked laugh.

The guard lifted the skin and drank deeply, a trickle of wine tracking down his chin into his beard. He swiped at Isabelle's waist, but she danced just out of reach, an unsteady giggle bubbling up. Edgar grunted and snatched the wineskin from Ned's hands, taking a deep draft himself.

"Don't hog it all, you smell-feast," he said, taking another drink.

Ned watched Isabelle weave in and out of the torchlight, reaching a blind hand for the wineskin. "Don't you hog it all, neither, you pig's ear."

"There is plenty to share," Isabelle declared, dancing back toward them.

"Have a drink with us, lass," Edgar said, holding out the wineskin toward her. "Go on, it is Lammas Day, is it not?"

Isabelle smiled nervously, moving unsteadily on her feet. She knew she should get closer, tip the wineskin higher while they drank, but she couldn't bring herself to suffer their touch. "Methinks I've had a bit too much of the fine grape already this evening. Perhaps I should scurry along back home. It is much too late for a lonely girl like me."

"Stay, birdie," said Ned, snatching at the edges of her dress to draw her in. "We'll celebrate the feast with you, won't we, Ed?"

"I'm sure we could find some way to keep you entertained," Edgar said with a boisterous laugh, his eyes following Isabelle in a way that made her want to plunge into the moat and scrub her skin raw. What if she had mixed the dwale wrong? They should have been out by now, and yet they were still scrabbling at her skirts, their fingers blunt where they grazed her skin. She shivered, grabbing the wineskin and lifting it high.

"To Lammas Day!" she declared, shoving it toward Ned and sloshing a few drops over his beard as her hands shook.

"Lammas Day awaits," Ned said. He grabbed the wine, trapping her hands beneath his as he took a deep draft. His eyes slid closed on a sigh, and as Isabelle jerked her fingers free, he slouched forward slightly, the weight of him knocking her back and pinning her to the ground.

"Don't hog the lass, neither, you lout," Edgar grumbled, leaning forward and adding his weight to the pile.

"Get off me," Isabelle breathed, panic stealing the air from her lungs as all pretense of the drunken barmaid fled under the crush of the two guards. She shoved at their shoulders, their armor cold and heavy and tearing little runs in the fabric of her skirts. Their only response was a chorus of snores that rattled their chest plates and splashed little drops of saliva on her dress.

"Help, please," she said in a small, tight voice. She couldn't have the castle guards finding her like this, but if she did not escape the weight of these men soon, she would scream. She needed to give the signal, but she barely had enough air in her lungs for breathing. She would not let things end this way, though, smothered to death under a pile of snoring body hair. So she shoved an elbow into Ned's side and sucked in as much air as she could manage, blasting out the two-note whistle Little John had taught her back in the camp. It came out weaker and more off-key than when she practiced, but she could only hope it was enough.

"We've got you, lass," said a voice so close she gave a yelp of surprise.

Little John appeared beside her, his hose and tunic dragging with the extra weight of river water still trapped within its weaving. He dug his fingers under the armor of both guards, hauling them off her and dragging them into the shadow of a nearby building out of sight. Isabelle scrambled up, heaving in a deep, relieved breath as she beat her hands against her skirt, knocking away the invisible weight of the men. Helena appeared from the shadows beside Little John, surveying the heap of beards and armor as she stepped around them.

"Ugly brutes, aren't they," she said conversationally. "Must have been a chore getting them to sleep."

"You cannot fathom," Isabelle muttered.

"Quick now, lads," said John to Adam and Little, appearing behind Helena with Patrick. "Get the keys."

Adam shuffled through Edgar's pockets, his lip curling in disgust as the man's mouth fell open on a snore. "You all right, Isabelle?"

She nodded, the buzz of adrenaline loosening her joints and keeping her hands constantly moving. Now that the danger of the guards had passed, her body did not know what to do with the energy flowing through it. She had done it—she played her part and disarmed the guards all alone, and now she was moments away from meeting her father.

Dressed as a barmaid.

"I am going in with you," she said to Adam, peering over his shoulder as he sorted through the ring of keys looking for the correct fit to the dungeon gate.

"No, you're not." Adam grunted with impatience as another key refused to turn the lock. "You would be far too great of a distraction down there. Most of those men haven't seen a woman in years, much less a woman looks like you."

Isabelle did not realize until then that it was possible to be flattered and offended in the same breath. "You know I must go with you," she said. "After all we have been through."

"You're too much of a risk. Wait here for us to come back up with Robin. Then we get the hell out of here before anyone else knows what's happening. You go down there, you're liable to cause trouble. And we've got enough of that already."

Isabelle set her jaw but did not reply. She knew Adam spoke reason, but her fingers drummed against her thigh restlessly as he finally unlocked the gate and led John and Little down into the dungeon depths. Helena and Patrick waited beside her, in and out of the shadows along the adjoining walls, their eyes trained on the top of the north end of the wall for the next rotation of the guards. Isabelle could not keep still, pacing to and fro before the gate as if she could will the others to appear. Her fingers knotted together and apart, her knuckles popping loudly in the stillness punctuated only by Edgar's snoring.

"Would you stop that?" Helena snapped at her after the tenth time she nearly stepped on the girl's toes. "You look suspicious enough as it is, no need to draw more attention."

"Apologies," Isabelle said, rooting her feet to the ground. She couldn't control her hands, though, and they wove intricate patterns around each other as the minutes stretched out.

What would she say to him? *Do you remember me, Father, your long-abandoned daughter? Of course you do not.* Her stomach burbled and twisted, and without realizing it she began pacing in a small path again. *Hello, Father. Would you care to accompany me to Kirklees so I can sell your life to the Wolf to save Mother?*

"How long exactly does it take to free someone?" she asked after what felt like hours had passed. Ned and Edgar continued their blissful snoring, but she had no idea how long the effects of the concoction would last. And she did not want to be there when they woke up. The air was heavy with the scent of the impending rain, and somewhere close by a fresh warning rumbled low through the clouds.

"Depends on what they find down there," said Helena. "With Robin, anything's likely."

"Should we check on them?" Isabelle asked. "Perhaps they need our help."

"Have faith," said Patrick.

Isabelle paced back and forth, her gaze flicking between the sleeping guards, the gate, and the top of the wall. Time leached away, the chill of the night crawling over her skin and settling on her bones with an insistent grip. Ned gave a snort and rolled over, exposing the handle of a knife stuck in his belt. Isabelle grabbed the weapon, the weight surprising her. The hilt was wrapped in leather, and the blade was long enough to span the length of her forearm.

"I am going down there," she said, tightening her grip on the knife. "Something is wrong. I can feel it."

"You're not going anywhere," Helena said as she drew her sword. "Stay here and I'll check on them."

"Both of you stay put," said Patrick. "I'll check on them."

Before any of them could make a move, the dungeon gate swung open. They all spun, weapons at the ready, as John emerged with Little and Adam.

"Where's Robin?" Helena demanded.

"Small problem, that," said Little. "Apparently he's not here, either."

"Not here?" Isabelle asked in desperation. "Where the bloody hell is he?"

Adam lifted one brow. "The priory is well and truly behind you, isn't it?"

She pointed the knife at him in warning. "Where is he?"

Little John scratched at his woolly beard. "It took a bit of persuading, but we learned from one of the prisoners below that he's the private guest of the sheriff now."

"Where?" Isabelle asked.

John nodded to the keep, towering over them on the raised hill.

"Oh bloody bother," Helena said, throwing her hands up. "He might as well be taking tea with the queen in France."

"What do we do now?" Isabelle asked. "If the sheriff has him, that is bad, yes?"

"It's not good," John agreed.

Helena set her hands on her hips. "So the sheriff's got Robin, we've got no way in, and we just wasted half the night on a fruitless rescue attempt. Any more good news?"

"I've got an idea," Adam said slowly. "It's ill-advised and more than a little foolhardy, but it just might work. Little, do you still have the dungeon keys?"

Little held up the ring with a jangle. "What's this plan of yours?" he asked.

Adam grinned. "We're going to need a distraction."

CHAPTER
SEVENTEEN

Isabelle crouched under the eaves of the castle chapel as a crack of lightning lit the sky, a rolling boom of thunder signaling the imminent rainstorm. The chapel stood on the north end of the castle grounds, the wall of the building so close to the castle wall she could barely squeeze into the shadows.

The castle motte loomed over her like a specter, the massive hill of raised earth and rock meant to protect the castle's most important inhabitants from invading armies. A narrow bridge patrolled by soldiers crossed the small river serving as a moat and turned into stairs that climbed up the side of the hill toward the keep at the top, a mishmash construction of partial stone foundation and thick timber walls with narrow window slits where the castle kept its weapons, gold stores, and—most recently—infamous outlaws. More soldiers patrolled the top of the keep, the curve of their longbows invisible in the dark at least fifty feet up. But Isabelle knew they were there.

"It is impossible," Isabelle whispered, shaking her head.

"Not impossible," Adam said, leaning against the wall beside her. "Improbable, maybe. Impractical, definitely. But not quite impossible."

She pointed to the narrow flight of stairs leading up the hill. "Even if we were to clear the wall at the bottom, which is teeming with soldiers, by the way, we would still have to scale the hill with no cover, break into the keep, where there are likely more guards, find Robin, and do it all again to escape. And we will be surrounded on all sides by the rivers."

Adam's mouth curled into a smile as he leaned in close. "When you put it like that, it does sound closer to impossible. You'll just have to have faith, sister."

Isabelle sighed. "We are all going to perish this evening. Those soldiers will pick us off before we make the bridge."

"No, they won't," said Adam. "That's what the distraction is for."

"Where is this distraction, anyhow?" she asked, craning her neck just far enough out to watch the men atop the wall. "How shall we know when Little has done it?"

"Oh, we'll know well enough," Adam said, tracing her line of sight. "Though he is taking his blasted time."

"What if this does not work?" Isabelle asked, her voice so much smaller than she wished. "What if we cannot free him? What will they do to us?"

Adam was just a smudge of green against the white wall of the chapel, but his eyes shone as he reached out a hand, his fingers rough with calluses but his touch gentle as he slid them along her cheek, cupping the side of her face. The air buzzed with an unspent crackle of electricity, building in the clouds and tingling across Isabelle's skin.

"These men don't deserve your fear, Isabelle," he said, brushing his thumb across her cheekbone. "You're stronger than the whole bleeding lot of them. Don't you forget that."

Isabelle drew in a deep breath, but before she could respond, a shout went up on the wall to the east, near the dungeons. They both spun toward the sound as the area above them exploded into action, the men clanking away from the chapel toward the source of the disturbance. Their plodding movements turned into a frenzy of activity, snatches of barked orders filtering down to their hiding place. All along the wall, there was howling and weapons waving, men running to and fro as more cries went up. She glanced back at Adam, who stood with his sword drawn behind her.

"He released *all* of the prisoners?" she said.

Adam rolled his eyes. "Little was never one to do things by halves. It should keep their lot busy for the next few hours trying to round up the worst of them. You see the others?"

Little John was easy enough to pick out even in the growing chaos, the big man at least a head taller than everyone around him in the courtyard as he pushed through the servants rushing out of the bakery and brewery screaming and seeking shelter. Helena and Patrick flitted among their ranks, the Irish boy and the black-haired girl already headed for the narrow bridge up to the keep.

"Godspeed them," Isabelle whispered, watching their progress with her breath caught in her throat.

They sprinted across the bridge, the way temporarily clear of guards. For a moment they were lost to Isabelle's sight as the castle wall blocked her view of the bottom of the motte. She curled her fingers into a fist and pressed her fingernails into her palm, every muscle tensed as she waited for them to reappear on the stairs. Lightning flashed, throwing the hill into relief and momentarily blinding her.

"Where are they?" she asked Adam when she could stand it no longer.

"Patience, sister," Adam murmured, though his brows were drawn down.

Another crack of lightning forked through the sky, illuminating the stairs in white brilliance. Isabelle was startled to find the two figures already halfway up and rising fast. Her relief gave way to horror as a call went out from the keep, the watch fires blazing to life. The lightning had betrayed their position and made Patrick and Helena vulnerable to the keep defense. The first arrow struck the stairs behind Helena, another one following closely and landing just before Patrick's next step.

"Damn," Adam swore, breaking from the cover of the building and sprinting toward the gate leading to the keep. "John! They've spotted them!"

Little John barreled through the remaining crowd as Adam raised his sword, both shouting to call the attention of the guards away from Patrick and Helena. The arrows halted for a moment, the guards temporarily confused by which of the approaching attacks posed more danger. But Isabelle knew their time was short. She could hardly help by running after Adam, but if she did not do something they would all end up dead.

She gazed about, desperate for anything to aid their cause, when her eyes fell on the watch fires on the wall overhead. The guards had not returned to their posts, and the shouting from the direction of the dungeons indicated it would be some time before they did. This section of the wall, at least, was clear.

She ran around the chapel until she found a stack of empty crates piled against the chapel wall. Scrambling over the moldy wood, mindless of the tearing at her skirts and the scratches across her arms and legs, she scaled the small pile until she caught hold of the edge of the chapel's roof. She hauled herself up, running toward the castle wall. The gap was only a foot or two, a daring jump with her skirts hampering her, but she had no time to second-guess herself now. She grasped her skirts in one hand and jumped, sailing through the open air.

She hit the top of the wall with a tumble, knocking her head against the stones. A buzzing started in her ears, but Adam's shouts below brought her around. She stumbled to her feet, listing dangerously close to the crackling fire. Adam and John had made it across the bridge, their progress stopped short by another hail of arrows.

"Adam!" Isabelle shouted, the word snatched away on the rising wind and smothered by the thick air. She ran along the wall until she was just below the keep, the arrows thudding inches deep into the rocky side of the motte. She kept running until she found what she was looking for, a discarded bow and a scattering of arrows stuck into a wooden stand beside it.

"Come on," she muttered to herself, crouching beside the bow and ripping at the hem of her skirts. She chanced a look over the wall. An outpouring of guards filled the mouth of the keep, spilling out toward the top of the stairs, where her friends waited. Time was running out.

She growled and set her teeth along the thickest edge of the hem, wincing at the mud that filled her mouth. The fabric tore away in a long strip, leaving a ragged gap along the bottom of the dress. *They will never have use of this dress again,* she thought with a momentary satisfaction. She tore another strip for good measure and wrapped the strips around the arrowheads, knotting each piece tight into a bundle. She ran to the closest watch fire, nocking the arrow to the bow and dipping the bundle into the flames.

"Please work," she begged as the fabric sputtered and hissed, clods of dirt dropping into the fire as the threads danced in the heat. The small tongue of fire gutted out, and for a moment Isabelle feared her plan was ruined. But the fabric caught in little orange ridges, the flame licking hungrily into the depths of the wadded bundle.

She raised the bow and drew back the string as far as it would reach, aiming the arrow high above her head toward the keep. She could not see Helena or Patrick, no longer heard Adam or Little John as she waited for the shot to come clear. She thought back to the last time she had shot like this, blindfolded and desperate in Sherwood. She was guided by a primal instinct now, just as she had been then. The flame hissed and crackled as she released the arrow, speeding it along with a blind prayer.

At first it looked as if the flame had died out, or that the arrow had fallen short of its target, and her heart sank. Soldiers swarmed the stairs leading down the side of the hill, and no doubt they would soon reach the wall where she stood. She had only a handful of arrows left; it wouldn't be enough to make her escape. Not that she would have anywhere to run.

But then a long tongue of orange fire crawled up the side of the keep, just at the base where the new timber construction met the stone foundation. The fire raced up the length of the first floor, branching out and covering a patch of the lower keep in flames in a shockingly short time. Isabelle took up the other arrow, dipping it into the watch fire. This arrow she loosed with only a brief sighting, the flame slicing through the dark night and thudding into the other side of the tower near the top. The fire caught immediately.

The shouted commands broke into a confusion of voices as the first of the soldiers spotted the flames crawling their way up the wall with the vicious intent of an invading army. The hail of arrows stopped as the men turned their attention to beating back the fire. Flaming bits of timber rained onto the dewy grass like the wrath of God, distracting the soldiers crowding the stairs.

"Isabelle!" Adam shouted from below, grinning up at her. "You beautiful fool! Hurry up, before the whole thing burns down!"

Isabelle spotted a stairwell several feet away and raced toward it, her stomach turning over with excitement. She flew down the stairs, unmindful of the wind beating against her tattered skirts. All along the motte was chaos, the fire eating away at the exterior of the keep with a ferocious determination. Soldiers atop the keep rained down buckets of water, kept there for just such an emergency, and though it sliced through some parts of the fire, the wind helped pick up the flames and carry them across the blackened patches. Patrick and Helena were nowhere to be seen, but Adam and John had survived the onslaught of arrows, and even Little had somehow found his way to the fight. All three were now taking the steps at a run on the heels of the fleeing soldiers.

"You might have waited to burn the place down until we were leaving," John said, his breathing steady even at the steep upward pitch of the motte. He shouldered several guards out of the way as they barreled forward, the men tumbling down the steep hill.

Isabelle sucked in a breath as she tried to match his pace, too winded to answer. The heat of the fire blasted her chill skin as they reached the top of the stairs. She pressed a hand to her mouth.

"I did not mean . . ." she said, trailing off as the fire nearly scorched her face.

"You're not the first or last to burn this place down," Adam shouted, sweeping an arm around her shoulders and swinging her out of the way of a soldier running past. "Let's find Robin and get the hell out."

CHAPTER

EIGHTEEN

⊱━━━━━━━━━⊰

The air inside the keep hung heavy with smoke and the confusion of screaming servants. Isabelle choked back a cough and ducked low, keeping her gaze narrowed on Adam's back as he pressed through the archways leading into the heart of the keep. They reached a tight spiral staircase that was thankfully built out in stone, the smoky air speeding them along.

"What about Patrick and Helena?" she asked.

"They'll be fine," Adam said.

"Probably," added Little.

"Probably?" she cried. But then they were racing up the steps and she had no more breath to ask. With horror it occurred to her that she might have set fire to the room where they were keeping Robin, and he might have had no way to escape.

She tumbled into Adam as they reached a sudden landing. Axes lined the wall in front of them, no doubt for the castle's defense, but here they were useless against the fire. The stairs continued up, most likely to the top of the keep, where the soldiers still battled the fire. An archway led off to the left, the air here clearer of smoke for the moment, but the floors and walls were built entirely of timber. They wouldn't be safe for long.

"Any idea where the sheriff is holding Robin?" Adam asked John. "Hell if I know," the big man said.

"This way!" came a voice down the hall, Patrick and Helena appearing a moment later, weapons still drawn.

"I am so glad to see you alive," Isabelle said as they met in the middle of the hallway. "Both of you."

"Save the celebration until we're alive and out of here," Helena said. "The sheriff's quarters are this way."

"Should we not be worried about the fire?" Isabelle asked as they passed what looked like living quarters, an ornate four-poster bed taking up the center of the room. She wondered if King John slept in that bed when he visited.

"It's mostly burning the outer wall of the keep for now," said Patrick, trotting along in front. "But we won't have long until it finds its way in here. Where did the fire come from, anyhow?"

"The sister here, in a moment of brilliance," said Adam.

"And to think I almost missed it freeing the prisoners," Little added with a grin.

"What a shame that would have been," Helena said dryly.

"Here," Patrick said, stopping before a door. "Sheriff's quarters."

John nodded grimly and wielded his sword, the rest following suit. Isabelle had left the bow behind on the wall, a thoughtless action for which she chided herself now. She hung back behind Adam, balling her hands into fists and readying herself for whatever she was to face. John leaned forward, pressing one ear to the slim crack between the doors before he nodded again. He threw his shoulder against it, the wood cracking and giving way.

They stormed in, weapons brandished high and war cries rising from their throats. The room, however, was empty save for a long table at which a compact man sat, his rich clothes glittering in the soft light of a nearby fire. A plate of partially-eaten chicken sat before him, a succulent thigh lifted halfway to his mouth as he surveyed them with a raised eyebrow.

Isabelle had never seen anyone so strikingly dressed, a turban wrapped around his head and his fingers decorated in glittering rings of gold and jewels. His clothes were soft white, pearly and studded with gleaming bits of decorative metal. His blue eyes were crystalline as frosty water and twinkling with mirth. Little John stopped midroar, sword hovering in the air as he surveyed the strange scene. He dropped the weapon a fraction, staring hard at the man. The man, for his part, raised the thigh in salute with a brilliant smile.

"John, my good man, what a surprise," he said in a crisp accent with only the hint of a Scottish burr. It was not what she expected out of this strange man's mouth.

John's sword lowered a few inches more. "Robin?" he said dubiously. "What are you . . . They said in the dungeons the sheriff had you."

Robin, if Isabelle was to believe Little John's incredulous introduction, waved his hand around the room. "And so he does."

"We thought he'd learned your true identity."

Robin snorted. "Hardly likely, the man is thick as a bramble bush. A gracious host, though, and his cook is to be highly commended. This chicken is excellent."

Little John stared long at the man, his face betraying no emotion. "So the sheriff didn't bring you to the keep because he learned you were Robin Hood."

Robin shrugged one shoulder. "I should think I would have received a far less welcoming greeting were that the case. No, I thought it would rather be in my best interest if he had someone more compelling with whom to spend his time."

Little John sighed, dropping the tip of his sword to the ground. "He thinks you're the bloody horse sheikh."

Robin gave a bow from where he sat, drawing a swath of the white cloth over the lower half of his face so only his eyes were showing. "Prince Alik of Arabia, at your service. I was just negotiating a herd of our finest stallions for my release when he was called away on urgent business. Seems someone has let his prisoners loose and set his keep on fire."

John shook his head. "I thought he had you on the rack."

"Well, he certainly had me over a barrel with his equestrian demands. The man wanted forty stallions. As if I were made of horse meat."

"Robin," John said, sounding pained. "We're in a bit of a hurry. We need to go."

Robin held up a hand. "Just a moment. This chicken is cooked superbly. It would be an insult to the cook not to clean the meat off the bone."

Little John sighed. "The bloody keep is on fire. Can you not take the leg with you?"

"John, I never eat and run," Robin said, sounding insulted. "It's bad for the digestion." He leaned forward, looking past the bulk of the big man to the others. "What in heaven's name are you lot doing in York?"

"Not rescuing you, apparently," Helena said, sheathing her sword. She jerked one thumb over her shoulder. "The sister here has urgent need of you. Apparently that's worth us nearly getting our gizzards shot out by the castle guards."

"Since when have we gained a sister in our ranks . . ." Robin began, but he trailed off as his gaze landed on Isabelle. A lump lodged painfully in her throat, and every hair on her body stood at attention as her skin prickled to life. He rose slowly, all pretense of flippancy gone.

"Isabelle, what in God's name are you doing here?" he asked.

Isabelle froze. *He knows me. How does he know me?* The others turned to her, as shocked as Robin. Isabelle cleared her throat and clasped her hands in front of her to stop them from shaking. How many days had she practiced this? How many times had she imagined this very meeting? Perhaps not under such unusual or dire circumstances, but with the same urgency and emotion. Now that she was here, though, now that *he* was here, nothing she had imagined felt right. What could she possibly say to this man? Where should she even begin?

Robin, it seemed, felt no similar sense of conflict, because he swept across the room, pulling the covering off his face and taking her by the shoulders. "What has happened, love? Where is your mother?"

Isabelle took in a shuddering breath, her reasons for being there coming into focus. "The Wolf has her."

He held himself perfectly still, no expression playing out across his features to give her any indication of what he was thinking at the moment. Not that she could have read this strange man even if she tried. Only his eyes moved, flickering over her face as if she were a manuscript to be deciphered.

"Where?" Robin asked, the word so brittle it cracked like glass against her ears.

Isabelle hesitated. She could tell him everything, right now. He was, after all, Robin Hood. If anyone could stage a daring rescue, it was him. But the Wolf's cold promise still sat like a stone in the pit of her stomach, dragging her down to his murky depths with its weight. "In Kirklees. That is why I have come. To ask your help in . . . freeing her."

"Right," Robin said, clapping his hands together with purpose. "Point me in the direction of the nearest exit that is not currently on fire."

"Hang on," Helena said, holding up a hand. "How is it you know the sister? And you, sister, why have you been playing at not knowing Robin this whole time, asking us questions about him and the like? What's going on?"

"We can get to all that back at the camp, lass," said Little John. "The keep's not any less on fire the more we bicker here."

"No, that's twice now we've put our lives in harm's way for her, and she's done nothing but lie this whole time." Helena pinned Isabelle down with a cutting glare. "We deserve the truth. Why are you really here? What's really going on?"

Isabelle's gaze darted from Robin to Adam, but if she meant to find some measure of comfort or support, it was not there. Adam stood with his arms crossed, his legs braced wide and his gaze narrowing on her in a way that threatened to pierce her through. Even Patrick looked doubtful where he stood just behind Adam, his brows drawn down in a frown.

"Helena has a point, sister," Adam said with quiet intensity. "What's going on?"

Smoke crept into the room, stinging her eyes and drawing tears. "Please understand I never meant to . . . to lie, or keep the truth from you. Thomas said you would be in greater danger if you knew the truth. And I had only just learned it myself, I was not even sure it *was* the truth. I wanted to tell you, so many times. But I could not risk your lives."

"Couldn't risk our lives?" Helena snorted. "What in bloody hell do you think we've been doing this whole time? Having a bit of a lark?"

"What is it you're not telling us?" Adam asked.

Isabelle glanced at Robin, who watched her with a searching curiosity. No doubt finding her lacking. She pressed her eyes closed on a sigh.

"Robin is my father."

Patrick drew back sharply as Helena hissed a curse. Adam's gaze on her burned like a tongue of flame, but she couldn't bring herself to meet his eyes. Little leaned toward Adam, his face a mask of confusion.

"I think I've just had a fit," he said. "Did she say 'father'?"

An ominous crack rocked the floor beneath them, more smoke pouring in between the wooden beams. John rapped his fighting staff against the floor, checking the integrity of the timber. He gave Robin a look.

"Won't hold much longer," he said.

"Then neither shall we," Robin said, his tone surprisingly jovial despite the tension in the room. "Come along, my Merry Men, before we are all as perfectly roasted as this fine fowl."

CHAPTER

NINETEEN

———————▶

Robin's white robes swirled as he strode toward the door, leading the others out of the sheriff's chambers and into the hall beyond. Something about his movements reminded her of Patrick and Adam, each step quiet and efficient. Of course, he had probably been the one to teach them. What could she have learned, had she grown up knowing him? The others started back toward the wall of axes and the spiral staircase, but Robin waved them off, continuing down the corridor in the opposite direction.

"I know a better way out."

They followed him as tendrils of smoke chased them down the hall, the smoldering scent of burning wood everywhere. Robin moved with unerring speed, turning unexpected corners and finding tucked-away staircases that led down through the keep. Isabelle had only a brief chance to wonder how he was so acquainted with the castle keep, when he stopped before another set of doors. If she had to guess, Isabelle would say they were on the ground floor, in the very heart of the building. A thick lock secured the handles together, and the others drew in a collective breath.

"This doesn't look like a way out," Little John said.

"We shall find the exit soon enough," Robin said with twinkling eyes. They were magnetic, those eyes, drawing her in with the promise of great mischief and adventure. "Only a slight but very necessary detour that will lift all your spirits."

"Is this . . ." Little trailed off, touching the door with reverence. "How did you find it?"

Robin gave a shrug. "As I always do. A bit of snooping, a bit of lurking, a good deal of bribing. John, if you would please?"

Little John gave a grim smile as he lifted his sword, bringing the hilt crashing down on the metal lock. The shackle cracked in two, falling away from the door handles. Patrick and Helena pulled at each handle, the doors creaking as they revealed the room's glittering interior. Adam sucked in another breath.

"Bloody hell," he breathed out. "You found it."

"Found what?" Isabelle asked, bewildered.

"The Yorkshire gold stacks," said Robin. "The entire wealth of the sheriff of York resides in this room. Quick now, Merry Men, before the whole place burns down."

The others flowed into the room, sweeping stacks of coins into their pockets. Little rattled like a set of cathedral bells from his various hidden pockets, and even Helena's normally harsh expression softened and twinkled against the light of thousands of gold coins. Isabelle's fingers twitched once, curious to feel the smooth weight of so many gold pieces, but the vow of poverty the novitiates took was instilled deeply in her, even if she had never taken the vow herself. She balled her hands into fists to stop their wandering.

The others suffered no such moral qualms, taking gold by the handful. Isabelle watched it all with a growing sense of dread, as the world burned around her. A week ago her greatest sin was nodding off during midnight prayers; now she had set a castle keep on fire and helped a gang of outlaws rob the gold stores of the sheriff of York. After freeing all the prisoners from the dungeon. Did she even understand what was right anymore? Perhaps the Wolf was right, and Robin needed to be stopped. After all, this man was a stranger. A very strange stranger.

Who spoke to her as if he knew her.

"Isabelle, love, would you be a lamb and fetch me that sack over there?" he asked, sweeping an armful of coins into the loose folds of his robes.

She crossed the room perfunctorily, sure that the smoke had done more damage to her mental faculties than she realized, and retrieved the bag for him. He dumped the coins into the sack with a great clatter, giving her a wink.

"That should do the trick quite nicely." He raised his voice. "Let us make haste, Merry Men, before we are smelted along with the rest of this gold."

The others refused to meet her eyes as they filed out after Robin, all of them clinking with each passing step. Only Adam glanced at her, but as her eyes met his, she wished he hadn't. It gutted her worse than their avoidance. Little John dropped a heavy hand on her shoulder in what she thought was meant to be sympathy, shaking his shaggy head.

"Come on, then, lass," he said, guiding her out of the room.

They passed through more abandoned chambers and corridors, the smoke getting thicker the closer to the outside they came. Isabelle feared they would never find their way out and would indeed go down with the keep, but then they turned a corner and were standing before the main doors. The smoke was so heavy here she could hardly breathe, and they all crouched low to make their escape.

Outside was chaos, the entire front of the keep burning and throwing down chunks of hot charcoal. Robin led them through it all like a ghost in his white robes, skirting around the outside of the keep toward the unguarded backside. It was difficult for Isabelle to keep her footing along the steep grassy motte, and more than once her heart jolted as her foot slipped, threatening to tumble her a hundred feet down into the river. But she managed to follow the others until they were on the backside of the keep, the water glittering below. Robin tilted his head up, frowning at the plumes obscuring the night sky.

"You could have shown a bit of discretion, John," he said.

Isabelle bit her lip, studiously avoiding the gaze of the others as Robin crouched on the grass, studying the river spread out below them. He moved to the right a few steps and then doubled back, muttering to himself as he walked, tilting his head and tapping at his chin.

"What is he doing?" Isabelle whispered.

"I hope he's not doing what I think he's doing," Adam said pointedly to Little John, glancing back at the smoking keep. "I think I'd rather brave the fire and gate guards."

Isabelle sank into herself at the cut, feeling invisible as Robin snapped his fingers and raised his index finger triumphantly.

"Here is best," he announced, rejoining their small group. "We will need a bit of a running start, no doubt, but the motte is steepest here."

Adam groaned. "I'll try my luck with the sheriff's men."

"Nonsense," Robin proclaimed. "You will almost assuredly clear the rocks below."

"Almost is not the same as definitely," said Helena, peering over the steep edge into the water below. "How do you know it's even deep enough to jump here?"

"Because I've jumped it before," Robin said. "If you're feeling squeamish, John can give you a little push."

"Do you mean for us to jump off this cliff?" Isabelle asked.

"It does seem a bit ludicrous, Robin," said John. "That's at least fifty feet down, maybe more. And if we hit those rocks, we'll drown."

Robin shrugged. "Then the answer is simple, my good man. Do not hit the rocks."

"I don't like the sound of that," John said, but Robin had already taken off at a run, sailing over the edge and disappearing into the darkness below. Isabelle rushed forward as Robin hit the surface with a plunking sound, the waters billowing out in waves. She held her breath waiting for him to reappear, and he eventually bobbed up to the surface, a white speck against the black surface, waving his arms over his head.

"Well, damned if it didn't work," John mused.

"I'll go next," Little said with an eager look in his eyes, letting out a whoop as he sailed over the edge.

"Idiot," Helena muttered.

John made the jump next, his bulky form hurtling toward the water like a bolt. The water erupted with his entrance, a small wave dousing Robin and Little before the big man rose to the surface. Patrick jumped next, his dive into the water barely causing a ripple. Helena followed after, splashing about below as she made her way to the surface with more than a little irritation. Adam looked to Isabelle.

"I don't often find myself saying this, sister, but Helena is right," he said, his voice heavy with disappointment. "We gave you our trust, our colors, and our lives. And all you gave us was a lie."

Isabelle drew a breath to respond, even though she had no adequate response to give him, but he ran for the edge in three long strides, sailing over the cliff. She shivered in the sudden quiet, her heart hammering against her ribs and her breath coming fast as she contemplated the bobbing figures in the river far below.

I could leave now, she thought. *Spare them any further danger. They would no doubt be relieved to be rid of me. Adam just said as much. Or I could turn myself over to the sheriff of York now, throw myself on his mercy to help free Mother.*

But a voice grew within her, terrified and exhilarated, that wanted to follow them over the cliffs and into whatever dangers they faced next, because she'd never felt more alive than when she was on the edge with them. If she walked away now, she would never know her past. And her mother would have no future.

No, there was only one way out, and it was over those cliffs.

With one last heaving breath, she pushed off the wall of the keep, running as fast as she could over the cliff's edge. The water hit Isabelle with an impact so forceful that for a moment the world went black, her lungs deflating as the frigid depths turned her muscles to stone. She hung there, suspended in a world without air or sound, the weight of her skirts dragging her down. The chill of the night was nothing compared to the unrelenting freeze of the river.

A strong pair of hands hooked underneath her arms and hauled her up, breaking the surface of the water with a splash. She sucked air gratefully into her lungs, her arms and legs coming to life as she fought to keep above the water. The clattering of her teeth filled her head as the world took shape around her once again, Adam's angry face coming into focus.

"Can you not swim, either, Isabelle?" he asked, giving her a little shake.

"There are not many opportunities for leisurely swimming lessons in priory life," she panted, shivering from the cold. "I thought I did rather well, considering."

He sighed forcefully. "How many times do we have to save your life?"

She met his gaze, his breath warming her frigid cheeks. "You could have let me drown."

Adam gave her a long look, his eyes as fathomless as the waters around them. His hair spiked wildly about his head and droplets clung to his lashes. "I think you've got more water than brains left in your head, sister."

But he did not let her go, hooking an arm around her and keeping her close, the cold water tangling their clothes together. The others paddled around them, Helena's lips a dark blue even in the murky light. Little John was so calm he looked as if he stood on a rock below, and for all Isabelle knew, he did. If any of them could reach the bottom, it was him. Patrick made graceful little strokes in a figure eight between them, happy as a frog. Little and Robin were nowhere in sight.

"Would you stop that?" Helena said to Patrick, her words muffled by her chattering jaw. "You're like a bloody river otter."

"Just trying to keep myself warm," Patrick said placidly, daring a smile in her direction. "Reminds me of the waters in Liuerpul. Father Donnell took a dip every morning. He said the water invigorated the blood."

"I feel as if my blood has frozen solid in my veins," Isabelle said, shivering. Patters of rain struck the surface of the river, biting into her scalp and face as a great peal of thunder tore through the sky above.

"Where's Robin?" Adam asked, floating away from her and taking his warmth with him. She had to stop from physically reaching out for him. "And Little? Don't tell me he cracked his head on a rock."

"I don't know where they are, but if we're meant to swim to shore, someone's going to have to tow me," Helena said. "I stopped feeling both my legs about five minutes ago, and these blasted coins are like mud bricks in my boots."

A shadow detached itself from the little waves lapping against the motte, the shape bulky and rounded in the glimmering light of the fire overhead.

"What the hell is that?" Helena asked, somehow on her guard despite the frigid temperature. Isabelle even caught the flash of a knife under the surface of the water.

Adam's gaze narrowed as the figure drew closer. "Of course he has a boat stowed away here."

Robin and Little pushed the small rowboat forward, swimming with long strokes until they reached the group. Robin patted its glistening hull proudly.

"Always keep one handy," he said. "You would be surprised how much use she can be. I've grown rather fond of the old dinghy, I must confess. She has gotten me out of more than one sticky situation I would rather not explain to the gate guards."

Little John held the side of the boat steady as Robin vaulted in, pulling the others in after until they were all crammed into the small vessel. Isabelle shivered uncontrollably now, her wet clothes and damp skin exposed to the whistling wind blowing the storm in from the west. She missed the warmth of Adam's lean body pressed against her, his back turned to her now as he took a seat at the front. Helena at least looked similarly miserable in her soaked tunic and hose. Robin fished a pair of oars from beneath the plank seats and handed them over to John, who fitted them into the oarlocks and pulled them toward the shore with powerful strokes.

Isabelle surreptitiously watched Robin as the boat sailed on, all of them huddled against one another in the increasing downpour. Even waterlogged in his costume, there was an air of unpredictability about him. She could not tell if it was dangerous or thrilling, or perhaps a potent mix of the two.

"So, Alik of Arabia," Adam said, raising his voice over the rain. "I've not heard tale of him."

Robin sighed and leaned back, propping both hands behind his head as if he were idling on a summer pond and not fleeing a burning castle in a storm. "I came by a man in Lincoln who was selling Saracen swords of a fine variety. I had not seen their like since the Crusades, and a pesky nostalgia induced me to purchase one. The man was rather a crafty salesman, I think, for he also carried with him a set of robes and that fine turban. He spotted me as the collector I am and offered them up at a tantalizing discount. I could hardly turn down the opportunity for such an adventure."

"Was it adventure that got you thrown into the dungeons?" Helena asked.

Robin waved one hand lazily. "A simple misunderstanding that would have been cleared up posthaste were it not for the inconvenient intervention of the sheriff's men."

Having just encountered those men, Isabelle would not have used the word "inconvenient" to describe them. But Robin seemed as much at ease dripping wet in the bow of a tiny ship as he did layered in sumptuous robes feasting on chicken in the sheriff's quarters. She wondered if there were anywhere in England he would not look so self-assured. She could hardly say the same for herself; the wind helped shuttle them to shore but did nothing for the cold that frosted over her hair and skin. Her toes sloshed in her boots, painfully numb and inflexible, and her fingers would not bend without her knuckles cracking.

Robin and Adam hopped out of the boat as it neared shallow waters and dragged it ashore, the gentle lolling of the vessel stopping so suddenly that Isabelle still felt herself swaying to its movements. The guards seemed to have finally put out the worst of the fire at the keep with the help of the rain. Billowing clouds of smoke rose up in the distance, covering their movements as they disembarked. Robin and Little John dragged the boat behind a nearby building, burying it beneath old crates.

"All in all, not a bad outing," Robin said, wringing water from his turban and setting it askew on his head. "Shall we return to camp? I am positively famished after such an invigorating swim."

CHAPTER

TWENTY

Despite the late hour and the freezing rain pouring down their necks, the Merry Men of York threw a feast to honor the return of their wayward master. The men stoked up a blazing bonfire upon their return, the ale flowing and the bread and cheese still warm from whatever hearth they had stolen it. The nets made of leaves were thick and kept the rain from extinguishing their fire, and it was cozy enough that Isabelle could almost forget the sopping mess of fabrics still clinging to her skin.

Any merriment she might have enjoyed seeped out of her bones as the others gathered on the far end of the bonfire, turned in toward each other with no break in their ranks for her. She found her way to a secluded copse of trees and gratefully exchanged the barmaid's dress for her Lincoln greens, but now they felt all wrong. Too tight, and scratchy, as if even the clothes were rejecting her.

Her teeth chattered mercilessly, and she was sure she would not be warm ever again even if she stepped into the heart of a bonfire. She stood there a while longer, shivering and rubbing the wool of her sleeves vigorously against her arms to try and bring some life back to her skin. She could not face the carousing men and their gleeful fire just yet, for she didn't trust herself enough to keep her composure.

I deserve their scorn and more, she thought, crouching into a ball and laying her cheek on her knees. *If they knew what I was planning, they would have left me to burn along with the keep. A liar who would betray her own father.*

Her father. Robin Hood. Robert of Huntingdon. Her mother's husband. For the thousandth time since leaving Kirklees, she wished her mother were there. She wished she could ask how they met, who he was, what it was that had drawn Marien to him in the first place. They seemed like opposite ends of the world—Marien so calm and collected, Robin a carousing force to be reckoned with. But she had never known her mother to make a poor choice, and so there must have been something in Robin that attracted her to him. Something that made her give up whatever life she had before to protect his secrets.

She could just see him through a small break in the trees, moving among his men with masterful ease, slapping them on the back and raising pints in their honor, all with a mischievous gleam in his eye. Those sparkling blue eyes that seemed to capture everything at once and make a farce of it. He had exchanged his white robes for the Lincoln greens, but they made him no less fascinating. He was not a tall man, but he filled the camp with his voice and his presence, goading Little John into a pitifully off-key rendition of "The Milkmaid's Lament" as the other men in the camp covered their ears and pitched their empty mugs at the pair.

She turned her head away, curling more into herself and her misery. She had never been part of something so powerful, a bond that carried the Merry Men through the hardest times and lifted them up in brotherhood. And now she never would be, not after the lies she'd told. And certainly not after she lured Robin to Kirklees.

You could tell him the truth, said the practical voice that always sounded suspiciously like her mother. *He is the outlaw Robin Hood. If anyone could save her, he could.*

She had just played a part in his rescue from the bowels of one of the country's strongest keeps, after all. If they could free Robin from York Castle, perhaps they could free Marien from Kirklees. Her mother could join the Merry Men, and they could live in Sherwood as a family, finally together.

But there was no mistaking the cold certainty in the Wolf's eyes: He would tear this country apart and burn every tree to the ground to find Robin, no matter who got in his way. If he was willing to hang her mother, what would he do to the Merry Men? To the people like Thomas who protected them? What would he do to her friends? Whatever answers Isabelle could fathom, none of them boded well for her or her family.

"Isabelle, love," someone said, giving her shoulder a gentle shake.

Isabelle started awake, her back aching and a crick in her neck. For a confused moment she could not place where she was, or how she had gotten there. A blanket covered her shoulders, tucked in at the edges to protect her from the chill. Except it was not nearly so chilly now, with faint sunlight streaming in through the trees above. She turned her head just as Robin sat back on his heels, smiling at her.

"Care to take a walk with me?" he asked.

Isabelle rose slowly, working out the kinks of a night spent sleeping curled in a ball. Robin looked resplendent, his eyes bright and his face fresh in the late-morning light. The sun burnished his hair to a dark auburn flecked with bits of gold, and in the full light of day, she could easily see the sharp, aristocratic lines of his hooked nose and lean jaw. He carried a longbow with him, and a great curved horn hung from his belt, the end capped in silver and gleaming white. The same horn Little John had blown when she met him.

"Where are we going?" she asked, her thoughts still thick with the cottony web of her dreams.

"To see a few old friends," he said, slapping her on the shoulder. "Come along, the day is far too bonny to waste under the trees."

She followed him out of her sheltered copse, the clang of swordplay reverberating throughout the camp. The Merry Men filled the trees with their fighting, paired in groups of two or three or four, each carrying their weapon of choice and taking turns in the ring while others called their encouragement. She spotted Adam and Little sparring in the thick of the group, Patrick and Helena standing on the sidelines calling out suggestions, mostly for Little. Helena caught her eye and turned her back resolutely, continuing her conversation with Patrick. The Irish boy met her gaze for a moment before turning to Helena to reply. Somehow she preferred Helena's scorn to the deep disappointment etched on Patrick's face.

Robin led her out to the main road, whistling a soft, cheerful tune as they went, his step quick and light despite the muck created by the previous night's rain. Isabelle moved at a considerably heavier pace, her heels squishing into the mud and splattering her hose with flecks of mud.

"You've lost the bow I gave you," he said, breaking the long silence between them.

Isabelle looked up, startled out of her own swirling thoughts. "Pardon?"

He glanced at her empty shoulder. "Your favorite bow. It's gone. And your quiver, too, by the looks of it. Don't tell me you've gambled it away as part of your new outlaw life?"

"No, it was taken—" She turned to him sharply. "How do you know about my bow?"

He arched a brow at her. "I carved it myself, didn't I?"

Isabelle shook her head. "No, a traveling peddler gave it to me."

"Oh, you mean the traveling peddler who always has a special little treat for his special little dolly girl," Robin said, his voice shifting and his shoulders curling over as the muscles in his face tightened and relaxed into a mountain of wrinkles that made him look considerably older. He hardly looked like himself. In fact, he looked rather like—

"*You* are Old Man Peddler?" she asked incredulously, rocking back on her heels. "The batty old fool always clanging his pots about?"

Robin relaxed his face, his expression returning to normal, if a bit indignant. "I never thought of him as batty, really. Just a bit eccentric."

"A bit?" she said. "You were always pinching my cheeks, calling me dolly girl. And asking about Mother. It was quite off-putting. I thought you were a hundred years old."

"With all the vim and vigor of a spry young man," Robin said wistfully.

"With all the vim and vigor of a perverted old man." Isabelle resumed walking, struggling against the rising tide of emotion within her. "All these years, and it took the Wolf for me to truly know you. Why such secrecy? Why did you never tell me the truth?"

Robin's expression grew serious. "If you had met the Wolf, you would not ask."

"I *have* met the Wolf."

Robin's eyes cut to her. "I believe it's time you told me the truth of why you are here."

Isabelle's heart lurched guiltily at that, and so she deflected with a question of her own. "Who is Robert of Huntingdon?"

Robin's forehead crinkled as his eyes widened. "I've not heard that name for many a year now."

"Is it really you?" Isabelle leaned toward him, intent on the answer.

Robin did not reply for several moments, his gaze lost somewhere in the murky middle of the horizon. She began to think he would not answer, when he spoke in a soft, almost regretful voice.

"I suppose at the very least I owe you the truth." He took a deep breath. "Once upon a time, in another life, I was Robert of Huntingdon. Eldest son of the Earl of Huntingdon."

"Earl?" Isabelle gasped. Thomas had said he was a hoity-toity person in the nobility, not a full-fledged *earl*. She shook her head. "Thomas said King John sent the Wolf to kill you before I was born. Why?"

He waved a hand. "It's a rather boring tale of the intricacies of inheritance law and the importance of feudal standing."

"I would rather welcome being bored for a change," Isabelle said pointedly.

Robin sighed. "Couldn't we talk of something else? Perhaps how lovely the day is, or the curiosity of grass growing?"

Isabelle leveled him with a look, and Robin sighed again. "You look just like Marien when you do that. Very well, the boring parts it shall be. Sixteen years ago—could it really be sixteen? It feels like only yesterday."

"Perhaps to you," Isabelle retorted. "It has been a lifetime for me."

Robin tilted his head. "A fair point. An Isabelle-lifetime ago, King Richard the Lionheart sat on the throne, and his sniveling little brother John Lackland wanted it. Richard was always away, fighting some war or another, and John had nothing better to do than fritter away his brother's winnings in gluttony and convince himself he would be a better king. So he formulated a plan to stage a coup and take the throne.

"As you might imagine, there were those who were less than pleased with John's actions. The rebel barons did not rise overnight. Most of these barons have been fighting against John since before he took the throne, your grandfather chief among them."

"You mean your father?"

Robin shook his head. "No, I mean your maternal grandfather. Marien's father. Robert Fitzwalter, leader of the rebel barons."

That knocked the wind out of her sails. "Mother is from the gentry as well?"

"Of course," Robin said with a sideways glance. "Where do you think she learned her disdain for them? Not from her father, mind you. The man is a blustery wind on a chill day. But you do have to admire what he's accomplished with the barons now. You know, he'd be quite proud of you, if he knew of you. Setting the castle keep on fire in York, you've no doubt saved him the trouble of doing it himself."

How could she not know her entire family history? Her father the Earl of Huntingdon, her mother the daughter of Robert Fitzwalter, leader of the rebellion against King John?

"I suppose it was inevitable I would find myself at the end of a royal sword, wasn't it?" she said faintly.

Robin grinned. "It runs in the blood."

"So why did John consider you a threat to his coup?"

Robin grimaced. "That's the boring, complicated part. In a very long, roundabout way, the earldom of Huntingdon had a claim to the throne of Scotland. My father was David of Scotland, a prince and heir to the throne at one point. It's more of a ceremonial right than anything else now, but at the time it meant something to John. The English and the Scottish have never been amicable in the best of times, and the King of Scotland was worried John might not stop at his brother's throne. In a show of solidarity with the barons, my father arranged for me to marry Fitzwalter's daughter. We were young and untried, and everyone thought they could control us."

"I cannot imagine anyone controlling Mother," Isabelle said. "Or you."

"Yes, the whole business went rather poorly from the start," Robin agreed. "Your mother hated me, and I had no intention of marrying. But as such things do in youth, our passion turned from hatred to love, and we agreed to be married. It was a strong alliance between the rebel barons and the Scottish throne, and it must have made old Lackland very nervous indeed."

A shiver ran over her skin. "Because he sent the Wolf to kill you."

Robin nodded. "Wherever John Lackland went, Sir Roger of Doncaster slithered along in his shadow. Mind you, he always loathed me. The man did not even have the muscles in his face required to smile. He just sort of lifted his top lip and bared his teeth. My father used to say he smiled as if he had just smelled something most foul. I was arrogant in my youth, and I never thought he would come for me directly. I let my guard down, and he slipped through."

"What happened?" Isabelle asked breathlessly.

Robin's eyes hardened. "He burned down our home with us inside it. They tried to make it look like an accident, but they did a poor job of it. Kicked over a few pots in the kitchen and lit the tapestries in the hall on fire. As if a flaming goose would have sauntered out of the kitchen and stopped to admire a woodland scene."

Even though she knew how this story ended, her breath still came in quick, shallow bursts. "But you did not die."

"No, I did not. The fire consumed enough of the house that we only had to help it along in the eastern wing to cover our escape.

We used the bodies of two servants who had been caught in the kitchen as decoys. We spent many months in a perpetual state of flight, staying with trusted friends when we could and making our home in the wilds when we could not. But eventually Marien was far enough along with you that I could not have her running about the forest, hiding for her life. I was desperate to find a safe haven, and so I turned to a distant cousin who served as prioress at Kirklees. I tried to convince Rosamund to let me stay disguised as a sister, but she was appalled at the suggestion. Something about violating the sanctity of the vows and disturbing the sisters' communion with God."

Isabelle smiled faintly, imagining Sister Catherine's horrified reaction were she to discover a man living in their midst.

Robin shrugged. "So I escaped to the wilds of Sherwood, where I found men made even more desperate than myself by the toll the monarchy was taking on them. Richard was an incredible soldier but an abysmal king. He left his subjects vulnerable to his brother's greedy attacks. They needed hope and discipline, and I was embarrassingly full of both at such a young age. And so, here I am."

Isabelle's head swam with questions, the most inane of which rose to the surface. "Does this mean I am a princess?"

He gave her a wry smile. "Only in my heart, love. I am afraid I left that life long ago, and took you with me. My younger brother, John, holds the title of earl now. Ah, here we are."

He held his hands out to encompass the meager gathering of cottages before them, many of the thatched roofs falling in and missing support beams along the top. The people drove their sheep and hung their washing as townspeople did all over the country. It was a small hamlet, the citizens grim and weary. Their faces were smeared in various shades of grime, their backs hunched as they shouldered their burdens. After the opulence of the sheriff's gold stores in York, the sight of his people suffering in resigned silence raised the heat in Isabelle's blood.

"What are we doing here?" she asked.

"We are here to repay an old friend," Robin said.

CHAPTER
TWENTY-ONE

Robin moved into the town with his light step, giving a wave to those he saw. Their faces brightened as he passed, many breaking out in wide grins and lifting their hands in salute. Some of the people called to him by name, shouting across the fields to be heard.

"You know these people?" Isabelle asked.

"I have need of many friends in my waning outlaw years," Robin said, clapping a passing farmer on the shoulder. "You never know when you might require a pile of hay to hide under while the soldiers pass."

Isabelle lifted her brow. "Are these people not afraid of incurring the sheriff's wrath?"

Robin shrugged one shoulder. "He barely manages disdain for them. He would not imagine any of them might have an original thought of their own, much less the temerity to defy him. Rather works in my favor most days. Here we are."

He ducked into the opening of a small hovel, the roof collapsing in places where the constant rain had eaten away at the thatching. Isabelle had borne witness to the crumbling exteriors of the poorer abodes in Kirkleestown when she accompanied her mother to tend the sick, their hearths cold because they could not gather the wood, their floors unswept because their brooms kept moldering. But still this home fared worse than those in her memory, seeming to be held together by not much more than the mysterious will of the Almighty. The people of Kirkleestown were starving; what would happen to the people of this nameless village?

She took a moment to adjust to the dim interior as she stepped inside, but Robin's boisterous laugh drew her toward the far end. A rail-thin man stood among a collection of patched burlap sacks filled with grain or some other staple. It was an odd dichotomy, such a starved-looking man among so much food. But his eyes were bright and quick, and he matched Robin's laugh with a surprisingly full-bodied one of his own.

"That, my friend, is why my wife is in charge of the household expenses," the man was saying. "Or so she tells me."

He looked up at Isabelle, his eyes widening. "Who is this lovely young woman?"

Robin lifted his chin and pulled back his shoulders, his eyes shining. "This glorious creature is my daughter, Isabelle. Isabelle, this is Harry."

The man's eyebrows shot up as a warm blush spread across Isabelle's cheeks. "Your daughter? I should say she must have her mother's looks."

Robin gave another laugh. "That she does, my friend."

Isabelle inclined her head, acutely embarrassed to be discussed in such a manner. "Pleased to meet you, sir."

Harry gave her a low bow, which seemed particularly ridiculous considering the ruinous state of his home. "The pleasure is all with me, miss. But what brings you two here in Little John's place?"

Robin waved one hand dismissively. "The wind, my good friend, the wind calls and I am but her slave to answer. Well, that and the promise of a spot of good fortune. Speaking of which, I find myself with a pocket full of coin and an empty belly. Have you a spare sack or two of your fine meal?"

The man frowned, looking about the small space. "All of this is held for the collector. We barely had enough to fill our own table this harvest. I cannot risk being turned out of our home, not with the new wee one."

Robin scratched at his chin, pursing his lips in contemplation. "How much do you owe the tax collector?"

"Ten sacks," Harry said heavily. "Would have been twenty if he had his way."

"What does that tally to? Three pence a sack?"

Harry nodded. "And a surplus tax of a penny on top of it. As if we should be punished for a good harvest."

Robin dug into his pocket, producing a handful of gold coins Isabelle recognized from the sheriff's coffers. "I should think this would cover your troubles, would it not? And a bit extra for the wee one."

Harry's eyes went even wider, accenting the thin lines of his long face. "Robin, I can't . . . 'Tis too generous. The collector will want to know where I got this."

"And you shall tell him a passing nobleman had a craving for flat cakes and insisted you accept his gold for your grains. Though these collectors tend to lose the power of speech in the presence of shiny baubles."

Harry cupped his hands as Robin dropped the coins, folding his long fingers over the gold in wonder. Robin scratched his chin, contemplating the bags of grain.

"I am afraid in my hunger I have been overzealous in my purchases," Robin said. "The Merry Men could hardly eat ten sacks of grain before the wheat rotted away, and I would be loath to see such fine meal go to waste. I do not suppose you know anyone hereabouts who would benefit from such a supply?"

Tears stood out in Harry's eyes as he gave a solemn nod. "I will see the grain put to fine use among the townspeople. And thank you, Robin. From the bottom of our hearts, thank you."

Robin gave a wave. "I should be thanking you for alleviating me of the burden of carrying ten sacks back to the camp." He lifted one of the sacks and tossed it over his shoulder with a grunt. "Now I remember why I send John on these errands. Good day, Harry."

Harry gave a smile and bowed to Isabelle. "Good day to you, my friends."

Isabelle waited to speak until they had cleared the hovel. "Will the sheriff not be suspicious of how he came by the gold?"

Robin gave a small laugh. "The sheriff will have his hands full trying to rebuild the keep before King John's next visit. He'll need that gold too badly to ask where it came from. This way the townspeople at least get a decent meal out of it."

Isabelle shook her head. "When you took that gold, I thought . . . Most men would keep such wealth for themselves."

Robin shrugged. "What use have I for gold? The earth is my floor, the heavens my roof. The Merry Men my company. What more do I need that gold would buy?"

Isabelle followed him through the hamlet as he dispensed the sheriff's gold, many of the townspeople brought to tears at the sight of a single coin that was worth more than they could earn in a lifetime. And everywhere the people blessed Robin, forcing what gifts upon him they had to give, until he was burdened with sacks of grain, stacks of cakes, simple pieces of pottery, and skeins of wool.

"This is not what I imagined of the outlaw lifestyle," Isabelle said, carrying a sack of wooden cups and bowls with her. "I expected far more carousing and highway robbery."

"There's plenty of that, too," Robin said with a wink. "We've one more stop to make."

Isabelle followed him to the edge of the hamlet, where an old man worked out in the open, his hair thick and gray. He leaned over a worktable, his lean arms browned from the sun, stripping the bark off a long piece of wood. He looked up at Robin's clattering approach, shielding his eyes against the sun.

"Well, look what the rains washed in," he called in a scratchy voice.

Robin grinned. "I see they can't wash you out."

"I'll be clinging to this place like a drowned rat until God himself puts me down," the man said. Robin clasped his forearm, shaking it heartily. "Good day, Robin."

"And a most excellent one to you, Matthew. I have need of your craftsmanship today." He nodded toward Isabelle. "My daughter has misplaced her bow."

"Ack," the old man said, squinting at Isabelle. "And are you sure she deserves a replacement? A bow is family. You can't simply go about losing one."

Isabelle reddened. "I did not lose it," she said. "It was taken. Rather forcefully."

The old man grunted, but he turned away and disappeared into his small cottage. When he stepped back out, he held a simple bow, the wood so expertly planed and smoothed it reflected the clouds. She drew in a half breath, reaching out for it reverently.

"This is the most beautiful thing I have ever seen," she whispered, running her hands along the shining grain.

"Better be," Matthew grunted. "Took me near two weeks to craft it. That one was a stubborn wood."

"Matthew is the greatest bowman round these parts," Robin said. "When I'm not here, of course."

"Ye've never accepted a challenge from me, so who's to say," said the old man.

Robin tilted his head in concession, flipping him two gold coins. "For your trouble, and any future troubles that might come your way."

The old man grunted again, the coins disappearing from the table in the blink of an eye. "She'll be needing a quiver as well."

The quiver, if it was possible, was even more beautiful than the bow. The outside was simple and unadorned, but the stitching was tight and neat, the leather perfectly cured to a beautiful golden-brown hue. She shouldered the quiver, stretching the bow to its full extent to test the tension. It was a heavier weight than her last, requiring all her concentration to pull it, but it fit perfectly into the groove of her hand.

"Thank you so much," Isabelle said, not knowing any better words to express her true gratitude to the old man or Robin.

"Shall we test it out?" Robin asked.

Isabelle looked up, and for an absurd moment she thought she might cry. "You want to go shooting with me?"

"Why would I not? You are my daughter. I am the greatest bowman of England. It is my paternal duty to make sure you live up to the name of Hood."

The woods around York were much sparser than Sherwood, the canopy cover giving way to rolling hills as they left the road. The township was but a speck in the distance, though Isabelle imagined she could still see smoldering clouds over the keep. Robin kept a brisk pace down each hill and up the next, the grass thin and marked with rocks. Isabelle's stomach grumbled, reminding her that she had skipped breakfast. She was about to protest walking any farther, when they crested a tall hill, the land stretched out like a rumpled blanket below them.

"Here?" Isabelle asked as Robin finally stopped, leaning over and trying to catch her breath. "But there is nothing to shoot here."

"No, there is nothing easy to shoot here. If I wanted to see you shoot a target at thirty paces, I would not have brought you so fine a bow for your fifth birthday."

Isabelle took a last huffing breath and straightened, turning in a slow circle to survey the land. She could see nothing but hills all around, the city a smudge against the blue horizon, and a few trees dotting the landscape. She shrugged, completing her circle, before something caught her eye and made her turn back.

One of the lone trees dotting the hills in the distance was nondescript except for a tuft of white against the trunk. Isabelle squinted and shielded her eyes, sure she was imagining the angular cuts of feather sticking out. She shook her head.

"Impossible," she said. "That tree must be at least seventy paces away, maybe more."

Robin shrugged one shoulder. "I suppose it is impossible for those who do not possess the skill necessary to make such a shot."

Isabelle gave him a narrow look. "You are goading me."

"I would not dream of such a thing."

She huffed, shading her eyes once more toward the tree. "How do I know you shot from this hill? You could have shot from that one over there closer to the target."

"I could demonstrate now, if you like. Setting aside your intimation that I am a liar and a cheat, of course. Come, now, let us see your stance."

"My stance? Whatever for?"

"Their stance is the bowman's declaration of intention. A poor stance ruins even the best of aim."

Isabelle planted her feet, feeling a bit foolish as she lifted the bow and drew the string back with the first three fingers of her right hand. She settled down into her ribs, rooting herself to the earth and focusing on the tree rather than the tip of the arrow. A fair archer tries to measure the gap between the tip of the arrow and the target to gauge for distance. An excellent archer intuits the distance and focuses solely on the target.

"Not bad," Robin murmured. "Though I am surprised your mother would let you get away with such a slouching posture."

Isabelle sighed, releasing the tension on the string to rest her muscles. "She does not let me get away with it, but I cannot shoot right when I try to hold my carriage up as she does."

Robin waved his hand. "She told me on more than one occasion that I would grow a hump if I continued to slink about like that while shooting."

Isabelle laughed. "She told me my spine would grow crooked if I did not stand straight."

"It is refreshing to know her habits have not changed. Now, then, let us test that slouching mettle of yours."

Isabelle took up her stance again, but now her hands were shaking and her eyes kept cutting back to Robin, standing so close and watching her so intently. Suddenly she was aware of every bad angle, every stray hair tickling at her nose, even the fatigue in her arm from his rescue the previous evening. Every distraction that could make her miss the shot. She chewed on the inside corner of her mouth, the tree in the distance swimming out of focus.

"Shall I tell you how your mother and I came to be engaged?" Robin asked casually.

Isabelle jerked her head around, her arm releasing the tension in the bow with relief. "I would very much like to hear the tale."

Robin gave a faint smile, his gaze drifting toward the scuttling clouds in the sky. "The first time I met your mother, she threw a knife at my ear."

Isabelle blinked. "What?"

He waved his hand. "I deserved it. It only nicked me, though it bled like a wild boar. I still have the scar here." He rubbed a small white line across his right ear fondly. "Your mother was the one who patched me up, though. I think she felt badly after all that."

"Perhaps that is where her gift with healing began," Isabelle said. "Though I cannot imagine Mother harming anyone. Even if they deserved it."

"I was a terribly arrogant young man, as all firstborns tend to be. When her father came to my father to suggest the union, I rejected her. I said I could do better, and I would marry for my own pleasure, not for any political machination."

Isabelle sucked in a breath. "Oh, I do not believe Mother would have liked that."

"Oh, no, she did not," Robin agreed. "She gave me my nickname, you know. Robin. She said I was just like one, puffed up with importance, brain the size of a pea, singing my own praises. I believe I told her she was like a drab little crow, plain and squawking. That is what earned me the knife."

Isabelle winced. "I still cannot imagine it."

"Your mother was a force to behold," Robin said, smiling widely. "She told her father in no uncertain terms that she would never marry me, as I was her inferior in every way. And when her father told her she would do as she was bid . . ." He shook his head. "Fitzwalter is a formidable man, but I have never seen him so cowed as he was by his daughter when she told him what she would do if he tried to force her hand."

"What did she say?" Isabelle asked breathlessly.

"Oh, it's certainly not fit for tender ears such as these," Robin said, tweaking one of her earlobes. "But I must say, I fell in love with her in that moment, watching her stand her ground with your grandfather. I knew I would never meet her like in another woman. I had to marry her. But of course she wouldn't have me, not after I'd made such an ass of myself."

Isabelle leaned forward, the new bow momentarily forgotten. "What did you do?"

Robin gave her a sly smile. "I did what I do best—I charmed my way into her heart by every means possible. I wrote her poems, brought her flowers from the farthest reaches of the forests in Huntingdon, threw feasts in her honor. She refused every single one."

Isabelle pressed a hand to her lips. "She would not."

"She most certainly did," Robin said with a sage nod. "Once, she even returned a packet of poems eviscerated into shreds, and said they would be better served as bedding for the cows. It occurred to me then that traditional courtship rituals would not stand with Marien. I needed to employ a more ingenious means to secure her hand. So I challenged her to a competition."

"What kind?"

"The kind I was sure I could win, of course. A shooting match. She could choose the location and the target. If she bested me, I would abandon my suit immediately. But if I bested her, she would accept my proposal."

Isabelle only knew of Robin's prowess with the bow through his reputation, but she had witnessed her mother's skill firsthand for years. Marien was the most challenging competitor with a bow—methodical, patient, steady, sure with her hand and her eye. She had never outshot her mother, not once.

"I shall tell you, Isabelle love, I've shot in the blinding rain from atop a charging horse, through a canopy of trees at fifty paces, even once across a keep to cut through a hangman's noose. But shooting against your mother . . . that was the most difficult shot of my life."

Robin stared at the targeted tree in the distance. "She did not make it easy on me, either. She chose a target just like this, a stubby little tree nearly a hundred paces away on a blustery day in poor light. And wouldn't you know, your mother hit that target dead-on, straight through the eye of the tree. Didn't even give me an inch of room. If I was going to win her hand, I would truly have to earn it."

He paused, watching the tree in the distance, until Isabelle could not stand the quiet any longer. "And did you? Did you earn it?"

Robin turned to her, spreading his hands wide. "Well, you're here, aren't you?"

"What did you do? How did you best her?"

Robin grinned. "I split her arrow."

"Oh," Isabelle said with a faint trace of disappointment.

"Five times in a row."

"Oh," Isabelle breathed.

"Hardest bloody shot of my life," he said with a chuckle. "Well, shots. But I would make them again in a heartbeat. I thought she would be furious, accuse me of showing off again, but when I landed the last shot, she only gave me a little smile and told me to publish the banns. And then I knew she'd been leading me about by the nose all along, making me think it was my own idea."

"She is terribly good at that," Isabelle agreed.

"So, shall we test out that new bow of yours now?" Robin suggested.

This time as she turned to face the tree, the light sharpened and the trunk came into focus, her arm steady and her aim true. She pulled back as far as she could, the string creaking under the pressure she exerted on it, and when she could pull it no farther, she released, the arrow slicing through the air with a whistle. She held her breath for the second it took the arrow to reach its destination, an inkling of doubt keeping her fingers tight around the handle. But as the arrow found its mark, burying itself deep in the trunk of the tree to join the other tuft of white, the doubt exploded into a frisson of triumphant energy. She turned to Robin with suppressed glee to find he was grinning wide enough for both of them. He doffed his cap and bowed low.

"A brilliant shot!" He swept her up in a fierce embrace before holding her out by the shoulders. "You do me proud, daughter."

In that moment of pure, unaffected joy, Isabelle knew the truth. She knew she would not turn this man over to the Wolf. Not after everything she had seen today, all the good he had done, the generosity he had shown her. She could not betray him.

"I need your help," she said, the words rushing out of her.

"Of course, love, anything," Robin said.

Isabelle took a deep breath. "The Wolf will kill Mother if I do not turn you over to him. I need your help to rescue her."

CHAPTER
TWENTY-TWO

The whole story tumbled out of her in a torrent of words, from the errant shot in Kirklees to the Wolf's terrible ultimatum in Lincoln. Robin listened with a growing tension, a growl escaping him when she detailed her meeting with Sir Roger. He paced the small hill as she spoke, his blue eyes narrowed in concentration.

"I should have done away with that man sixteen years ago," he said, simmering with rage. "If he has harmed a solitary hair on Marien's head . . . This time I will not make the mistake of leaving him alive."

"You cannot kill the king's right hand," Isabelle said.

"There's a great deal I can do, just watch," Robin promised.

Isabelle shook her head. "The king and the rebel barons are poised on the edge of a war. Any action could tip the balance, and they will not be the ones to pay the price of battle. It will be people like your friends back in the hamlet and the townspeople of Kirklees."

He pointed a finger at her. "That kind of talk is your mother's influence."

"And she is right," Isabelle reasoned. "I have been to Lincoln.

It is crawling with soldiers and mercenaries. If you could even get to Sir Roger—"

"I could certainly get to him," Robin scoffed.

"Even if you could," Isabelle continued, "it would be almost impossible to get back out without someone discovering him and capturing you. And then what good have you done? Besides which, his men still have Mother. If something were to happen to him, what would stop them from . . . from harming her anyway?"

Robin nodded, resuming his pacing, head bent in deep thought.

"If your men could pluck you from the armored bosom of the sheriff of York, surely they could steal Mother away from a mere priory? And if it is a matter of sneaking into the priory undetected, I know at least half a dozen ways in. And another half a dozen not even the sisters know about."

Robin arched a brow at her, looking every inch the marauding outlaw. "Isabelle, my darling, your devious mind does me proud. When did Sir Roger say to deliver me to Kirklees?"

"By the end of the week," Isabelle said.

"Right," Robin said with a nod. "Then we will need to make haste to beat him there."

By the time they returned to the camp, the clashing of swords had given way to the clanking of mugs and crackling of cooking fires. Isabelle's stomach let out an unladylike growl at the smell of charring wood and fatty meats dripping into the flames, and Robin gave her a nod.

"I could not have put it better myself," he said.

The men had laid out the feast over several large stone tables, the heaps of food making her salivate. Robin took up a spot beside a large roasted duck, waving her in to sit beside him. She sighted Helena and Patrick at the next table, Adam and Little across from them. It felt odd, sitting beside Robin instead of the others, but at the same time it felt like the most natural place for her. The Merry Men passed her dishes as if she were just another member of the crew.

"I must see to travel arrangements with Little John," Robin told her after he'd cleared his plate three times over. "We'll leave at first light. Perhaps you could take the time to mend some fences?" He glanced meaningfully at the next table.

Isabelle shook her head. "They will never forgive me. Certainly not after they learn that I intended to . . . to betray you."

"Nonsense," Robin scoffed. "If they could not forgive you for such an understandable oversight, they would not be very good friends, would they? I do not choose my Merry Men because they hold grudges, love."

But as he disappeared among the men to find Little John, Isabelle could not even bring herself to look across the table. However confident Robin was that they would forgive her, Isabelle had seen their faces. She had used them, lied to them, betrayed their trust, and endangered their lives. She had been a victim of betrayal at the hands of girls loyal to Sister Catherine enough to know that the hurt often ran deeper than forgiveness could reach. She was not sure she could accept their forgiveness, even if she earned it.

She wished she could talk to Adam, unburden herself and ask for his help as she should have done from the beginning. He was so strong and sure, so much stronger than she had been. He would know what to do, how to protect Robin and save her mother. Her gaze traced over the breadth of his shoulders and down the planes of his back, her heartbeat picking up at the thought of running her hands over those muscles and testing their strength. He was too much of a distraction, always turning her thoughts away from what they should be.

She took her new bow and skirted the feasting tables, retreating to the fields where the men had left their weapons propped against trees or lying on the ground. Robin had given her a full quiver of arrows, but it was the swords and staffs that drew her attention. The others moved with such ease and grace, as if they'd been practicing their entire lives. And Helena had been right about her lack of knowledge in hand-to-hand combat; a bow was fine if you needed to shoot a tree at seventy paces, but it would not protect her from mercenaries like Blade.

She picked up a nearby sword, surprised by how light and manageable it was. She tried to hold it with one hand as Adam had done, but it only took a few practice circles for her forearm to protest the movement. She gripped it with both hands then, holding it before her and darting forward with chopping motions, trying to get a feel for the weapon.

"If you're looking to learn swordplay, your first lesson is that's not how you hold it."

Isabelle whirled around, the tip of the sword swishing past Patrick's nose where he stood behind her. The Irish boy took a hasty step back, putting up both hands in defense.

"Patrick!" she said, dropping the point down. "I am so sorry. Are you all right? I had no idea you were there."

"Yes, I'm realizing now that was my mistake," Patrick said with a faint laugh. "Helena is always on me about not sneaking up on her, only I never mean to. It's just how I move."

Isabelle nodded, setting the sword aside. "I suppose it was foolish to think I could learn to use a sword just by watching Adam and Little fight once. I should leave such fighting to those of you who are properly trained."

Patrick crossed his arms, a frown creasing his brow as if he were wrestling with what he wanted to say. "A knife is your best bet on account of your size. Staffs are fine for big men like John who can give you a good walloping, but the blade cuts through flesh no matter what size you are. Plus, they're easy to tuck away in all sorts of hiding places."

"I have never used a knife for anything other than kitchen work," Isabelle said.

Patrick took a deep breath before pulling a knife from the top of his boot. He handed it to Isabelle, and she turned it over to survey the double-edged blade. It was heavier than the one she used at home, the hilt wrapped in leather and studded in iron at the end. The blade was a few inches longer than the span of her hand. She touched the pad of one finger to the tip and drew it back quickly, the edge already shearing into her tender skin. It sent a surge through her, a powerful and respectful fear. This was an instrument intended for damage. Patrick watched her as she familiarized herself with the weapon, clearing his throat politely.

"Lesson number two, you're not holding the knife right, either."

Isabelle frowned, moving her wrist. "What is wrong with how I am holding it?"

"Well, nothing, if you're cutting a chicken. But to cut a man, you need to keep your wrist straight, like this." He adjusted the position of the blade in her hand, holding up his own weapon in the same fashion. "And bring your left foot back. Make yourself a smaller target."

Isabelle did as he said, moving her hips so that she faced him at an offset angle. She held the knife out before her as he matched her stance, starting in a slow circle around her.

"There are two ways to attack with a knife," he said, mimicking each movement as he spoke. "You can stab straight forward, or you can slash. If you're going to stab, go for the soft parts below the ribs. You don't want to hit a bone."

He poked at her stomach below her ribs in example, the cool tip of the knife scratching at her through the wool. The contact prickled her skin in warning, and she took an involuntary step back. Patrick waited patiently as she caught her breath, eyeing his weapon warily. He moved through more combat positions, showing her how to turn the blade and change her grip with each attack to strike at all angles. The blade grew heavier and heavier in her hand as they worked, her arm and shoulder aching.

"Don't leave your back exposed," Patrick warned after sidestepping one of her attacks.

Isabelle huffed, lowering the knife. "Perhaps this was a mistake."

Patrick shook his head, taking up his stance again. "The Merry Men never quit, Isabelle. Let's go again."

They sparred for several minutes more, and gradually, Isabelle came to anticipate Patrick's moves before the knife could reach her, letting his blade graze her only a few times as she learned to watch for the flickering of his eyes, the ripple in his shoulder before he drove the knife forward. At last she found an opening in his defenses, smiling as the tip of her knife found its target in the hollow of his neck.

"Very good," Patrick said, his eyes rounded in surprise. "This might be the weapon for you after all."

Isabelle stepped back with a smile, holding the knife out to him. Patrick shook his head.

"Keep it," he said. "I've got a dozen others like it."

"Thank you," she said, tucking it into the top of her boot as he had done. She straightened, lacing her fingers together nervously. "Patrick, I am so terribly sorry for not telling you the truth. All of you. It was cowardly."

"Nobody thinks you were a coward, sister," Patrick said. "We were only hurt you never trusted us enough to tell us the truth." Isabelle nodded, studying the ground at his feet. "Trust is not an easy thing for me. I have never belonged to anything like the Merry Men. You would lay down your lives for each other, all of you. And you accept each other, regardless of your past. Regardless of who or where you came from. I have never . . . I have never imagined I could be part of such a thing."

"The others will forgive you," Patrick said, echoing Robin's words from earlier in the evening. "I forgive you, for what it's worth."

Isabelle looked up to him gratefully. "It is worth a great deal."

Patrick smiled. "Give them time. They'll come around."

"Even Helena?"

Patrick's smile widened. "Even Helena. For all her prickly talk, she's really quite soft once you get to know her."

Isabelle twisted up her mouth, trying to imagine it. "Forgive me again if I do not entirely believe you."

"Well, maybe 'soft' isn't the right word," Patrick conceded. "But she's loyal, and caring, and she'd throw her sword down for any of us. Including you. And not just because you're Robin's daughter. Because you're one of us now. The Merry Men take care of their own."

"Thank you, Patrick," she said softly. "For everything."

CHAPTER
TWENTY-THREE

B y the time Isabelle awoke the next morning, the camp was in
a frenzy of activity. The Merry Men sharpened swords, crafted
quivers of arrows, thunked staffs against trees to toughen their
edges, and wrapped the remains of the previous evening's feast
in delicate cloths to keep it protected for the journey. Little John
directed the men as Isabelle approached.

"What is going on?" she asked, dodging out of the way of a man
hauling a sack that clanged like armor.

"We're breaking down the camp," John said, setting his shoulder
to a massive rock table and shoving it over to clear room.

Isabelle looked about, bewildered. "Whatever for?"

"Robin's orders. Seems we've got a prioress to rescue."

Isabelle's eyes went wide. "The entire camp is coming to
Kirklees? I had thought . . ."

Little John cocked his head at her. "You had thought we'd just let
the two of you go face the Wolf of England alone?"

"Well, no . . ." Although that was exactly what she had thought.
She shook her head. "Where is Robin?"

"Getting the horses," John said, his massive bulk moving another
table out of the way.

Isabelle frowned. "Will he be playing the horse trader from Arabia again?"

Little John grunted. "Not if he knows what's good for him."

"Won't we . . ." Isabelle gestured around the camp, which was looking more and more like an ordinary meadow by the minute. "I don't know, attract attention? All of us thundering out of here on horses?"

John leaned against one of the overturned rocks. "You ask a lot of questions."

Isabelle met his gaze. "You give very few answers."

"The Merry Men know how to move about undetected," said Adam behind her. She turned to find him carrying a brace of swords. "Or didn't you learn that from Robin's rescue?"

"You mean the one where we released all the prisoners and set the keep ablaze?"

"*You* set the keep ablaze," he reminded her. He gave a nod to John, who pushed himself up off the rock with a grunt and moved to help the men with their weapons. Isabelle didn't quite miss the big man, but she wasn't ready to be alone with Adam, either. She chewed the inside of her lip as he sat down, taking a sharpening stone to the first blade.

"Does this mean you are coming along as well?" she finally asked.

He didn't look up from his work, just gave a noncommittal noise.

"So you know what is to happen, then?"

"I've an idea."

She looked about the camp at the men moving with purpose, feeling useless in the middle of so much activity. She slipped her quiver off her shoulder and began checking the fletching on her arrows to give her hands something to do. When she swallowed, it was overloud and forced, making her cringe. Why did he make her feel so clumsy, like a new fawn?

"I see you found yourself another bow," Adam said after several minutes of quiet.

She startled at the sound of his voice. "Oh, yes. Robin . . . My father procured it for me."

Adam lifted a brow but did not look at her. "So it's 'my father' now, is it? Odd you couldn't make that switch before."

Isabelle took a deep breath. "You are still angry."

"What do I have to be angry about?" Adam asked, moving the stone down the blade in long strokes. "That you didn't tell us who you were, or why you were here? Or that you were planning on turning over our master to a murderous nobleman?"

Isabelle dropped her eyes, her stomach turning. She wished there were something she could say in her defense, something to explain the torture she'd endured while agonizing over the decision. Or the fact that she had made the right choice, in the end, by telling Robin the truth instead of handing him over to the Wolf. But Adam was right; she had planned to betray her father before she knew him. It was a knowledge about herself that she would have to live with forever.

"I understand that you cannot forgive me," she said quietly. "If it is any consolation, I can never forgive myself."

Adam frowned up at her, his hand stopping midway down the blade. "I never said I couldn't forgive you."

"But what you just . . . You said—"

"I said I was angry. With plenty of good cause. But I didn't say I didn't understand why you did it. And I didn't say I would never forgive you." He leaned forward, his dark eyes holding her captive. "You wear the greens, Isabelle. You took the oath. You belong to us no matter your past. That's what you keep missing. You're not on the outside anymore. You're part of us now."

Her breath stuck in her chest, a tight bubble that expanded into a wave of pressure washing over her, sending tears into the corners of her eyes. It was a feeling so precious, so novel and fragile, that she feared if she released the breath the illusion would shatter. She'd never had anything that mattered so much to her before. It had been one thing to dream of something greater while trapped in the daily miseries of the priory. It was another thing entirely to live in it, here and now, and be charged with the care of it. She had already made such a mess of things; could she really belong? She so desperately wanted to.

"Go on, then, Adam, you're going to make the sister cry," came Little's voice. The tall boy dropped on the rock beside her, giving her shoulder a hearty slap. "I'll trounce him for you if you like, making a girl cry."

Isabelle laughed, the pressure in her chest releasing with the sound. "I think I shall be all right, thank you."

Little shrugged, leaning back with a deep stretch. "You just say the word, sister, and I'll have my staff swinging."

"As if you could land a blow," Adam said.

"Oi, I'll knock you clear off that rock, you just watch."

"Cut it out, Little, before you earn yourself a smack on the head," said Helena, appearing with Patrick. She looked at Isabelle, arms crossed. "How is it I've been an outlaw all my life and I haven't managed to make half as many enemies as you? And the king's right-hand man, at that."

Isabelle nodded faintly. "Apparently I have also been an outlaw all my life, if it is any consolation to you."

Patrick smiled. "Lucky for you the Merry Men specialize in gaining the advantage on powerful enemies."

Isabelle could not keep the smile from bubbling up to her face. "Shall I take this to mean you are all coming to Kirklees to help rescue my mother?"

"You do have a tendency to get yourself in trouble when we're not around," Adam said.

"And even more trouble when we *are* around," Little added. "You'll need our help saving you from that as well."

Isabelle looked to Helena hopefully. "And you, Helena? Will you forgive me for not telling you the truth?"

Helena rolled her eyes. "Of course I will, you blighter. I'm not one to hold grudges."

The boys scoffed, each one turning into a cough as Helena glared them down.

"Thank you," Isabelle said, her heart overflowing for the first time in a very long time.

Helena waved off her thanks. "If you cry, I'll take it all back."

Robin returned shortly after, leading a team of horses that the men loaded up with supplies and weapons. Isabelle gave the beasts a wide berth as she sought out Robin, the memory of her last ride with Adam still fresh in her mind. Thankfully she did not see the wild mare among their ranks, though many of the horses looked like they would trample her if she looked them directly in the eye. She found Robin with Little John, discussing logistics.

"I've more than a passing familiarity with the priory," he was saying to the big man, sketching out a crude map in the dirt with a stick. "The gatehouse is here, but he'll most likely have it heavily guarded. These are the dormitories here in the back, and Marien's chamber is here in the middle. It's most likely where he would keep her, since he can block the staircases leading in and out. We'll have to—"

"That is not where Mother keeps her chambers," Isabelle

interrupted. She pointed to another place on his sketch. "That is where Mother keeps her chambers. She moved them to be next to me. And that building," she said, pointing to another section of his sketch, "is no longer there. It caught fire during a storm last year after lightning struck it."

Robin frowned at her. "Did you need something from me, Isabelle my love?"

Isabelle cocked her head at him. "It seems you rather need something from me, Father. When is the last time you were in the priory proper?"

Robin cleared his throat. "Well, some time has passed, but I assure you, my memory is as good as any map."

Isabelle crossed her arms. "Really? Because you have put the orchard on the wrong side of the chapel."

"Have I?" Robin murmured, looking down to his sketch. He turned his head one way, then the other. "Oh. Yes, I see I have. Well, that's a minor detail."

"Not minor if you consider there are several unrepaired breaks in the orchard wall through which we could gain entrance, instead of going through the main gate. Which you said would be heavily guarded."

Robin took in a breath, pausing as he considered the map. "Well, yes. Hmmm."

Little John gave a chuckle. "She is your daughter true, Robin."

Robin crossed his arms, leaning back. "All right, then, Isabelle, what is your plan?"

Isabelle smoothed the sketch with her boot, obliterating his work, and held her hand out for the stick. He handed it over with a frown, and she quickly mapped the basic layout of the priory. "Our most advantageous point of entry would be here, on the far side of the orchard. There is a break in the wall there just behind an English oak. It will provide perfect cover to move in and out without detection."

Robin lifted a brow at her. "And you would know this how?"

She smiled demurely at him. "Because I have used it often enough myself."

Robin shook his head. "You rebellious child."

Isabelle pointed to the center of the map. "This is Mother's chamber in the dormitories. She is on the second level, in a separate room from the main dormitory. It would be the perfect place for Sir Roger to put his men, since there are no windows and his men can station themselves at the day stairs just beside it."

"So how do we get to her, then?" Little John asked.

Isabelle traced the stick up a half inch. "Here, at the far end of the dormitory. There is a section of loose stones in the corner I used to crawl through when I had nightmares. I doubt the Wolf or his men know about it. There are several windows into the dormitory. I can easily scale the wall there to get in and out. I've done it hundreds of times."

Robin raised both brows. "Hundreds of times? What manner of priory is your mother governing there?"

Isabelle set her hands on her hips. "The information is coming to our aid now, is it not?"

Robin tilted his head in concession. "A fair point. So the men and I will scale the wall—"

"Not you," Isabelle said. "Me."

Robin scoffed. "As if I would send you into the Wolf's clutches ever again. No, I shall be the one to rescue Marien."

Isabelle squared off with him. "No, you shall not. *You* are the one he truly wants. If you go in and are captured, we have no means of saving you or Mother. He will have what he wants, and he will kill you both. It cannot be you."

He faced her, his expression equally resolute. "It will absolutely be me."

"The lass has a point," said Little John mildly.

Robin turned to him in horror. "You as well, John?"

The big man shrugged. "I'm not saying we send her in, but you're the one he wants. Don't seem very wise to give him the opportunity."

"I know the priory best," Isabelle protested. "I will be able to move quicker and surer than any of your men."

"I will not put you in danger alone," said Robin.

"That's why we'll go with her," Adam said, approaching their huddle. Little, Patrick, and Helena stood behind him. "We'll keep her safe, Robin, and we'll get the prioress out. You know you can count on us."

Robin shook his head. "It is too great a risk. If he were to capture you, any of you . . . I am responsible for your protection."

"And we're responsible for yours," replied Adam. He tilted his head toward Isabelle. "And hers. Isn't that what you told us the Merry Men stand for?"

Robin narrowed his gaze. "I knew you were far too clever to take on. I told John so the moment I saw you in those stocks in Locksley. I said that was a boy who found trouble."

Little John scratched at his beard. "If I'm remembering, you said it was a compliment."

"Well, of course it was a compliment," Robin said, throwing up his hands in exasperation. "At the time. It has since come around to cause me no small amount of trouble."

Isabelle laid her hand on Robin's arm. "I can do this, Father. Please. Trust me."

He looked at her, his blue eyes clouding over with worry and doubt that both frustrated her and warmed her heart. Finally he sighed, shaking his head.

"I shall be right outside the walls with the full force of the Merry Men," he said. "If there is any trouble, even a stray guard, you raise the cry. Do you understand?"

Isabelle nodded, stepping forward to give him a tight hug. "Thank you, Father."

Robin turned to Adam. "You are responsible for my daughter," he said, his voice surprisingly thick. "Take the absolute best care of her. She is worth all of us and more."

Adam nodded, his eyes gleaming as he looked at Isabelle. "I'll protect her with my life. I swear it."

Her breath hitched in her chest under the intensity of his gaze, his eyes dark pools she felt could drown her. She took a deep breath, her body prickling with awareness, and looked away. She dashed her boot through the drawing, returning it to dirt once more.

"It is settled, then?" she said.

The others nodded, their expressions determined as they set off for the horses and Kirklees Priory.

CHAPTER
TWENTY-FOUR

They rode the horses hard through the morning, splitting off in groups as soon as they reached the road to avoid suspicion as they traveled. Isabelle was happy to let Adam take the reins, even if it meant an uncomfortable amount of thigh contact under her father's watchful eye. Little, Helena, Patrick, and John rode with her, Robin leading another group of men to the south to scout the woods around the priory and set up defenses. The trip was not quite so hard as the first time, but by the time they stopped to let the horses rest and get water, her legs were once again cramped and sore. She reached down to massage her calves in her boots, pulling out the knife hidden within so she could better get to the muscle.

"What are you doing with Patrick's knife?" Adam asked, rubbing down their horse as it drank deep from a creek.

"He gave it to me," she said, tucking it into the top of her boot and stretching her aching back. "As you all keep pointing out, I cannot rely on my bow arm alone for protection."

Patrick and Helena moved their horses down the creek toward a stand of tall grass for the horses to eat, and both John and Little stretched out in a patch of sunlight, falling into a snoring sleep immediately. Adam tied their horse up, his brow furrowed.

"If you are going to deprive Patrick of one of his weapons, I hope you at least know how to use it," he muttered, turning away from her.

"I do," she said, prickling at his tone. "Patrick showed me how."

Adam stopped and swiveled to face her, crossing his arms with a doubtful look. "Really?"

"Yes, really," Isabelle said defensively. "I must learn to defend myself. And Patrick was the most helpful of all of you."

Adam narrowed his gaze. "Was he, now? And why is that?"

Isabelle shrugged. "Because he is . . . knowledgeable. And clever. And patient."

"And you figured he wouldn't be a challenge," Adam said.

"No," she said succinctly. "Not that I owe you an explanation, but Patrick best understands the limitations of my size. I have seen the way you and Little fight. We cannot all just bludgeon our way through our enemies."

Adam raised a brow. "So that's what you think I do, just bludgeon?"

"No, of course not, you are the most magnificent fighter I have ever seen," she said. Heat rose up her cheeks as the implications of her words illuminated the space between them. Adam took another step forward, his expression warming even though he kept his arms crossed.

"Well, let's see how good of an instructor Patrick is," he said, his voice low and thrumming with an intensity that harmonized with something speeding up in Isabelle. "Show me what you know."

The warmth drained away from her. "What, here? Now?"

Adam nodded, unlocking his arms to draw a long knife from his belt and gesturing for her to take the first strike. Isabelle hesitated, her fingers loose around the dagger's hilt.

Adam lifted one brow. "Unless you are afraid of a real opponent?"

She frowned, tightening her grip. "Patrick was a real opponent."

"Patrick went easy on you. I will not."

"That much I believe," Isabelle said, shifting her feet and taking up the defensive position Patrick had taught her. Adam surveyed her stance critically, his eyes running the full length of her body up and back down.

"Not bad," he said, reaching for her elbow and repositioning it. "Keep your elbow down like this to protect your ribs."

She had thought nothing of it when Patrick corrected her stance, but now, every time Adam touched her, she lost track of his instructions. He adjusted her feet and stepped back, holding his own knife at the ready. A slight tremor danced along the edge of her blade as she stepped forward into her first strike, which he resoundingly deflected. He frowned at her.

"I hope he taught you better than that."

Her shoulders stiffened. "I am only just beginning."

"Well, it'll be over soon enough if you fight like that."

She set her teeth and moved again to strike, but again he knocked her dagger away as if swatting a fly. Patrick had made it seem easy enough, but each time Adam's blade glinted toward her, she cringed involuntarily. She stepped back, frustration bringing tears of embarrassment to her eyes, and balled her fist around the knife.

"This is why I asked for Patrick's help," she said, her voice trembling in shame.

Adam was quiet a moment as she fought to control the quivering in her hands. Of course she could not learn to fight like them after only one brief lesson. She would have no hope against the mercenaries keeping her mother; they would shred her in ribbons before she could even draw her own knife.

"I'm not trying to upset you, Isabelle," Adam said finally, blowing out a breath. "In all honesty, you're not doing so bad. Your stance is solid, you've got a good grip, and you're doing a sight better than Little ever does protecting your ribs. But it's a whole different thing, fighting someone who means to harm you. Even with everything I taught Abigail, she still couldn't . . . I failed her. I wasn't there for her when she needed me, I couldn't keep her safe. Try as I have—and believe me I've tried damn hard—I haven't been able to keep you safe, either."

Isabelle stared at him willfully. "It is not your job to keep me safe."

Adam threw up his hands. "I know it's not my bloody job, but I want to."

"Oh." Isabelle's fingers unclenched, the tension going out of her jaw and shoulders at the defeat on Adam's face. The idea of Adam worrying about her was strangely thrilling, and her heart picked up its pace as she longed to reach out a hand and smooth away the frown forming between his brows. He let out a frustrated grunt and turned away from her, pacing a few steps away and then turning back.

"You have to be better than good," he said. "You have to be something they don't expect. You have to surprise them."

"Then show me something surprising."

Adam narrowed his gaze on her, but she did not break this time, meeting his eyes steadily. "Fine," he said, turning his back to her. "Grab me from behind."

She stepped forward hesitantly as Adam set his hands on his hips and waited. She floundered for a few moments, wondering how she was expected to get a firm hold of him. But then she remembered Blade twisting her arm behind her back and pressing the knife to her throat when he caught her on the roof in Lincoln, and she stepped up behind Adam and grabbed him as Blade had grabbed her. She tried not to put too much pressure on his arm, afraid of causing injury. Adam sighed.

"Like you mean it, sister."

She glared, wrenching his arm up harder, and was rewarded with a small grunt. She had to stretch up on her toes to bring the knife over his shoulder and press it to his throat, but she at least had a good grip on him. He wriggled his arm, but she increased the pressure, holding him in place.

"That's better," he said. "A little overenthusiastic, but better. You ready?"

"For what?" she asked, but then he was moving so fast she had no time to react. In a blur he twisted out of her grip and stepped behind her, sweeping her off her feet and dropping her within inches of the ground. She tensed, bracing for the impact, but he cradled her by her back and shoulder in a low dip. She scrabbled to grab hold of him as he swept her back up, setting her on her feet but keeping hold of her waist.

"I have no idea what just happened," she said, breathless.

"That's the point. I'll show you again, slow this time."

He gave her instructions as they moved through the positions, stepping behind her and setting his hip against hers to use as a fulcrum to throw her down. She focused hard on his words, trying to set aside the painful awareness where their thighs touched. He swept her back and again she fell, but he caught her inches from the ground, his long fingers trailing down her arms as he pulled her up.

"Have you got it?" he asked.

She nodded, though she was not at all sure. "I think so."

"Good, now you try," he said, stepping behind her.

Her first attempt was pitiful, and Adam was quick to say so. She tried two more times, each time throwing herself off-balance instead. The frustration rose again, but she tightened her heart around it, using it to fuel her concentration and block out the sensation of Adam's arms around her and the awareness of her own frailty beside him.

Adam was mid-instruction on another attempt when she pulled at his arm and twisted her hips, stepping behind him and grabbing his tunic to throw him down. His eyes widened as she turned, the force of his fall dragging her down as her hands tangled in his tunic. He landed with a thud, and she dropped on top of him, his face twisting with a grunt of pain.

She pulled up, her hands splaying over his chest. "Are you all right? I am so sorry, I was trying to take you by surprise as you said, but then I could not let go. Did I hurt you?"

"Only my pride," he said with the faintest hint of a wheeze. "That was brilliant, Isabelle. You're brilliant."

He put his hands on her hips, and whatever she meant to say next shattered against the feel of his fingers along her lower back, the length of him pressed against her and his heart thumping away beneath hers. She dropped her gaze to his jaw, his cheeks darkened considerably with stubble that lent him a disheveled air of wildness. She couldn't bear to meet his eyes, though she could feel them burning into her, her chest rising and falling in time with his as her head spun in wider orbits. She had been staring at his mouth too long, filling the space between them with too heavy a silence. One hand swept up her back, tracing every indent in her spine and tightening something insistent and excruciating in her. Her hands slid up his chest and over his neck, brushing against the stubble on his chin. His skin vibrated with life under her fingertips.

A twig snapped nearby, followed by the soft nicker of the horses. Isabelle sprang up and stumbled back as if Adam had caught on fire, the heat exploding over her face as she desperately wished for some hidden alcove in which to bury her mortification. Adam leapt to his feet in one swift movement, but he turned his face away from her, lines of tension running across his shoulders and down his back. Patrick and Helena emerged from the trees, their expressions making it clear that the twig was broken on purpose.

"We should go soon, if we want to reach the priory by nightfall," said Patrick, studiously avoiding both of their gazes. Helena, for her part, fairly gloated.

"Before anything else gets out of hand," she said, looking Isabelle up and down. Isabelle was sure she would burst into a thousand scattered ashes of humiliation at the look. "Or into hand, as the case may be."

CHAPTER
TWENTY-FIVE

Isabelle quietly asked to ride with Patrick the rest of the way to Kirklees, but the distance did nothing to stop the heat that suffused her skin at the memory of Adam's body beneath her, his hands sliding along her back. She thought the burning shame of it must be lighting her up like the full moon, but if the others noticed her discomfort, they said nothing. Helena did hum a suspiciously chipper tune as they rode along, though.

What was she thinking? Here she was, on her way to rescue her mother from England's cruelest nobleman, and all she wanted was to touch Adam's cheek again and feel his rough stubble against her soft fingertips. It must be the nerves that were getting to her; her mind was only trying to distract itself from what was to come. But every time she caught sight of Adam, her fingers twitched at the desire to bury themselves in his wavy locks.

She was losing her mind. She was absolutely losing her mind. There was no other explanation for how he drove her to the point of distraction and set her nerve endings on fire by simply looking at her. Oh, she could just imagine Sister Catherine's snide little lip curl if she saw her now, dressed as an outlaw and intimately familiar with a young man. There weren't enough floors to scrub or prayers of penitence to appease the sister now. Not that she wanted to any longer.

Her discomfort shifted into a sharp sense of apprehension the closer they drew to the priory. Unlike the ancient oaks of Sherwood, these woods were familiar; she recognized the mossy trunks and the lean squirrels and the cooing larks. The apprehension grew as the road curved away and then back again, and her heart kept a pacing drumroll the lower to the horizon the sun dropped. She was returning home.

Kirklees Priory sprawled over the land before them, the low wall and meager buildings sending a jolt of recognition through Isabelle as her gaze swept over her home. It seemed at once familiar and foreign, as if someone had picked up the entire estate and moved it a few feet to the left. The buildings were smaller than she remembered, but whether that was because she was looking at them from a distance or because her knowledge of the world had expanded she couldn't decide.

Little John signaled a halt and led them toward a copse of trees beside the road, the foliage providing just enough cover for their horses. The others dismounted and quickly tied up their horses, and Isabelle waved off Patrick's offer of help in favor of dismounting herself. It was neither graceful nor efficient, but she managed to reach the ground on her own and keep her feet under her.

"It'll be dark soon," John said, pulling a few loaves of bread and cuts of meat from his pack. "Eat now."

"I'll check the perimeter," Patrick said, melting into the trees.

Adam handed Isabelle a chunk of bread and meat along with a skin of water. The idea of putting anything in her stomach at the moment was far from appealing, but she saw the wisdom in their advice. She couldn't be sure when she would next have a chance to eat.

"What's the plan, then, sister?" Little asked, munching happily away on his share as if they were going out for a midnight stroll.

Isabelle paused in her chewing, looking at their expectant faces. "What do you mean?"

Adam swept his hand toward the shadowy hulk of Kirklees Priory, his mind turned to the business at hand. "You're the expert here."

The four of them were looking at her—at *her*—to guide the way. This was her home, her territory, and she had insisted on leading them. But how? It was one thing to know the layout of the priory buildings and the secret ingresses and the perfect path through the orchard to stay under cover of the trees. But what did she really know about evading mercenaries and staging rescues? Surely they did not expect her, of all people, to be in charge?

Be braver than you feel. Her mother's hands on her cheeks, the rushed intensity of their embrace, the storm of fear and worry in her eyes. Her jittery apprehension gave way to a growing anger and resolve at the thought of her beautiful mother, the always judicious and compassionate prioress, being kept a prisoner in their home. Something hardened and solidified within Isabelle, and as she took a deep breath in, it felt as if she drew in the strength of the earth around her. A greater purpose filled her lungs and infused her blood, and she nodded at the reflection of determination in her friends' gazes.

"There is a break in the priory wall along the back side of the orchard," she said. "To the northwest behind a large English oak. The stones are still there, but they are easy to remove. Unless the Wolf's men have discovered it, that will be our best way in."

Patrick emerged from the shadows, a second form taking shape behind him. Robin's expression was grave, though he gave Isabelle a wink when his eyes landed on her.

"Well, it's about time you lot arrived," he said in a low voice. "Here I was thinking I would have to do all the heroic rescuing myself."

John leaned back against a tree trunk. "What's it look like?"

Robin shook his head. "The Wolf did not take any chances. There are at least forty men patrolling the ins and outs of the priory, and from what we could see of the dormitories, he's got half of them guarding where the sisters sleep. Probably where he's keeping Marien."

Little John looked up to the darkening night sky. "Won't be long now."

Isabelle nodded, her body buzzing with nervous energy. "I am ready."

Robin laid a hand on her shoulder. "It's not too late to change your mind, Isabelle. There's no shame in letting us handle it."

Isabelle shook her head resolutely. "She is my mother. I will be the one to set her free."

Robin took her by both shoulders, pulling her in and kissing the top of her head. "I couldn't be prouder of you. You're everything a father could wish for."

"You embarrass me, Father," Isabelle whispered, blushing deeply as she glanced at the others.

"Oh, go on," he said, waving them off. "If a father can't honestly praise his daughter before his Merry Men, what good are they?"

"I thought it was touching," Little said solemnly.

"That's because you're a fool," Helena said, the words slipping out as they always did. But when she caught Robin's look, she cleared her throat. "That is to say, you would be a fool if you did not find it touching."

Isabelle stifled her smile. Robin tightened his grip on her shoulders, his blue gaze piercing.

"You have the blood of kings and rebels within you, love. Let it rise to meet the call."

Adam stacked the last stone back in place on the orchard wall, the late-autumn harvest of apples sweetening the air around them as a gentle breeze rustled the leaves. The moon peered through patches of dense clouds, lighting the thinning trees with a spooky, ethereal quality. Isabelle had wandered among these trees thousands of times in her childhood at all hours of the day and night, but it was now more dangerous than any of her other nighttime forays.

"Are you sure they will be all right out there?" she whispered to Adam, rising up on her toes as if she could see over the brick wall. "The woods do not provide the same coverage here as they do in Sherwood."

Little snorted beside her. "If anyone should be worried, it's the poor bastard who finds himself afoul of the Merry Men."

"They'll be fine," Adam said. "It's we who need your worry. Where to now?"

Isabelle swallowed, checking the neat rows of trees leading up to the dormitory. Her heart thumped as each sway of the trees and creak of the branches imbued the night with sinister unrest. Somewhere beyond where they crouched, dozens of mercenaries waited with sharpened swords and keen eyes. How could she hope to outwit them?

"Have faith, Isabelle," Adam murmured against her ear. "We're with you."

She nodded, taking a deep breath and ordering her senses back into submission. She couldn't lose her determination now, not when her mother and father were relying on her.

"Follow me," she said, her steps making no sound as she set off through the orchard.

The heavy clouds concealed their movements as they ran, snaking toward the main buildings of the priory. The sisters would be at matins, and the midnight prayer gathering would give them time to gain access to the dormitory. They reached the edge of the orchard, ducking for cover behind a discarded cart used for hauling apples to the cellarium.

Indistinct figures moved through the arched openings of the dormitory building leading to the cloister within. Isabelle held her breath until the mercenaries passed out of sight, their pace steady and brisk. The slotted windows overhead were no more than black holes in the stone. Isabelle stared hard at the darkened window of her quarters but could make out no movement or light within.

"The last window on the left," she whispered, pointing up.

As soon as the patrol moved out of sight, she sprinted across the open space, throwing herself flat against the wall into the shadows. She listened for any approaching footsteps before running her hands over the stones, searching for a familiar grip. It had been over a year since she had done this, but her fingers remembered the way, and soon she had her first handhold. She set her toe into the jutting stone at the bottom of the wall and pushed up, blindly reaching for the next stone far to her right.

She continued up the wall, her feet and hands moving as surely as a spider climbing a familiar path. Without the encumbrance of her habit, it was a faster ascent than she was used to, and she reached the lip of the window in only a few seconds. She peered over the edge, but all was darkness within, so she hauled herself up and tumbled inside.

The familiar smells of the dormitory greeted her as she rolled onto her feet, dusting straw from her hose and righting her bow over her shoulder. She inhaled the sweet scent of lemon and lavender from the sisters' soaps, the tang of incense left burning in the church, and the musty straw of their pallets. Patrick landed with a whisper behind her, pivoting around the room with quick movements as if he expected someone to leap out of the shadows.

"No one is here," Isabelle whispered. Her room was separated from the rest of the sleeping quarters by flimsy walls constructed of thin slats of wood, and she caught glimpses of the room next door through the cracks. "They will have gone to matins by now. They should not return until the bells chime again."

"Bloody guards," said Helena from the window as she crawled in. "Nearly ran right across the path of one walking the perimeter outside. The dogs are everywhere."

"Did you see that?" Little whispered, his head popping up below the window. "Oi, Helena, you nearly cost us the whole bit."

"Shut up," Helena snapped. "He came out of nowhere."

"You've been holding out on us, sister," Little continued, folding himself over to fit through the narrow window. "That was brilliant, climbing that wall as you did. You're a natural Merry Man. Though I suppose that's true enough anyway, isn't it?"

Isabelle smiled with chagrin. "I did become rather adept at sneaking in and out at night. Priory life can be a bit . . ."

"Imprisoning?" Helena offered.

"Boring?" Little added.

"Constraining," Isabelle replied.

Adam appeared at the opening of the window, eyeing the narrow passage with doubt. "Maybe I can squeeze myself through the eye of a needle when I'm done here."

"It's not that bad," Little said. "I managed it."

"Only because you're all height and no width." Adam wedged

himself through the window, grunting as his shoulders popped free of the narrow frame. He stepped into the room, looking around curiously. "So this is your room, Isabelle?"

Her cheeks colored red, and she was grateful for the low light. "Was my room, yes. The loose section of wall to my mother's chamber is over here."

"All right, we've got to do this quiet and quick," Adam said as he and Little took up their positions beside the wall. "Otherwise we'll have the whole place down on our heads. Little and I will pull these stones. Patrick and Helena, be ready to move. Isabelle, get your mother and get her out, quick as you can."

Isabelle nodded, shaking the jittery tension out of her hands as Little pulled the first stone. He and Adam worked fast, piling up each rock neatly beside the wall and revealing the dark interior of the adjoining room. Isabelle crouched low, peering into the void, a nervous spiral of dread rising from her stomach and up the back of her throat. It was too quiet, everything too still. Why was there no light?

"Something is wrong," she whispered, just as Little stuck his head through the small opening they had created. She knew the response before he drew back, his expression grim.

"Bad luck, sister. Your mother's not here."

CHAPTER
TWENTY-SIX

"Where else could they hold her?" Adam asked.

Isabelle shook her head, pushing back on the panic that threatened to rise up within her. "I . . . I do not know. I thought surely this would be . . . I do not know."

"Patrick, check the rest of the dormitory and the cloister below," Adam said.

Patrick nodded, moving on silent feet out of the room. Isabelle pressed her arms into her sides, trying to wrangle her thoughts. Where else could they keep her mother? What would Robin do?

"The chapter house," Isabelle said, looking up. "The sisters use it for confession and penance. It is on the ground level, on the opposite end from here, and it faces the inner cloister. Perhaps the Wolf thought it would be a more secure location to keep her."

Patrick slid back into the room. "I count at least ten guards below. There's a room on the far end that has two guards stationed right out front."

"The chapter house," Isabelle confirmed, her heart sinking further.

"You got any other secret ways to get in there up your sleeve?" Adam asked.

Isabelle shook her head. "There is nothing but solid stone beneath our feet. There are the night stairs at the far end of the dormitory leading down to the cloister toward the chapel. The sisters will take those stairs from the chapel when they have finished matins." Adam peered out into the open dormitory. "We'll have to take our chances. Little, do you think you could draw the guards off the door long enough for Isabelle to slip in?"

Little laced his fingers together, cracking his knuckles. "Be my pleasure."

"You can't just go in there with your staff swinging and start cracking heads," Helena said. "You'll bring the entire lot of mercenaries down on us."

"We don't have much of a choice," Adam said.

"What about a distraction?" Patrick asked. "I could cause a disturbance down at the other end of the dormitory, chuck some rocks or something. That ought to get their attention."

"Wait," Isabelle said, crossing to the small chest beside her sleeping pallet and rummaging around inside. She pulled back, holding up a habit with a fine coat of dust from lack of use. "My spare habit. A bit short around the ankles, but it should do the trick. I can pass through the cloister as if I am just leaving services and ask the guards for help, draw them off. Then one of you could get into the room to find my mother."

"What if the Wolf's men recognize you?" Patrick reasoned. "If those mercenaries in Lincoln knew you, it's possible these men could, too."

"Well, it is not as if you could pass for a sister," Isabelle pointed out. "I do not have a spare wimple to cover your head. What other choice do we have?"

"Patrick's right," Adam said, scratching at his chin. "We can't risk the guards recognizing you."

Isabelle looked down at the habit in her hands, shaking out the skirts again before lifting her eyes to Helena. The girl stood with her arms crossed and her feet braced apart, more like a swaggering outlaw than a pious sister of the order. It seemed the others had drawn a similar conclusion, however, for they all stared at Helena expectantly. She furrowed her brow in confusion.

"What?" she demanded.

Isabelle held up the habit with a little shake.

Helena's eyes narrowed. "Oh, I'd rather lick a dead bird."

"You are the only one of us who could conceivably pass for a sister without getting caught," Isabelle whispered.

"I don't do the disguises bit," Helena said. "I'm not like the rest of you with the fake accents and ridiculous stories. Just give me a good clean shot and I'll take it."

"That's not true," Patrick whispered, taking one of her hands in both of his. "You're the cleverest of us all. We need you to do this, and you can. Please, Helena."

The girl shifted uncomfortably under Patrick's steady attention, the tense moment stretching out between them across the heavy bootfalls of the patrol below. Finally the girl's shoulders relaxed and she scowled at Isabelle, snatching the habit from her outstretched hands.

"If a single one of you so much as snorts, I'll cut your tongue out," she said, shoving them out of the small room.

"There is a well on the far side of the cloister," Isabelle whispered, leaning her head out of the narrow confines of the stairwell to gesture to the small stone enclosure. "Tell them the handle has stuck, and ask if they can help you unstick it. It often sticks in the wintertime and can be stubborn as a mule to draw back up."

"Maybe for hands that are more used to prayer than hard work," Helena muttered, pulling uncomfortably at the front of the habit. "How do you wear these bloody things? I feel like I'm going to trip just trying to cross the walkway."

"You grow accustomed to it," Isabelle said. "And it won't be for long, just enough to draw the guards away from the door. The chapter house is situated along that wall. If the men give you any trouble, simply continue around the cloister to the chapel on the far side. The sisters will still be in prayer and you can slip past the chapel and return here. Just stay clear of the other sisters. They will know you are not one of them and raise the alarm."

"If they give me any trouble, I'll give it right back," Helena said grimly, patting the sword belted to her side under the habit. Isabelle had talked her out of carrying her bow and quiver, but the girl would not part with her short sword or the daggers stuck into her boots. Isabelle could hardly blame her.

"You'll do brilliant," Patrick whispered behind them, briefly laying a hand on Helena's shoulder. "As you always do. And we'll be here waiting for you."

Helena twisted to look at him, a rare shadow of doubt passing over her features as she touched her fingers to his. But then the girl caught sight of Little grinning behind him in the stairwell and her scowl returned.

"One word, Little, and you'll need a funnel to pour your ale down your throat," she said.

Little shrugged, though he wiped the grin from his face. "Might be an improvement."

"Go, quickly," Isabelle said. "The sisters will be back soon."

Helena nodded, dropping her head and muttering to herself as she scuttled across the walkway surrounding the grassy expanse of the cloister. Isabelle held her breath as the girl passed under the first archway, nearly barreling over a mercenary crossing through. He tilted his head, looking after Helena, and Patrick and Little pressed forward behind Isabelle, ready to step into the fray. But Isabelle held up her hand, staying their actions and her own heartbeat as the mercenary shook his head and resumed his watch.

A shadow passed along the wall only a second before another mercenary crossed the threshold to the stairwell, so close Isabelle could smell the rot of meat and wine on his breath. She flattened herself against the stones, closing her eyes and praying as hard as she could that he would not give the stairwell more than a cursory glance. Her heart thumped loud enough that it was all she could hear, obliterating even his footsteps, but several seconds passed and she wasn't seized from her hiding spot.

She opened her eyes with a sigh, the lingering scent drifting away as the man continued on his path. The relief lasted only a few seconds as the low rumble of speech reached her from somewhere beyond the stairwell. She couldn't make out the words at first, but her stomach clenched at the undeniable tenor of suspicion in the voice.

"—not a bloody farmer, woman," he said, his words clipped and harsh. "You want a well fixed, fix it yourself. Get out of here."

Helena's response was too low for Isabelle to make out the words, but she winced at the general tone. It sounded neither pious nor subservient. Patrick stiffened beside her.

"What did you say to me?" the man's voice rang out, clear and angry. He moved into view, and Isabelle leaned forward a hairsbreadth to catch sight of Helena. The girl stood under an archway, her head bowed but her shoulders raised, the mercenary between her and the stairwell. The man took another step forward, grabbing her roughly by the arm.

"You sniveling little chit, I'll teach you to show respect to your betters," he said, drawing back as if to slap her. Helena's hand flattened against the habit, where she wore her short sword, her fingers drawing the hem up to access the weapon. Patrick's sword slithered loose of its scabbard, Adam and Little only a breath behind. Two more guards blocked Helena, their expressions hard and bleak. Isabelle's heart slammed against her ribs.

"Sister Helena!" she cried out in a shrill, nasally voice. It sounded tight and uncertain, and she forced that familiar note of pompous superiority into it. "What is taking so long? I requested water for our sisters in prayer. I did not intend you to fetch it from the river!"

Helena's head shot up in surprise, which one of the mercenaries mistook for guilt. He prodded her in the back, a grin spreading over his face. "You're in for it now, lass."

"Sister Helena, have you gone dumb as well as deaf?" Isabelle continued in Sister Catherine's voice. "Where is our water, please! The sisters are so parched Sister Margaret can hardly speak her prayers. Do not dillydally."

Helena muttered something that sounded like it was coming through her teeth, her shoulders still raised in a defensive posture.

"What was that? Speak up, child, the Lord Almighty himself cannot hear you."

"I said the bucket is stuck," Helena ground out.

"The bucket is—oh, for heaven's sake, Sister Helena, ask those fine gentlemen to help!"

"I did," Helena continued, her voice pitching higher. "They refused to help me."

"They would do no such thing, would you, gentlemen? We simply must have water for our sisters in prayer, I insist. Help Sister Helena with the bucket."

"That's not our job, miss," said one of the mercenaries, though he sounded doubtful of himself.

"Yes, I see your job is to parade on an endless loop about my cloisters, disturbing the peace of all of us, causing a ruckus on holy grounds. And yet you cannot complete a simple task such as hauling up a pail of water? Shall I speak to your master about your manners?"

Isabelle winced, worried she had gone too far with Sister Catherine's admonishments. She held her breath in the small eternity of silence before the mercenaries spoke again.

"No need for that, miss. We'll help her fetch the water."

"Good," Isabelle cried, her voice pitching even higher with relief. "Bring an extra bucket for our troubles, if you would."

The men grumbled, but they followed after Helena to the well on the far side. Little clapped Isabelle on the shoulder. "Bloody brilliant, sister."

"It is not over yet," Isabelle murmured. "I still need to reach the chamber doors without being seen."

"Quick, before they get back," said Adam.

Isabelle nodded, the staccato pace of her heart sending energy thrumming along her nerve endings as she slipped out of the stairwell. Her mother was one unguarded door away, and all she had to do to reach her was move lighter and faster than air. Her blood hummed, fingers dancing in time to her heartbeat as she flew across the open space and pressed herself against the first stone pillar, the open air rushing past her as if to expose her. The shadows hung deep between each arch, the chamber doors seeming a mile away from where she crouched.

She glanced back to the stairwell as Adam waved sharply toward the next pillar, signaling for her to move. She nodded and darted across, not even daring to breathe as she reached the arch. Another guard clomped by where she had stood seconds before, his heels thudding against the packed earth. She waited a few breaths before collecting herself, moving to the archway that stood before the chapter house door.

Adam signaled again, and she sent a prayer into the heavens above as she closed the distance to the door, setting both hands on the heavy knob. It grated loudly as she turned it and the screech seemed to echo all around, but as she glanced back, it was obvious it had only sounded so deafening to her. She twisted the knob desperately and it gave way, the door shuddering open.

She tumbled inside the room, throwing her body against the door to drive it shut again, the movement echoing. Three small windows let in only a smattering of light at the far end of the empty room, and it took several moments for her eyes to adjust. Something within her cringed at the impression of columns and benches along the walls, the site of so many of Sister Catherine's cruel punishments for her. She preferred to castigate the novices in the chapter house as if she were the prioress herself. Isabelle shook off the specters of her past, moving beyond the first column as she pressed deeper into the room.

"Mother?" she whispered as she moved. No sound greeted her, but she was not sure if that was a comfort or a concern. A narrow table lined the wall in the back of the chamber, where her mother would sit while the sisters made their confession, a collection of letters scattered across the surface. These letters were fresh, as was the single candle burning beside them and the block of sealing wax still partially melted. Maybe her mother was not in as much danger as she feared if they were allowing her correspondence. Still, there was no sign of her mother here. Where had they taken her?

She hurried to the table, scanning the letters to search for any clue of her mother's whereabouts, when the door behind her creaked open. She froze, caught out in the open with nowhere to hide as the door shut, trapping her with whoever had entered. She reached down to her boot, sliding Patrick's knife from the top and gripping it tightly as she turned to face the intruder. But it was not a mercenary who greeted her with pinched lips and narrowed eyes.

"Sister Catherine, what are you doing here?" Isabelle asked in disbelief, taking in the sister's attire. "And why are you wearing my mother's robes?"

CHAPTER
TWENTY-SEVEN

———➤

"Isabelle," Sister Catherine said, her tone even more pinched in surprise. "I should ask what *you* are doing here in *my* chapter house."

Isabelle narrowed her gaze. "What do you mean, *your* chapter house? You are not the prioress."

Sister Catherine contemplated her for a moment, tapping her index finger against the length of the rosary she kept at her belt. She glanced at the letter Isabelle still held in her hand, her mouth tightening into a thin line. Isabelle crumpled the paper against her tunic protectively.

"Much has happened since you were arrested for attacking that poor soldier carrying out his duty," Sister Catherine said, sweeping across the room toward her.

"Why are you wearing my mother's robes?" Isabelle ground out again.

Sister Catherine sniffed. "These are not Marien's robes anymore. They are mine now."

Isabelle pressed harder on the paper. "What do you mean?"

"After you were arrested—"

"For protecting the villagers of Kirklees," Isabelle objected.

"For shooting a soldier," Sister Catherine said sharply. "The soldiers came here to speak to all of us. To find out if there were any more . . . renegade elements within our congregation."

"I am not—"

"Do not interrupt," Sister Catherine said sharply. "Marien refused them entry to the priory, which I told her would only anger the soldiers and bring them back in greater numbers. And of course, it did. They returned, with reinforcements."

The Wolf. She bit her tongue to stop from saying it aloud.

"And then, when you disappeared from their custody, it was determined that your mother helped you escape."

"Why would anyone think that?"

Sister Catherine tilted her head to Isabelle with a knowing look. "Well, it certainly was not any of us."

"No, it was not," Isabelle said curtly.

"The men arrested your mother, and the sisters needed a guiding light in her reckless absence. They elected me as prioress in her stead."

Isabelle shook her head. "You have always envied my mother's position. Of course you would swoop in like a vulture the moment you saw an opportunity. These men are killers, Sister Catherine. And all you care about is gaining a title."

"How dare you speak to me in such a manner," Sister Catherine said, drawing herself up. She gave Isabelle a withering look. "You cannot imagine what the sisters have been through because of you and your mother's selfish actions. And now you come sneaking in, dressed like an absolute heathen, endangering the sisters once again. I should call the guards on you."

Isabelle pointed the knife at Sister Catherine. "You will not do anything of the sort."

Sister Catherine's eyes went wide in shock, then narrowed. "You insolent little bastard."

"Tsk, tsk," Isabelle said. "Such language from a sister of the order."

"I always knew you were no better than a common gutter rat," Sister Catherine said. "Resorting to violence to get what you want."

"I do not want to hurt you, Sister Catherine," Isabelle said. "But I will, if I have to. I need to find my mother. Where are they keeping her?"

Sister Catherine drew her robes in around herself. "Why should I tell you anything?"

Isabelle took a deep breath, willing herself to be patient. "Because you can have the priory as I know you always dreamed. I only want to see my mother safe, far away from here. Please."

It stuck in her teeth, begging this horrible woman for help, but she would get on her knees and tear her hair out to save her mother. Sister Catherine eyed her up and down.

"I do not think well with a knife thrust in my face."

Isabelle lowered the blade. "I am sorry. Please, Sister Catherine. Please help me. Where is my mother?"

The sister tapped her fingers against the beads of her rosary once more, her eyes flicking toward the door and back. Isabelle wasn't sure she really could harm the woman if she tried to call out for help, but she hoped she would not need to.

"It is no use trying to free her," Sister Catherine said, though her tone had turned thoughtful. "They keep her under lock and key all hours of the day, with more of these foulmouthed savages guarding her."

Isabelle pressed her eyes closed, praying she was not too late. "Where?"

Sister Catherine sighed. "In the cellarium."

Isabelle shivered involuntarily. Anywhere but underground. "Can you get me there?"

"Of course not," Sister Catherine said, horrified. "And if I were caught aiding you, what would happen to the sisters then? What would happen to me? I would rather be stabbed."

Isabelle pushed her annoyance back. Sister Catherine always got under her skin in just the right way, but she could not let the woman cloud her judgment now. She needed to get to the cellarium.

"Where are you storing the apple harvest?" Isabelle asked.

Sister Catherine looked confused. "In the cellarium, of course."

That is how I will reach her. Isabelle looked about the room. "Do you have a spare habit?"

"Only my old one," Sister Catherine said slowly. "Why?"

"I need to borrow it," Isabelle said.

"What for?"

Isabelle wouldn't dare to reveal her plan to the sister, especially not when she barely trusted her not to call out to the guards at any minute. "Because it is my only way of getting out of this room without raising suspicion from the guards patrolling outside. If they catch me in here with you, it will be both our heads in the hangman's noose."

Sister Catherine paled considerably before moving toward a trunk in the far corner of the room, digging toward the bottom to locate the habit. *She probably hoped never to wear it again,* Isabelle thought. *No doubt she jumped at the opportunity to take Mother's place when the Wolf arrived.* But she had no time to consider Sister Catherine or her petty machinations, and so she accepted the garment gratefully.

She donned the habit, agonizing for only a brief moment before setting her bow and quiver aside. She could never pass as a sister carrying such a weapon, despite how vulnerable and empty it made her feel to have them out of her possession. She tucked

Patrick's knife back in her boot, which would have to suffice for now. It took some wrangling to pin Sister Catherine's wimple in place, but she hoped it would obscure her features enough that the guards would not bother with her.

"It really is no use trying to rescue her," Sister Catherine said, watching Isabelle dress. "They have several men on guard at all hours. How would you possibly get past them?"

"That is not your concern," Isabelle said, adjusting the belt around her waist. "You will stay here when I leave, then return to the dormitory without a word to the soldiers."

"Without so much as a 'please,'" the older woman sniffed. "I see your manners have deteriorated further in your lawless absence."

"Sister Catherine," Isabelle said, hesitating beside the candle that was now close to guttering. "I know we have not always seen eye to eye in the past, but I appreciate your help. And I am sure my mother appreciates your efforts to protect the sisters in her absence."

"Of course," Sister Catherine said, lifting her chin. "It is my sacred duty."

Isabelle slipped out the door, keeping her head down as she made for the shadowed arch. The two men on guard were still gone, which she hoped meant they had moved to another location and not that they had fallen prey to Helena's sword. She dodged between the pillars again, avoiding the guards' attention as she made her way to the stairwell. She could not see Adam and the others in its shadowy depths, but she gestured in the direction of the cellarium and held up a hand, hoping he would understand the signal. She cast one glance back at the chapter house doors, but Sister Catherine did not emerge. She might not be a great help, but at least she wasn't raising the alarm.

Isabelle bowed her head and stuck to the shadows, pressing her hands together and murmuring Ave Marias over and over. They were half meant as a means of disguise, and half meant as a very earnest plea to the heavens. She passed two guards on rotation, but she lowered her head and prayed harder, the veil obscuring her face. The men did not stop, and she reached the kitchens on a quick exhalation of gratitude to the Virgin.

Sister Catherine was right; they had six men stationed around the kitchen, two on the door outside and another four lounging within, guarding the doors down to the cellarium. Isabelle hovered around the corner, watching the bored men as they picked at their teeth and cleaned under their nails with the wicked ends of their knives. It was possible her plan was madness, but she had no better idea for reaching her mother. She took a deep breath, smoothed her hands down the rough skirts of Sister Catherine's habit, and stepped into view.

"Evening, good sirs," she said in a soft voice, keeping her head lowered and her eyes on the ground.

"No one allowed down there," said a man in a bored, flat tone. "You know the rules."

"Yes, I . . . Yes, of course. It is only that . . . Sister Catherine has sent me? To begin the preservation of the apple harvest?"

The man grunted. "Why would the prioress send one of you in the dead of night?"

Isabelle gritted her teeth at the man's tone. "We always do our preservation at night, sir. The cooler weather makes for sweeter apples. We have only just completed matins laud. I could come back with Sister . . . with the prioress, if that would help?"

"Not that old bag," another of the men muttered. "Go on, then, let the girl pass. What's one sister going to do?"

"We have our orders," said the first soldier, but he didn't sound as if he felt strongly about them.

Isabelle's heart pounded, and she had to move her tongue around her mouth to keep it from going dry. "Please, sir, if we do not start the preservation soon the apples will rot, and we will lose our entire harvest. There are many poor souls in the neighboring towns who depend on our apples for their sustenance through the winter."

"Just let the sister pass," said another of the mercenaries, with a thick scar where his eye should have been. "Come on, I fancy a game of bones. I've got the coin. Who's in?"

"I'll take that play," said another of the men, producing a set of dice carved out of ivory.

The first man sighed, rolling his eyes as the men laid out their coin to start the game. "All right, sister, do your harvesting. But be quick about it, yeah? No talking to the prisoner."

It was jarring to hear her mother referred to as the prisoner, and she couldn't imagine what it had been like for her, buried in this cellar for so many days now. She had spent less than a night in her prison cell, and it still gave her nightmares. She would get her mother out of there, even if she had to fight through every mercenary in this place to do it. Which she hoped would not be the case.

Isabelle nodded and the man fished a key from his tunic and unlocked the thick chains around the cellarium doors. Isabelle willed her hands to stay by her sides as he unwound the chains slowly, every muscle in her body wanting to rip them free and throw the doors wide. He drew the last of the chains out, the hinges creaking as he pulled the door open.

"Go on, then."

"Thank you," she said, ducking to descend the short flight of steps. The door clanged shut behind her as she reached the hard-packed earth of the cellar floor, making her jump with fright. For an irrational moment she wanted to spring back up the stairs and throw the doors wide to breathe deep of the outside air, but she would not let fear get the best of her.

"Who goes there?" came a gentle but suspicious voice, one so familiar it brought tears to Isabelle's eyes. She turned away from the steps, her heart soaring.

"Mother?" she whispered.

"Isabelle?"

Something bumped her and Isabelle startled before grasping for her mother. Marien's hands fumbled blindly but found their way to her shoulders and then her face, pausing over the wimple and lightly brushing the tip of her nose. Her mother gave a strangled cry before drawing Isabelle into her embrace.

"My dearest, dearest daughter," she murmured, her voice a thick confusion of emotions. "My Isabelle."

Isabelle melted into her mother's embrace, burying her face in her neck and letting the worry and tension of the last week slip away, just for the moment. Despite all the Wolf's efforts, her mother was still alive, her scent of lemon verbena and mint rising above the musty atmosphere.

"We are going to get you out of here," Isabelle whispered.

Marien drew back sharply, and though Isabelle couldn't see her expression, she could feel the tension in her hands.

"You cannot be here, child," she said, her tone urgent. "You must go, now. Before they know you are here."

"It is all right, Mother, I borrowed a habit from Sister Catherine and told them I was here to preserve the apples. They suspected nothing."

"Sister Catherine? No, Isabelle, you do not understand. They are expecting you. You have to go. Now."

"Expecting me?" Isabelle echoed, just as the chains rattled in the door, the click of the lock loud and clear in the cellar.

TWENTY-EIGHT

"**N**o," Isabelle whispered, flying through the darkness toward the doors, her fists pounding against the surface. "No! Let me out! Please! Don't lock me in here! Let me out!"

She screamed it over and over, but if they heard they did not care. They were probably laughing, just as the soldiers who captured her laughed when they threw her in that potato cellar. The walls pressed in, her fists against the wood loud and close and the air wet and stifling, her breath coming in ragged bursts as hot tears coursed down her cheeks.

"Please!" she screamed, raking her fingernails against the door. She tore off her borrowed wimple, the neck threatening to choke her. "Please let me out!"

"Isabelle!" her mother said, dragging her back from the door. "Isabelle, stop! You will hurt yourself. Please, my darling, stop."

"They have to let me out!" Isabelle cried, clawing at her mother to free her. "I cannot stay down here. I will die. I will suffocate! Let me out!"

"Isabelle!" her mother said sharply, her voice cracking across Isabelle's panic like a whip. "Stop that this instant."

Isabelle turned into her mother's arms, sinking against her in a sob. "They cannot leave me here," she said, the panic threatening to surge up again. "It is like being buried alive. I cannot stand it, Mother. I cannot stand it!"

"I know, child, I know," her mother said, her voice soothing, her hands smoothing down her hair. "But you can stand it, and you will. You must be braver than you feel."

"I tried, Mother, I tried," she said, feeling suddenly helpless and small in her mother's embrace. "I tried to be brave and strong like you, like my father. But I have only made things so much worse."

Her mother stiffened slightly. "What do you know of your father?"

Isabelle drew back, trying to take in a full breath of the musty air. "I know everything. I know about Sir Roger, and Robin, and the fire. I know that the Wolf will hang you if I do not bring him my father."

"Sir Roger is not going to kill me," Marien said with surprise.

"Of course he is," Isabelle said. "He told me himself in Lincoln. He said if I did not bring Robert of Huntingdon to him by the end of the week, he would have you hanged."

"Well, he might have threatened to do so, but he has no intention of killing such a valuable bargaining chip," Marien said. "He plans to use me to force my father to give up Rochester Castle."

"What is Rochester Castle?" Isabelle asked, her confusion pushing the panic aside.

"Rochester is a key port location, and King John needs it if he has any hope of beating the rebel barons in a war. My father currently controls Rochester Castle, but Sir Roger hopes to force him to turn it over to him by using me as ransom." Marien sighed. "These sorts of political tiffs are why I was happy to give up the nobility all those years ago."

"Your father, Robert Fitzwalter," Isabelle said slowly, trying to put the pieces back together. "Leader of the rebel barons."

"I see someone has been giving you a history lesson as well," said Marien.

"Yes, it has been an edifying few days." Isabelle shook her head, though her mother could not see it in the dark. "But why would Sir Roger tell me he was going to hang you if he intended to use you as bait?"

"I assume to lure Robin here as well," Marien said. "Which, thank goodness, reason at least prevailed with one of you."

Isabelle hesitated. "Well . . ."

"Do not tell me," her mother said, her voice threaded through with irritation.

"He is here as well."

Marien gave an exasperated sigh. "That man, always insistent on rescues in silly costumes. We could have settled this years ago if he had simply accepted the Scottish throne as his father intended and dealt with King John then. He would rather play king of the outlaws."

And though there were far more pressing matters at the moment, Isabelle could not help but ask the question that had been weighing on her for days. "Why did you not tell me who I was? Who my father was? Why did you not trust me to know any of this?"

"It was never about trust, dearest," her mother said. "Look at the danger to your life just this past week. I would not have put that on you for the past sixteen years. I know you are cross with me now, but someday you will have children of your own and you will understand the lengths you go to for their protection."

"Yes, and we see how that has turned out."

"You have grown far too much like your father, and in such a short time," her mother said in a sharp tone. "How does he fare, the foolish man?"

"He is . . ." Isabelle struggled to fit the swelling of emotions filling her chest into words. "He is a constant surprise. Clever yet caring, boisterous yet contained, a man of the people and a man apart. And did you know he visited me all these years in disguise? Dressed as a peddler?"

"Ah, the peddler. My least favorite of his characters. Always banging about with his pots. I preferred when he would play the wayward knight."

"What is the wayward . . . You knew it was Father? All those times he brought me gifts, made me my first bow, you knew it was him? And you never said a word?"

"Of course I knew it was your father. Did you honestly think I would let a stranger teach you how to hold a bow? Although I should never have let him give you your first lesson—I have not been able to get the slouch out of your stance since."

"Mother!" she sighed, but in that moment she could understand what had drawn her parents to each other, all those years ago. The spark that flew between them, even after years and miles apart.

"I have a great many questions," Isabelle said. "*After* we are free from this wretched cellar."

"I do not doubt it," her mother replied. "I have many myself, including whose foolhardy plan it was to attempt my rescue in the first place. Your father should know better than to expect Sir Roger to leave anything to chance. If he lured you here, he had a good reason for it."

"What possible reason . . ." Isabelle drifted off as all the pieces finally came together, each link in the chain locking her up tight. "Of course. I was a fool. A complete and utter fool. How could I be so blind? With both of us captured, he has everything he needs to force Father to surrender to him now."

She dropped her head into her hands on a helpless moan. It was the Wolf who had set the trap for them, and she had stepped so willingly into it. A flush of shame washed over her. What had she done?

"Your father is as clever and resourceful a man as there ever was," Marien said, her voice fierce in the darkness. "Whatever Sir Roger has planned for him, he will be more than a match for it."

"We must escape," Isabelle said. "We have to warn him, before it is too late."

"I have a great many skills, Isabelle, but breaking through locked and chained doors is not one of them. I already searched for weapons and there is nothing here. We are defenseless."

Isabelle reached down to her right foot, giving a sigh of relief as her hand found the hilt of Patrick's knife. She crept along the line of apple crates until she found the cellarium door. On impulse she pushed against the wood, but it did not budge, faint cracks of light showing through where the edges of the boards did not quite meet. A sliver of someone's back blocked the view through the cracks. She could see no one else besides the single guard.

"It looks as if they have left us only one guard," she said, retreating from the door. She could not allow herself to worry about where they had sent the others now. She laid her hands on the edge of a crate, the crisp sweetness of apple floating up. "If we can get him down here, we could overpower him and make our escape."

"And if you are anything like your father, I suppose you already have a plan for that," Marien said.

Isabelle grinned, picking up an apple and running her thumb over its knobbly surface. "I suppose I do."

CHAPTER
TWENTY-NINE

Isabelle dragged a heavy-bottomed cooking pot into position behind a stack of crates nearest to the cellarium door, rusty patches of metal flaking to the ground from the cracked rim. She gripped the handles and hefted it to waist height, reassuring herself she could wield it when the time came. Satisfied that it would do as a makeshift weapon, she set it back down and skirted around the boxes toward the center of the cellarium, where her mother waited.

"Are you ready?" she whispered.

"Isabelle, I understand your time among the outlaws has given you a glimpse into their audacious ways, but this is perhaps a tad reckless," her mother said, doubt threaded through her tone. Isabelle did not need any more light to know there was a small crease of worry between her mother's eyebrows. "This is our entire harvest for the priory. If we destroy these apples—"

"We will not destroy them," Isabelle whispered, trying to infuse her voice with enough confidence that it left no room for her mother's doubts. "We will only destroy the crates to make them *think* we are destroying the harvest."

"But if the stores are damaged in the attempt—"

"They will not be," Isabelle said, growing exasperated. "Please,

Mother. You trusted me enough to send me to Sherwood. Trust me now."

Her mother took in a slow breath, no doubt pursing her lips as she always did when considering important priory decisions. But then she let it out on a sigh. "Very well, Isabelle. But do please try and be careful."

"I shall try," Isabelle muttered, before picking up the nearest empty crate and smashing it on the ground. It landed with a terrific crack, the wood splintering and launching in several directions. She slammed it down once more for effect, the impact vibrating up her arms.

"If they will not release me, I will make them regret it!" she screamed, pitching her voice toward the door. She waited a moment before reaching for another crate, smashing it over the remains of its predecessor. "I shall make mash of their harvest until they all starve! They cannot do this to me!"

She handed the crate over to her mother, who hesitated only a moment before demolishing it against the earth. Isabelle gave another wild scream, running around the crates to where her cooking pot waited in the deep shadows. She had left one more empty crate beside the pot, and she lifted it over her head and hurled it at the cellarium doors with all her might. It crashed against the doors, tumbling down the few steps and landing off to the side. She waited for any sign of life from the other side of the door, her hands reaching down to grip the pot handles as her mother laid waste to another crate with impressive force.

The lock jangled and the door burst open, flooding the underground room with light. Isabelle winced against the fresh source of light as she hunkered lower, peering at the man through the gaps in the crates. She could not see her mother from where she crouched, but she could imagine her straightening up at the sight of the scowling mercenary, the wreckage of crates piled at her feet.

"What in hell is going on down here?" he demanded, charging down the three short steps into the cellarium. The toe of his boot hit a loose apple, sending it rolling forward. "You, quit that! What are you doing?"

"Destroying the fall harvest, obviously," Marien said in her best prioress tone, cool and dismissive.

"Don't you give me cheek," the man growled, taking another few steps forward. He was now in line with Isabelle's hiding place, the thick smell of leather and unwashed skin drifting between the apple crates. "You can't go destroying all that food."

"And why not?" Marien asked, as if it were the most foolish question in the world.

"Because it's our bloody food, too!" the mercenary groused, glaring about suspiciously. His gaze narrowed. "Hang on, where's the girl?"

"What girl?" Marien asked.

"The sister, came down here for the harvesting," he said. "The one the Wolf told us to lock up. Where is she?"

"Oh, you mean my daughter," Marien said. "She is not here, obviously. Perhaps you should have done a better job securing her."

The man charged toward Marien, taking her by the shoulders and dragging her toward him. "If that girl's gone missing, it's your head that will roll, not mine."

Isabelle hefted the pot and stepped out from her hiding place, lunging the few steps across the cellarium to where the man stood with his back to her and using the momentum to raise the pot over her head and bring it down directly on the back of his skull. It connected with a slick crunch before thudding to the ground, a piece of the rim cracking apart at the impact. The man pitched forward, and Marien had just enough time to step out of the way before he collapsed in a heap. She held her fingers before his nose.

"He is breathing," Marien said. Isabelle was surprised at the rush of relief that ran through her. She did not want to add murder to her list of skills acquired in recent days. "That will be quite the goose egg you gave him when he comes around, though."

"I would wager he deserved it," Isabelle replied.

"I hope for everyone's sake we do not run across any other guards," Marien said, pulling his sword belt loose before straightening up, carrying a dagger from his tunic in her other hand. "I do not think your pot could handle it."

"What are you going to do with his blades?" Isabelle asked.

"Hopefully nothing," Marien said. She fastened the belt around her waist. "But if required I shall use them as they were intended. In any case, he no longer has need of them."

"What do you know about wielding a sword?" Isabelle asked incredulously.

Marien lifted one brow. "Apparently you did not receive the full history lesson," she said. "Time enough for that later."

They crept up the cellar stairs into the abandoned kitchen, locking the cellarium door behind them. Isabelle cracked the door to check the walkway beyond. She counted five mercenaries making their patrols through the cloister, their attention focused away from the kitchen doors. She drew it shut again, leaning against it as she gathered her thoughts.

"We need to get to the dormitory and find my friends," she said. "Then we can slip out my window and get back to the wall where Little John waits."

Marien watched her curiously before comprehension lightened her features. "I always wondered how you managed to sneak past my room without awakening me."

Isabelle's heart gave a guilty lurch. "What makes you think I snuck out?"

Marien gave her a level look. "Darling, I was Robert's wife long before I was your mother. I am not ignorant of his or your penchant for late-night wanderings."

"Why did you never stop me?"

Marien shrugged. "I thought you needed your privacy as he did. Besides, the guilt of sneaking out made you exceptionally devoted to your chores the next day."

Isabelle sucked in a breath before realizing she had nothing to say, so she closed her mouth. She cracked the door once more, waiting for the closest guard to complete his circuit before darting to the cover of the nearest pillar. This trek through the arches proved easier than the first, as she knew when to move and where to stand to avoid being seen. Marien moved without a whisper beside her, as silent and quick as Patrick ever was. Not even the white of her habit gave her away as they advanced toward the dormitory stairs. Once they reached the shadowy alcove Isabelle let out a pent-up breath and leaned against the wall.

"Mother," she whispered, shaking her head as Marien appeared beside her a moment later. "You move just like the . . . I had no idea . . ."

"I know, dear," her mother said, giving her a distracted kiss on her brow. "I can be quite impressive when the situation calls for it. But where are your friends? I thought you said you left them here."

"I did," Isabelle replied with a frown. She searched the shadows of the dark corridor leading up to the dormitory but could pick out no distinct shapes. "Perhaps they already returned to the orchard wall."

Even as she said it, though, she knew it couldn't be true. They wouldn't abandon her. What if they learned she had been captured, and had been taken themselves trying to rescue her? A dozen scenarios ran through her mind, none of them doing anything to set her nerves at ease.

"We need to check the priory," she said. "I cannot leave here without them."

Marien nodded. "I will check the dormitory, you check the chapel, and we shall meet back at your room." She kissed Isabelle again on the forehead. "Be more than careful, dearest."

And then she was gone, floating up the stairs into the dormitory above. Isabelle suddenly felt very alone, the thud of boots and someone's distant snoring the only sounds within the priory. But then she thought of Adam and the others, possibly in danger or searching for her as well, and she squared her shoulders. She would not let fear guide her, not anymore.

Quickly as she could, she made her way toward the chapel entrance, heart pounding as she nearly stepped into the path of a passing mercenary. She made it to the doors and darted in, pressing herself against the wall, out of sight. The recently extinguished wicks still smoldered in the bank of candles by the door, cool gray tendrils of smoke rising toward the high ceiling. The pews stood empty, rows of sentinels stretching toward the altar at the far end of the room. A preternatural stillness reigned within the sacred space until someone grabbed her from behind, clamping a hand over her mouth and dragging her back into the shadows.

CHAPTER
THIRTY

She waited just until her feet gained purchase before biting down hard on the fingers pressed to her mouth, stepping behind her attacker and sweeping her arm back as Adam had taught her. The man fell with a grunt, his grip on her arm dragging her down on top of him. But this time she was prepared, drawing up her leg and whipping the knife from her boot to press it to his throat.

"Isabelle, it's me!" her attacker hissed as she leaned forward on the blade. "I never would have taught you that move if I'd known you would use it exclusively on me."

She let her breath out in one great whoosh, pulling the knife away from Adam's throat. "Are you mad? I thought you were one of the Wolf's men. I nearly sliced your throat open."

"I didn't want you screaming and drawing them down on us," Adam said as he sat up. "But clearly I should have been more worried about my own neck. Where in bloody hell have you been?"

"It is a long story," she said. "I shall explain later, but right now we need to get out of the priory as quickly as possible. The Wolf has set a trap for Robin and we need to warn him. Where are the others?"

"Hiding," Adam said with a general wave. "After you disappeared the sisters returned and we had to move. We've been waiting over an hour for you to come back. Little wanted to go in swinging, of course, and Helena only just stopped him by threatening to bash his head in. I've searched nearly every nook of this blasted place looking for you, which wasn't easy with the mercenaries thick as ticks on a doe out there. Did you at least find your mother?"

Isabelle nodded. "She is waiting for us. We can slip out the way we came in. Get the others and meet us back in my room."

Isabelle rose to retreat to the chapel doors, when Adam took her by the wrist, pulling her close. He buried the fingers of his other hand in her curls and pulled her forward, wrapping an arm around her waist as he lowered his mouth to hers. At first it was only warmth and wetness, and she wasn't quite sure what to do with her mouth, but then he tipped her head up, parting her lips with his and starting a fire that burned away any lingering thoughts in her head. It simmered low in her belly and sent her fingers sliding up the rigid planes of his back, the chill of the night set alight with the need to keep his mouth against hers forever. Warm breaths filled the space between them as he drew back, resting his forehead against hers.

"With your habit of getting in trouble, I wasn't sure I would have another opportunity," he said, a slight pant to his whisper. "For heaven's sake, Isabelle, be more careful this time."

"I am . . . I will . . ." Her thoughts scattered and collided as the heady memory of the fit of his mouth over hers and the warmth of his chest still filled her mind. Adam seemed to sense her disorientation, for he pulled back with a grin.

"I see I've finally discovered something to render you speechless."

She gave a huff, scowling as a litany of words rushed to fill the empty space in her mind. But before she could give shape to her thoughts, a voice rang out from the cloister, filtering in through the chapel door.

"Well, well, little sweetling, I found you again," it called.

Isabelle's hands tightened around Adam's shoulders, her fingers digging into the muscle as panic flooded her system.

"Blade," she whispered. "The mercenary from Lincoln who attacked us in the Wounded Lion. He is here."

"I know you're about somewhere," Blade continued, his voice taunting. "Come out, or your mother loses her pretty face."

Isabelle bolted for the chapel door, but Adam caught her, hauling her back before she could throw it open and reveal herself. Through the crack she glimpsed a dozen mercenaries surrounding Blade, though that was not what drove a shard of ice into her heart. Blade held Marien by the throat, the tip of a dagger pressed into the soft hollow beneath one eye.

"Don't be daft," Adam hissed. "He's goading you."

"He has my mother!" she said.

"And he'll have you, too, if you just go rushing out there like a fool," Adam said. "We need a plan."

"I'm waiting," Blade called from beyond the door. "What should go first, do you think? An ear or an eye? She's got a spare one of both. You'll hardly miss it."

"Isabelle, you must run," her mother's voice called out. "He cannot kill me. You know what you must do. I will be fine."

"Kill you, no," Blade mused. "But maim you, well, I suppose that's up for debate."

"We have to do something," Isabelle said, struggling against Adam and her own realization that he was right. She couldn't just rush out there heedlessly; she would be playing right into Blade's hands. But what could she do? They had only the dagger Patrick had given her and Adam's sword. She did not even have her bow to make a stand; not that she could have stopped all of them before they overwhelmed her.

Think, Isabelle, think, she chided herself, running through a dozen scenarios. What would Father do?

"Where are the others?" she asked.

Adam gestured outside. "Hiding about the cloister."

"Can you get to the roof without Blade and his men seeing you?" she asked. Adam nodded. "Good, find Helena and take her with you. Be ready for my signal."

Adam frowned but nodded again, slipping silently into the shadows. Isabelle set her hands on the door handle, her breath coming fast and short. She was either going to save her mother or doom them all.

You can do this, she thought, taking a deep breath. *Be braver than you feel.*

"I am coming out," she called, before pushing open the door. She took a few steps forward, her gaze darting over the assembled mercenaries. There were more than there had been when she first entered the chapel, and they flanked the square walkway.

Blade gloated as he jerked his head to the men standing on either side of her. They stepped forward, grabbing her roughly by the arms and holding her fast. She didn't fight them, willing her gaze to stay on Blade. She was pleased to see he had at least suffered a deep cut across one cheek, no doubt Marien's handiwork. She wasn't sure how much time Adam needed to reach Helena and get to the roof, but she hoped it would be sooner rather than later.

"Well, well, little dove," said Blade, moving forward a few feet and dragging Marien along. He lowered the knife but kept a firm grip on her neck. "You're in quite a lot of trouble, trying to fly your coop. See, you cost me a good man on watch, and my men aren't pleased having to roust you out like this."

"Isabelle, run," her mother said, voice low and gravelly. Isabelle didn't meet her gaze, afraid she would lose all resolve at the terror threaded through her voice.

Blade shook Marien roughly. "Nothing out of you. You're not safe yourself."

"Take your hands off her," Isabelle hissed.

Blade met her gaze, deliberately squeezing his fingers tighter. "I will do what I damn well please with this one, and you besides. You're not the one calling the shots here. The Wolf's got you right where he wants you, and your dear da, too. His head will be on a pike before you break your next fast. But that will be the least of your problems when I get done with you. Huntingdon won't be coming to save you now. You're all alone."

"Well, then, it seems we both have a problem," Isabelle said, pushing her voice to the highest corners of the cloister. "Because I did not come alone."

A single arrow sliced through the air, grazing Blade's ear before thudding deep into the grass behind him. He cursed, releasing his grip on Marien to clutch at his injured ear. The prioress took advantage of the momentary distraction and elbowed him hard in the gut, springing toward Isabelle.

Isabelle dropped to the ground, dragging the two guards with her. Their heads met with a crunch, and she rolled out of their grip, whipping the dagger from her boot as she came to her feet. Marien had drawn her own dagger from somewhere in the folds of her habit, and they pressed together, shoulder to shoulder, as the men closed around them in a threatening circle.

"You little bitch," Blade snarled, still holding his ear. A fine trickle of blood ran between two fingers. "I will flay you and your friends alive."

He lurched toward her as another arrow bit into the earth at his feet. Isabelle pressed closer to Marien, flashing her dagger at an approaching mercenary.

"That was your final warning shot," she said. "If you take one more step, my friends will shoot you through the eye. Lucky for you, you still have a spare."

"Search the priory!" Blade shouted. "Tear it apart if you have to, but find whoever dared to take that shot and bring them to me. Alive. And you men, crossbows at the ready. Fire at any shadow that moves."

Marien drew Isabelle under her arm and backed toward the safety of the chapel wall as the men's attention turned to the rooftops. Blade wheeled on the two of them, lifting his dagger and pointing it directly at Isabelle.

"Don't move a muscle. You're not going anywhere. My men will find your friends, and when they do I will make you watch as I strip every inch of flesh from their bones while they scream for death. The Wolf only needs the prioress alive, not you."

"That may be," Isabelle said. "But if you try to stop us now, there is no way you will live to see the outcome. Let us go."

"Never," he said.

"Then it seems we are at an impasse," Isabelle said, heart thumping hard.

"Perhaps I could be of help," said Robin, stepping from the shadows at the far end of the cloister.

CHAPTER
THIRTY-ONE

"**F**ather, no!" Isabelle cried. "It is a trap. You must get out of here now!"

"Darling, of course it's a trap," Robin said. "These sorts of gatherings always are."

"That man is Robert of Huntingdon," Blade called out. "Pretender to the Scottish throne and an enemy of King John. Seize him!"

Robin held up a hand as the men rushed to do his bidding. "I would rather you not," he said. "I just had this tunic spun up in Lincoln and the threads are still fresh. I would be sorely disappointed to ruin it."

The men faltered, taken aback by Robin's casual confidence and friendly tone. Even the most hardened among them glanced toward Blade, conflicted by the shift in the balance of power. Blade snarled out a curse, grabbing for the sleeve of the nearest mercenary and shoving him forward.

"I said seize that man!" he spat.

"I would stay my hand, were I you," Robin said to the mercenary. "If you were to draw your sword, I would necessarily draw my bow, and I do not think you would be pleased with the outcome of such a challenge. Unless you are a fool and do not recognize the Lincoln greens."

The man blanched and stepped back, his sword thunking into its scabbard. Robin gave a satisfied nod as the rest of the men paused, hands still perched on their sword handles. Some of them even drew away from Isabelle and Marien, and Isabelle pressed the advantage by creeping forward, pulling her mother along with her. Blade watched all this with increasing tension, mottled red spots standing out across his face and neck.

"Cowards!" he shouted, brandishing his sword high. "If you will not take him, I will."

Robin's hands moved in a blur as he whipped his bow from his shoulder, nocking an arrow and letting it fly at the mercenary. The white fletching whipped through the short space between them, slicing the tender inner flesh of Blade's sword hand. He cried out, his sword falling to the ground as he cradled his injured hand to his chest.

"You bastard!"

Robin clucked his tongue, lowering his bow but keeping hold of it. "If you are going to enter into a contest of skill, be sure you are the more skilled man. Now, if we are quite through with all this posturing and shouting, perhaps we can discuss our true business this evening."

The men parted farther as Robin strolled toward Isabelle and Marien. Isabelle was not sure if she wanted to throw her arms about him or slap him. Even if he had brought the rest of the Yorkshire camp into the cloister with him, they were vastly outnumbered, their advantage tenuous at best. And yet Robin looked as relaxed and confident as ever, as if he were feasting among the Merry Men and not surrounded by enemies.

Robin's gaze ran over Marien's face in a caress so intimate that, despite their immediate danger, warmth crept up Isabelle's neck. Marien smiled a little, the severity of her expression melting, before she reached her free hand out to briefly touch his chest. In that moment Isabelle would have torn the hearts out of every man there to preserve the thin bonds holding her family together. Robin gave her a wink before pivoting on his heel, spreading his arms wide toward the men.

"What a fine collection of hired swords Sir Roger has gathered for his cause," he called out, his voice rebounding off the cloister walls. Isabelle was surprised it did not wake the sisters sleeping in the dormitory above, but she supposed the wisest among them were keeping the rest well and truly hidden. "Why, such fine soldiers as yourselves must be chafing under the deadweight of playing nursemaid to a handful of pious sisters. Have you not heard there is a war afoot in the country? There is gold to be made for an industrious lot such as yourselves if you were but free to pursue it!"

"Don't think your flowery words will tempt my men, Huntingdon," Blade snarled. "We're sworn to the Wolf and King John. We're not your wood-cutting Merry Men, happy to scamper off into the forest with our tails between our legs. We are real men."

Robin shook his head slowly. "Luck is on your side that I am the Merry Man who heard such insults. Were it Little John, friend, your head would have already bidden a fond farewell to the rest of you."

Blade turned a shade paler at that, but whether from the blood trickling down his hand or Robin's words, Isabelle was not sure. The other mercenaries shifted restlessly, glancing over their shoulders. Robin held his arms wide once again.

"I come with a proposition for anyone wise enough to take it," he said. "It will require nothing of you except to stand aside and let me leave here with my wife and daughter, and in return it will pay out quite handsomely."

Robin drew a sack from his belt, the coins clinking with the promise of wealth. The gathered mercenaries fairly salivated at the sound, their eyes following Robin hungrily as he moved to the center of the grass field in the cloister, giving the sack a shake for good measure.

"I have here two dozen gold pieces," he called out, loud enough that even those beyond the cloister could hear. "And a thousand more waiting with my men outside. Enough to make each of you rich."

Robin turned back toward the mercenaries standing beside Blade. "If you let us leave here unharmed, the gold is yours to split among you as you see fit. That is more of a promise than Sir Roger could ever make you, for even if his king wins his war against the barons, John Lackland is still a desperately broke man. I should think you lot are smart enough to realize a handful of gold today is worth ten times the promise of a coin tomorrow."

The men shifted uneasily, the truth of Robin's words sinking in. The war with the barons started over King John's insatiable appetite for the finer things in life, and he was draining the country's coffers to finance his losing battles in France. What pitiful earnings could they hope to accrue stuffed away in a priory?

"Any fool even considering taking your money would be hanged for treason," Blade said. "The Wolf will see to it himself."

Robin shrugged. "Who among us has not committed a little treason here or there? The king hardly has the wherewithal to consider a crime as petty as treason at this juncture. Last I heard he is on his way to Rochester Castle, hundreds of miles from here. What would the Wolf even know of it?"

"I would know a great deal," came a voice from the far side of the cloister. Isabelle's heart twisted as the glimmer of hope she had been nursing since Robin's appearance was snuffed out by the Wolf's gaunt form emerging from the shadows. Robin stiffened before relaxing back into his wide-legged stance, the moment over so quickly she wasn't sure it had even happened.

"Sir Roger, how kind of you to join us," Robin said.

The Wolf turned his black-eyed scowl on Robin. "I am disappointed, Robert. Look at you. Robin Hood, outlaw king of Sherwood? Though it is the only thing you were ever fit to be king of, a pathetic collection of ragged castoffs fleeing their responsibilities to play about in the woods." He lifted one long finger in Robin's direction, turning his furious gaze on the collected men. "I will double the promised pay to the man who arrests these three in the name of the crown. And you can keep the stolen gold he has promised when I am done with them."

Avarice lit a fire in the eyes of the men surrounding them, and the mercenaries pressed in. Isabelle raised her paltry knife, taking stock of their surroundings. Her gaze flitted up to the roof of the church, where she hoped Adam still stood watch with Helena, but she could not make out any shadows moving up there. She prayed Patrick was keeping Little far away where he could not go charging foolhardy into this fray. What had Robin been thinking?

Robin sighed. "I had hoped we would all prove reasonable men and it would not come to such a juncture. But it seems you lot are swayed only by blunt force. Did you really think I would come so woefully unprepared?"

He lifted the white horn from his belt and blew three short blasts, the sound shattering the night air around them. Shadows detached from the interior walls and materialized into the Lincoln greens as the Merry Men from Yorkshire and Sherwood crowded behind the mercenaries, trapping them in the open courtyard of the cloisters. Some of the mercenaries attempted to draw their weapons but found themselves at the sharp end of a sword instead. Little entered the cloister beside his father, both of them ducking to avoid the low arch of the walkway as they flanked Sir Roger. More figures rose from the pulpy light of dawn along the rooftops, and Isabelle's heart skipped as she recognized Adam's tall form on the church roof. Hope and fear surged through Isabelle in equal measure.

"Impressive, are they not, for a pathetic collection of ragged castoffs?" Robin said dryly. He jangled his sack of coins for emphasis. "Now you men have a choice. You can die for free under Sir Roger's orders, or you can live and line your pockets with enough gold to see yourselves comfortably back to France, well out of John Lackland's reach. Seems an easy enough choice to me, though perhaps I am spoiled by the luxury of living."

The answer was obvious across the calculating expressions of the mercenaries. With the exception of Blade—who had retrieved his sword and now held it in his left hand, the injured one tucked into the side of his hauberk—the men were already lowering their crossbows and resheathing their swords. Robin loosened the straps on the coin bag and tossed a few pieces to the nearest mercenaries, sealing their fate. The men at the fringes edged past the Merry Men, slipping away. Isabelle took firm hold of her mother's hand, hardly daring to breathe.

"Do not leave this courtyard!" the Wolf shouted, rage enlivening his features. Little and Allan A'Dale moved forward a step, their staffs hovering over the thin man's shoulders. "Do not play into their foolish attempts at bargaining. If you abandon your posts now, I will find you all and hang you for treason against the crown. Hold your positions!"

But the mercenaries did not even hesitate as they filed out of the cloisters, the blades of their weapons growing cold in their sheaths. They knew a better deal when one was presented.

"And that is what comes of buying your loyalty," Robin said, sauntering off the grass toward Isabelle and Marien.

"If you think you have outwitted me, Huntingdon, you are a fool," the Wolf hissed. "I will tear every stone from every town in the whole damned countryside and turn every poor villager out of their stinking hovels until I find you. And when I do, I will make you rue each braggartly word you just spewed. You are a vermin to be extinguished, and I will purge your kind with fire."

"I should think the only vermin that will need extinguishing are the ones that infest the prison cell you shall shortly find yourself in," Robin said, his expression turning hard. "I have already sent word to Robert Fitzwalter and the rebel barons that King John's most valued advisor has been taken prisoner and awaits their judgment."

"Your pathetic impudence knows no limit," the Wolf hissed. "I would never submit to your crude attempt at peasant justice."

"Oh, by all means, put up a good fight," Robin said, spreading his hands wide. "The Merry Men would be happy to give you a demonstration of their peasant justice."

The Merry Men sent up a deafening cheer at the steel in their master's voice, lifting their swords and bows aloft as a current of wild energy shot through each man gathered. Isabelle let out her own elated whoop, raising her dagger in triumph. The mercenaries who had not yet left braced against the unbridled recklessness of her cry, their hands automatically shifting to their weapons. It did not escape Isabelle's attention that they were still in a tightly confined space with two warring factions, and she attempted to rein in her joviality.

"Let us return to Sherwood, Father," she said, loudly enough to set the mercenaries' minds at ease. "And leave Sir Roger to the rebel barons."

"That is a splendid idea," Robin said expansively. "Marien, my love, what a perfect daughter you have raised."

"She has far too many of your tendencies to be perfect," Marien said, but she smiled.

Isabelle tucked the borrowed knife into the top of her boot and took her father's hand, linking their little family. She smiled, a warmth she had never known suffusing her chest despite the menace of the remaining mercenaries. Her family was at last whole.

A flicker of movement over Robin's shoulder caught her attention, drawing her eye to where the Wolf stood. He snatched the crossbow of the nearest mercenary, lifting it level with Robin's exposed back.

"Damn you to hell, Hood," he hissed, just before firing.

CHAPTER
THIRTY-TWO

The bolt shot out with a *crack*, and Isabelle only had time to jerk Robin's arm to the side before it struck, the tip driving through his back and protruding from his shoulder. He grunted and slumped forward, dragging her down to the ground. Blood spattered against her tunic.

"Father!" she gasped.

It proved to be the opening note of a violent symphony as the walkways around them erupted in fighting. The Merry Men fell on the mercenaries, fighting their way toward the Wolf even as he disappeared into the shadows surrounding the cloister. The peace of the grassy enclosure shattered, filled with the ring of clashing swords and shrill battle cries. Marien knelt beside Isabelle, and together they pulled Robin into the relative safety of the chapel doors.

"Damn that poxed cur," Robin grunted, holding one hand to his shoulder even as Isabelle tried to support him. Marien knelt by his side, her expression calm as she took on the role of healer, her fingers making quick work to assess the extent of his wound.

"It is a clean shot, no bone," she said, as if this were another farmer impaled on a thresher and not her husband shot by a crossbow. "Can you breathe?"

"Not bloody well," Robin groused, but he staggered to his feet. Isabelle looped his good arm over her shoulder, wrapping her arm around his back to support him as he took a step. The Merry Men had formed a protective ring around them, shoulder to shoulder as the mercenaries put their considerable skill to work. The bag of gold had fallen to his feet, but Isabelle did not bother to pick it up.

"My bow," Robin wheezed, already reaching for the quiver across his back. He winced with the movement, and Marien put a firm hand on his shoulder to stop him.

"You cannot fight right now," she said. "If you do not tend the wound, you could risk greater injury. We need to get you to the infirmary. I have supplies there."

"I am not leaving my men," Robin said, setting his teeth in a grimace.

"I will stay," Isabelle said.

"Absolutely not," Marien and Robin said simultaneously.

"I am fine," Robin continued, though his skin had paled considerably and a faint sheen stood out along his brow. "It is not the worst I have had to fight through."

"You are not staying, either," Marien said in her best prioress tone. It brooked no argument from the sisters, and it seemed to have a similar effect on the king of the outlaws. "You will both come with me to the infirmary."

Isabelle drew in a breath and straightened her shoulders, careful not to jostle her father. "I am staying here. I will not leave my friends until I see them to safety. Besides, no one knows the secret ins and outs of the priory like I do. Not even you, Mother. I can protect the men."

"I will not let the Wolf lay a hand on you ever again," said Robin.

"Neither will I," Isabelle replied. "Please trust me, both of you. I can do this."

Marien and Robin shared a long look, an unspoken communication flowing in the quirk of Robin's eyebrows and the press of Marien's lips. Isabelle knew her mother well enough to understand the struggle playing out over her features, but she was surprised at how easily she could read Robin's thoughts in the minor tics of his face. Finally Marien gave a little huff.

"Entirely too much like you to be perfect," she said.

Robin smiled, grimacing again. "Lead them well, love."

Isabelle gave him a determined nod, gently moving his arm to drape it over Marien's shoulders. Her mother pulled him in close, wrapping her arm around his waist to support him. He leaned in close to her, lifting his nose just enough to breathe in the scent of her hair. Something in the movement brought a lump to Isabelle's throat, but she pressed it down and tapped the shoulder of the nearest outlaw.

"Follow them to the infirmary," she said. "Do not let anything happen to them."

"Aye," the man said with a nod. They ducked to the outskirts of the walkways, dodging swinging cudgels and whistling swords as they went. Isabelle held her breath as she watched them reach the far end of the cloister and disappear toward the infirmary.

Everywhere arrows and swords flew with brutal efficiency, each slicing of flesh and crunching of bone sharp and distinct. A few prone forms littered the open space of the cloister, the blades of grass torn and matted with blood. Frantically, Isabelle scanned the faces of the fallen for any familiar features, her feet frozen into immobility as the savagery of battle stormed around her. It was one thing to promise Robin that she could protect the Merry Men, but how could she hope to lead them to safety?

Someone shouted her name as she stood there by the chapel doors, rooted to the ground. She turned her head dumbly as the sound came nearer, and just caught sight of Adam dropping down several feet away, his expression a warning as someone grabbed her from behind.

"Got you, little bitch," Blade growled in her ear, dragging her back even as he pressed a blade to her throat with his uninjured hand. "I don't care what the Wolf's said now. This one's for me. I'm going to enjoy your blood on my hands."

You have faced outlaws, soldiers, mercenaries, and the king's own right hand, said a firm voice in Isabelle's head. *You will not be brought low by this pig scum.*

Isabelle grabbed his good hand with both of hers and pulled down, sinking her teeth into the meaty pad of his thumb. They ripped through layers of flesh as warm blood slicked over her tongue. Blade howled in pain as she executed the maneuver Adam had taught her, stepping behind and throwing him to the ground, her knee landing hard in his gut. She spat his blood back on him as Adam reached them, sword pointed to Blade's throat.

"Give me a bloody reason," he said, eyes burning.

"Go to hell," Blade snarled, lurching for Isabelle again.

"Good enough," Adam said, driving his sword deep into Blade's gut. Isabelle fell back with a half cry, the grunt of Blade's last breath already embedding itself in her memory. The mercenary's jaw went slack, his eyes rolling back in his head as he slumped back down to the ground. Adam had been so fast, so brutally efficient. Isabelle shook with the violence of it as he drew his sword out, wiping the blood on Blade's sleeve with a grimace.

"We need to get the men out of here," Adam said.

But Isabelle could not stop looking at Blade. Could not stop tasting the lingering tang of his blood on her tongue. Adam glanced back at her, taking her hand in a tight grip as he stood.

"Isabelle?" he said, his voice gentle but insistent.

The sound of her name on his lips brought her back to the present. "Where are Patrick and Helena?" she asked, willing the tremor out of her voice.

Adam pointed to the roof, where a wave of outlaws descended on the open melee. Helena hurtled into the thick of the fighting, a blur of dark green as her short sword caught a mercenary's blade in a down strike. Faster than he could regroup, she spun, her sword arcing around and slicing into his exposed armpit. He grunted at the impact, bringing his other arm down hard on her shoulder. Helena dropped to one knee, hand whipping to her belt to pull a small knife. She spun again, driving the knife up into his belly. The man crumpled in half as his hose darkened with blood.

Patrick still crouched on the roof, his bow arm blurring as he fired shot after shot into the mercenaries, picking off one man just as he raised a cudgel over Helena's head. She lifted her sword to Patrick in thanks before swinging it at the next man, catching him in the gut. Little fought beside his father, a head taller than everyone else on the field. The mercenaries were no match for the sword Little now wielded, his height lending a savage crunch to the sound of the blade as it drove down into the shoulder of his opponent. The man clutched at the wound and fell to the ground crying out, a spray of red coating the grass at his feet.

Isabelle pressed forward to where Helena and Little fought, ducking under a swinging cudgel as Adam brought his sword up to meet the blow, driving the man back. "Helena!" she shouted. "Little! We need to get the men out of here!"

"How?" Helena called back. "The pigs have the exit."

"There is a door behind the altar in the chapel," Isabelle called, dodging under the blade of one mercenary even as another swung a cudgel back, knocking the first unconscious. "If Patrick and the others can pin them down from the roofs, we can escape through the door and barricade it from outside. Then we can make it to the orchard wall."

"We don't know if John's still holding it," Little shouted.

As if summoned by his name, the big man came barreling into the fray, wielding his staff with a great roar that rattled the priory stones. He shook off four men, knocking them senseless and giving another great battle cry. He was fearsome enough a sight that even the most scarred of the mercenaries blanched at his appearance.

"I guess that answers that," Little said, swinging a fist into someone.

"Helena, get to Patrick!" Isabelle commanded, already running toward the chapel doors. "Little, get your father and fetch the men. I'll secure the door!"

The others nodded as she sprinted through the field, slipping on the slick grass and falling once to her knee, her hand coming up red from the grass. It was enough to turn her stomach, the crumpled bodies and metallic scent of blood, not knowing who it came from as it mixed on the sacred green of the cloister. This place, dedicated to prayer and healing, now desecrated with the base violence of man. There was no penance, no litany of prayers she could offer to make up for what had been done. Neither would her spiritual guilt help save the men still standing, so she steeled herself and kept running, crossbow bolts whizzing past her ear like wasps.

The chapel doors stood partially open as she had left them what seemed like hours ago. The interior was dim, the orange edge of dawn spreading its long fingers down the wall from the high windows overhead. Isabelle sprinted down the length of the pews to the altar, eyes whipping to either side for any sign of hidden attackers. She leapt onto the altar with a quick sign of the cross, tearing aside the drapings to locate the door tucked into the back wall.

"Come on," she muttered, scraping her nails along the stone. Not even her mother knew about the door, and Isabelle had only found it by accident while taking a prolonged break from scrubbing the flagstones. What it had been used for previously she could not imagine, but it would serve her purposes well now.

"There!" she grunted, her fingers falling into the slight grooved edge of the door. She dug her fingers in hard, her joints aching against the strain of trying to pull the stone loose. The door slid forward a few inches, scraping over the ground as the rusted hinges groaned against the intrusion.

"Open, damn you," she muttered, setting one boot against the wall and heaving back with all her might.

"Such language in a church," said a voice behind her. She nearly lost her grip whipping her head around, drawing her leg in to reach for her knife, but Adam stood behind her grinning. "How many prayers of penance will that be?"

Six other Merry Men stood behind him, panting as they crowded around the altar. Two of the men were being carried by their friends, their heads bloodied and hanging down. Isabelle dug her fingers farther into the opening and dragged the door the rest of the way open.

"Out this way and west to the orchard wall," she commanded. "Did John leave it open?"

"Aye, I'm to lead the men out and post watch," said one of the men. "The archers have got the mercenaries pinned down outside, and we're getting the wounded out quick as we can. Not that there's as many of us as there are of them."

"What about the Wolf?" Isabelle asked. "Where is he?"

"I'll find him," Adam said, already heading toward the chapel doors.

Isabelle sucked in a breath as the men ducked out of the hidden door, more trickling in through the church entry. The fighting had died down outside, no doubt thanks to Helena and Patrick's efforts, but she knew where the Wolf would go. "Adam, wait! The infirmary. We have to get to the infirmary."

"Little!" Adam called to the chapel doors, where the tall boy was just making his appearance. "Watch the door and make sure the men get to safety."

Little gave a wave of acknowledgment, taking up his position as another group of Merry Men filtered in through the entrance.

"The men will be all right?" Isabelle asked, following after Adam.

"I'll see to them," Little said. "You've done a brilliant thing here, Isabelle. You're saving our hides tonight."

"Thank you," Isabelle said to both of them, overwhelmed for a moment.

"No thanks needed among brothers," Little said. "Or sisters, you know."

Isabelle flashed him a small smile as they passed out of the chapel into the cloister. A hail of arrows rained down from the roof just as they emerged, striking the chain mail armor of the mercenaries still left. Isabelle raced down the covered archways under the dormitory toward the far end of the cloister, Adam shielding her from the fighting. She veered to the right in the direction of the infirmary.

"Wait," she said, stopping before the door to the chapter house. "I need my bow. I left it here earlier."

"Be quick about it," Adam said, turning toward the fighting and brandishing his sword. "I'll guard the door."

Isabelle nodded, slipping into the dark room. It took a moment for her eyes to adjust, but enough light came through the small window that she could just see the curve of her bow propped against a far corner of the wall beside the desk. She took the bow and quiver, slinging both over her shoulder. The stacks of letters stirred as she passed, and she paused as one fluttered open, the very same letter she had picked up before Sister Catherine appeared. The wax seal was broken in half, nothing more than a colorless blob in the dim light. A fragment of the seal caught her attention and she bent down to inspect the figure stamped into the cold wax. A wolf's head, broken clean through the middle.

Isabelle snatched the letter up and scanned the contents, only catching bits and phrases like *keep the prioress and her child ignorant of your machinations* and *you shall make a far greater prioress than her*. Sister Catherine had been corresponding with the Wolf. She probably threw the doors open herself for the mercenaries when they arrived. But Isabelle's heart stumbled and raced as her gaze trailed to the last paragraph of the tightly looped script.

I thank you for the service you have done your king and your country, most especially the loyalty you have shown me. Were it not for you, my darling, Robert of Huntingdon and his brood of traitors would have gone undiscovered, left to foment their revolution in the quiet of your sacred priory.

"It cannot be," she breathed, the letter drifting out of her hands to the desk. Sister Catherine had betrayed them. It had not been Isabelle's confrontation with the soldier; somehow Sister Catherine had discovered their secret, and brought the Wolf down on them.

"Mother," she breathed, before racing out of the chamber and tearing past a surprised Adam, willing her feet to carry her faster to the infirmary before the Wolf and Sister Catherine could reach them.

CHAPTER

THIRTY-THREE

A dam called after Isabelle, but she did not hear him as she sped
up, could not hear anything but the pounding of her feet and
the breath exploding from her lungs and the refrain playing like a
litany. *It cannot be, it cannot be.*

The passage stretched out interminably before her, and the
harder she ran, the farther away the door to the infirmary became.
Adam's steps echoed distantly behind her, but she was going too
fast for him to catch up. Sister Catherine could not have escaped
the chapter house without anyone noticing, could she? The Wolf
could not have slipped through the Merry Men's fingers. Surely
her mother and father were safe. But the rationalizations felt more
like a plea, and they did nothing to settle the erratic beat of her
heart or the fear hazing her thoughts.

Her first indication that something was wrong was the slumped
form lying halfway through the infirmary door keeping it propped
open. She recognized the Lincoln greens with mounting dread and
did not need to see his face to know it was the outlaw she had sent
to take care of Robin. She stopped only long enough to check that
he still had a pulse before stumbling over his legs to get through
the door. A cramped stairwell spiraled up to the infirmary.

Isabelle had the wherewithal to draw an arrow from the quiver so hastily slung over her shoulder and nock it to her bow, though she could not draw her elbow back in the narrow passage. Her ragged breathing bounced off the close stone walls, but her feet made no sound in their soft leather boots as she ascended the stairs. A clatter and crash of breaking glass tinkled down from the room above. Her heart pounded so hard it made her chest hurt, but she willed her steps to slow as she reached the top, something solid striking the ground with a curse.

Isabelle lifted her bow as she cleared the stairwell, steeling herself for whatever scene she might find. In the far left corner Marien struggled with Sister Catherine, a knife clasped in the sister's hand as she tried her best to strike at Marien. Isabelle's mother deftly deflected each blow, but she followed the glistening blade with sharp eyes. Sister Catherine bumped into a healing table beside her, knocking more glass bottles onto the floor and releasing their pungent woodland aromas.

Isabelle swung her bow from one corner to the next, where the Wolf and Robin stood only inches apart, sword blades locked together. A heavy sheen of sweat covered Robin's face, and his skin had gone an ashy gray, the dark stain of blood across his shoulder dipping down toward his belt. He leaned forward on his sword, trying to use his body weight to force the Wolf back. But his injury limited his motion, and Sir Roger managed to sidestep Robin's blade.

"Stop!" Isabelle shouted, her voice ringing out as she drew back on the bowstring. She leveled the arrow tip at the Wolf's chest. "Or I will shoot you through the heart."

"Shoot him, and your traitorous mother dies," Sister Catherine called from the other side of the room, where she had finally gained the advantage, the knife pressed against Marien's neck.

Isabelle swung the bow toward Sister Catherine. "Then I shall shoot you first."

"Shoot her and I will see you all burn," rasped the Wolf. "You should have burned in that fire sixteen years ago, Huntingdon. You cannot stop the destiny of the mighty. You are but a handful against an army of thousands."

"We do not have to stop an army of thousands," said Isabelle, narrowing her attention on Sister Catherine. "Just you."

She released her bowstring as Adam burst from the stairs, hurtling toward the Wolf. The arrow caught the sister in the shoulder, ripping her away from Marien. The dagger clattered to the ground and Isabelle rushed to her mother as Adam and Robin turned on Sir Roger. Adam had the advantage of height and youth, and with Robin's help disarmed the nobleman, forcing him to his knees at swordpoint. Robin swayed on his feet but stayed upright.

Isabelle pushed past the broken bottles on the floor to her mother, pulling her into a hug and drawing her away from where Sister Catherine lay on the floor moaning.

"Are you all right, Mother?" she asked frantically.

"Yes, of course, I am perfectly fine," she said, drawing Isabelle in. "What a foolish, brave thing you have done. Thank goodness you have your father's tendencies."

"You will never get away with this," spat the Wolf, his black eyes coming alive with the heat of his wrath. "The barons could never hope to defeat King John. And when he quashes their petty rebellion and imprisons every last one of them for their mutiny, I will gladly pull the ropes that strangle your wife and daughter. Hanging will be a kindness compared to what I will do to you."

"What a terribly menacing thing to say," Robin huffed, some color returning to his face. "Now I shall not visit you in prison.

Unless the barons choose a more permanent punishment for you. Then I shall be front row with my best Lincoln greens on."

The Wolf's eyes blazed. "You would not dare."

"I very much would." Robin lowered himself into a crouch, unmindful of the wound pulsing in his shoulder. Isabelle made to rush over to him, but Marien held her back. "You should have let Robert of Huntingdon stay dead, Sir Roger. But now you have earned the wrath of Robin Hood, and he is a rather vengeful fellow."

"And yet too much of a coward to kill me himself," the Wolf said.

Robin smiled. "Death will be a kindness compared to what the barons will do to you."

He straightened up, nodding at Adam. "Find Little John. I have a feeling Sir Roger will require his considerable skills to cooperate."

"I will never cooperate!" Sir Roger snarled, surging up from his kneeling position with the flash of a stiletto knife drawn from the hidden folds of his tunic. He fell on Robin, both of them crashing to the ground with the knife pinned between them. Adam gave a shout, grabbing the Wolf by his collar and hauling him back, but already a sticky pool of blood glued their tunics together, dripping between them as the fabric separated.

"Father!" Isabelle cried, crunching through broken glass to reach Robin. Her hands hovered over his chest, shaking too much to find the source of the bleeding. "Where is it? Where is the wound?"

"Not on me," Robin grunted, nodding toward where the Wolf slumped against Adam's hold. The hilt of the stiletto protruded from his chest, driven up at a sharp angle into his heart. Blood leaked around the handle, staining the front of his tunic as his mouth hung slack and his eyes rolled toward the ceiling.

"Is he . . ." Isabelle could not bring herself to finish the question, but Adam gave her a grim nod as he lowered the body to the ground.

"Shame," Robin said, his voice faint. "Fitzwalter will be disappointed he missed the opportunity to kill Sir Roger himself."

"Oh, Father!" Isabelle threw her arms around him, drawing back when he grunted painfully. "What is it? Are you all right?"

"Just my shoulder, love," he groaned, giving her a pained smile. "I should think it will require a great deal of rest and relaxation to recuperate."

"And a few barrelfuls of ale," Adam added.

A primal scream ripped through the infirmary as Sister Catherine staggered to her feet, her brown eyes slitted and glowering in her pale face. Isabelle gripped the handle of her bow, her fingers finding their way to the string as the sister dragged herself across the worktable.

"You ruined everything I worked so hard to build," she hissed at Isabelle. "That soldier should have struck you down instead of putting you in that pathetic potato cellar. I told Sir Roger he was weak."

Isabelle drew back sharply. "You set the soldier on me?"

"You and your mother left me no choice," Sister Catherine spat. Her eyes cut to Marien, hatred pulsing like a heartbeat in her words. "I found one of your disgusting letters in Rosamund's things after she died. I knew all about your shameful, traitorous past. I warned her the night you showed up at our door, *with child*, that you would bring nothing but trouble to our sacred priory. But of course she did not listen, and instead she allowed you to poison our community with your treachery. When you forced us to open to the villagers—allowing strangers on our hallowed grounds!—it was too far. I was the only one brave enough to stop you."

"By bringing a murderer to the priory!" Isabelle exclaimed, heat rising within her. "My mother did not poison anything, it was you who poisoned the sisters. Against her, against me, against everything the order is supposed to stand for. The villagers needed us, they needed our healing, our food, our care. But all you cared for was yourself! For too long you have stolen joy from every possible moment of our lives, but I am not afraid of you. You are small and cruel, and your cruelty has no place here."

Sister Catherine glared at her. "How dare you, you impudent little—"

"Isabelle is right," Marien said, her voice tired but firm. "I have tried to look past your constant attempts to undermine my work as prioress, to try and find the good within you. But you have buried it too deep. Or perhaps it was never there to begin with. But you no longer have a place at Kirklees, Catherine."

"I no longer . . ." Sister Catherine lurched back from the table, drawing herself upright. "I was here long before you, and I will be here long after!"

Isabelle drew up her bow even as Sister Catherine raised her arm, the knife clutched in her white fingers. It arced away from her as the arrow hit her square in the chest, but Isabelle could only hear the sister land with a muffled thud as Robin pushed her out of the way, the knife slicing between them and clattering to the ground behind her.

"Isabelle, are you all right?" he gasped, sounding truly terrified.

"Are you injured?" her mother asked, her face appearing over Robin's shoulder.

"Yes, I mean, no," Isabelle said, her hands shaking. "I am all right. I did not mean to . . . she was going to hurt us."

A burble of laughter sounded from the other side of the table, and the four of them moved forward to where the sister lay in a spreading pool of sticky blood. Foamy red spittle bubbled up over her lips as she laughed again, her chest spasming with the effort. She looked to Marien, her dimming eyes full of hate.

"An eye for an eye," she wheezed on another laugh. "A lover for a lover. The blade was dipped in hemlock. It needs but one cut." Isabelle frowned, turning to her mother, but Marien was no longer looking at Sister Catherine. The color drained from her mother's face as she lurched forward to catch Robin before he crashed to the ground. They crumpled in a heap together, Robin's weight dragging Marien down as Isabelle dropped to her knees beside them.

"Father!" she said, hands fluttering over his face and neck. "What is it?"

"Robert, no," Marien said, her voice a hush of horror at the thin red line of blood welling up on his neck.

"The knife," Isabelle said, her mind skittering to a halt. What had Sister Catherine said about the knife? *Dipped in hemlock.* "Hemlock! Mother, the knife was poisoned with hemlock."

"I know," Marien said, cradling Robin's head in her lap. Her voice was distant, her hands smoothing his brow.

"We must do something!" Isabelle cried.

"What can we do?" Adam asked. "What do you need?"

Isabelle shook her head, trying to remember the distant, failed lessons with her mother. "Hemlock, what does hemlock do? Something about the liver? No, is that henbane? It is the muscles. The heart! Hemlock stops the heart! If we could find something to . . . I do not know, to keep his heart beating, or make it beat faster? Mother, please help me! I cannot . . . I am not the healer. I need you."

"Isabelle," her mother said. She looked into her daughter's eyes, her own glittering like the infinite deep of the seas, and it was in that abyss Isabelle knew. There was no cure.

"Marien . . . my love . . . we were so close," Robin wheezed.

Marien smiled, tears coursing down her cheeks. "We always were, my dearest heart."

Robin's skin had paled considerably, and his chest shuddered with each labored breath. His eyes drifted to Isabelle, and he used what little control he had of his facial muscles to twist his mouth into a wry smile. "Oh, Isabelle, I am so very sorry."

Isabelle shook her head, her throat closing and her eyes burning. "No, Father. I will not let you leave me. Not after all it has cost me to find you."

Robin's eyes drifted closed, and he lifted them again with effort. "I do not regret a single thing in my life that has brought me to you. The love I have carried for both of you has sustained me through all these hard years. You have made me Robin Hood."

Isabelle took his hand, the tendons tight and brittle. "Father, please. Please, do not leave me."

Robin dragged a labored breath in, his eyes drifting shut again. The lids fluttered, but stayed closed. "You must know . . . how proud . . . you have made me."

She squeezed Robin's hand as a sob rose from her core, his pulse jumping erratically under her fingertips, slow and then fast and then painfully slow again. She squeezed his fingers as hard as she could, as if she could infuse her own life back into his flesh and open his eyes, hear his laugh one more time. Marien bent down and pressed her lips against his, her tears falling down his cheeks.

"Goodbye, my love," she whispered.

Robin took a ragged, shallow breath in, the air sliding out of him on a sigh. Isabelle waited as a hollowness opened in the center of her chest, threatening to drown her in its darkness as the seconds stretched out into eternities. But his chest did not rise again.

THIRTY-FOUR

The day of Robin's burial dawned leaden and somber, the clouds hanging low as the sky wore its own mourning in swaths of gray against the pale sunlight. Isabelle slipped out of the hidden door of the chapel, still swept open from the Merry Men's hasty escape the day before. The Merry Men had routed the mercenaries from the premises just as dawn broke, their cheering turned to ashes in their mouths as it fell to Isabelle to share the news of Robin's death. She had sat vigil through the night with her mother as they wrapped Robin's body in clean linens with the help of a few of the sisters who offered, and laid him out on a simple wooden litter.

Fatigue like a deep well pulled at every part of her so that each thought and action moved with the thickness of honey, the weight of them suffocating. She walked on silent feet into the orchard. The oak tree held court in the far corner, the wide leaves already taking flight on the late-autumn wind for far-flung destinations. Isabelle pushed the branches aside and stepped under the protective canopy of the tree, the branches twisting around one another above. The heavy wool of her habit shielded her from the bitter

cold of the morning, though her feet were numb. The branches of
the oak scratched at her shoulder as she approached the trunk, her
heart as numb as her limbs.

Nestled in a shallow hollow of the trunk was a collection of
small wooden figurines, each crafted with a keen eye and a loving
hand. Knights on horses with lances raised in triumph, ladies with
billowing skirts waving brightly colored favors, jesters pulling hilar-
ious faces. Baubles gifted to her from a batty old peddler, always
passing through, always knowing exactly what she needed to cheer
her most. The sisters were not allowed personal possessions, so
she had tucked them into the hollow of the tree for safekeeping,
away from the prying eyes of those loyal to Catherine, who would
gladly have turned her over for an extra glass of wine with their
supper.

They had been her companions through the lonely passage
of childhood, these exquisite figurines, telling her stories of the
greater world. A world of color and joy instead of chores and piety.
Only now did she know they told her a different story entirely, of
a father's love and longing for what he could never have. For what
she would never have again.

She wanted to scream, but her throat was too raw, her eyes too
hot, and her lungs too heavy. She closed her fingers in a tight fist
around the figurine of the knight and smashed it against the tree,
her knuckles bruising and the skin breaking as she pounded her
fist against the trunk over and over, growling through her teeth as
she tore her fingers. The tip of the lance bit into her palm, embedding itself deeper with every blow.

"Why?" she cried out to the oak, her hands opening and dragging
along the bark as she sank to her knees. The figurine rolled to the
ground, the knight helpless on his side.

She dropped her forehead to her thighs, curling in a tight ball as if she could compress the pain raging through her. Here in this magical spot where she once dared to dream she now allowed herself to grieve, sobbing into the rough wool of her robes. The cold ground numbed the pain of her bloodied knuckles, and she dug her fingers into the dirt.

"I am so sorry," she sobbed, shaking. "Take me, please. Take me instead."

But the magic of the oak floated away with its leaves, leaving nothing to answer Isabelle's plea.

Marien took Isabelle by the hand as Little John, Allan A'Dale, Little, and Adam took up the stretcher and carried it through the priory toward the orchard. She said nothing of the blood crusted over Isabelle's knuckles, only held her fingers gently in her own cool hands. The Merry Men crowded the spaces between the trees, their faces pale as their master passed. Isabelle felt the weight of their gazes, for the moment crowding out her own thoughts as they passed out of the orchard into the woods.

The men stopped at the edge of the clearing, lowering the litter as Helena and Patrick stepped from the crowd to meet them. Helena looked small and fragile for the first time since Isabelle had met her, her black hair unbound and flowing down her back, in a simple dress of green wool belted at the waist with her short swords. Even with her weapons belt, the flowing lines of her hair and the dress lent a softness to her features.

Helena held out a longbow to Isabelle. She took the smooth wood in both hands, the bow surprisingly light for its great length. It stood taller than her, shaped for Robin's height and arm strength. A tremor rippled through her hands as she touched the string, as if the last vibration of its former master passed through her. Patrick presented her with a single arrow, fletched with snow-white feathers.

For a moment she could only hold the bow in one hand and the arrow in the other, as if her mind could not put the two objects together. They felt so foreign, the bow much larger and the string carrying more tension than she was used to. What right had she to wield it? She turned to her mother, holding them out.

"You should shoot it," Isabelle said, her voice small.

Marien took her by the shoulders, pressing a kiss to her forehead. She blinked back a wave of tears, one trembling over the edge of her lashes to course down her cheek. "He would want you to do it, dearest. I have faith in you."

She turned from her mother to face the great expanse of trees ahead, the deepest wells and thickets of her childhood within their depths. She nocked the arrow to the string and lifted the bow to the unblemished expanse of the sky, her arm trembling with the force required to draw the string back. The arrow arced out with a great hum, tearing across the heavens and piercing the deep green of the woods in the distance.

"To the west, Merry Men," Little John called out in his deep voice.

The sun had risen to its apex in the murky sky by the time they reached the arrow. It landed in a small clearing, the trees parting just enough to allow the sunlight to dapple the brittle grass beside a trickling stream. It was a beautiful and fitting spot in Isabelle's estimation, quiet and far removed from the town and the priory. The men set about their task of digging Robin's grave with a solemnity the sisters would have envied, their spades biting into the earth in a rhythmic harmony.

Marien looked almost fragile in her grief, her eyes bluer and her long blond hair paling in the week since Isabelle first fled Kirklees. Isabelle had rarely seen her without a veil covering the long locks, and it shocked her how much they were like her own. Deep lines etched around Marien's eyes and mouth, and though she looked calm, Isabelle knew her mother well enough to see the dull edge to her energy as she waved away the men's offers to find her a comfortable place to sit.

Despite the similarities in their hair, Isabelle didn't imagine she looked anything like Marien at the moment. She couldn't remember the last time she'd washed her face, and dark circles of insomnia pressed under her eyes. Her fingers were cold and stiff, a sure sign of impending rain. She felt as if she'd aged a hundred years in a few days and her brittle bones would snap in a breeze.

The men finished digging and took up the litter, standing over the deep hole. Allan stepped forward, intoning a prayer as they lowered Robin's body into the ground. Each of the men took a handful of dirt, standing at the four corners of the grave with their hands extended.

"To my greatest friend, Robin," said Allan, "who gave me purpose when I thought I had reached my end. Most of us came to this life as desperate men, fleeing the law and abandoning what home we had for a cold dirt bed and an empty belly. Robin took us in and forgave us our pasts, and in turn made us better men than we could ever have been on our own. He inspired us to inspire the people, and for that I'll always be grateful."

He opened his hand, the black earth crumbling over the white sheet in little patters. Little John cleared his throat.

"Robin was a blustering, maddening, brilliant bastard," he said, and several of the men chuckled in agreement. "He could get blind drunk and shoot straighter than anyone, he always found the last cask of wine in the high sheriff's stores, and I never saw him pass a mother or child he didn't give a coin to if he had one. And if he didn't have one, he bloody well remembered their names and brought two round later. To Robin, the true king of Sherwood."

He dropped his dirt into the grave, bits of the earth sticking to his palm as he lowered his hand.

Adam held out his hand, struggling to hold back the emotion rippling over his features. He swallowed once, forcefully, before speaking. "Robin saved me when I thought I was beyond it. When I thought I was beyond anything. I was only alive before him, not really living. The Merry Men have given me a purpose I didn't think I deserved. May you have tricked your way through the pearly gates, Robin."

Each of the men stepped up to deliver their own wishes for their fallen master, filing past Isabelle one by one. A dozen of them, and then a dozen more, until Isabelle lost track of their individual stories and they blended together in a tapestry of love and loyalty and loss. The grave was nearly filled when the last of them had paid their respects, the earth soft and loamy. The men piled rocks over the fresh grave to keep out foraging creatures, the rectangle of stones the only marker for the great man who lay beneath them.

When the last of the stones had been laid, Marien gave Isabelle's hand a squeeze before letting it go to kneel before the grave. She whispered a few short words, the moment so intimate that many of the men respectfully turned their eyes from the scene. Isabelle found that she could not look away from her mother's bowed head, her curls glistening with a fine mist that had begun to fall. When she rose again, it was slowly, her hand still lingering low as if to keep touching the earth forever.

Several moments passed before Isabelle became aware of the press of dozens of gazes on her, the attention of the men turned toward her expectantly. She looked from her mother to the others, at a loss for what she should say or do. What did they expect of her? What could she say that would heal the wound she had caused? She stepped forward, lacing her fingers together to keep them from shaking.

"I find myself at a loss for words, which may surprise some of you," she said, glancing at Adam, who gave her a tilted smile. "You all knew Robin so much better than I. All I had of him were a few precious moments. And now they shall have to last me a lifetime."

The words stuck in her throat, lodged there like a dam that protected her from a flood she couldn't bear to face. She swallowed hard and continued.

"But what I did learn from Robin in those moments was that we do not have to let the constraints of our past define our future. My father was born a nobleman, but he rejected power and wealth and chose instead the earth as his bed and the stars as his roof. He fought for those oppressed by men he once called peers." She took in a shaky breath. "He gave up his life to protect those he loved. I could not possibly live up to such a legacy, but it is the very least I owe him to try. Whatever the rest of the country may think of him, I am proud to be his daughter."

She stepped forward, laying her hand on the stones covering his grave. "I love you, Father," she whispered.

When she straightened, Allan was there beside her, holding out the great curved horn Robin had carried. The last time she had seen Robin blow it, he had raised the Merry Men to save her from the Wolf. How many lifetimes ago did that feel now, only a day later?

"You must blow the horn, Isabelle," Allan said, and for a moment his tone was so gentle, so like her father's, that it pierced her through.

"Why me?" she asked.

"Because you are his kin. It is your right."

She reached fearful hands out for the polished surface, taking it from Allan. It was heavier than she expected, the curved sides thick and smooth and narrowing as they curled around toward the mouthpiece. She lifted it to her mouth, taking a deep breath before closing her eyes and wishing her father on to the afterlife as she blew with all her strength.

"To Robin Hood!" the men shouted around her, lifting their swords into the air. Allan gave her a nod, and again she blew on the horn as they called out, the sound echoing through the woods. When she blew the third and final time, just as Robin had done in the priory, the leaves rustled and carried the cry of Robin Hood until it seemed the very trees took up the call.

Isabelle stood alone beside the pile of stones marking her father's grave, a humble resting place for such a legendary man. The Merry Men had dispersed to procure food for the evening's feast, their mood carried along by a sense of purpose. Her mother spoke with Allan and John, both of the big men bowing their heads reverentially to the prioress. Patrick and Little gathered wood for the cooking fires while Helena and Adam filled their quivers to hunt food for the feast honoring Robin that night. She could feel Adam's eyes on her as she stood there, a question as much as an invitation, but she couldn't meet his gaze. She couldn't look at any of them right now. When he disappeared into the woods with Helena, Isabelle pressed her eyes closed against the sigh that slipped out of her.

"You did well by your da, lass," said a gruff, low voice beside her. She looked up, startled, to find Little John kneeling at the gravesite. He set a gold coin on top of the pile of rocks. "He would have been proud."

Isabelle fidgeted with the rope that bound her habit, the ends fraying beneath her worrying fingers. "What pride is there in what I have done?"

Little John sat back on his haunches, considering her from his position beside the grave. "I knew Robin a long time, lass. Seen him through plenty of stupid stunts that should have been the end of him but weren't. He knew the life he led. We all do." He looked down to the stones. "I lost a sister and a mother to a bitter winter and empty stores of food, and nearly lost myself in the grief and shame. It was Robin pulled me out, and told me what he'd tell you now were he here. We go on not because we have to, but because we want to. We live the life we would have wanted for them."

He rose to his feet, laying a heavy hand on her shoulder. "Robin would want you to go on, lass. He'd want you to find happiness."

"But how can I go on?" she whispered, her voice catching behind a thick lump of tears. "How can I find happiness with only half a heart?"

"That's your own path," Little John said, laying a comforting hand on her shoulder. "Can't any of us walk it for you. But we'll be beside you all along. The Merry Men stand with their own."

"Thank you," Isabelle said, wiping at her cheeks. "But I will not be returning to York. Or Sherwood. My place is here, with my mother."

Little John frowned. "I thought you said you weren't a sister."

Isabelle shook her head. "I am not. Yet. But I intend to take my vows as soon as I am able. I may not be a gifted healer, but I can still serve the community here in other ways. And since it seems the king is set on war with the barons, the people here will certainly need our help. My mother cannot do it alone."

Little John glanced at the prioress still talking to Allan. "I think your mother can handle herself. You sure this isn't about something else?"

Isabelle looked down at her feet, down to the simple arrangement of stones. The lump rose again, threatening to undo her resolve. Threatening to undo her.

"This wasn't your fault, lass," Little John said in a soft voice.

Some small part of her could hear the ring of truth in his words, but the pain was still too great. Robin died saving her. He gave up the life he knew to protect her before she was even born. How could she face the Merry Men every day carrying that weight in her heart? It was difficult enough to look at the sadness weighing her mother down; how could she watch her father's closest friends go through their grief knowing she was the one who caused it?

"Kirklees is my home," she said, her voice shaky. She looked up to the big man imploringly. "I must return to the priory. Will you . . . Will you tell the others goodbye for me?"

"You don't want to do that yourself?" he asked. "They'll return soon enough, and you and your ma still have to eat."

Isabelle shook her head. "I cannot . . . I have caused them enough trouble already. I should think they would be glad to be rid of me by now. Helena most of all."

She tried to laugh, but the sound was so small and sad it turned into a sigh. Little John's gaze on her was like being buried under all the rocks at her feet.

"Please," she whispered. "I cannot face them. Not after all they have done for me, after all I have done. Tell Adam . . . Tell them all I am sorry. Please? For everything."

He sighed, his brows coming down in a deep furrow, but he nodded his agreement. Isabelle fled his side, waiting until she was deep within the sightless embrace of the trees to give release to the tears made of her heart and her bones, the tears that dissolved everything within and left her hollowed out. The tears that made her nothing more than a vessel for boundless grief.

CHAPTER
THIRTY-FIVE

Isabelle waited until the snores of the sisters in the dormitory took on a deep, even rhythm before slipping out of her room. She crossed the long hall with quick, efficient steps Patrick would have envied. Not that she needed to bother with such stealth, considering most of these sisters slept like they were hibernating for the winter. She did not begrudge them their rest, though, after a long day caring for the sick and starving who had flooded their halls since the king and his barons officially declared war on each other. Marien and Isabelle had worked hard to regain the trust and peace of the sisters who remained after Catherine's death—those whose beds had not been mysteriously vacant the morning after the mercenaries departed. It had taken hours of prayer and nights of tears and weeks of scrubbing to clean the dark stains from the cloister walls, but Isabelle had gladly gotten on her knees to scour those stones. When her hands worked, her mind did not.

She found her way to the stairwell leading down to the cloister, a light mist falling across the grass and turning it to icy shards in the cold. A whisper of fabric was her only warning as a shadow appeared beside her, and she had her knife drawn and raised before the soft scent of lemon verbena and mint gave her mother away. Marien raised a delicate eyebrow at the long blade hovering inches from her throat. Isabelle sighed, lowering the weapon and shaking the tension out of her limbs.

"Must you sneak up on me like that?" Isabelle asked in a whisper, glancing about the empty walkways. "One of these times I might actually hurt you."

"I should hope whoever gave you that knife taught you better than that."

Isabelle cut her eyes to the glittering courtyard, not wanting to think about Patrick or Adam or the others. She tucked the knife back into the holder she had fashioned for it on her belt. She still wasn't as efficient with the knife as she was with her bow, but she used the time after matins to practice when she could not get back to sleep. No one would catch her unaware ever again.

"Where are you heading at this early hour?" her mother asked.

"To the chapel," Isabelle said. "I could not sleep."

"Ah, that is a shame," her mother said with a small sigh. "I was rather hoping you were attempting to sneak out of the priory."

"Mother!" she said in a shocked whisper. "It is not safe, you know that."

"It is not safe anywhere in the country now, my child," her mother said sagely. "Not with a war on. Do you know, my father told me the rebels have invited Prince Louis of France to invade the country? They would rather a foreign prince take the throne than give up everything to the king's mercenaries. Imagine that, a Frenchman on the English throne."

"He cannot be worse than John Lackland," Isabelle said bitterly before she could catch herself. She glanced at Marien as they began walking toward the chapel side by side. "Not that I care a fig for the political machinations of the king."

"Yes, I know," her mother said with a nod. "As you vehemently insisted to my father when he visited last month. What was it you told him? That you would sooner set yourself alight on a sacrificial bonfire than take up a claim to the Huntingdon title or the Scottish throne? I do not believe a woman has ever spoken in such a manner to my father. Other than myself, of course."

"I do not want anything to do with the nobility," Isabelle said, thinking back to that first meeting with her grandfather. He was an imposing man, built with the same steely gaze and intractable will as her mother. He did not take kindly to her words, though she could have sworn he fought back a smile when she spoke them. "I have seen the damage such power and entitlement can cause."

"You have seen the worst it can do, but that does not mean all men wield it with such brutality." They reached the chapel entrance, the smell of melted candle wax filling the space. Her mother turned to her. "There are those that can do great good. My father is one. You could be another."

Isabelle shook her head, approaching the bank of prayer candles the sisters kept at the back of the chapel. A half-burned taper stuck out of a cup of sand at her feet and she extracted it to touch its wick to another candle's, sharing the flame between them. The little flare sputtered and grew to life, and she buried the taper in the sand, crossing herself and offering up a short prayer before facing her mother.

"That is not the life for me," she said simply, her voice hushed and reverential in the hallowed space. Without Sister Catherine there to scold her, the elegant beauty of the place made it a refuge. "And I should think you of all others would understand, as I know Grandfather asked you to return home and you refused."

Marien gave a noncommittal murmur, lighting her own candle and pressing her hands together in brief prayer. Isabelle wanted to ask what she prayed for, if they prayed for the same thing, but she stayed quiet until her mother was finished. When her mother faced her again, she looked at Isabelle with one of her searching gazes, the kind that could pierce right through every defense Isabelle put up. Her shoulders tensed against the intrusion.

"I took my vows, and I cannot betray them," Marien said. "My life is in my work, and these women need my guidance. This winter will be harder than ever on the people here, and it is our duty to care for them. And while I know you have a good heart, my child, I also know it is not here in Kirklees."

"That is not true," Isabelle said, turning toward the nearest pew. She sat down, folding her hands in her lap. "You cannot deny I have dedicated myself to my duties more than ever."

"Yes, I know," her mother said, taking up a seat beside her. "You have been the soul of piety and devotion."

Isabelle gave a small sigh, the edges tinged with irritation. "So why do you deny me the right to take my vows and become a sister?"

"Because I do not think you actually want to *be* a sister," her mother said.

"Of course I do," Isabelle countered, though she could not bring herself to look at her mother as she said it. "What else would I be?"

Her mother took a deep breath, letting it out slowly. "You have not touched your bow since you returned," she said in a soft voice. "You do not shoot, you do not hunt."

Isabelle's jaw tightened. "I have not felt much like killing lately."

Her mother paused for several moments, letting the hush of the chapel envelop them. When she spoke again, she laid a strong hand over Isabelle's own. "I miss him, too."

A wave of emotion built in Isabelle's chest, climbing up her throat with a ferocity that threatened to split her apart if she let it past her lips. She curled her hand into a fist under her mother's soft touch and clenched her teeth together, pressing it back down into her stomach. Marien gave a soft sigh.

"Isabelle, you cannot bury these feelings until they choke you."

"I am not burying anything," Isabelle snapped. "I am fine."

"No, you are not," Marien said, just as firmly. "You are angry and heartbroken and scared, if you would just let yourself feel it."

"I do not want to feel it! I cannot bear . . ." She swallowed hard against the lump that stuck steadfastly in her throat. "I am fine."

"Is that why you will not even say your father's name?"

Isabelle looked to her mother in surprise. "I do not know what you mean."

Marien met her look straight on. "I see you picked up some of Robert's more irritating qualities. He was always most stubborn when he was wrong."

"I am not . . ." Isabelle took a deep breath, struggling for control. "What good would it do to speak of what has already passed? I only wish to move forward."

"Well, you certainly cannot do that by standing still." Marien brushed a lock of Isabelle's hair back behind her ear as she always did when her daughter was discomfited. "I understand grief, dearest, but what you have taken upon yourself is far beyond that. It is almost as if you believe you do not deserve to be happy."

"How can I be happy? Knowing what I have done?"

Marien frowned. "What is it you have done?"

And there it was, behind her teeth, filling her mouth with the bile of recrimination. She couldn't hold it back any longer, couldn't bury it under the routine of chores or the fatigue of labor. Salty tears rose up in stinging waves, filling her head with their roaring.

"It is my fault," she whispered, her voice thin and high. "If I had been paying closer attention, if I had gone with you to the infirmary, if I had realized the full extent of Sister Catherine's betrayal, he would still be here. And if I had never existed, you would never have come here and been torn from the love of your life. How can I be happy?"

Marien sat in stunned silence, her deep blue eyes sweeping over her daughter's face, contorted in agony. The words sat like a stone in the pit of Isabelle's stomach, the cancer she had carried for weeks. But her mother reached out, touching her cheek, her lips lifting into a smile so warm it erased the tired lines from her eyes and mouth.

"Isabelle, my dearest heart. Your father was not the love of my life, and neither was I the love of his. *You* are the love of our lives. I will always love Robert, but the love we felt for each other was a drop in the ocean of the love we have for you. And there is no hellfire we would not walk through, no trial we would not endure to see you safe. And happily so. Never doubt that. Your father and I made a fine match, but we were not whole until you."

Marien reached for her then, and at her mother's knowing touch, Isabelle could no longer deny the tears, or the pain that rushed them to the surface. Marien enfolded Isabelle in her arms, laying her cheek against her daughter's head as Isabelle's grief washed through her and out of her, pouring onto the stones of the empty chapel.

At first she cried for her father, for the family she would never have and the small collection of memories she would treasure; but as those tears were exhausted, a melancholy settled in her, a restlessness of spirit that had nothing to do with Robin's death. It was the same selfish thought that had plagued her since her time in Sherwood, that insinuated itself into her mind when she was most tired and least guarded against it. She shifted uncomfortably in her mother's embrace, as if she could shrug it away. Marien sat back again, regarding her daughter with a keen eye.

"Do you know why I have never let you take the vows of poverty, chastity, and obedience?" she asked.

Isabelle slouched into herself. "Because I am not yet worthy."

"If Sister Catherine was deemed worthy, you certainly are by a thousandfold," her mother said dryly. "But that is not why. I have not allowed you to take your vows because I want it to be your choice. You have had so few of them in your short life, and many were forced on you. But this one does not have to be. You said it so eloquently yourself: The constraints of our past do not have to define our future. The Wolf is gone. Sister Catherine is gone. And much as it breaks both our hearts, so is your father. You are no longer bound to this place, to this life. You are free."

Isabelle dropped her eyes to the candles, the flames low and fat in the cold air. "So you wish me to leave Kirklees?"

"Of course I do not wish such a thing," said Marien, an edge of reprimand to her tone. "Were my wishes the only ones to be considered you would have stayed a little girl, my shadow companion. But my greater wish for you is that you find your place in the world. If that place is here, in Kirklees, the sisters will welcome you into their ranks with open arms. But if it is not, if another calls to your heart, then you must go."

Isabelle twisted her fingers, unwinding them in a slow gesture of doubt. "Even if another place called to my heart, which I will not admit that it does, it hardly matters. The Merry Men do not need me. They need strong leaders like Adam, and strong bow arms like Helena's. I would only get in the way."

"I would not be so sure of that," said Marien with a hint of a smile. "I have seen my fair share of hooded figures about the priory when they think they are being discreet. The sisters have not had to refill supplies in the village for weeks because someone keeps leaving mysterious donations of food and clothing."

Isabelle frowned. "Why would they do that?"

Marien nodded toward the chapel doors. "Perhaps you should ask him yourself."

Isabelle twisted in the pew, her heart leaping painfully in her chest at the tall, lean figure filling the chapel opening at the edge of the candlelight. Marien leaned forward and pressed a kiss against her temple, smoothing one hand down her hair and giving her a gentle smile.

"I love you, my infuriating daughter," she said, giving her another kiss. "Find the place that calls your heart."

Marien rose and swept out of the chapel, briefly touching Adam's shoulder before disappearing. Isabelle stood and skirted the pews to the center aisle. Adam gazed up in bemused wonderment at the sturdy wooden arches holding the roof of the chapel aloft.

"Huh. I guess I won't burst into flame upon crossing consecrated grounds again. That's one in Patrick's favor."

His voice sounded deeper and richer than she remembered. The memory of him had been soft and regretful, the thought of his smile or the feel of his arms around her. This boy who stood before her was real, and rough with that realness.

"Why are you here?" She'd forgotten how tall he was, and had to tilt her head back to meet his eyes.

"To see you."

"To see me? Why?"

"Well, because it's been two months and you haven't been to see us, and the others were starting to get the impression you'd forgotten all about us, or that you didn't care anymore. So I thought I'd come and remind you."

Isabelle let her gaze travel toward the bank of candles. "I did not forget you."

"So it's that you don't care?"

Isabelle frowned at him. "Of course not."

Adam leveled her with a look. "Then what is it keeping you away?"

"I have been busy."

"Yeah, so have we. But one of us still made the time to come see the other, didn't I?"

She squared her shoulders and lifted her chin. "I see your manners have not improved with time."

He crooked one side of his mouth in a grin. "Time was never a factor in my manners."

Her blood started a dangerous race at the curve of that grin, and she turned to hide the flush crossing her face. In the sacred chapel, no less. She blew out the candle she had lit, busying her hands to keep them from reaching for him.

"I appreciate the great distance you have traveled to come see me, but I cannot return to Sherwood at the moment," she said, sounding far less convinced than she intended. "Perhaps later, when things have settled."

"Things aren't likely to settle anytime soon," Adam said, crossing his arms and watching her. "King John's finally taken Rochester Castle after spending the last month nearly tearing the thing apart stone by stone to get it. And we've got word from Tuck that Prince Louis is sailing toward England's shores with an invading army. Things are likely to get far worse before they settle."

"All the more reason I must remain here, and vigilant," said Isabelle. "The country is at war and there are enemies everywhere. Just because Robin is gone does not mean I am safe. Robert Fitzwalter is still my grandfather. And King John's closest advisor is dead because of me."

Adam waved a hand. "John doesn't know you had anything to do with the Wolf's death. Not after the Merry Men got done setting him up to look like his carriage took an unfortunate detour into a deep lake." Adam shook his head, clicking his tongue. "Poor bastard, got to watch out for those ruts after a rainstorm. And anyone who could have said otherwise is halfway across the continent now with a pocket full of coin."

He was dismantling her conviction one piece at a time, pulling apart the walls she had constructed to keep herself contained these past two months. The hopeful part of her that she'd pressed into the far corners of her mind surged forward, practically begging to be let free. But it hurt so much to hope, too much to let it overcome her again. She turned away from him.

"I cannot return," she said, sadness weighing down each word. "I am sorry."

"We need you, Isabelle," Adam said, his voice rough. "We need your clever brain and your wicked shot and your passion for helping people."

"You are talking about Robin," she whispered.

"No, I'm not," he said forcefully. "I'm talking about you. The girl that stood up to a camp of outlaws and challenged for her place among them. The girl who took on the most powerful man in the country and beat him. The girl who stared down a soldier of the king to protect innocent people. We've got our hands full helping the rebel barons and protecting the people of Sherwood. No one knows about Robin's death besides the Men, and we can't let anyone find out. The people need something to believe in now more than ever. We need Robin Hood to live on, even if the man himself is gone. But I'm too tall and Little's a terrible shot. Helena's the only one with a bow arm good enough to pretend to be Robin, and she won't let any of us hear the end of it. We need you." He cleared his throat. "I need you."

Tears pressed against her closed eyelids, and her throat filled with a surge of emotion so powerful it made her hands shake. She opened her mouth to speak, but it was too much. She was too overcome.

"And if that's still not enough to convince you to come along, then I'll challenge you for it," Adam said after a moment.

She turned, finding her voice through her surprise. "What do you mean?"

"I mean that I, Adam of Locksley, challenge you, Isabelle of Kirklees, to a shooting competition. I make the best shot, you come back to Sherwood. You make the best shot, you can stay and do whatever it is you love doing here." He glanced about. "Scrubbing floors, I guess."

"But I do not even have my bow with me," she said, spreading her empty hands wide.

"Lucky for you, I always come prepared." He motioned to the open door of the chapel as a voice floated in from outside.

"Tell her to hurry up 'cause we're freezing our toes off out here," Little called out. "And other vital parts not needing to be mentioned."

Adam cast his eyes up. "Thank you, as always, Little. I was handling it."

"Well, handle it faster," Little called back. "You could snap my nose right off my face at the moment."

"Let me know if you want me to," Helena said.

Patrick appeared in the door, his expression chagrined. "Apologies, Isabelle." He cast his eyes up at the altar. "And to you, Lord. I tried to keep them quiet. We didn't want to pressure you."

"Yes, we did," Helena said, stepping in beside him. She wore heavy furs wrapped around her legs and across her shoulders. "Come on, then, sister, we haven't got all day. And I'm tired of carrying this about."

The girl unslung a longbow from across her shoulder, striding into the chapel to hand it to Isabelle. Patrick followed along after her, still looking slightly guilty.

"Don't forget to kneel," he murmured to Helena.

"Why would I do that?"

The Irish boy looked horrified as he bowed his head. "She doesn't mean that, Lord."

Isabelle ran her fingers in wonder along the string of her father's bow. Little hurried into the chapel after them, huddling near the bank of recently extinguished candles as if their smoke would bring some small warmth. He rattled a quiver of white-tipped arrows at her.

"Made them myself, with a bit of help," he said, passing the quiver.

"More than a bit," Helena said.

"It's the thought that counts," Little replied.

"So what is it to be, then, sister?" Adam asked. "Do you accept the challenge?"

Isabelle looked to each of their expectant faces, exhilaration burning the cold from her cheeks and racing through her veins. A lightness she hadn't felt in months lifted her chin and drew her shoulders back as she looped the quiver over her chest. She pressed her lips together to keep a straight face even though a smile pulled at every other part of her.

"I suppose I have no other choice," she said. "I have a reputation to uphold, after all."

Adam gave her the bow, matching her expression. "This way, then, champion."

They left the chapel, giving the dormitory a wide berth as they headed toward the orchard. Adam nodded to a tree on the far edge, taking up his stance.

"Closest to hitting that knot dead in the center wins the challenge," he said, drawing an arrow and pulling back on his bowstring. "And you'll understand if I don't wish you luck."

His arrow struck true to the center, the fletching rippling from the impact. Little grinned and slapped him on the back as Patrick murmured his quiet praise. Only Helena kept her arms crossed and looked to Isabelle expectantly. It was a different sort of challenge, but Isabelle recognized it immediately. And as she stepped up to take her own shot, drawing back on the string that had launched a hundred legends, the call of the challenge sang like a chorus in her mind.

"I have missed wearing a truly good pair of hose," she murmured to Adam as she let the arrow fly, splitting his in two. She took a deep breath, admiring her handiwork as the others waited behind her. She turned to them with an expectant look.

"What was it you said about a high sheriff terrorizing the people of Nottinghamshire?" She shook her head. "That will not hold. Not for Robin Hood."

Adam's eyes gleamed. "No, it won't."

She cocked her head at the four of them. "Shall we see about setting this brute to rights, then?"

"Oh, I think I'm going to like this Hood," said Little with a grin.

Isabelle matched her grin to his. "I think I am, too. To Sherwood, my Merry Men."

ACKNOWLEDGMENTS

The journey of a book is a strange one. I spent eight years crafting a story I hope you'll devour in a single afternoon. So many people touched and shaped that story along the way, cutting and digging and honing it into something I'm wholeheartedly proud of. For a perfectionist like me, it's been a surprising and delightful discovery.

My thanks, first and foremost, to my critique partners—Anna Sargeant, Christina Johnson, Bryn Schulke, and Lindsay Funkhouser. You ladies have kept me sane, encouraged me when I thought I couldn't go on, and made this story what it is today.

To my agent, Elizabeth Bewley, thank you for taking the dream I thought long dead and giving it new life. Your championing of this book helped me rediscover my love for it, and you brought it to my absolute dream home. My thanks to everyone at Sterling Lord Literistic.

To my editor, Kieran Viola, I have enjoyed literally every step of this process and I know that's thanks to you. Your suggestions were deep and thoughtful, and took the baton and carried it over the finish line. You have made this process a dream, and I know how rare that is. I'm so grateful to work with you.

To the rest of the team at Hyperion, especially editorial assistants

Mary Mudd and Vanessa Moody, cover designer Phil Buchanan, publisher Emily Meehan, editor Laura Schreiber, and copy chief Guy Cunningham—thank you all so much for your kind, loving handling of this story. You have all helped turn a little story from my mind into a book that exists out in the world.

My thanks to Michelle Hauck and Amy Trueblood for connecting me with my agent through their Sun vs. Snow contest. These women work tirelessly to support the community, and I only hope to be able to give back as much as they have given me.

To my fellow writers, my friends through the Austin SCBWI, the Roaring Twenties debut group, and especially Shannon Doleski and Prerna Pickett, thank you. It's been an unexpected gift to find communities that love the craft of storytelling as much as me.

I owe a debt to my family that can never be repaid, but I'm hoping seeing their names in a Disney book will at least be a decent down payment. To my mom, Linda, who shared stories with me early on and is basically to blame for this whole thing. To my dad, Vincent, who taught me a love of discovery and adventure that finds its way into my stories no matter how much they terrify me. To my brother, Matt, for being my biggest hype man and keeping me humble. To Granny B, who always made quiet spaces for me to dream; and to Grandpa B, who was first in the family to know about this book but never got to read it. To Gigi and Pop, for always being willing to watch my little heathens when I need the help.

To those two little heathens, Max and Lily, this book also couldn't have existed without you. I didn't know how to write a mother until I was one. Papa and I were happy, but we weren't whole until you.

And finally to Joe, who I always swore wouldn't get a dedication because I'm a stubborn Taurus. But of course you do, because where would I be without you? This world was a lonelier place before you. It's you and me, kid.

TURN THE PAGE FOR A SNEAK PEEK
AT JENNY ELDER MOKE'S
NEXT GASP-WORTHY NOVEL!

CHAPTER ONE

Sam let the first door chime go unanswered, occupied as she was with the stack of delicate books cradled in her arms. The second chime earned a grunt of displeasure from her as she scanned the shelves for the first edition of John Locke's *An Essay Concerning Human Understanding* she had repaired last week. She spotted it, tucked safely between Kant and Machiavelli. The third chime rang so insistently that she tipped the book forward too hard and it dropped to the floor with an ominous *crack*.

"Oh dear," she said, crouching down to retrieve the book. "Mr. Locke, I apologize. And I swear to you if it's the butcher's boys again, I will take the broad side of his cleaver to their rear ends myself."

The spine appeared unmarred, which was more than Sam could say for her disposition as she stacked the book on top of the others and jostled to a standing position. She tottered to the front of the shop and set them down on the desk. In the window stood the rounded figure of Clement's postman, his face pressed to the glass and obscuring the gold lettering across the door. She checked off each book on her inventory list, letting him freeze in the early January snows of rural Illinois, before crossing to the door and unlocking it. A blast of cold drove it open like an unwanted guest.

"Yes, Georgie, what is it you need?" she asked, shivering back from the chill.

"Got your mail," Georgie huffed, bustling past her to drop his sack on the desk. He trod in drifts of snow across her pristine carpet, and she swept the more offensive piles back out the door as she swung it shut.

"That's why I had the package drop put in, Georgie," Sam said. "So you can leave them in a protected box without them getting soaked by the melting snow you're tracking in."

"It's colder than a brass toilet seat in the arctic out there," Georgie replied, leaning against his mailbag like he planned to stay. He peered into the stacks behind Sam. "It's toasty in here, though. Must be nice for you, being tucked up in this place all day."

"We keep the temperature stable for the books," Sam said, her patient tone fraying at the edges. She had plenty to do before her long walk home in that same snow, and she couldn't do it as long as Georgie was here chewing the cud. "Extreme heat and cold damage the leather. You said you had my mail?"

"Oh sure." Georgie ducked his head into the thick canvas sack. "Couple of these are too big, wouldn't fit through the slot."

Sam was sure his bell ringing had far more to do with the warm interior of the shop than with any oversize packages, but it was too late for that. Here he was already, invading her space and upending the careful equilibrium she maintained. He didn't care that there was the rest of the inventory list to get to, plus the packages to prepare and send to Mr. Peltingham in London and Mr. Burnham in Oslo, never mind the repairs to the copy of *Medieval Remedies for Cistercian Monks* they had received at the shop last week. She didn't have time for Georgie Heath and the trail of muddy snow he dragged everywhere.

He pulled a small collection of boxes from his sack—none of them, as Sam suspected, too large for the mail slot—with an exotic array of stamps across the front. Sam's heart rate picked up when she spotted Mr. Studen's scrawled handwriting. He always had the best finds in Paris. She grabbed her letter opener and sliced through the thick paper.

"Books," Georgie said, in the same tone his father used when talking about the neighbor's marauding hogs. "Always books, isn't it?"

"Yes," Sam said with a happy little sigh, extracting Mr. Studen's letter along with his latest find. "We *are* a bookshop, Georgie."

Oh, clever Mr. Studen. She smiled at the first few lines of introduction, a jumble of letters and pictographic marks. He'd sent her another cryptogram, with a small note dashed off at the top that read *I'm sure to stump you this time.*

He wasn't, but she appreciated the challenge.

Georgie gave a snort. "I don't know what we need with a bookshop here in Clement, anyhow. We've already got a library."

"A collection of old family Bibles does not count as a library," Sam said, reaching for a pencil and paper. It looked to be a straightforward monoalphabetic cipher despite the distraction of the pictographic marks, but she didn't want to underestimate Mr. Studen so quickly.

Georgie shrugged. "I was happy enough to give that stuff up the second I walked out of Mrs. Iris's schoolroom for good."

"*Madame* Iris," Sam corrected.

"*Madame,*" Georgie said in a gross mockery of the French madame's accent. "Pa says a book is only good for propping open a door or knocking a fella out."

"Well, I would expect no less from the man who led a town-wide protest when Mr. Steeling hired a Frenchwoman to teach at the schoolhouse," Sam murmured, making a list of the most frequent letter appearances and the most common letter groupings in the cipher. Georgie craned his neck around, squinting at Mr. Studen's neat handwriting.

"What is that?" he asked. "Some kind of gibberish?"

"It's a cipher," Sam said. "A code. It's meant to keep a message hidden."

The last word she said pointedly, looking up at the intrusion of his person on her space. If Georgie noticed her intention—which Sam was positive he did not—he didn't do anything to address it. Instead he scooted in closer, wrinkling up his nose like his father's prize hog.

"Well, how do you know what it says?" Georgie asked.

"You need a key," Sam murmured, writing out a few attempts at the letters she thought she might have deduced.

"Do you have the key?"

"No."

"Well, then how do you know what it says?"

Sam let out a sigh. "I don't, Georgie. Not yet. I have to decrypt it, which would be much easier to do without so much distracting chatter."

Georgie rocked back. "I get it, this is like those things you and Jo and Bennett used to do, out at the Manor, right? Those treasure hunts you'd make up."

"We didn't make them up, Mr. Steeling did," Sam said, setting down her pencil and folding the letter closed along with her deciphering attempts, away from Georgie's prying eyes. "And I haven't done those in years, not since we were children."

Georgie shrugged. "Maybe you and Joana can put one up now that she's in Clement again."

Sam drew back. "Jo's in town?"

"Yeah, didn't you know it? I figured she would have come to see you straightaway. You were the only one she ever bothered with. Maybe she's too good for you now, too, after being at that fancy academy in Chicago."

Joana Steeling was back in Clement and she hadn't come to see Sam. So, she was still mad about the fight. Sam had tried so many times to explain why she couldn't go to the academy with Joana—first in person, and after Joana left, through half-finished letters—but Joana couldn't understand. It was so easy for her, the heiress of the Steeling fortune, to spend late nights in shady speakeasies flirting with the boys, getting into and out of trouble. But Sam could never live like that. Most likely Joana had found her people at Marquart Academy. It didn't surprise her that Joana had moved on, but it did surprise her how much it hurt hearing about it from Georgie Heath.

"If you see Jo, tell her we're out at the old barn most nights, me and Pete and the gang," Georgie said, oblivious to Sam's discomfort. "They might have those swanky speakeasies up in Chicago, but nobody's calling the G-men on us. We do what we want, all night if we want it."

"Sounds a dream," Sam said tiredly. "But I've got work to do, if there's nothing else."

"Oh, right, got your newspaper here," he said, ducking back into the bag and pulling out a copy of the *Chicago Daily News*. Sam's attention snagged on a small headline tucked into the right corner of the front page: *TUT OPERATIONS RESUMED.*

"The curse of the mummy has been lifted," she murmured, leaning closer to read the rest of the article.

"Are they still writing about that thing?" Georgie asked, glancing at the paper. "The grave or whatever?"

"Yes, they're still writing about the tomb of Tutankhamen," Sam said dryly. "It's the greatest archaeological discovery of our time."

Georgie waved her off. "I don't see any point in all that old stuff. Who cares? They're all dead anyway."

Sam had no intention of explaining the historical significance of Howard Carter's recent discovery of Tutankhamen's tomb. No one in Clement would understand, except her boss, Mr. Steeling. He shared Sam's fascination with all things ancient and lost. He spent much of his time traveling overseas to exotic places like Greece to join archaeological excavations. Places she would only ever read about in the *Daily News*. She snapped the paper closed and placed it on the desk, looking at Georgie expectantly.

"Well, I suppose that's all," Georgie said, gazing forlornly out at the brutal white of the main street of Clement.

"Yes, well, enjoy your evening in the barn with the other boys," Sam said, picking up his sack and putting it on his shoulder, using the movement to push the rest of him toward the front door. They both squinted against the cold wind that burst through when she opened the door.

"All right, all right, I'm off," Georgie said, the winter wind turning him chapped and irritable again. "You tell Jo—"

"Will do, thank you, Georgie," Sam said, swinging the door shut and throwing the dead bolt.

She took a deep, cleansing breath of the temperature-controlled interior of the store, the soft scent of the oiled leather covers restoring her sense of self, before turning her attention to the stack of recent arrivals. Her eagerness to discover new friends outweighed her obligation to the packaging list or the pang in her gut about Joana returning home and not coming to see her.

She had just begun to sort the packages when a smaller one slipped out from the press of the others, the paper soiled and the corner torn away. It looked as if it had been through a monsoon, the writing so faded it was a wonder Georgie had known where to deliver it at all. And judging by the various interpretations of the address scribbled across the front, she wasn't sure the bookshop had been the package's first delivery attempt. How long had it been in the system, knocked from one place to the other, before it got to her? There was no return address. She held it up, a small puff of dry earth sifting onto the desk.

"What a terrible journey you've been through," she tutted. "Let's get you fixed up."

She carried the package to the repair room in the back. The work lamp there glowed a bluish white. A humidifier hummed beside it, giving the occasional ping in the relative silence. She sat at the worktable and opened the package. A little avalanche of dust and desiccated plant parts came sliding out along with the enclosed item.

The book was small, barely larger than her hand, the cover in such disrepair that Sam feared it would disintegrate if she so much as gave it a stern look. She had seen plenty of books in a variety of conditions since she started working at Steeling's Rare Antiquities, but this had to be the worst state of deterioration she'd ever witnessed. It looked as if the book had been buried in someone's back field and dug up by a stray goat.

"Who would do such a thing to you?" she wondered, her chest aching at the violence the book had encountered on its journey. "Well, whatever ills have befallen you, you're safe here now."

There was nothing in the package to indicate where it had come from, no letter of provenance or introduction from a buyer explaining what the book was or why they had sent it. The mystery of it had her pulling out her tools, for the moment abandoning the other new arrivals. She took her brush and went to work, tilting it up to sweep softly along the outside edges, collecting a tidy pile of earth and sediment.

Already she knew it would need a rest in the humidifier to loosen up the pages and hopefully restore the faded writing within. Once she had sufficiently cleaned the outside, she began her preliminary inspection of the interior. The pages were so waterlogged she could hardly pry them apart, but with the aid of a scalpel and a level of patience bordering on stubbornness, she managed to loosen one enough to pull it open.

The writing was, as she suspected, faded and illegible in many places, but that wasn't what drew her attention to the book. It was the hasty sketch of a cat on the open page, the graphite strokes thick and dark and tearing through the paper in some places. She could even see smudges where the lead must have broken. Whoever drew this cat must have had very strong feelings about it.

Except that, the longer she stared at the image, the less it actually looked like a cat. At least, not like any ordinary house cat. The proportions were all wrong—the ears too sharp and pointed, almost like horns; the jaw too long and narrow, more fitted to a dog. And then there were the eyes. They were nothing more than blank page, but the longer she stared, the more they seemed to burn, two desolate holes radiating a promise of danger. Awareness prickled down her legs and across her arms, as if a wayward slip of icy January wind had found its way into the shop. But it wasn't the wind. It was the way the cat kept staring, even when she slid the book aside. Those sightless eyes were on her, always on her, and in a fit of fear she slammed the cover shut.

"Don't be such a fool," Sam muttered, though she made no attempt to open it again. "It's only an old book. What's the harm?"

Georgie was putting her on. He must be. This was exactly the kind of prank he and Pete and the other boys would pull back in Madame Iris's schoolroom. Leaving notes with rude poems, knowing she would mistake them for clues to a new treasure hunt at

Steeling Manor, the hunts Mr. Steeling created for his children and Sam. They must be bored to tears after the last snowstorm, getting pickled out there in his father's barn every night. They were probably watching through the front window, waiting to see her come tearing out of there screaming.

But there was nothing at the door save the whistle of the winter wind and the last rays of a dying sun. The darkness looming outside made the malevolence emanating from the book so much worse, and Sam was acutely aware of how alone she was just then. She hovered in the doorway of the workroom, not wanting to come any closer to the odd little book.

"What are you?" she whispered.

But whatever secrets the book had, it held them as tightly as the dust wedged into its pages. Sam chewed at one corner of her lip, weighing her options. She could try to chase down Georgie, force the book back on him, and make him deliver it to Steeling Manor. But the shop was the last stop on his route; he was probably halfway back to the barn by now, and halfway into a flask of his awful bathtub gin. The boy could be surprisingly agile when getting away from work. She could leave it until the next time Mr. Steeling came by to check on the new arrivals, but that could be weeks from now and Sam didn't want it hanging around.

No, there was nothing for it. She would have to deliver it to Steeling Manor herself. Which meant facing her fears, and potentially her former best friend.

"Oh, Sammy girl, what have you gotten yourself into?" she sighed, tucking the book into her satchel and pulling the strap across her chest like a battle shield.

CHAPTER TWO

Sam knew she had made a terrible mistake when the third car nearly ran her off the lane leading up to Steeling Manor. One car in Clement was an anomaly; two cars a statistical improbability. Three cars could only mean one thing.

A party.

Sam's fears were soon confirmed as she reached the large circular drive in front of the Manor and spotted the fleet of fine cars parked around the massive water fountain. Within it three women stood back-to-back, their bare arms raised to the sky, glittering daggers of ice dripping from the buckets in their hands. The facade of the manor house was no less impressive, painted in a brilliant white with a wraparound front porch held up by sweeping columns in the Greek Revival style. Freshly fallen snow lined the edges of the lawn, making it look like a Christmas-village set piece. The sight of the wide windows framed by robin's-egg-blue shutters made Sam's head ache, and even though she knew it was not the season for them she could have sworn she smelled Mrs. Steeling's English roses.

But she wouldn't think about those flowers, or the treasure

destined to be buried forever beneath them, or that last fateful hunt left unfinished. She had a job to do.

Now that she was closer to the house, she could hear what the crunch of snow under her shoes had hidden before—the tinkle of champagne glasses, the rumble of idle conversation punctuated by an occasional laugh. The faint strains of a horn.

Definitely a party.

Sam sighed, already regretting so many things, and waited for the recent party arrivals to disappear through the front door before braving the porch. She pounded a fist against the massive glass-and-steel double doors, entirely too loud and fast, and stood back to wait in a jittery silence. The butler drew the door open, his professional decorum covering up the half-second glint of surprise in his gaze.

"Ms. Knox," he said in his smooth English accent that always sounded slightly disapproving. Or maybe that was only ever directed at her and Joana. After all, he was always the one catching them using Cook's good ladle as a digging trowel.

"Hi, James," Sam said on a sigh.

"Are you here for the soiree?" James asked, his gaze sliding over the raggedy edges of her father's old winter coat and the loose pair of work trousers she'd put on under her skirt so the snow wouldn't pile up in her socks.

Sam shook her head, burrowing deeper into her coat. "Absolutely not. I received a strange book at the shop that I need Mr. Steeling to see."

A faint crease appeared along James's otherwise smooth forehead. "I am afraid Mr. Steeling is indisposed."

Sam moved from one foot to the other, the resolute energy that had carried her there quickly dissipating under the butler's steady gaze. "Well, of course I can see that now that I'm here, only I didn't know it when I left the shop. Maybe I could just leave the book in the library? I'll be quick, I promise. I don't want anyone here catching sight of me either."

The crease in his forehead deepened. "I see. I will show you to the library."

"That's all right, James," Sam said, already moving past him into the foyer. "It's only been a few years—I still remember the way."

But Sam hesitated in the marble entryway, the cacophony of voices echoing against the hard floor like a physical impediment. Just beyond the foyer, the party guests moved, sparkling and sleek in their floor-length dresses and tailcoats. Deep within the house, a band played something new and heavy on the brass, the dancers whirling in and out of view as they moved their feet in double time to keep up with the tempo. Mr. Steeling had expanded his collection of rare goods since the last time Sam had been there; the walls were lined with numerous restorations of precious Greek pottery. And it seemed Mrs. Steeling had finally convinced him to swap out the massive stone lions that used to guard the staircase with tall porcelain vases. But underneath all those decorative changes, it was still the same manor house. Her second home for so much of her childhood, until she couldn't stand the sight of it anymore.

No, no, that wouldn't do. No need to retread those memories, not tonight. Sam took a deep breath, keeping her eyes wide open, and dodged through more arriving guests toward the staircase leading to the second floor. Several people looked at her askance, taking in her well-worn clothing and the drifts of snow still piled over the toes of her shoes. She increased her speed, practically running up the steps. She found the library straightaway, just past a full suit of English armor from the thirteenth century. Sam ran her fingers over the word BIBLIOTHECA in thick brass letters above the door handle before pushing it open, slipping in and pressing it shut. Only after she had inhaled the leathery scent of so much knowledge could she release the knot of tension twisting her gut. At least until someone said her name.

"Sam?" The voice was warm and deep, like a swirling pot of chocolate, and terribly familiar. Sam stiffened and whirled about, her satchel banging against her hip under her coat.

"Bennett?" she said, the name slipping out halfway between a plea and a sigh.

Bennett Steeling rose from behind his father's desk situated in the center of the library, the shelves of books reaching another twenty feet overhead. He wore a black tailcoat, the shirt white and crisp and the jacket tailored to fit his broad shoulders and narrow hips. His hair was styled back in soft waves, nearly black like Mrs. Steeling's, his eyes the color of champagne by candlelight, a beautifully light brown with sparkling patches of gold. Sam cataloged all these details, comparing them with the precious collection of memories she had hoarded for the two years he had been gone to college in Chicago.

"I didn't know you were coming tonight," he said. He waved to the door, seeming to encompass the whole house beyond it. "I thought these kinds of things didn't interest you anymore. Jo said you hadn't even been to the Christmas party in the last two years. Between the two of us, I think my mother is starting to take it personally that no one but the mill workers show up for her parties anymore."

He said it lightly, as a joke, but it prodded something deep and tender within her, a wound she preferred to leave alone. It had always been so hard to come back here ever since the telegram from the War Office seven long years ago. Her mother had walked the mile and a half from their house after receiving it, her hands still red and her dress still damp from the hot laundry. And there Sam had been, playing at being a code-breaking explorer, not knowing the war had taken her father and changed her life irrevocably. For those last fateful minutes, she was still just a girl seeking an adventure.

Sometimes she thought about getting a spade and digging up that last treasure, just to be done with it. It hung like a loose thread in the tapestry of her consciousness, always snagging her when she brushed past the memory. The urge was nearly overwhelming, even now, after so many years away. She hated the idea of anything left undone, especially the hardest of all their treasure hunts. But she never could do it. Maybe she didn't want to find out she had been wrong all along, and the statue was never really buried there. Or maybe she didn't want to dig it up after all these years and find out nothing really changed.

"Sam, everything all right?" Bennett asked, because of course it had been too many moments since he had said anything and she had stood there mired in a memory.

She was suddenly and painfully aware of the plainness of her appearance—her threadbare white shirt that had been through the wringer so many times the tint of her skin showed at the elbows; her thick khaki skirt that was too tight in the waist and came too far above her knee, but had no more fabric to let out; the hasty bun she had fastened that morning, trying to tame the kink of her auburn hair into some kind of recognizable shape. Bennett looked like a Greek god made flesh, a marble statue come to life, and she probably looked as if she'd spent the last hour tilling the back fields and cleaning out the feeding trough.

Oh, the work trousers. She should have slipped them off the second James sniffed at them. Maybe she could slip them off now without Bennett noticing. Except she and Bennett were the only ones in the library, as far as she could tell, and he was looking right at her. It wouldn't do to start shucking items of clothing now.

"Oh, yes, sure, everything's fine," Sam said.

He circled the desk and came to stand before her, his eyes sweeping down to her feet and back up to her face. One corner of his mouth crooked up. "You've gotten taller."

She could melt into the warm edges of the way he said that, swim around in the chocolate timbre of his voice. It had gotten deeper since he'd left, she was sure of it. It had expanded and aged like the fine French wines Mr. Steeling was always rumored to be smuggling into his parties. She could listen to Bennett talk for the rest of the night, but if she didn't say something soon, he would think she had been brained by their old mule in his absence.

"I . . . You're back? From Chicago? I didn't know."

Bennett tucked his hands into his pockets, that small smile still turning up one corner of his mouth and threatening to take Sam's knees out from under her. "Only for the evening. I skipped out on the Christmas party this year as well, and Mother gave me hell for it. Said that I came home so little these days she was starting to forget she even had a son. Which is ridiculous, of course, because she comes up to Chicago at least once a semester to do all her shopping, but you know my mother. She might have left the stage, but it never left her. Anyway, since I'll be gone for the semester, I figured I'd better come home and make the appropriate rounds."

"Gone?" Sam said, her voice pitching up in dismay. "Where will you be gone? I mean, why will you be gone? Where are you going?"

"To help one of my professors—Professor Wallstone—with a survey in Ireland."

Sam's eyebrows went up. "Professor Barnaby Wallstone?"

"You know of him?"

"Of course. I read his article in last year's *Archaeological Digest* about Linear B and the possibility that it could be a form of ancient Greek."

Bennett winced. "That article didn't win him any friends in Sir Arthur Evans's camp, especially the part where he criticized Sir Arthur for keeping his cache of tablets under lock and key and thwarting the efforts of any would-be decipherers. He received a shocking amount of hate mail and nearly had his tenure revoked."

"Oh, but I think he might be right," Sam said. "He made some compelling arguments around the syllabary and its parallels to Mycenaean Greek of the later time period. I know Sir Arthur has first right of translation as the discoverer of the tablets, but he's been promising the next volume of Scripta Minoa for ages. It really has impeded progress, to Professor Wallstone's point. But I thought Wallstone's expertise was in Greek and the classics. What is he doing in Ireland?"

Bennett gave a small sigh. "Professor Wallstone has a bit of a reputation at the university for his . . . side projects. He spent a semester researching the standing stones in Ireland and Wales on a lark. The administration wasn't pleased about him abandoning his classes to graduate students, apparently. Now he's got it in his head that he wants to excavate a potential Neolithic passage tomb in the mountains outside of Dublin. He's convinced it might have been a worship site for the Druids. Don't mention it to my mother, but really I came home to raid Father's collection on Celtic lore and symbology."

"Which ones did you pull?" Sam asked, the topic shifting her attention away from how the collar of his shirt made his jawline look so appealing. She skirted around Bennett to examine the stack on the desk, reaching for the topmost book and propping it up on either side to take the pressure off the spine. She tapped the pages. "Conway is a good one, though I find his writing style a bit blustery."

"He does tend to go on," Bennett conceded, joining her on the opposite side of the desk. "After a year and a half at the University of Chicago, though, I'm used to it. All the professors talk at you like they're lecturing, even in casual conversation."

"Oh, you're studying ogham, too," Sam said, pulling the book out from beneath Conway's formidable tome. She traced a finger over the branch-like formations of the ogham characters on the page.

Bennett tilted his head up in surprise. "You know about ogham?" He pronounced it differently than her, the *gh* sounding more like a soft *w*. She turned warm with embarrassment; that's what came of learning so much of her vocabulary from books. The pronunciations were always spotty at best.

"I read Robert Stewart Macalister's theory that it originated in Italy, based on secret hand signals the Druids used to communicate," Sam said quickly, hoping to move past her mistake. "Isn't it also called the Celtic Tree Alphabet?"

"Yes, the ancient Celts used it to approximate the characters of their spoken language, since they had no written language," Bennett said. "They mostly used it to mark graves and property lines with people's names. And there are these stones, all over Ireland and Scotland and Wales, that have ogham characters inscribed on them."

"It's so incredible," Sam said, "that these stones have lasted for thousands of years, with secret messages hidden in plain sight. Imagine finding one for yourself and discovering its meaning for the first time in centuries. What a thrill that would be."

Bennett's gaze turned warm. "You never could resist a good mystery. I remember you would go for hours, days, hunting down one of Father's buried treasures. You'd forget to eat, to sleep. It used to drive Joana nutty. I'm surprised you haven't flown the coop by now to seek your own puzzles to solve in the greater world."

"Oh, I . . ." She shook her head, as if that might shake some of the stuffing out of it. "No. That's all . . . It was just childhood fancy, those treasure hunts. I'm not going anywhere. I could never . . . The shop needs me. Who would tend the books if I were gone? Georgie Heath? His father would have the pigs feasting on their delicate interiors by nightfall."

Bennett laughed, the sound of it creating a sensation that expanded in her chest like a new collection of stars. "Yes, but imagine his dismay when they began quoting Chaucer the next morning."

Sam smiled, the heat of it radiating out of her skin. "It would finally class up the barnyard."

"Well, it's a shame the shop needs you so much, because Professor Wallstone could have used a mind like yours at the Hellfire Club," Bennett said.

Sam lifted both brows, the hairs on the back of her neck rising. "What is the Hellfire Club?"

"Well, technically it's called Montpelier Hill, but the locals call it the Hellfire Club, after a group of nobles that used to meet there in the early 1700s." Bennett moved the book with the ogham figures, tapping on an entry in the book below it. "It was a hunting lodge built in 1725, and local legend has it the man who built it tore out the stones of a Neolithic passage tomb to make it. The place is supposedly so cursed that a storm blew the whole roof off right after it was built. So they just tore more rocks out of the passage grave and put a stone roof on it."

"Cursed," Sam echoed, suppressing a shiver. No self-respecting scholar would believe in curses, even if she did want to draw a little closer to the warmth of the massive fireplace.

"It's all a bunch of superstitious nonsense, of course," Bennett said, leaning against the edge of the desk. "The curse, I mean. The passage tomb is quite real, or so Professor Wallstone believes. Convincing the rest of the administration has been more difficult."

"Why is that?" Sam asked, studying the squat, grainy structure of the Hellfire Club lodge in Bennett's book. Even in tiny black-and-white form, a sinister air hung over it. But maybe that was just the clouds looming in the background.

"The university just opened the Oriental Institute a few years ago, and their focus is on the Near East, especially now with Howard Carter's discovery of Tutankhamen's tomb. But Professor Wallstone is . . . very determined." Bennett frowned as if this were an argument he'd had with himself several times over.

"You think he's wrong?" Sam asked softly.

Bennett shook himself. "No, no, of course not. He's brilliant, and the excavation of a Neolithic passage tomb would have great historical significance. But sometimes his side interests become obsessions. And this one has been particularly engrossing. Anyway, he's gone off to Dublin to do a survey of the site himself, without a license or the university's support, but he'll need assistance. So I've agreed to go along. Someone's got to watch out for him."

"Oh, well, that's . . . something." Sam didn't know what *something* she thought that was. She didn't want to think about the searing disappointment of losing Bennett so soon after he'd finally returned to Clement; and she had absolutely no intention of examining the frisson of interest running along her spine at the idea of digging out the remnants of an ancient passage tomb. That part of her life was long past.

Bennett shook his head, straightening up. "But you didn't come here to listen to me go on about my studies. What was it you needed?"

"Oh, you weren't going on at all, I find it fascinating," Sam said, before catching the enthusiasm in her tone. "What I mean is, I hope you have a good trip. I got a book at Rare Antiquities, a strange one. There was no return address on the package, no letter of provenance inside, nothing. It couldn't have come from any of our regular sellers, and the inside of the book . . . Well, I thought I should bring it to Mr. Stee—uh, your father—right away."

She pulled the package from her satchel and handed it to Bennett. He frowned at the faint trace of handwriting on the front.

"This came to the shop, you said?"

Sam nodded, taking a half step forward and craning her neck to look at the lettering. Did she miss something? "Yes, just this afternoon. Why?"

Bennett tapped a finger on the package. "Because I recognize this handwriting. This is from Professor Wallstone."

Sam drew back in surprise. "Your professor? I thought you said he was in Ireland?"

"He is," Bennett murmured, sliding the book out. He made to open it, but Sam grabbed his arm.

"Please don't," she said, cringing at the barest sliver of page visible beneath his finger. She gave a little embarrassed laugh. "I mean, don't open it while I'm here."

"Why not?"

Why not indeed? Sam could hardly admit her fears when he had just dismissed the superstitions of the locals so disdainfully. And she probably *was* being ridiculous. Too much time alone in the stacks, devouring all those articles about the curse of the mummy in Egypt. Still, she had no desire to look at that cat—if it could really be called that—again.

"I don't—" she began, but she was saved from her attempt at an excuse by the creak of the library doors and a confident, brassy voice just outside.

"Bennett, you old bore, Daddy sent me to shake off the dust and round you up for handshakes and baby kissing," said Joana Steeling, sauntering into the library like she sauntered into every room. With more confidence than Sam could have ever mustered. Joana looked like she'd stepped right out of the pages of a Butterick catalog, all tall and long, elegant lines in a brilliant scarlet evening dress. She had cut her hair short, the pageboy style popular with Hollywood starlets, the golden finger curls framing her face.

"Oh. Sam." Her expression softened in surprise, an awkward silence stretching out between them as Sam tried and failed to come up with something to say to bridge the gap.

Sam chewed nervously at her lip, running her hands along her satchel strap. "Jo, hello. Georgie said you might be home. I . . . You didn't say."

Joana's expression shuttered as she swept past Sam to link her arm through Bennett's like she was a prison guard tasked with his transport. The hem of her gown brushed over the piles of melting snow Sam had tracked in. "Yes, well, I'm not a dusty old book, so I didn't think you'd care. Bennett, Daddy's waiting. You know he hates waiting."

Sam drew back sharply, stung by the casual barb. Joana had always been the best at them, they'd just never been aimed directly at Sam before. Bennett frowned, glancing back at the stack of books even as Joana dragged him toward the door.

"I've still got a lot to do before I leave," he said. "I really don't have time for Father's kissing up."

"Make time," Joana said grimly. "If I have to laugh at another joke about the length of hemlines these days from a rotund bald man with sour champagne breath, I'll burn the whole place down. Give them something else to talk about."

"I've just received an important package from my professor in Ireland," Bennett insisted. They stalled at the library doors, and Joana glared at Sam like this was somehow all her fault. Which, to be fair, it was. But it wasn't like Joana could know that. "Sam brought it from the shop."

Sam cringed. "I didn't know it was from your professor."

"It's important that I go through it, Jo," Bennett said.

Joana rolled her eyes. "More important than making sure Daddy pays your tuition next year?"

"I wouldn't expect you to understand," Bennett said dryly. "Since you got yourself expelled from the academy after a single semester."

"What?" Sam gasped. "Oh, Jo, what happened?"

"Don't you 'oh, Jo' me," Joana said, stabbing a finger in Sam's direction. "That school wasn't worth my time anyhow. Full of dew droppers and killjoys, stuffier than a leather couch. Maybe if you had come with me I would have stuck it out, but I'm better off without it."

Sam took a full step back, the implication of Joana's words sinking into her chest and tugging at her heart. "I should go," Sam said, her voice shaky. "I've got to get back to the shop."

"I bet you do," Joana muttered. She gave Bennett's arm a little pinch, dragging him through the library door. "Read your little books later, Bennett. You know the way out, don't you, Sam?"

Joana didn't wait for Sam's answer, and Sam only waited long enough to be sure Joana wouldn't see the shimmer in her eyes before hurrying out of the library. She shoved past James, his surprise showing in the faint creasing around his eyes, but she didn't stop to apologize for her rudeness. She'd made a fool of herself, but that could hardly be helped now. At least she still had the shop— she would always have the shop. The books didn't judge her.

Her steps slowed as she reached the main street. It was so dark with all the storefronts closed up for the evening, the deep stillness broken only by the crunch of her boots through the snow. A single crow cawed somewhere in the distance, startling her enough that she doubled her pace.

A little restoration work was just what she needed to settle her nerves. She reached the front door of the shop, fishing for her keys as she grabbed the handle. But it turned freely, the door opening with a soft click. She was sure she had locked it. Something tugged at the edges of her awareness, a prickle of warning as she stepped into the darkened shop. Her eyes needed time to adjust, but her feet knew the way into the stacks. She was just outside the workroom door when a rumble of deep voices spilled out, along with the stray beam of a lantern.

Someone was in the bookshop.

ABOUT THE AUTHOR

Jenny Elder Moke writes young adult fiction in an attempt to recapture the shining infinity of youth. She worked for several years at an independent publisher in Austin, Texas, before realizing she would rather write the manuscripts than read them. She is a member of the Texas Writers' League and has studied children's writing with Liz Garton Scanlon. She was a finalist in the Austin Film Festival Fiction Podcast Competition in 2017 for her podcast script, *Target*. When she is not writing, she's gathering story ideas from her daily adventures with her two irredeemable rapscallions and honing her ninja skills as a black belt in Tae Kwon Do. Jenny lives in Denver, Colorado, with her husband and two children.